D0977136

After
the
Parade

A NOVEL

Lori Ostlund

Scribner
New York   London   Toronto   Sydney   New Delhi

Scribner
An Imprint of Simon & Schuster, Inc.
1230 Avenue of the Americas
New York, NY 10020

This book is a work of fiction. Any references to historical events, real people, or real places are used fictitiously. Other names, characters, places, and events are products of the author's imagination, and any resemblance to actual events or places or persons, living or dead, is entirely coincidental.

Copyright © 2015 by Lori Ostlund

All rights reserved, including the right to reproduce this book or portions thereof in any form whatsoever. For information, address Scribner Subsidiary Rights Department, 1230 Avenue of the Americas, New York, NY 10020.

First Scribner hardcover edition September 2015

SCRIBNER and design are registered trademarks of The Gale Group, Inc., used under license by Simon & Schuster, Inc., the publisher of this work.

For information about special discounts for bulk purchases, please contact Simon & Schuster Special Sales at 1-866-506-1949 or business@simonandschuster.com.

The Simon & Schuster Speakers Bureau can bring authors to your live event. For more information or to book an event, contact the Simon & Schuster Speakers Bureau at 1-866-248-3049 or visit our website at www.simonspeakers.com.

Interior design by Akasha Archer

Manufactured in the United States of America

10 9 8 7 6 5 4 3 2 1

Library of Congress Cataloging-in-Publication Data is available.

ISBN 978-1-4767-9010-7
ISBN 978-1-4767-9012-1 (ebook)

For my students, who make me hopeful

Where you come from is gone, where you thought you were going to never was there, and where you are is no good unless you can get away from it.

—FLANNERY O'CONNOR, *WISE BLOOD*

It is an odd thing, but everyone who disappears is said to be seen at San Francisco.

—OSCAR WILDE

After
the
Parade

December

1

Aaron had gotten a late start—some mix-up at the U-Haul office that nobody seemed qualified to fix—so it was early afternoon when he finally began loading the truck, nearly eight when he finished. He wanted to drive away right then but could not imagine setting out so late. It was enough that the truck sat in the driveway packed, declaring his intention. Instead, he took a walk around the neighborhood, as was his nightly habit, had been his nightly habit since he and Walter moved here nine years earlier. He always followed the same route, designed with the neighborhood cats in mind. He knew where they all lived, had made up names for each of them—Falstaff and Serial Mom, Puffin and Owen Meany—and when he called to them using these names, they stood up from wherever they were hiding and ran down to the sidewalk to greet him.

He passed the house of the old woman who, on many nights, though not this one, watched for him from her kitchen window and then hurried out with a jar that she could not open. She called him by his first name and he called her Mrs. Trujillo, since she was surely twice his age, and as he twisted the lid off a jar of honey or instant coffee, they engaged in pleasantries, establishing that they were both fine, that they had enjoyed peaceful, ordinary days, saying the sorts of things that Aaron had grown up in his mother's café hearing people say to one another. As a boy, he had dreaded such talk, for he had been shy and no good at it, but as he grew older, he had come to appreciate these small nods at civility.

Of course, Mrs. Trujillo was not always fine. Sometimes, her back was acting up or her hands were numb. She would hold them out toward him, as though the numbness were something that could be seen, and when he put the jar back into them, he said, "Be careful now, Mrs. Trujillo. Think what a mess you'd have with broken glass and honey." Maybe he made a joke that wasn't really funny, something about all those ants with bleeding tongues, and she would laugh the way that people who are very lonely laugh, paying you the only way they know how. She always seemed sheepish about mentioning her ailments, sheepish again when he inquired the next time whether she was feeling better, yet for years they had engaged in this ritual, and as he passed her house that last night, he felt relief at her absence. Still, when he let his mind stray to the future, to the next night and the one after, the thought of Mrs. Trujillo looking out the window with a stubborn jar of spaghetti sauce in her hands made his heart ache.

Aaron picked up his pace, almost ran to Falstaff's house, where he crouched on the sidewalk and called softly to the portly fellow, waiting for him to waddle off the porch that was his stage. At nine, he returned from his walk and circled the truck, double-checking the padlock because he knew there would come a moment during the night when he would lie there thinking about it, and this way he would have an image that he could pull up in his mind: the padlock, secured.

A week earlier, Aaron had gone into Walter's study with a list of the household items that he planned to take with him. He found Walter at his desk, a large teak desk that Walter's father had purchased in Denmark in the 1950s and shipped home. He had used the desk throughout his academic career, writing articles that added up to books about minor Polish poets, most of them long dead, and then it had become Walter's. Aaron loved the desk, which represented everything for which he had been longing all those years ago when Walter took him in and they began their life together: a profession that required a sturdy, beautiful desk; a father who cared enough about aesthetics to ship a desk across an ocean; a life, in every way, different from his own.

Though it was just four in the afternoon, Walter was drinking cognac—Spanish cognac, which he preferred to French—and later

Aaron would realize that Walter had already known that something was wrong. Aaron stood in the office doorway, reading the list aloud— a set of bed linens, a towel, a cooking pot, a plate, a knife, cutlery. "Is there anything on the list that you prefer I not take?" he asked.

Walter looked out the window for what seemed a very long time. "I saved you, Aaron," he said at last. His head sank onto his desk, heavy with the memories it contained.

"Yes," Aaron agreed. "Yes, you did. Thank you." He could hear the stiffness in his voice and regretted—though could not change—it. This was how he had let Walter know that he was leaving.

Walter had already tended to his "nightly ablutions," as he termed the process of washing one's face and brushing one's teeth, elevating the mundane by renaming it. He was in bed, so there seemed nothing for Aaron to do but retire as well, except he had nowhere to sleep. He had packed the guest bed, a futon with a fold-up base, and they had never owned a typical couch, only an antique Javanese daybed from Winnie's store in Minneapolis. Winnie was Walter's sister, though from the very beginning she had felt more like his own. Sleeping on the daybed would only make him think of her, which he did not want. He had not even told Winnie that he was leaving. Of course, he could sleep with Walter, in the space that he had occupied for nearly twenty years, but it seemed to him *improper*—that was the word that came to mind—to share a bed with the man he was leaving. His dilemma reminded him of a story that Winnie had told him just a few weeks earlier, during one of their weekly phone conversations. Winnie had lots of stories, the pleasure—and the burden—of owning a small business.

"I'm a captive audience," she had explained to him and Walter once. "I can't just lock up and leave. People know that on some level, but it suits their needs to act as though we're two willing participants. Sometimes they talk for hours."

"They are being presumptuous, presumptuous and self-involved," Walter had said. Walter hated to waste time, hated to have his wasted. "Just walk away."

Aaron knew that she would not, for he and Winnie were alike: they understood that the world was filled with lonely people, whom they did not begrudge these small moments of companionship.

The story that Winnie had called to tell him was about a customer of hers, Sally Forth. ("Yes, that's really her name," Winnie had added before he could ask.) Sally Forth and her husband had just returned from a ten-day vacation in Turkey, about which she had said to Winnie, pretrip: "It's a Muslim country, you know. Lots of taboos in the air, and those are always good for sex." Sally Forth was a woman impressed with her own naughtiness, a woman endlessly amused by the things that came out of her mouth. The first morning, as she and her husband sat eating breakfast in their hotel restaurant and discussing the day's itinerary, her husband turned to her and requested a divorce. Winnie said that Sally Forth was the type of person who responded to news—good or bad—loudly and demonstratively, without considering her surroundings. Thus, Sally Forth, who was engaged in spreading jam on a piece of bread, reached across the table and ground the bread against her husband's chest, the jam making a red blotch directly over his heart. "Why would you bring me all the way to Turkey to tell me you want a divorce?" Sally Forth screamed, and her husband replied, "I thought you'd appreciate the gesture."

Winnie and Aaron had laughed together on the phone, not at Sally Forth or even at her husband but at this strange notion that proposing divorce required etiquette similar to that of proposing marriage—a carefully chosen moment, a grand gesture.

Sally Forth and her husband stayed in Turkey the whole ten days, during which her husband did not mention divorce again. By the time the vacation was over, she thought of his request as something specific to Turkey, but after they had collected their luggage at the airport back home in Minneapolis, Sally Forth's husband hugged her awkwardly and said that he would be in touch about "the details."

"I feel like such an idiot," she told Winnie. "But we kept sleeping in the same bed. If you're really leaving someone, you don't just get into bed with them, do you?"

And then, Sally Forth had begun to sob.

"I didn't know what to do," Winnie told Aaron sadly. "I wanted to hug her, but you know how I am about that, especially at work. I actually tried. I stepped toward her, but I couldn't do it. It seemed disingenuous—because we're not friends. I don't even like her. So I just let her stand there and cry."

As Aaron finished brushing his teeth, he tried to remember whether he and Winnie had reached any useful conclusions about the propriety of sharing a bed with the person one was about to leave, but he knew that they had not. Winnie had been focused solely on what she regarded as her failure to offer comfort.

"Sometimes," he had told her, "the hardest thing to give people is the thing we know they need the most." When he said this, he was trying to work up the courage to tell her that he was leaving Walter, but he had stopped there so that his comment seemed to refer to Winnie's treatment of Sally Forth, which meant that he had failed Winnie also.

He went into the bedroom and turned on the corner lamp. The room looked strange without his belongings. Gone were the rows of books and the gifts from his students, as well as the Indonesian night table that Winnie had given him when he and Walter moved from Minnesota to New Mexico. It was made from recycled wood, old teak that had come from a barn or railroad tracks or a chest for storing rice—Winnie was not sure what exactly. For Aaron, just knowing that the table had had another life was enough. When he sat down on his side of the bed, Walter did not seem to notice. That was the thing about a king-size bed: its occupants could lead entirely separate lives, never touching, oblivious to the other's presence or absence.

"Walter," he said, but there was no reply. He crawled across the vast middle ground of the bed and shook Walter's shoulder.

"Enh," said Walter, a sound that he often made when he was sleeping, so Aaron considered the possibility that he was not faking sleep.

"Is it okay if I sleep here?" he asked, but Walter, treating the question as a prelude to an argument, said, "I'm too tired for this right now. Let's talk in the morning." And so Aaron spent his last night with Walter in their bed, trying to sleep, trying because he could not stop thinking about the fact that everything he owned was sitting in the driveway—on wheels nonetheless—which meant that every noise became the sound of his possessions being driven away into the night. He was reminded of something that one of his Vietnamese students, Vu, had said in class during a routine speaking exercise. Vu declared that if a person discovered an unlocked store while walking down the street at night, he had the right to take what he wanted from inside. Until then, Vu had struck him as honest and reliable, so the nonchalance with which Vu stated this opinion had shocked Aaron.

"That's stealing," Aaron blurted out, so astonished that he forgot about the purpose of the exercise, which was to get the quieter students talking.

"No," Vu said, seemingly puzzled by Aaron's vehemence as well as his logic. "Not stealing. If I destroy lock or break window, this is stealing. If you do not lock door, you are not careful person. You must be responsibility person to own business." Vu constantly mixed up parts of speech and left off articles, but Aaron did not knock on the desk as he normally did to remind Vu to pay attention to his grammar.

"But you did not pay for these things," Aaron cried. "I did. We are not *required* to lock up our belongings. We do so only because there are dishonest people in the world, but locking them up is not what makes them ours. They are ours because we own them."

Vu regarded him calmly. "When the policeman comes, he will ask, 'Did you lock this door?' If you say no, he will not look very well for your things. He will think, 'This man is careless, and now he makes work for me.'"

"I'm not saying it's a *good* idea to leave your door unlocked, Vu. I'm only saying that the things inside are mine, whether I remember to lock the door or not." Belatedly, he had addressed the rest of the class. "What do you guys think?"

They had stared back at him, frightened by his tone. Later, when he tried to understand what had made him so angry, he had come up with nothing more precise than that Vu had challenged the soundness of a code that seemed obvious, inviolable.

Aaron got out of bed to peek at the truck parked in the driveway. He did this several more times. Around three, having risen for the sixth time, he stood in the dark bedroom listening to Walter's familiar wheezing. Then he put on his clothes and left. As he backed the truck out of the driveway with the headlights off because he did not want them shining in and illuminating the house, the thought came to him that he was like his mother: sneaking away without saying good-bye, disappearing into the night.

All along their street, the houses were lit up with holiday lights. That afternoon, as Aaron carried the first box out to the truck, Walter had blocked the door to ask, "Whatever is going on here?," adding, "It's nearly Christmas." In the past, Aaron would have made a joke along the lines of "What, are you a Jew for Jesus now?" They would have laughed, not because it was funny exactly but because of the level of trust it implied. Instead, Aaron had continued loading the truck without answering, and Walter had retreated to his study.

It was quiet at this hour. Driving home from the symphony one night several years earlier, he and Walter had seen a teenage boy being beaten by five other boys in the park just blocks from their house. Though Albuquerque had plenty of crime, their neighborhood was considered safe, a place where people walked their dogs at midnight, so the sight of this—a petty drug deal going bad—startled them. Walter slammed on the brakes and leaped from the car, yelling, "Stop that," as he and Aaron, dressed in suits and ties, rushed toward the fight. The five boys in hairnets turned and ran, as did the sixth boy, who jumped up and sprinted toward his car, a BMW, and drove off.

Later, in bed, Walter joked, "Nothing more terrifying than two middle-aged fags in suits," though Aaron was just thirty-five at the time. They laughed, made giddy by the moment and by the more sobering realization that the night could have turned out much different. Walter got up and went into the kitchen and came back with two glasses of port, which they sat in bed—the king-size bed—drinking, and though Walter insisted on a lighthearted tone, Aaron took his hand and held it tightly, reminded yet again that Walter was a good man who cared about others.

When Aaron got to the park, he pulled the truck to the curb and turned off the engine, which seemed very loud in the middle of the night. He sat in the dark and cried, thinking about Walter asleep in their bed down the street.

Aaron was in Gallup buying coffee when the sun rose, approaching Needles, California, when he fell asleep at the wheel, awakening within seconds to the disorienting sight of the grassy median before him. He swerved right, the truck shifting its weight behind him, and found himself on the road again, cars honking all around him, a man in a pickup truck jabbing his middle finger at him and screaming something that he took to be "Asshole!" He was not the sort who came away from close calls energized, nor did he believe in endangering the lives of others. He took the next exit, checked into a motel in Needles, and was soon asleep, the heavy drapes closed tightly against the California sun.

But as he slept, a series of thuds worked their way into his dreams. He awoke suddenly, the room dark and still, and he thought maybe the thudding was nothing more than his own heart. It came again, loud and heavy, something hitting the wall directly behind him. *A body,* he thought, and then, *Not a body. A human being.*

He reached out and felt a lamp on the table beside the bed, then fumbled along its base for the switch. From the next room, he heard a keening sound followed by the unmistakable thump of a fist meeting flesh. He slipped on his sneakers. Outside, it was dusk. He ran down a flight of steps and turned left, into the motel lobby. The woman at the desk was the one who had checked him in. He remembered the distrustful way she looked at him when he burst in and declared that he needed a room, so exhausted he could not recall his zip code for the paperwork.

"Call the police," he said.

She stared at him.

"You need to call the police. A man in the room next to me is beating someone up—a woman, I think, his wife or girlfriend. Someone."

He could see now that beneath her heavy makeup, she was young, maybe twenty, the situation beyond anything for which either her receptionist training or meager years of living had prepared her. "Nine-one-one," he said slowly, like he was explaining grammar to a student. He reached across the counter, picked up the receiver, and held it out to her. She looked left and right, as if crossing the street. He knew that she was looking for someone besides him.

At last, a switch seemed to flip on inside her. She took a breath and said, "Sir, you're in room two-fifty-two, correct?" He shrugged to indicate that he didn't know, but she continued on, his uncertainty fueling her confidence. "It must be two-fifty-three, that couple from Montana. But they had a child with them? Is there a child?" she asked.

"Just call," he said, and he ran back outside. When he got to room 253, he hesitated, the full weight of his good-fences-make-good-neighbors upbringing bearing down on him. He raised his hand and knocked hard at the door. The room went silent, and he knew that something was very wrong.

"Hello?" he called, making his voice louder because he had learned early on in teaching that volume was the best way to conceal a quaver.

The receptionist came up the steps and stood watching, afraid, he knew, of the responsibility they shared, of the haste with which she had wedded her life to his. "Key?" he mouthed, but she shook her head. He stepped back until he felt the walkway railing behind him and then rushed at the door, doing this again and again until the chain ripped away and he was in.

The receptionist's name was Britta. He had heard her spelling it for the policeman who took down their stories as they stood outside the door that Aaron had broken through minutes earlier.

That night she knocked at his room door. "It's me, Britta," she called, without adding qualifiers—"the receptionist" or "we saved a boy's life together this afternoon."

When he opened the door, she said, "I came to give you an update on Jacob," but she was carrying a six-pack of beer, which confused him.

Still, he invited her in because he could not sleep, could not stop picturing the boy—Jacob—lying on the floor as though he simply preferred it to the bed, as though he had lain down there and gone to sleep. There'd been blood, and the boy's arm was flung upward and out at an angle that only a broken bone would allow. The mother sat to the side, sobbing about her son from a distance, from the *comfort* of a chair. She was not smoking but Aaron later thought of her that way, as a woman who sat in a chair and smoked while her husband threw her son against the wall. It was the husband who surprised him most: a small, jovial-looking man with crow's-feet (*duck feet* a student had once called them, mistaking the bird) and a face that seemed suited for laughing.

He and Britta did not drink the beer she had brought, though he could see that she wanted to. "It's still cold," she said hopefully as she set it down. She would not go further, would not slip a can from the plastic noose without his prompting. She was an employee after all, used to entering these rooms deferentially. Aaron was relieved. He had left behind everything that was familiar, but at least he recognized himself in this person who would not drink beer with a teenager in a cheap motel room in Needles, California.

The beer sat sweating on the desk between the television and the Gideon Bible. "Were you reading the Bible?" Britta asked, for of course she would know that it was generally kept tucked away in the bottom drawer of the desk. He felt embarrassed by the question, though he could see that she considered Bible-reading a normal activity, one to be expected given what had happened earlier.

"Not really," he said, which was true. He had spent the last three hours *not really* doing anything. He had tried, and failed at, a succession of activities: sleeping, reading (both the Gideon Bible and *Death Comes for the Archbishop,* his least favorite Willa Cather book, though he periodically felt obligated to give it another chance), studying the map of California in an attempt to memorize the final leg of his trip, mending a small tear that had appeared in his shirtsleeve, and watching television. When Britta knocked, he had been sitting on the bed listening, the way he had as a child just after his father died and he lay in bed each night straining to hear whether his mother was crying in her room at the other end of the house. Some nights he heard her (gasping sobs that he would be reminded of as an adult when he overheard people having sex) while other nights there was silence.

"Where are you going?" Britta asked him.

"San Francisco," he said.

She nodded in a way that meant she had no interest in such things: San Francisco specifically, but really the world outside Needles. He tried to imagine himself as Britta, spending his days interacting with people who were on the move, coming from or going to places that he had never seen, maybe never even heard of. Was it possible that she had not once felt the urge to pack up and follow, to solve the mystery of who Britta would be—would *become*—in Columbus, Ohio, or Roanoke, Virginia? It seemed inconceivable to him, to have no curiosity about one's parallel lives, those lives that different places would demand that you live.

They sat in silence, he at the foot of the bed and she in the chair beside the desk. He did not know what to say next. "Do you like working at the motel?" he asked finally.

"It's okay," she said. "It's kind of boring most of the time, but sometimes it's interesting."

"Give me an example of something interesting," he said, his teacher's voice never far away. "Other than today, of course."

"Today wasn't interesting," she said. "It was scary. I threw up afterward. Weren't you scared at all?"

"Yes," he said. "Actually, I was terrified."

She smiled, and then she began to cry. "Do you think we did the right thing?" she asked.

"What do you mean?"

"I don't know," she said. "My boyfriend—Lex—he said that it was none of our business. And my boss is this Indian guy—he's all in a bad mood now because he said it's bad for business for people to see the cops here."

Aaron's first impulse was to ask what her boss's ethnicity had to do with the rest of her statement, but he did not. He sensed no malice, and the question would only confuse her. "Listen," he said sternly. "We definitely did the right thing. Okay? We saved a boy's life."

His voice broke on the word *saved*. It seemed he had been waiting his whole life to save this boy, though he did not believe in fate, did not believe that everything in his forty-one years had happened in order to bring him here, to a run-down motel in Needles, California, so that he might save Jacob. No. They were two separate facts: he had saved a life, and he was alone. He had never felt so tired.

"I need to go to bed," he said, and he stood up.

Britta stood also and picked up her beer, leaving behind six wet circles on the desktop. "He's in a coma," she announced as she paused in the doorway. "Jacob. So you see, we might not have saved him. He might die anyway."

Aaron leaned against the door frame, steadying himself. "At least we gave him a chance," he said. Then, because he did not have it in him to offer more, he offered this: "You're a good person, Britta, and that's important."

They were standing so close that he could smell alcohol and ketchup on her breath. He imagined her sitting in a car in an empty parking lot somewhere in Needles with her boyfriend, Lex, the two of them eating French fries and drinking beer as she tried to tell Lex about Jacob while Lex rubbed his greasy lips across her breasts.

"Good night," Aaron said, gently now. He shut the door and pressed his ear to it, waiting to slide the chain into place because he worried she might take the sound of it personally, though later he realized that she would not have thought the chain had anything to do with her. It was a feature of the room, something to be used, like the ice bucket or the small bars of soap in the bathroom.

When the telephone rang, he sat up fast in the dark and reached for it. "Hello," he said.

"Front desk," said the man on the other end. He sounded bored, which reassured Aaron. "You have the U-Haul in the parking lot."

"Yes," said Aaron, though the man had not inflected it as a question. "Is something wrong? What time is it?"

"You'll need to come down to the parking lot. Sir." The "sir" was an afterthought, and later Aaron knew he should have considered that, should have weighed the man's reassuring boredom against that pause.

"Now?" said Aaron. "Is something wrong?" But the line had already gone dead.

He looked at the bedside clock. It seemed so long ago that he had been lying beside Walter, worrying about the truck, yet it had been only twenty-four hours. He dressed and ran down the steps to the parking lot, where a man stood beside the truck. Aaron had parked under a light—not intentionally, for he had been too tired for such foresight—and as he got closer, he could see that the man was young, still a boy, with hair that held the shape of a work cap.

"What's wrong?" Aaron asked. The boy lifted his right hand in a fist and slammed it into Aaron's stomach.

As a child, Aaron had been bullied—punched, taunted, bitten so hard that his arm swelled—but he had always managed to deflect fights as an adult. It was not easy. He was tall, four inches over six feet, and his height was often seen as a challenge, turning innocent encounters—accidentally jostling someone, for example—into potential altercations. He did not know how to reconcile what other men saw when they looked at him with the image preserved in his mind, that of a small boy wetting himself as his father's casket was lowered into the ground.

The boy hit him again, and Aaron dropped backward onto his buttocks. "What do you want?" he asked, looking up at the boy.

"I'm Lex," said the boy.

"Ah, yes, Britta's friend."

"*Boy*friend," said the boy.

"Yes, of course," said Aaron, but something about the way he articulated this angered the boy even more. He jerked back his foot and kicked Aaron hard in the hip. Aaron whimpered. He had learned early on that bullies liked to know they were having an effect.

"What was she doing in there?" asked the boy.

"Where?" said Aaron. "In my room, you mean? We were talking. She was telling me about Jacob, the child we saved this afternoon."

"So why was she crying then?"

"Crying?" said Aaron.

"She was crying when she came out. I saw her. I was right here the whole time, and I saw her come out of your room. She was crying, and she wouldn't talk to me."

"Well," Aaron said, trying to think of words, which was not easy because he was frightened. He could see the fury in the boy, the fury at being in love with someone he did not understand. "You do realize that people cry. Sometimes we know why they are crying, and sometimes we do not. Britta had an extremely hard day. She saw a child who had been beaten almost to death."

The boy looked down at him. "She was in your room. You can talk how you like, mister, but she was in your room."

Aaron realized only then what it was the boy imagined. "I don't have sex with women," he said quietly. He thought of his words as a gift to the boy, who did not have it in him to add up the details differently, to alter his calculations. Behind him, Aaron could hear the interstate, the sound of trucks floating past Needles at night.

"What?" said Lex. "What are you saying? That you're some kind of fag?" His voice was filled with wonder.

Later, when he was in the U-Haul driving away, Aaron would consider Lex's phrasing: *some kind of fag,* as if fags came in *kinds.* He supposed they did. He did not like the word *fag,* but he knew where he stood with people who used it, knew what they thought and what to expect from them. He had nodded, agreeing that he was *some kind of fag* because the question was not really about him. Lex's fist somersaulted helplessly in the air, his version of being left speechless, and he turned and walked away.

Aaron's wallet was in his back pocket, the truck keys in the front. He could simply rise from the pavement, get into the truck, and drive away. He wished that he were that type of person, one who lived spontaneously and without regrets, but he was not. He was the type who would berate himself endlessly for leaving behind a much-needed map and everything else that had been in the overnight bag. He went back up to his room, checked beneath the bed and in the shower, though he had not used the latter, and when he left, he had everything with which he had arrived. He drove slowly away from Needles, waiting for the sun to catch up with him.

2

"Tell me what you want, Aaron," Walter had periodically insisted, his tone turning impatient these last few years, the words no longer an invitation but a way of chiding Aaron, of suggesting that he wanted too much—or worse, that he had no idea what he wanted. But in the beginning of their lives together, back when they were two discrete people, Walter's motives felt easy to read: *Tell me who you are,* he seemed to be saying. *Tell me what you want from this life.* Only later had Aaron understood that his real motive in asking was to discover how he might serve as benefactor to Aaron's wishes and ambitions and, in doing so, bind Aaron to him.

Walter had first posed the question on a Sunday afternoon, as they drove toward Moorhead, Minnesota, where Walter was a language professor—French and Spanish, Italian in a pinch—at the university. Though it was hard even to imagine such a time now, they were strangers then, two men (one just barely) occupying the intimacy of a car. Aaron had spent the first five years of his life in Moorhead. It was there that his father had died, his death causing something to shift in Aaron's mother so that soon after, the two of them had moved to Mortonville. Aaron still had memories of the house his family had lived in and the street where his father died, enough to make his arrival with Walter a homecoming, even though he thought of what he was doing that day as running away. It was all a matter of perspective: whether one was focused on leaving or arriving, on the past or the future.

In the midst of pondering this, he heard Walter say, "Tell me, Aaron. What is it that you want?"

"I want a different brain," he had answered.

He was eighteen and bookish, this latter the adjective that he would employ as an adult—euphemistically—to indicate that he had not yet had sex. He did not mean that he actually wanted a different brain but rather that he wanted to fill the one he had with knowledge and experiences of which he could not yet conceive but was sure existed. Walter had laughed, not unkindly, but the laughter had upset Aaron, a feeling that was underscored by the music playing on Walter's cassette deck. It was classical music, which Aaron had never known anyone to listen to, not like this: in the car, for *pleasure*. People in Mortonville listened to country music and rock, hymns and patriotic songs, though they did not discount such things as classical music and poetry. Most of them were proud that their children could recite nine poems by the end of sixth grade, a poem a month. They saw these poems as proof that their children were getting educated, for they were practical people who did not expect education to be practical, did not expect it to make their children better farmers or housewives. If it did, it was probably not education.

When Aaron was nine, Mrs. Carlsrud had assigned each student a classical composer, about whom the child was expected to deliver an oral report. He was assigned Sibelius, who was a Finn, a Swedish Finn, a distinction of importance in Mortonville, where most people were either Scandinavian or German. The Scandinavian block was dominated by the Norwegians and Swedes, who were seen as separate groups, except when discussed beside the Finns; the Finns were technically Scandinavian, but they were *different*. All of them, every single Finn in Mortonville, lived east of town, a self-imposed segregation. They even had their own church, which sat atop a hill amid their farms.

The first day of the presentations, Ellen Arndt stood at the front of the classroom holding a small stack of recipe cards, from which she read two parallel pieces of information: "Tchaikovsky was a Russian and a homosexual." Three children giggled, and Sharon Engstrom raised her hand and said, "What's a Russian?" When Mrs. Carlsrud replied that a Russian was "someone from Russia, a communist," Sharon Engstrom said, "Then what's a homosexual?," shifting her focus to the second noun, which included the word *sex* after all, and the same three children laughed.

"That is not relevant," said Mrs. Carlsrud, her reply suggesting to Aaron that homosexuals were worth investigating. He planned to ask his mother about the word after school, but when he arrived at the café, their café, she was preparing the supper special, meatballs, and because she did not like to be asked questions when she was busy, he waited until the two of them were closing up that night.

"What does *homosexual* mean?" he asked as he filled the saltshakers.

"What makes you ask?" said his mother. She was running her hands under the bottoms of the tables, looking for improperly disposed of gum.

"Today, Ellen Arndt said that Tchaikovsky was a Russian and a homosexual, and Mrs. Carlsrud said that Russians live in Russia but homosexuals aren't relevant."

"Well," his mother said. "It means he likes men."

"Why isn't it relevant?" he said.

"That's just something Mrs. Carlsrud said because she didn't want to talk about it," said his mother. Then, she turned off the lights in the dining room and went upstairs, which was what she did when she didn't want to talk about something.

The first time Aaron and Walter met was on a Saturday morning when Walter came into the café for breakfast. He was alone, for his weekend fishing trips to Mortonville were solitary affairs. Aaron was fifteen. He later learned that Walter was thirty, twice his age, though Aaron, like most teenagers, had no sense of what thirty looked like. Walter stood by the door, waiting to be seated, which was not the custom at the café, so Aaron finally approached him and asked whether he needed directions.

Years later, as he walked through the Castro, Aaron would be struck by how many gay male couples looked alike, the narcissistic component of love driven home in stark visual terms, but he and Walter were opposites. Aaron's hair was blond and fine, and already, at fifteen, he wore it in a severe right part, while Walter's hair that day was unevenly shorn, with dark, curly patches sprouting out along his neck and across the top. When Aaron next encountered him, his hair would be long and frizzy, though just as inexpertly cut. Over the years, Walter would come home with one bad haircut after another, the *bad* part the only constant, but when Aaron asked why he didn't try a different salon, Walter would reply with a shrug, "Nobody around here knows how to cut Jew hair anyway."

Walter was short, just five eight, his weight concentrated in his lower torso and thighs, and as Aaron stood before him for the first time that morning in the café, Walter had to tilt his head slightly back to look up at Aaron. "Directions, no," Walter said. "What I need is a hearty breakfast."

Aaron paid close attention to Walter that morning. He noted that Walter was left-handed, though he would later learn that he was left-handed only for eating. Walter cut his food with his right hand, holding his fork in the left, but did not take what he called "the unnecessary step" of switching the fork to his right when he transported each bite to his mouth. His parents, who had both been refugees from Nazi Germany, had taught him to eat this way, like a European. He told Aaron that during the war, American spies—men who spoke perfect German—had been caught because of this simple slip, the shifting of the fork from left hand to right. Later, under Walter's tutelage, Aaron would become a left-handed eater also. Even as he evolved into his own person over the years, he would find the Pygmalion aspect of their relationship—habits such as these, established early on—the hardest to shed.

Walter carried a book, which he sat reading. Aaron had never seen anyone read while eating, not in public. Of course, the regulars sometimes glanced at the newspaper, making comments about crop prices or sports, but Walter read as if nothing but the book existed. Aaron often wished that he could bring a book to the table, especially as the meals that he and his mother shared became increasingly silent, but his mother forbade it. When he refilled Walter's coffee cup, Aaron looked down at his book and was shocked to see that it was not in English. Sensing his interest, Walter held the book up. "Camus. Have you read him yet?" Aaron shook his head, and Walter said, "Well, Camus is a must, but I guess I've officially lost my adolescent enthrallment with existentialism. I'm finding it quite tedious this time around." He sighed the way other men sighed about the weather or a hard-to-find tractor part. The adult Aaron would have laughed at Walter's transparent need to prove himself to a fifteen-year-old boy, but the Aaron he was then felt the world shifting, accommodating the fact that it was much vaster than he had ever imagined, that it included people who read books in other languages and spoke of ideas so foreign to him that they, too, seemed another language.

For men perhaps more than for women, there is something aphrodisiacal about finding oneself on the greater-than side of an intellectual disparity, and years later, Aaron would learn that Walter had felt something during that first encounter, a sexual stirring that they never fully discussed because Walter was not comfortable talking about desire. Aaron did know that Walter had been introduced to sex by a man who followed him back to the dressing room while he shopped for school clothes with his mother in a department store in New York. He was fourteen. He had no bad feelings toward the man, but he told Aaron that the experience had shaped him nonetheless, had taught him to associate sexual gratification with furtiveness and haste and a lack of reciprocity. On those rare occasions when Walter did discuss sex, he always brought to it this same textbook-like dryness.

Aaron had felt desire that day, a desire that was in no way sexual. In fact, it had felt to him more potent than anything sexual could be, for sexual desire was, by nature, transient, a flame that grew large and went out. Admittedly, he knew very little of sexual desire, recognized it largely in terms of what he did not want but was led to believe that he should—girls. True sexual desire, he thought, was like an undershirt worn close to the skin and covered by layers of shirts and sweaters and coats.

Three years after that first meeting, when Walter brought Aaron home with him to Moorhead and introduced him to his circle of closeted friends, one of them, Jonas, commented coyly, "Oh my, look what Walter caught," and the others laughed as if they had known all along that Walter's weekend getaways were not really about fishing. Within the group it was common knowledge that Jonas was in love with Walter and that his love was not reciprocated, for various reasons, among them that Walter did not date married men, and Jonas *was* married, a fact that the other men snickered at behind his back. They could not imagine Jonas, with his pear-shaped body and hands as white and soft as sifted flour, atop a woman. Walter did not snicker. He was patient with Jonas, partly because Walter was a kind man but largely because he pitied Jonas, pitied him for having both a woman's body and a wife. Pity is a hard thing to bear, for it's never about love; pity is the opposite of love, or one of its opposites, since love has many. Still, Jonas bore it.

Aaron later understood that the men's campiness was a pose, a function of the fact that they lived their lives hidden and needed to make the most of these secret moments together, but at the time he had not known what to think of any of them—not even Walter, who was solicitous of his needs yet laughed along with Jonas's joke, allowing the implication that he and Aaron were sexually involved to stand as truth. In fact, during their first four years together, he and Walter did not have sex, not with each other. Aaron was in college and engaged occasionally in *sexual relations*—as Walter termed it, taking all the passion and dirt right out of it—with other young men, his first encounter with a boy from his British literature class. He had been drawn to the familiar look of the boy, whose name was Ken. They had groped and wrestled on Ken's dormitory bed one afternoon as they studied for their midterm, both of them losing their virginity to the other, but after he left Ken's room, still breathless, he knew that familiarity was not what he wanted from life. He did not want to engage in furtive sex with a boy resembling those with whom he had grown up, a sturdy blonde whose hands gripped him as they once had a cow's teat, a boy whose pillows smelled faintly of hay and gum. Still, it had pleased (and bewildered) him to know that a boy like that—like those who had shoved him around in the locker room while talking loudly about what their girlfriends did to their penises—desired him.

After Ken, there had been others, none of whom Aaron brought to Walter's house. He felt it would be wrong to do so, even though Walter treated him in the same avuncular manner he treated everyone else, without innuendo or any hint of desire. It was Winnie who finally set him straight. "Don't you see how much he loves you?" she had asked. Aaron said that he did not. "Fine," she said at last. "He told me that he's in love with you. Okay? But you must never, ever tell Walter that I told you."

It turned out Winnie was lying, not about the nature of Walter's feelings but about his having confessed them to her, though Aaron did not learn of her dishonesty until after he had seduced Walter the evening of his college graduation party, an event that left him inebriated and nostalgic and deeply grateful to Walter, who had paid his tuition and all of his living expenses, who had made it possible for him to occupy a different brain.

Aaron could smell himself in the cab of the truck, not the thick, musky odor of physical labor but a sickly smell suggesting something passive: fear and anxiety. As he drove, he thought mainly about Jacob, Jacob, who might already be dead. He could call the motel and ask Britta for an update, but he knew he would not, which meant that for the rest of his life, when he thought about Jacob, he would not know whether to think of him as dead or alive.

His right hip throbbed where Lex had kicked him. He imagined Lex in his work cap, striding into the lobby of the motel. "He's a fag," he would tell Britta by way of declaring his own love, and she would know then that he had been meddling. Perhaps that was the nature of love: either a person was not in it enough to care, or was in it too deeply to make anything but mistakes. Sad Café Love, he and Winnie called this kind of lopsided devotion, after the Carson McCullers novel. Most people, they agreed, could either love or be loved, for these two were like rubbing your stomach and patting your head—nearly impossible to accomplish simultaneously. Winnie did not have a Sad Café marriage. She was deeply in love with Thomas, her husband, and he with her. They were the most equally in love couple that Aaron knew, the sort that took turns with everything: not just with household chores and finances but even with bouts of self-doubt and sadness. Never did they seem to regard each other as competition, as so many couples begin to. When one of them made a comment at a dinner party, the other found a way to make it sound even wittier or more insightful. As a result, they were in high demand at social gatherings, but they rarely accepted invitations because they enjoyed each other's company best.

"Every time we go to a dinner party lately," Winnie had told Aaron not long ago, "there's always some couple that insists on bringing everyone else into their unhappiness. When Thomas and I fight, I don't want anyone to hear because I'm usually just saying stuff out loud to see what I think about it, but having witnesses changes everything."

"Yes," Aaron had said, "but when people are really unhappy, they feel like they need witnesses, some kind of permanent record."

He told her about a fiftieth-birthday party that he and Walter had attended for one of Walter's colleagues, a woman named Nina who taught German. Nina's husband, Peter, had planned the event, an elaborate affair that he referred to throughout the evening as his labor of love, but as he became drunker, he began to tell stories about Nina, secrets that he presented as charming little anecdotes: she had once locked their baby daughter in the bedroom with a mouse for two hours while she waited for him to get home to kill it; during a humid summer in Thailand, a mushroom had sprouted in her navel. After each story, Peter held his glass in the air while Nina sat with a tight smile on her face, inviting the guests to laugh along with her husband, who was too drunk to notice that nobody did.

"It was completely *Virginia Woolf*-ish," Aaron told Winnie, referring to the Albee play and not the author herself.

"They probably had a very passionate relationship in the beginning," Winnie said. "When couples start hating each other, everything goes but the passion. It just gets rechanneled."

Aaron met Winnie when he was nineteen, the summer after his

first year of college. One day Walter announced that his sister would be coming for the weekend. He had never mentioned a sibling.

"Are you close?" Aaron asked.

"We're not un-close. There's no underlying animosity, if that's what you mean. We're typical of many adult siblings, I suspect. Being close, as you put it, requires a certain commitment from both parties, and perhaps we lack the commitment."

Aaron thought of his mother and Uncle Petey, how they had gone years without speaking, not because they were angry at each other but because they too lacked commitment. His mother said that at the end of each day, when you were tired and just wanted to be left alone, you made a decision either in favor of being left alone or in favor of the relationship, and she and Petey had both chosen solitude. The good thing, she said, was that there were no hard feelings that way.

It turned out that Winnie was visiting because she and Thomas were moving to Minneapolis, where Thomas had taken a job as vice principal at a private school. When Aaron asked her whether they had chosen Minnesota to be closer to Walter, she laughed and said, "The sort of relationship we have doesn't require proximity."

"Walter didn't even tell me he had a sister," Aaron confessed.

"That sounds like Walter," Winnie said, sounding not at all upset.

After she left, Walter noted how well Aaron and Winnie had gotten along, offering this assessment without jealousy. It was the same way he sounded when Aaron asked to borrow a scarf or a bicycle helmet. "Take it," Walter would say. "I'm not using it. Someone should."

Now, Aaron was giving Walter his sister back. Walter had not indicated that he wanted his sister back or even that he felt she had been taken, but Aaron preferred to think of his motives in this way because he did not know how to tell Winnie he was leaving. She would want to know why. She would want to know everything. He had instead recorded his reasons in a notebook, cataloging them as though he had in mind a tipping point—25 or 41 or 100—the number of grievances that justified leaving.

Grievance #1: *Whenever Walter and I are sitting in a room together and he gets up to leave, he turns off the light on his way out. He claims that it is a gesture born of habit, something ingrained in him by his parents, but I cannot help but feel that his focus moves with him so that when he leaves a room, everything in it, including me, ceases to exist.*

He told me once, not unkindly, that this bothers me because I have "abandonment issues." I don't particularly care for therapy lingo, yet it struck me as a convincing argument. Still, I cannot help but wonder why Walter does not then take more care to avoid triggering my "issues," why he continues turning off lights as he goes blithely along to his study or the kitchen, leaving me there in the dark.

Grievance #14: *Walter insists on using the French pronunciation of all Anglicized French words, an affectation that I must admit has become a source of embarrassment for me, unexpressed of course, for I understand that I am the one who has changed. In other words: Once, at the very beginning of our relationship—before sex entered the equation, before I became the person I now am—we went grocery shopping together. There, I watched Walter ask one stock boy after another where he might find the "my-o-nez," watched and felt proud of his perfect pronunciation, proud of the fact that it never brought us one step closer to what we sought, a jar of bland, white mayonnaise.*

Grievance #86: *Last night we got together with three of Walter's friends from college. The Credentialists, I call them. Walter doesn't approve of the name, but I consider it apt. The first time we met, several years ago now, one of them, Harold, immediately asked where I had attended college.*

"I went to a state school in Minnesota, the one where Walter used to teach."

They had gone to Harvard. They said it apologetically—"at Harvard."

At dinner, they proclaimed the food "fabulous," and one of them said, "Remember how awful the food was in the cafeteria?" and another, Harold again, said, "It was dreadful, but that's the thing. Anyone else can say their college food was terrible, and nobody thinks they're talking about anything more than food, but if I say to a group of people—not you guys, of course, because we're all in the same boat—that the food was awful at Harvard, well, everyone just assumes that I'm not talking about the food at all. It's become a bit of a problem."

"That does not sound like a problem," I said.

There were 149 grievances in the notebook by the time he left, but the main reason that he was leaving, which he never recorded, was that he no longer loved Walter. He did not know how to consider this alongside the sheer longevity of their relationship, the fact that he had been with Walter more than half his life. Several years earlier, before Aaron began keeping his notebook, Walter had remarked during a walk one day, casually, "You know if you left me now, it would be like tossing these years aside, regarding them as wasted." There seemed to Aaron nothing worse than feeling you had wasted your life.

The day he stood in Walter's office reading aloud the list of items that he wished to take, after Walter said, "I saved you" and began to cry, Aaron went into his own office and took out the notebook. It seemed cruel to add to it in the home they had created together, but he took up his pen and composed Grievance #149: *He saved me knowing that there is no stronger way to bind another human being to you than by saving him. This is why I must leave.*

Most of his grievance cataloging had been done at Milton's, a diner on Central Avenue, where he had secretly been eating lunch every Friday for the nine years they lived in Albuquerque. He considered himself a regular, though he suspected that nobody else did. The true regulars fell into three categories: truckers, prostitutes, and the old men who lived in the Route 66 motor lodges scattered along this stretch of

Central. The truckers came and went, as did the prostitutes, though their comings and goings were dictated not by the road but by the law and their own bad luck. They sat in groups of three or four, talking without lowering their voices, even when they discussed the vicissitudes of business or the policemen who trolled for "freebies," which the women expeditiously dispensed in the front seats of squad cars. They did not rage against these circumstances, but instead spoke as if bad luck were a family member they could not envision their lives without.

It was the old men who intrigued him most. He knew nothing of their lives and had always been too intimidated to strike up a conversation, but he thought of them, collectively, as a cautionary tale. *Do not become comfortable with loneliness,* he told himself as he listened to them converse awkwardly while vying for the waitresses' attention. One of the men, whom he nicknamed Elmer, was obsessed with terrorism, specifically with the possibility that his flophouse motel might be the next object of an attack. This was right after 9/11, when terrorism was on everyone's mind, but the certainty with which Elmer asserted his theory left Aaron disheartened. Elmer held forth from the smoking end of the counter, waving a cigarette in the air to help his point along. Aaron had never seen him without one, and as he watched Elmer light each new cigarette from the butt of the last, listened to him wheeze and hack phlegm into his napkin, he wanted to scream from his booth that it was clear what would kill Elmer and it had nothing to do with terrorists.

One Friday Aaron arrived feeling particularly fed up with people's irrationality, for he had just sat through a faculty meeting. To add to his displeasure, the booths were full, so he was forced to take a stool at the counter, to the right of the smoking Elmer, who was putting forth his theory yet again for the bored cook.

"Excuse me," Aaron said loudly, turning to Elmer, who rotated slowly toward him. This close, Aaron could see that Elmer's eyes were rheumy, their greenness turned to milk, and he realized then that Elmer was just a very old man engaged in a last-ditch effort to bring meaning to his life. He gestured at the pepper shaker. "Pass the pepper?" he said, as though pepper were what he had wanted all along.

The next week, Elmer was not present. From his booth, Aaron heard one of the waitresses say to a regular, "Did you hear? The terrorists finally got old Dick." She inclined her head toward Elmer's usual spot. Aaron finished his breakfast burrito and set a ten-dollar bill on the table, anchoring it with his coffee mug. When he got out to his car, he put his head down on the steering wheel and sobbed. He had not known the old man, had not even bothered to learn that his name was Dick, so he was not sure where the grief came from, except that he pictured the old man alone in his motel room, smoking and peering into the parking lot, and he regretted that he had not argued with him.

Aaron had not thought of Elmer, *Dick,* in a couple of years, but the Friday before he left Walter, as he sat at Milton's for the last time, he looked around at the old men and what came to mind was Thoreau's observation that "the mass of men lead lives of quiet desperation." He was sure Thoreau had meant, literally, *men,* for Aaron knew that men lived far lonelier lives than women—with the exception, perhaps, of his mother, though he considered the possibility that she was no longer lonely, that she had left Mortonville (and him) all those years ago to escape loneliness. He had not read Thoreau in years, not since college. He was not interested in reading about nature, not because he disliked nature, but because he disliked the artistic tendency to interpret nature, to put nature into words. He felt that nature spoke sufficiently for itself. He did not care to discuss it or to listen to others discuss it, nor to read about it in prose or poetic form or to see it depicted in art, for nature did not puzzle him: the seasons changed in the same order year after year, animals reproduced, birds assembled nests, flowers bloomed. People, on the other hand, did perplex him, and because the mind is often like that, gravitating toward mystery and challenge, Aaron preferred people.

Here was the thing, the irony perhaps: he had been coming to Milton's these nine years in order to be alone. No one knew of his Friday ritual, especially not Walter, for how could he have explained to Walter that surrounded by these men, these lives-of-quiet-desperation men, he had acknowledged his own abiding loneliness. He ate a forkful of beans and looked around the diner, wondering whether anyone there would notice his absence and ask, "Does anyone know what happened to that quiet young fellow who came in every Friday and ordered the breakfast burrito with chorizo?"

He hoped so.

Aaron stopped to eat just after Bakersfield, at a place marked by an old door propped up beside the road, doorknob intact, painted with the words SALS FOOD. The apostrophe—what his students called "the *up* comma"—was missing, though he knew that the sign looked the same to most people with the apostrophe or without. He could not get over this, for all he could see was the missing mark; it was like looking at a face without a nose.

The parking lot was empty, which meant that he could position the U-Haul in front of the window. When he walked in, three waitresses jumped up from a booth and ran toward him, calling out, "Welcome. Merry Christmas." There were no other diners. They tried to put him at a small table with a fresh flower on it, and when he asked for a booth near the window, they became flustered. Aaron wanted to tell them that the flower was beautiful but the truck outside contained everything he owned in the world. He noted the bulge in his throat, the telltale quiver of his chin, and knew that if he did not pick up the water glass that had been set before him and drink from it right away, he would begin to cry. The three waitresses watched him, listening to his throat convulse loudly as he swallowed. When he set the glass down, one of the women—SHIRLEY said her nametag—refilled it and handed him a menu. They watched him study it, and Shirley wrote down his order—a breakfast burrito with chorizo—while Margarita stood to the side snapping photos.

"I'm sorry," said Shirley, nodding at Margarita. "You're our first customer."

"Ever?" he said.

"Yes," she said. "We just opened ten minutes ago. I'm sorry if we don't know what we're doing. It's our first time. We're sisters. That's our father." She pointed to a man wearing a chef's apron who stood in the doorway of the kitchen.

"Sal?" Aaron asked, and she nodded. He smiled at Margarita and hoisted his water glass as proof of their hospitality and his pleasure, evidence for their future customers, who would be looking at his picture—taped to the wall or the cash register—for years to come. "You're doing very well," he said.

"Thank you. Are you from around here?" she asked hopefully, though he could see that she did not think it likely.

"I'm passing through," he said, and he pointed out the window to the truck. "I'm moving to San Francisco."

3

Like most major cities of the world, San Francisco, Aaron would quickly learn, had developed its own brand of provincialism, which manifested itself in its citizens' unwavering belief that theirs was the only city where one would want, even dare, to be gay. Upon discovering that he had spent the last nine years in New Mexico, more than one San Franciscan had remarked, "So I guess you moved here to really be gay," a comment that annoyed but mainly perplexed him with its implication that, until now, he had been only going through the motions, *playing* at being gay.

"Actually, I came here because of a woman," he generally replied. This was true, for he had chosen San Francisco because of Taffy, whom he had met two years earlier at an English-as-a-Second-Language conference in El Paso, a three-day event aimed at connecting ESL teachers with overseas jobs. He did not tell Walter that this was the conference's emphasis, allowing Walter to believe that he was going off to learn yet another strategy for teaching the past unreal conditional. Aaron went with the goal not of securing a job abroad but of *entertaining* the notion, of talking to recruiters from Hungary and Japan as though he possessed the intention and the freedom to pick up and go. It was his first step toward leaving. Taffy, on the other hand, attended because Glenna, her girlfriend of twenty-five years, had broken up with her, which meant that Aaron and she were two halves of the same coin— the leaver and the left. They became inseparable, attending meals and events and group interviews together, prompting a recruiter from

Osaka to inquire, hopefully, whether they were married, *hopefully* because married couples were highly sought after, two-for-ones that were considered more stable. Aaron was afraid that even uttering a simple "no" would reveal the shock and horror he felt at considering the question, at imagining Taffy as his lover.

Her given name, the one recorded on her conference pass, was Hulda. It suited her far better than Taffy, which was, after all, not a name but a candy. One heard *Taffy* and expected a pink-hued, stickily sweet young thing and not a dour, obese woman in her fifties who wore too much red, unbecomingly, and often left her hotel room without wiping the sleep from her eyes or the toothpaste residue from the corners of her mouth, oversights that Aaron felt obligated to point out. He told himself that Taffy had been getting along just fine without him, yet each morning at breakfast he found himself mentioning the glob of lotion that clung to the side of her cheek or offering her his unused napkin while noting that she might want to give her nose one more good blow, all of which had imposed a level of intimacy with Taffy that he did not want.

"Not married," Aaron finally replied. "We're friends." This struck him as deceitful.

The recruiter, a trim Japanese man in his sixties, smiled at his response. Was he smiling at how long it had taken Aaron to respond, or because he considered friendship a virtue worth smiling about? Or was he suggesting Aaron had employed *friends* as a euphemism for *lovers,* which meant that the conversation was back where it had started. Generally, Aaron enjoyed these strolls across cultural lines, into territory where people and situations could not be easily read or categorized. It was one of the aspects of teaching foreigners that appealed to him, but this interaction had drained him.

On the final afternoon of the conference, as Aaron and Taffy worked their way, table by table, through the conference hall, a Korean recruiter informed Taffy that she would not find work unless she lost weight. "Diet," the delegate said, pronouncing the word with an odd inflection so that, at first, Aaron thought he was actually speaking Korean.

Smiling pleasantly, Taffy assured the man that she had no interest in teaching in Korea. "Crossed it off my list ages ago," she said, adding in a mock-friendly tone, "Korean food is not very likable." She laughed and slapped the man on the back, and as she and Aaron walked away, she whispered, "That'll get him. Koreans can't stand to have their food maligned." Then she slapped Aaron on the back. "Come on," she said. "We might as well get a jump on happy hour."

They left the sea of tables, each representing an opportunity to escape the lives to which they would be returning the next day, and once they were settled in the hotel bar, drinking beer and eating free nachos, Aaron said, "Don't you think the Korean recruiter felt bad about what you said?"

"I hope he did," said Taffy. "That was the point, after all." She licked a glob of greasy cheese from her palm. "What I wouldn't give for some kimchi right about now, but what are the chances of finding decent kimchi in El Paso, Texas?"

Aaron did not reply, and after a moment, Taffy said, "He started it, Aaron. The man insulted me. Do we agree?" Her voice was sharp.

Aaron nodded.

"And do I not have the right to defend myself?"

Aaron did not look at her or respond.

"Listen," she said. "Is it because he's Korean? Is that what this is about? You're going to sit there and make one of those bullshit cultural relativity arguments?" She let her voice drift up to a breezy falsetto: "'Oh, it's wrong for an American to call me a fat pig, but we need to excuse him since he's from a different culture.' Because I can assure you that there are plenty of fat Koreans who would feel just as humiliated as I did, and he knows that. And if he doesn't, well, it's time he learned."

She was breathing heavily, not even waiting for him to reply. "Or maybe you think I should be used to it by now. I'm fat, so I need to expect people to say things, right? It goes with the territory. Is that it, Aaron?" She pounded the table hard as she spoke, the basket of nachos hopping like a rabbit toward the edge. "Or maybe this is some male solidarity thing that I'm just not getting?" She studied him. "Somehow,

I don't peg you that way, but there you have it. Help me out if I've missed something."

Aaron thought about the ease with which the man had spoken, as though Taffy's body, her fat, were public domain, open for scrutiny and comment. He knew that he had hurt her more deeply than the Korean recruiter had because the recruiter was a stranger, while he was supposed to be her friend. Still, nothing changed the fact that he was put off by Taffy in a way that seemed beyond his control, repulsed not by her size or laxness in grooming but by something he did not fully understand, though he knew it had to do with the way she positioned herself in the world. She had told him at breakfast one morning that she taught only beginning ESL because she preferred the docility of students who did not yet comprehend what was being said to or expected of them. He imagined her as a child, the one always put in charge when teachers left the room because they knew she would report everything, caring more about this small measure of power than she did the goodwill of her peers.

Taffy dipped another chip into the cheese and opened her mouth wide to receive the whole dripping mess, then slapped her greasy hands across her thighs, thumping them like watermelons. "I'm fat, Aaron," she declared, bits of nacho flying from her mouth. He felt one land on his face but did not reach up with his napkin to brush it away because he thought that that was what she expected him to do. He glanced at the tables around them. More than anything, he wanted her to lower her voice.

"That's what Glenna always did," she said. "Looked around to see whether anyone was listening."

"Well, she probably couldn't focus on the conversation with people listening. It's like having two audiences, and they want completely different things. You want to know what I think, but everyone else wants to be entertained, and I don't care to be entertainment for a bunch of strangers."

This, in fact, was Grievance #78: *When Walter wants to win an argument, he waits until we're in public, knowing that the minute it gets heated, I'll back down. He claims there's no forethought involved, that he cannot*

stifle himself simply because there are others around. Still, I can't help but
feel that he seeks out an audience of strangers as a way to silence me.

After that, neither of them was in the mood for another beer. Aaron picked up the tab, and Taffy let him. The next morning, they ate breakfast together, and Aaron did not point out that Taffy's shirt was misbuttoned. They said good-bye outside the dining room, shaking hands and exchanging addresses, though Aaron did not think they would keep in touch. However, once he was back home, away from Taffy and the constant stoking of his aversion, Aaron found himself remembering their time together with remorse. Eventually, he wrote to her, a brief note offering standard pleasantries—"It was great to meet you"—clipped to an article about teaching incorrect grammar to ESL students to help them better fit in with Americans. They had discussed the subject at breakfast the first morning, bonding over their mutual indignation. He hoped that she would see the letter as an overture.

Several weeks later, he received a reply. "Thanks for thinking of me," her letter began. She went on to describe her new batch of students, one of whom had come to the school Halloween party dressed as Hitler. "It fell to me to speak to him about his costume," she wrote. "Imagine trying to discuss such a thing with nothing more than a few nouns and verbs at your disposal. Still, I believe that by the end of our conversation he realized the potential this had to hurt others." Aaron understood that he had been forgiven.

They settled into a routine, Aaron composing a letter at the beginning of the month and Taffy responding near the end. He preferred her as a pen pal, having just her words before him and not Taffy herself, nose dusted with doughnut powder. She was the only friend he had who was exclusively his, who had never met Walter. Everyone who knew Walter loved him, was taken in by the way he seemed to listen deeply before dispensing advice that sounded wise and obvious when tendered in his calm, mellifluous voice. Aaron began writing to her about Walter occasionally, indulging in a newfound openness. Two years later, when he wrote that he was leaving Walter, Taffy had not waited until the end of the month to reply. She wrote back immediately, a response that read in its entirety, "I can help with the transition if you are interested in moving to San Francisco."

He pulled up in front of Taffy's house around two on Christmas Eve, tired and wanting only to rinse his face and drink a glass of water, perhaps walk around the block to stretch his legs and soothe his hip, which had settled into a steady throb, but Taffy, who had been watching for him, came out and hoisted herself into the truck. She had arranged for him to rent a studio apartment in Parkside, a neighborhood near hers, from the Ng family. She had once taught Mr. Ng's nephew.

"Let's go," Taffy said by way of greeting. "Mr. Ng is expecting us."

They drove in silence except for her one-word directions—*left, straight, left*. Finally, Aaron asked what the studio was like. "Tiny," she said, explaining that it was actually the back third of the Ngs' garage, which had been converted into living quarters. "And dark. It's the fog belt, but you'll be just fourteen blocks from the ocean."

The houses on his new street appeared nearly identical: the main quarters sat over the garage and were accessed by a tunnel entrance on the right. When they arrived, Mr. Ng came out. "One rule," he said as he shook Aaron's hand. "You pay, you stay."

"Yes, well, I think I can remember that," Aaron said. "Certainly the rhyming helps." Neither Taffy nor Mr. Ng laughed. Aaron took out his checkbook and wrote a check for the security deposit and another for the first month's rent, an amount close to what he and Walter had paid for their mortgage each month. Taffy had explained that it was the cheapest rent he would find in the city, given his insistence on living alone.

Mr. Ng stared at the check, which had his New Mexico address. "Mexico?" said Mr. Ng skeptically.

"*New* Mexico," he said, and Taffy assured Mr. Ng that New Mexico was in the United States.

"Okay, okay," Mr. Ng said finally, as though he were granting a dispensation in accepting this as fact. "Here is key."

But it was not a key. It was a garage door opener. Mr. Ng pointed it at the garage door, which rolled up noisily before them.

It seemed that this basic principle—thrift over convenience—had governed the conversion. No thought had been given to soundproofing, for example, which meant—Aaron would soon discover—that he could hear the family walking above him, hear them talking and arguing and even snoring. A thin wall had been erected to separate the studio from the garage proper, which housed not just the Ngs' car but also, problematically, the garbage cans. Indeed, in the months to follow, Aaron would lie in his studio at night, imagining all the ways that he could die right there in bed: the Ngs' Toyota smashing through the wall and running him over as he lay reading; the house (and the family with it) buckling down on him during an earthquake; the ocean forgetting itself and rolling up these fourteen blocks, drowning him in his sleep.

Taffy left him to settle in by himself, which he did not mind. It took him seven hours to unload and return the truck and then find his way back via public transportation, but when he finally stood on his block holding noodles from a Thai take-out place, he realized that he could not remember his new house number. He walked back and forth, pausing at last in front of the house that he thought was the Ngs', and when he pressed the garage door opener in his pocket, the door rolled up. He ate the noodles with his fingers because the take-out place had forgotten to include a fork and he could not find the box that contained cutlery. Above him he could hear Chinese, a pleasant sound. He focused on it and tried not to think about Walter. The two of them had observed a Christmas Eve tradition: they made a Moroccan chicken with gizzard-and-artichoke-heart stuffing and Brussels sprouts, and as they ate, they talked about what they each wanted from the coming year. It was like making resolutions, except they always began with an analysis of the previous year's disappointments. The last couple of years, however, Walter had been less willing to focus on the past, to reveal what had frustrated or discouraged him. Instead, he raised his wineglass and announced, "I wouldn't change a thing about my life," which left Aaron struggling to articulate his own discontentment.

He was relieved that the telephone was not yet hooked up because he would have called Walter right then to let him know he had arrived safely, but he would not have stopped there. He would have turned contrite, explaining tearfully how sorry he was, and Walter would have slipped into his most comfortable role, becoming patient and forgiving. "It's fine," he would have said. "Just come home."

Aaron wiped his greasy hands on his jeans, crawled onto the unmade futon, and slept for ten hours. The next morning, the city felt at rest. It was Christmas. He appreciated that silence would be his first memory. Then, an ambulance passed outside, and he felt the same sick dread that he had felt as a boy, when a siren almost always meant tragedy for someone he knew. He supposed that soon he would once again stop noticing sirens, but that morning he lay on his mattress and sobbed because the studio was dark and unfamiliar and because he had never lived alone.

Taffy had arranged an interview for him at her school, the San Francisco English Language Center. They needed someone to teach an advanced class, she said, and the director, Marla, wanted to meet him the day after Christmas. Taffy did not tell him much about the school, just that she had been teaching there for three years, since Glenna left. She had quit her old job, thinking change would make Glenna's absence less noticeable, but instead she had found that going off to a new school each day and riding a new bus home to an empty apartment only made her miss Glenna more. She wrote this to him after he accepted her invitation to come, the only truly personal thing she had ever revealed. She was being kind, he supposed, letting him know that it would not be easy.

The school was on Anza Street, housed in a drab building from the sixties that bore signs of neglect. Marla was also in a state of disrepair. Half the buttons on her dress had been replaced with safety pins, and when she stood, she appeared to list to one side, though he realized later that her dress was missing a shoulder pad. She began the interview by explaining that she had a firm policy of hiring gay people, though she herself was not gay, because she believed they made better teachers. Aaron did not know how to respond, for he desperately needed the job but was not in the habit of ignoring questionable logic. He laughed in case she was joking, but it turned out that she was not, and the two of them sat there awkwardly. He immediately regretted laughing, not because he had hurt Marla's feelings, though there was that to consider, but because he had made a decision as he stared down at the road from the wheel of the U-Haul, a decision to stop second-guessing his own instincts. The decision had seemed doable there in the truck, where his needs were basic: he stopped when he needed to urinate; bought food when he was hungry; filled the gas tank when the needle neared empty. Most important, amid the monotony of satiating himself and the truck, there was Jacob, whom he had saved because he had trusted his gut.

He looked at Marla and blurted out what he knew to be the truth, "I'm a really good teacher," referring to the only part of himself that seemed intact.

"Good," said Marla. "Because you're hired." They stood up, shook hands, and Aaron thanked her.

"What were they studying with their last teacher?" he asked.

"Well," she said. "Nico's been sort of filling in lately, so I'm not sure what they're up to."

"And before that? What about with their regular teacher?"

"They had Noreen, but she left suddenly. What happened was, she was in class one morning, and her husband called." Marla's voice dropped, taking on the hushed, excited tone that people use to divulge someone else's secrets. "He said he'd fallen asleep with the baby on the bed next to him, and she'd rolled off and hit her head, but the doctor said it was more than that."

Marla took a breath, and Aaron cut in. "What was Noreen doing with them when she left?" He wanted to establish that workplace gossip did not interest him. He had worked at schools that resembled dysfunctional families and had always ended up in the role of the older brother whose repeated attempts to remain uninvolved made him the most sought-after family member of all.

Marla stared at him. "Ask the students, I guess."

The next morning, Aaron put on a tie, the green silk that Walter had given him on his last birthday. He did not always wear a tie to work, but he wore at least a shirt with a collar because he believed his students deserved to know that he considered teaching them a profession. He tried not to dwell on the tie's origins, yet he could not help but think of Walter as he stood in front of the mirror, tightening the tie around his neck. Aaron regarded the world as fraught with symbolism, a place where something as ordinary as knotting a tie became a commentary on one's life.

When he entered the classroom at nine sharp, carrying a satchel and wearing the tie, the class looked startled. Taffy later explained that the students were coming off two months with Nico, an octogenarian who could not teach at the school permanently because he made frequent trips to Cuba to visit his "young men." According to Taffy, Nico treated the classroom as a private salon: he arrived at ten because he considered nine an uncivilized hour and spent the morning passing around photos of his latest young man and demonstrating dance steps from the rumba and *danzón*. One morning, he had shown up in his Castro bar wear, a leather vest and chaps, though he had worn underwear, Taffy noted, perhaps in deference to the realities of the job, which required him to turn periodically to write on the board. "Nico's lived in San Francisco too long," Taffy concluded, but Aaron knew that he could spend the rest of his life here and never consider wearing chaps to class. Once, he and Walter had gone to a cowboy bar in Albuquerque, but after thirty minutes they left because Aaron could not bear the sight of men playing pool and dancing and sitting on barstools wearing nothing but chaps, their buttocks ripping away from the vinyl when they stood. "You can't be so squeamish," Walter had scolded him afterward.

"Nine o'clock," Aaron announced. "Time to begin class. My name is Aaron Englund." He turned to write his name in capital letters on the board. "I will be your teacher this semester."

"Like the country?" a student asked. The student's name was Paolo, and he was from Italy. In Italy, Paolo had taught mathematics for twenty-six years, and then one day, he decided that twenty-six years was enough; he would go to the United States, where he would spend his days riding Harleys. He would do this until all the money he had saved during those twenty-six years was gone. When Paolo spoke, which was often, he sounded like someone parodying an Italian accent, and his hands swung rhythmically in the air as though he expected those around him to pick up instruments and begin to play. Aaron tried to imagine Paolo standing in front of a classroom, leading students through the intricacies of math. He wondered how it was possible to go from being that man, a man who wanted numbers to add up, to being a man who embraced risk.

"That's England," Aaron said, enunciating the *e* before turning to write ENGLAND next to ENGLUND. "One vowel," he said. "The difference between me and a country." The students laughed.

The class was large, twenty students, but he went around the room learning their names and where they were from. He always did this the first day because he knew that it mattered, especially to those who were accustomed to being overlooked. There were five Brazilians—"Almost a football team," they joked—and three Thais, but he was most surprised by the Mongolians. He had never had a Mongolian student before, did not think he had even met a Mongolian, yet there were two in the class, both named Borol. When he said, "Borol must be a common name in Mongolia," the second Borol replied, "Not common," with a serious face and the voice of a Russian, and the first Borol laughed to let him know it was a joke. He realized that he had always thought of Mongolians as not the joking types. It surprised him to find that he harbored stereotypes of Mongolians.

"Well," he asked the class, "where should we begin? You must have questions. What's confused you lately?"

They all stared at him. They had no reason to trust him—his ability or his intentions—yet. In the front row, a handsome Brazilian named Leonardo raised his hand. In Brazil, Leonardo was a pilot, but here in San Francisco, he delivered pizzas, which the other Brazilians referred to as the Brazilian National Occupation. "Why are you studying English?" Aaron had asked each student earlier, and Leonardo had explained that it was his first step toward becoming a pilot in China.

"China?" Aaron said. He had not meant to sound so surprised. "Why China?"

"Is big country," Leonardo said.

"Yes," Aaron agreed, waiting for the explanation to continue, but Leonardo, he would learn, did not believe in explaining a point to death. He considered others capable of connecting the dots: a big country required lots of planes, planes required pilots. Leonardo's reticence would not benefit his English, but Aaron could not help but think that circumspection was attractive in a pilot. Aaron did not like flying, particularly the life-and-death bargaining he did with himself each time he got on a plane. When he imagined the people who sat in the cockpit, he did not want to think of them as chatty sorts who cared about entertaining one another. He wanted to think of them like Leonardo, less enamored of words than flight.

"You have a question, Leonardo?" Aaron asked.

"Yesterday," Leonardo said, "I hear my coworker say to my other coworker, 'I hope the boss wasn't mad.'" Leonardo leaned forward. "Is correct?"

"Yes," Aaron said apologetically, for he could see the point in question. "It depends on the situation, but yes, it is correct."

"Why?" Leonardo demanded, almost angrily. "Why he is saying 'hope' when it is past tense? Hope is about the future. This is what we always learn."

The other students nodded, asserting their collective will. Aaron could feel their frustration and beneath it their distrust, for they had been taught, rightfully, that *hope* described the future, yet here he stood, telling them that this was not always so. In just one hour, he had taken away more knowledge than he had supplied.

Aaron had discovered his love of grammar as a boy, when he first observed in these structures and symbols a kind of order, patterns that allowed words—his first love—to join together and make sense. He saw that he could open his heart and love grammar almost more, the way one loved the uglier child best because it required more effort to do so. He was known for explaining grammar in ways that made sense, for filling the board with sketches and equations and even cartoons that his students eagerly copied into their notebooks. He turned now and wrote: *I hope he wasn't mad.* Below the sentence, he drew a timeline, the past on the left marked *Know,* the future on the right, *Don't Know.*

"Here we are, between the past"—he pointed to the word *Know*— "and the future, which we don't know." He looked at them encouragingly. "Okay, now let's say one of the drivers mixes up a very big pizza order, and the next day everyone is wondering whether the boss was mad when he found out, but nobody actually knows whether he was mad because he came in after everyone was already gone. How would you say that?"

"I wish that he weren't mad," suggested Katya, the lone Russian.

"Okay," Aaron said. "Except that means he *was* mad, that I *know* he was mad." A few of the students nodded. "In this case, the boss's reaction is in the past, but we don't know it yet. We'll learn about it in the future, so we have to say, 'I hope he wasn't mad.'"

He looked at them, they looked back, and then several more nodded. He was relieved to be back in the classroom, where he felt clear about what was needed from him: his knowledge and his steadying presence. But teaching provided something he needed also, a period each day when his own life receded.

"If there are no more questions," he said, "let's take a break." He pointed one last time at the diagram on the board. "Remember, the nice thing about not knowing what has already happened is that we can keep hoping for the best."

"Even though outcome is finished?" said Katya with the fatalism of a Russian.

"Yes," he said, but he did not let himself think of Jacob, who might already be dead.

4

M̲r. Ng drove a UPS truck. Most nights, he pulled his car into the garage after his shift and stayed in it for several hours. Aaron found it unsettling to have him there, on the other side of the flimsy wall that he leaned against as he sat on the bed reading or eating dinner or preparing for class, especially since Mr. Ng did not seem to be doing anything in his car, except maybe sleeping. Of course, Aaron knew that Mr. Ng was putting off as long as possible the moment when he went upstairs and he and his wife resumed their screaming, furniture-shoving arguments. Aaron did not know what their arguments were about because he did not understand Cantonese, but he assumed money, because he had read somewhere that money was what most couples argued about. At the end of prolonged quarrels, the Ngs sometimes switched to English, as though inviting him into their problems. He hated this the most, the intimacy of lying in bed in his pajamas, listening to two people who were supposed to be nothing more than his landlords destroy each other in not one but two languages.

Despite the lost hours of sleep, Aaron began rising early. He thought it was his body's natural rhythm finally asserting itself, now that there were no one else's habits or needs to consider. As a boy, he had been an early riser, but that was because his mother was not, so the café's morning preparations fell to him. After she disappeared, he spent his senior year living with the Hagedorns, a family of night owls, and their schedule became his, which meant his memories of the year were clouded by exhaustion. Then, Walter came along, insisting that he call supper "dinner," and he had, for it seemed a different meal from the one that he and his mother had rushed through in the brief lull before the early-bird special began at five.

Walter considered it improper to dine before eight, though he favored nine, and while the supper that Aaron had shared with his mother was a mishmash of kitchen errors, dinner with Walter involved wine, always, and at least two courses, with salad served last. Afterward, they drank a nightcap, cognac, though Aaron would have preferred sherry. Most nights, Walter asked Aaron to read aloud to him after dinner, poetry usually, for they agreed on poetry, not just on its value but on which poets and poems they loved. Walter liked "Dover Beach" and T. S. Eliot and Richard Hugo's "Degrees of Gray in Philipsburg," to which he had introduced Aaron years earlier and which Aaron had since committed to memory. "You might come here Sunday on a whim. / Say your life broke down," Aaron would recite while Walter sat beside him, inhaling deeply, as though hearing the words were not enough and he needed to breathe them in also, breathe them in as Aaron exhaled them.

Aaron had always appreciated that Walter did not leave movies or concerts and immediately demand an opinion, and it was the same with poetry. They sat in silence after each poem, feeling whatever it was they each felt without having to put it into words. Eventually, they finished their nightcaps, rose, and got ready for, and then into, bed, the king-size bed, where they watched the news or read but did not have sex because Walter did not enjoy sex after dark, an indisposition he once explained by saying that he could never shake the feeling that he was being watched. Aaron assumed that Walter's fear was tied to something from his past, something he did not want to discuss, though at times he wondered whether it might not be a function of his collective consciousness as a gay man, a throwback to an era when gay men did everything furtively, when every look or word or touch had the power to destroy lives.

Despite Walter's fears, they had had sex at all hours in the beginning, sex at noon while the fire whistle blew, announcing lunchtime, and sex at midnight so that Aaron joked it had taken him two days

to come. Sometimes Aaron would visit Walter on campus, and they
would have sex there in Walter's office, a Latin professor on one side
of the thin walls and a young French professor on the other. Before he
bent Aaron over his desk or tipped him back in his reading chair, Walter pulled the shades and locked the door, but such precautions made
sense there, for neither of them wanted to look up as Walter thrust into
Aaron hard from behind to find a student in the doorway.

Aaron always fell asleep first, Walter beside him, reading or preparing notes for an article or keeping up with his correspondence,
for even after email came along, Walter continued to write letters by
hand, using carbon paper between the top page, the one he would
mail, and the bottom, the one that would go into a box marked neatly
with the year. The boxes of letters were lined up in their basement,
had moved with them from Minnesota to New Mexico. When Aaron
asked Walter why he kept the letters, he said that he anticipated
reaching a point in his life when the present offered nothing new, and
when that day came, he would bring up his boxes and read through
the story of his life, maybe finding even more pleasure in it the second
time.

Most mornings the smallness of his new apartment overwhelmed
him, the walls pressing in so that he could not read or grade papers or
even think. He began walking to work, giving himself an hour and a
half, even two hours, because he liked knowing that there was time to
linger, time to learn about his new neighborhood, where he felt daily
the surprise and pleasure of being an outsider. The signs on businesses
often announced themselves first in large Chinese characters, catering
to him as an afterthought, in English that was often grammatically
incorrect and rendered in small letters. Among his favorite business
names were these: Smartest Child, a tutoring center whose window
featured a photograph of a teenage girl in a beauty pageant gown, her
perfect SAT scores superimposed on her sash; 100% Healthy Dessert,
which he had tried once, intrigued by the pictures of syrupy concoc-
tions filled with beans and colorful tapioca worms and even more by

the menu descriptions promising enticements such as "promotes bowel movement"; and Happy Good Lucky, a tiny market on Taraval that advertised BEER ALL FLAVORS $9 and dissuaded shoplifters with a series of hand-lettered index cards, strategically placed, that read, HONESTY IS THE BEST PERSONALITY I APPRECIATE.

His favorite restaurant was T-28, a Macau diner, the name a handy mnemonic derived from its location at the corner of Taraval and Twenty-Eighth. At T-28, nobody asked how he was, only what he wanted. He found this deeply appealing and had eaten there every night his first week in San Francisco, drawn to the lack of pleasantries and inexpensive food, until the bubble burst: low on cash, he missed a night, and when he returned, the waitress slapped down his menu and said, "Hey, long time no see." He imagined her sitting in an ESL class, memorizing such expressions and waiting for an opportunity to use them, to say, "Breakfast special already finished. Early bird gets the worm." He did not begrudge her the chance to use her knowledge, but he missed the way it had been.

His morning walk took him down Noriega Street, where he stopped in front of a bank to read the exchange rates posted in the front window, noting which countries' currencies were listed, because this told him something about his neighborhood, and which currencies had risen or fallen, because this told him something about the world. From Noriega, he walked over several blocks to Golden Gate Park, where he lingered longest. Often, the bison were out, a herd that was kept there—in the middle of a city—to commemorate the lost American frontier. He liked to watch them and think about the irony of this. His last stop before exiting the park was a lake, man-made, where he sat on a bench watching a group of elderly Chinese doing tai chi, teenagers smoking pot before school, and a boy and his grandfather who came frequently, though not every morning, to motor a toy sailboat across the lake.

He preferred to begin his days in silence and found that walking to work eased him into the world. There was also the fare he saved by not taking the bus. He worried about money now that he was on his own, not because he had relied on Walter—he had not—but there was something reassuring about a household with two incomes. Mainly, he was avoiding the bus because of the twins, who were always on board. He had come to suspect that they had no destination, that riding the bus was what they did, the way that other people went to jobs.

The twins were identical. They dressed alike, usually in zippered, gray sweaters over emerald green cowboy shirts with snap buttons, and groomed each other like cats, one tamping down the other's cowlick with moistened fingertips, straightening his collar, rebuttoning his shirt, zipping his sweater to a point just above the heart. It was as though the public nature of the bus allowed them to more fully enter their own secret world. Aaron could not look away.

Twins were popping up everywhere. In class, Yoshi, who had recently become the father of fraternal twins, raised his hand to note that twins were highly unusual in Japan. Only here in America did you see twins with regularity, said Pilar, the Spaniard, turning Yoshi's children into a by-product of their parents' temporary expatriation. Several of her classmates nodded in vehement agreement.

Aaron knew that he should point out the obvious: the United States was nothing more than an aggregate of the world's populations and it seemed unlikely that the genetic capabilities of these same populations would change so drastically on American soil. But he did not disabuse the class of its theory, for he had noticed that the students were sometimes skeptical of his views on topics other than grammar. They would not be convinced, for example, that homelessness was not caused by laziness or that Americans did not all eat old food, as one of the Bolors had suggested.

"What is 'old food' anyway?" he had asked, perplexed by the deceptive simplicity of the words.

"Food that is old," another student said, because they all understood the charge being made. In fact, they had an arsenal of anecdotal evidence, stories of host mothers who prepared frozen waffles with expiration dates years past, of babysitting for families who ate around mold and expected them to do the same. He tried to explain that they were arguing from exception, assuring them that most Americans did not eat spoiled food or feed it to guests, but he stopped because he saw that they needed to believe these things. They spent their days cleaning houses and delivering pizzas to people who counted change in front of them, convinced of their dishonesty or inability to subtract, or, more likely, some combination of the two, being told—as they accepted a fifty-three-cent tip—how grateful they must feel to be in this country.

And generally they were grateful. They were young, most of them, and thought about their lives the way that young people do: with anticipation and the sense that their futures would build like symphonies, one great note following the next. But there was a difference between feeling grateful and having gratitude demanded of you.

Aaron encountered his first twins the summer he was five, when he and his parents embarked on a two-week vacation marked by long stretches in the car, six or seven hours at a time. It was hot that summer, and they rarely spoke as they drove, which had less to do with the heat than with the sort of family they were. Along the way, he learned to read his first words—*stop, population,* and *vacancy*—but mainly he stared at the back of his father's head, bristly with its policeman haircut. He had not realized, until then, how white his father's scalp was, like the inside of a potato at the moment it's split open.

"How much longer?" Aaron could not keep from asking. Prisoners, students, passengers on long sea voyages, children in cars: they all know well the slowing that occurs because their time does not truly belong to them. His mother gave cryptic responses involving *hours* and *minutes,* words that meant nothing to him, while his father threatened to pull over and give him "a good spanking" if he did not shut up, which did mean something. It was how his father spoke of spankings, employing the adjective *good* as though the spanking represented some obvious moral truth.

After several days of this, days defined by the heat and the sight of his father's head riding squarely before him, Aaron asked instead, "How many *Adam-12*s until we get there?," referring to a half-hour television program about policemen that he and his father watched each Saturday.

"Four," said his mother, too enthusiastically, and so the *Adam-12* system for telling time was established.

The vacation started at the Paul Bunyan Park in Bemidji, where cement statues of Paul and Babe the Blue Ox stood beside the shore of Lake Bemidji. The Englunds had visited the park twice before, the three visits merging in Aaron's memory so that years later he could not remember which time they saw a roller coaster being built or which time his father pointed to a family of four and leaned toward him, whispering, "Look, Aaron, there go some Jews." In the family photo album, there were three different shots of him standing between Paul and Babe, one to commemorate each visit, the changes in those young versions of himself obvious, despite the fact that whoever took the pictures (he assumed it was his father) had stood far back in order to capture the full height of Paul Bunyan, leaving Aaron an incidental presence at the statue's feet.

He did know it was during the last visit that his father became angry at him for refusing to go on the rides. "So you're just going to go through life a chickenshit?" his father asked as they stood to the side of the Tilt-A-Whirl, watching other children board the cars excitedly. In his pretend-casual voice, his father added, "Really, I don't see how you're going to manage in school." Aaron did not say that he wondered this also.

His father turned then and walked calmly away. At home he might have shouted or smashed a bottle on the floor, but he did not believe in being a spectacle, in providing strangers with that pleasure. Aaron was familiar with his father's stiff back, with the way his hands dove deep into his pockets and his feet kicked forward with each step, keeping an invisible can in motion, just as he recognized the way that he and his mother stood side by side, dazed by how quickly things could go awry. Only minutes earlier, his mother had turned to them, revealing a clot of yellow mustard on her ear lobe, a leftover from the hamburgers they had eaten while squeezed together on a bench. Aaron and his father had burst into simultaneous laughter, a rare occurrence that had encouraged all three of them, nudging them toward giddiness.

"Dolores," his father said, "were you feeding that hamburger to your ear?"

They laughed again while his mother dabbed at her ear with a tissue, using Aaron and his father as mirrors, asking, "Is it gone? Jerry? Aaron? Did I get it all?"

Years later, when Aaron thought back on that day, trying to see his father's anger as something predictable, he began here, hoping to understand the slow build of his rage, but when he remembered the way that his mother had giggled and spoken their names, he knew that she had been enjoying the attention, that his father's tone had been free of reproach. And so Aaron, too, had been happy. It was that simple and that treacherous.

Aaron and his mother waited, without speaking, for his father to return, and when it became clear that he was not coming back, they spent the afternoon at a free storytelling event about the life of Paul Bunyan. The storyteller—an old man dressed in a plaid lumberjack shirt—fidgeted as he spoke, his right hand rubbing the wrist of the left as though it had just been freed from handcuffs. He regarded the audience eagerly, too eagerly, when he thought he had said something funny. At the end, everyone rose and filed out of the hot room quickly.

"Stay put, and don't talk to anyone," Aaron's mother said, and she left too.

The storyteller regarded him nervously. "Young man, did you know that when Paul was just one week old, he was already so big he had to wear his father's clothes?" He chuckled. "Can you imagine?" Aaron thought about his father's shirts, which smelled of sweat that had worked itself deeply into the fibers. Even after his mother washed them, the odor remained, requiring only the heat of his mother's iron to rekindle it. Aaron smiled at the storyteller. It was not his fault that he thought Aaron might be intrigued by the idea of wearing his father's clothes.

The man shuffled out, and Aaron was by himself in the room. It was the largest room he had ever occupied alone, and the empty space gave freedom to his thoughts. What he imagined was his parents getting into the Oldsmobile and driving away without him, returning to their house in Moorhead (because his imagination was not equipped to send them elsewhere) while he established a new life here, sleeping under Babe's stomach when it rained and spending his days listening to the tall tales.

Into the room came two boys. He could still recall the shock he had felt as he looked at the boy on the left, taking in the severely upturned nose and knobby, receding chin, the blue eyes and unusually short lashes, and then saw the same configuration of unfortunate features on the other boy. They were around twelve, the age at which threatening younger children offered both pleasure and a way to subvert their own feelings of vulnerability. They spoke loudly and swaggered up to Aaron as if he had stolen something of theirs that they aimed to get back.

"Hey, asshole," said the boy on the right.

The other snickered and kicked Aaron's chair hard. "My brother's talking to you, asshole," he said.

"My mother told me not to talk to anyone," Aaron replied, his voice soft and overly polite. When he used this voice with his father, it only made him angrier.

The boys sat down behind him. "I heard that Paul Bunyan had a pecker as big as an oak tree," the one directly behind him said. He kicked the back of Aaron's chair, jolting Aaron forward.

His twin laughed. "Yeah, and nuts like basketballs."

The first boy leaned forward, his voice loud in Aaron's ear. "I heard a train thought his asshole was a tunnel—went in and never came out."

"Paul Bunyan was a fag," his brother said, and the boys slammed backward in their chairs, yelping like puppies.

Aaron's mother returned and glared at the boys. "We'll wait in the car," she said to Aaron, which meant that she had not found his father.

They left the park and walked up and down several streets, his mother pausing at each corner, giving careful consideration to all four directions. Her tendency, like his, was to leap to the worst conclusion; he felt her fear in the way she squeezed his hand tightly one minute and flung herself free of him the next. They rounded a corner and there was the Oldsmobile, the driver-side door open, his father's legs jutting into the street.

"It's about time," his father said when he saw them. "Four o'clock. What have you people been doing all day?" He called them "you people" when he found their actions as inexplicable as those of strangers.

Aaron and his mother got into the car. They said nothing because they knew that silence was best in the aftermath of his father's anger. Aaron fell asleep against the car door, too tired to worry, as he usually did, that it might spring open and send him tumbling into the road. When he awoke to the cessation of motion, he discovered that they were in front of a motel consisting of cabins and an office shaped like a wigwam, a VACANCY sign lit up in pink neon over its door. When his father got out of the car, the smell of rotting apples wafted in. He went into the wigwam and came back with a key, which he used to unlock one of the cabin doors, and they went inside. His mother quickly opened the windows, letting in the smell of the apples, which mingled with the smell his mother had been trying to air out, a sour odor not unlike the one that came from his father's feet when he sat in his recliner after working all day and ordered Aaron to pry off his shoes.

"Bed, Aaron," said his mother. He followed her into the bedroom, where she produced his pajamas and toothbrush from a suitcase. He'd felt such pleasure at seeing his possessions appear in these unfamiliar surroundings. They spent two nights there, hot, sleepless nights during which Aaron clung to the edge of the bed he shared with his parents because his father had not wanted to pay extra for a cot. The sickly sweet stench of rotting apples had intensified daily, its source an overly burdened tree that shed its fruit in a wide skirt outside their bedroom window. His father liked the smell, and the windows remained open.

The first morning, his father took him inside the wigwam, showed him a shelf of souvenirs—beaded necklaces, T-shirts, and miniature totem poles with eagle wings flaring out from the top—and instructed him to choose one. He considered each item while his father chatted with the old man behind the desk. When the old man shuffled over to a postcard rack near the door, passing gas with each step, Aaron's father turned to glare at Aaron as though expecting him to do something shameful, laugh perhaps.

"Did you find something, son?" he asked. He called Aaron "son" when there were other people around.

Aaron held up a beaded pouch shaped like a canoe with a zipper running from bow to stern. His father examined it. "That's what you want?" he said. "A purse?"

Aaron turned and grabbed the totem pole with eagle wings, mumbling "thank you" when his father paid for it, and they walked back to the cabin.

"A totem pole," said his mother. "Oh for cute."

She was sitting on the bed, stitching up a pair of his shorts that had split at the seam. He was a plump child whose clothes suffered routine outbursts, though as an adult, he would be thin, his childhood pudginess retained only in his hands. He handed his mother the totem pole, which she set on the sill of the open window. Each time Aaron awakened that night and saw it outlined there, wings spread, he could not help but feel that his mother had given it the option to flee.

The next morning, she packed their suitcases while his father sat on the bed and hurried her along, and then they walked across the road to a diner called Freddie's. Aaron was allowed to have pancakes, which they rarely had at home because his father hated them. They recrossed the road, and as his father loaded their suitcases into the trunk, his mother prepared three washcloths, wetting them and rolling them up inside a bread bag, which would be stored in the glove compartment for emergencies. She had done this the previous morning also. His father came in whistling and carrying a paper bag that the motel owner had told him to fill with the apples that lay scattered and rotting outside their cabin. The three of them gathered half a bagful, and while Aaron and his father waited in the car, his mother went back into the cabin, leaving the door ajar so that Aaron caught glimpses of her as she bent to peer under things. His father drummed impatiently on the car's roof, his thumps growing more thunderous when she finally appeared.

She got into the car holding a matchbook wrapped with black thread left over from mending Aaron's shorts. His father, weighing the delay against this bit of nothing, snatched the matchbook and flung it out the window.

The car was filled with the waxy, overripe scent of the apples and the smell of his father, who had not bathed at the motel because the bathroom had only a shower and he preferred a tub, where he could stretch out while Aaron's mother shampooed his hair and scrubbed his back until it turned red. His father gnawed steadily on the apples as he drove. Aaron tried to eat one, but his stomach was weak from the heat and the car's motion, and he managed just a few bites. He closed his eyes and pressed his brow against the window.

"Look!" he heard his father cry out, and he pulled away from the window and opened his eyes. His father's right arm was stretched awkwardly behind him, back over the top of the seat; in his hand, clutched like a baseball, was a half-eaten apple. Aaron thought that his father was offering him the apple, but as his eyes focused, he realized his father was showing him something: a worm that he had bitten in two, the half still in the apple wiggling frantically, the other half presumably doing the same in his father's stomach. Aaron did not know which half—the one he could see or the one he was forced to imagine—caused what happened next. His body convulsed, and then his father's arm was covered in vomit, *his* vomit, the pancakes and bacon and bits of apple all vaguely identifiable. His father took his eyes from the road to look at his arm as if he too were trying to sort out the ingredients of Aaron's breakfast.

"Jerry, pull over so we can get you cleaned up," Aaron's mother said, staring forward, as though reading the words from a sign up ahead.

His father veered onto the shoulder, braking with such force that the keys jangled in the ignition. He climbed out, holding his soiled arm away from him. As Aaron's mother worked to retrieve the wet washcloths from the glove compartment, jiggling its tricky latch, he yanked open Aaron's door and leaned in.

"Eat it," he said, mashing his arm hard against Aaron's mouth.

Aaron clenched his jaw, but the vomit leaked back in between his lips. He tried not to move it about with his tongue, but he could taste it, sour and bitter like a rotten walnut, and beneath that was the faint sweetness of the syrup and the bacon's clear salinity. He told himself that it had all come from him, but this realization only made things worse and he vomited again.

Then, his father was gone, replaced by his mother, who handed him one of the washcloths. "Clean yourself up," she whispered.

He pressed the cloth to his face, taking in its musty smell, and scraped it hard across his tongue. His parents were behind the car, and he boosted himself onto his knees so that he could watch them through the rear window. "See if I give a shit," he heard his father say, but a semi hurtled by, taking his mother's reply with it. At last, his father held out his arm and let his mother run a washcloth along it, the vomit piling up like snow before a plow. They drove away in silence, the washcloths in a heap beside the road, the remains of their emergency.

For two weeks they drove, his father staring at the road, his mother at maps. Aaron did not find maps appealing. "They're wonderful tools," his mother said, which made him think of hammers and drills and noisy activities like those in which his father engaged in the basement, activities that Aaron found as unappealing as maps. "You know," she added, "we couldn't make this trip without a map."

"Why?" he asked.

"Well, because we need the map so we know where we're going."

It had not occurred to him that his parents did not know where they were going.

The trip was marked by statues: a large otter in a park in Fergus Falls; the Happy Chef, who warned them to stuff cotton in their ears because he felt like singing; and Mount Rushmore, which featured the faces of very important men called presidents, whom he would learn about in school his mother said. His father held up a dollar bill, and Aaron was surprised to see that it bore the face of the man on the left, George Washington. His father said that George Washington had wooden teeth, as though this were the most important thing to know about him.

Bookending the trip were the Paul Bunyan statues, the standing one in Bemidji and the sitting Paul Bunyan in Brainerd, their final stop. It was there at the sitting Paul Bunyan's feet that something happened, a small thing that had nonetheless offered Aaron a glimmer of hope about his potential as a son. In the photograph that remained of that day, he was standing beside Paul's big, brown boot. He liked to imagine there was something unusual in his stance, defiant, though the look on his face was clear panic, the result of having been made to stand in line with the other children to meet Paul Bunyan while their parents waited to the side, eyeing them like 4-H calves at the fair.

He had watched as two girls in matching yellow bonnets approached the statue. "How old are you?" bellowed Paul Bunyan, and the older girl, her arm firmly around the other's shoulders, said, "I'm seven. How old are you, Mr. Bunyan?"

"Have you seen Babe, my blue ox?" asked Paul Bunyan, not mentioning his age.

Aaron tried to prepare for his turn by thinking back on what he had learned from the tall tales, but as the line moved forward, he realized that Paul Bunyan did not respond to any of the questions put to him. Finally, when only one child stood between him and the uncooperative giant, he began to sob. The slow simmer of his fear gave way to full-blown panic—like a teapot whistle shrieking inside him—and he leaped forward and kicked Paul Bunyan.

Immediately, he was sorry. "Did you feel that, Mr. Bunyan?" he asked in a voice meant to suggest contrition.

The only response came from the parents, in the form of enthusiastic laughter and clapping. A man in plaid shorts called out, "Knock 'im again. Bust his kneecaps," and as the parents cheered, his father pushed forward to stand beside him. More than anything else about the trip, Aaron remembered the warmth of his father's hand on his head.

"Hello there, what's your name?" Paul Bunyan shouted, his voice echoing from the area of his lap, but nobody was paying attention.

Aaron's father steered Aaron past the other parents, nodding at them casually, as if to suggest that his son provided such amusing fare daily. A burly woman with a large wooden cross riding atop her bosom called out, "You're a regular little David, aren't you?"

"My name is Aaron," he replied, and even this made people laugh.

5

The morning they left on the family vacation, Aaron's father had set his coffee cup on the table as he went out the door, triggering the usual response from Aaron's mother, who wanted to wash it right then, an argument that his father won by threatening to leave without her. When they returned two weeks later, the dirty cup sat where his father had left it, calling his parents to battle, but they averted their eyes and kept silent. In the days that followed, the truce established in front of the sitting-down Paul Bunyan hung over them, its fragility palpable. They sat at the supper table each night, afraid to speak, the hope that they had carried home settling on them like a yoke.

This went on for eight days. On the morning of the ninth, Aaron's father fell off a parade float and died. Aaron witnessed the whole thing, beginning with his father perched on the back rail of the float with three other policemen, waving and tossing candy, and ending when the tractor pulling the float lurched into a higher gear and his father tumbled backward, landing on his head in the street below. It looked so natural—his uniformed father rolling through the air like a scene from *Adam-12*—that Aaron thought it had been planned, until the float crashed to a halt, the Shriners in their go-karts veering wildly to avoid his father, their fez tassels going limp as horsetails. One of the other policemen leaped from the float, put two fingers to his father's neck, and, with something approaching awe in his voice, announced, "By God, Englund's dead."

It was not the first time Aaron had heard the word *dead,* but when he asked his mother exactly what it meant, she told him that *dead* was "a state, a permanent state." Flustered by her inability to make death clearer, she added, *"Permanent* means forever, Aaron." This made no sense, for when she went to the beauty shop, she got something called a permanent, which lasted just a few months, the curls uncoiling week by week. There was also the *dead* he associated with cold winter mornings, when his father would stomp back inside the house to pull on gloves, muttering, "The damn battery's dead." From the window, Aaron watched him lift the hood on his squad car and back the Oldsmobile out of the garage, attaching cables from its battery to the squad car's battery. Minutes later, his father drove off, the squad car's dead battery resurrected.

At the funeral, his father's colleagues gathered awkwardly around Aaron and his mother. They pressed pennies into his hand, which he slipped into his trouser pockets, alternating between left and right. That night he emptied the pennies into a bowl. As he dressed the next morning, indeed each morning, he redistributed the coins in the same way, enjoying the even weight of them. He came to think of death as this, the steady tug of pennies holding him down, keeping him balanced.

Technically, his father had died in the line of duty, and the funeral reflected this. At the cemetery, Aaron closed his eyes, enjoying the dizziness that overtook him as he stood above the gaping hole that would soon hold his father. The gun blasts, however, had come as a surprise and he wet himself, a warm sensation in his suit pants passing into his consciousness just as the echoes of the gunshots faded. In the days afterward, he and his mother rose and ate and slept, a routine punctuated by the sound of his mother crying in a room where he was not. One night just after the funeral she appeared with a framed photograph of his father, which she set on Aaron's night table in the spot where she usually set a glass of water. "He looks like this because he was squinting into the sun," she said, pointing at his father's small, scowling face.

His father glared at him as he lay in bed each morning, dry-mouthed, waiting for his mother to come for him. He always waited, a habit that had once been a simple function of age, though on his fifth birthday in March, everything changed. He had awakened early that morning and crept down the hallway to his parents' bedroom, planning to surprise them with his newfound independence, but standing in their half-open doorway, he witnessed a terrifying sight: his father, dressed in his police uniform, had his mother, his *naked* mother, pressed face-first against the wall, her legs apart, arms reaching upward. "Please, Officer," his mother said. As Aaron watched, his father handcuffed his mother. He knew what would happen next. He had heard his father run through the drill dozens of times. His mother would be put into his father's squad car, into the backseat, which was reserved for criminals, and taken to jail. He would be left alone with his father.

He went back to his room and lay with the covers pulled up to his chin. He stayed like that for what seemed a very long time. Finally, his door opened, and his mother peeked in. "Come on, sleepy boy," she said. "Time to get up. We have a birthday to celebrate." She held her index finger to her lips, the signal the two of them used to indicate collusion against his father. "Once your father's gone, we'll make pancakes." When she leaned over to pull back his covers, her body gave off a strange almond odor.

One morning, Aaron opened his eyes to find his father still staring at him from the nightstand. His mouth felt drier than usual, perhaps because he had been dreaming about the iron ore mines, which they had visited near the end of their vacation. They had stayed with Uncle Petey, who was twelve years older than Aaron's mother. Petey spent his days at his kitchen table sorting buttons for his wife, Charlotte, who was a seamstress. She was German; they had met when Petey was stationed in Germany after the war. Charlotte was so thin that you could see the bones of her spine beneath her cotton shirt as she bent over her sewing machine. Aaron's mother said she had always been this way, that she could not control her nerves except by smoking, and so, possessed of just one mouth, she had sacrificed eating. Everything in their house smelled of smoke.

Uncle Petey had once worked in the mines, but his mine had

stopped producing and become a tourist attraction, which Aaron and his parents toured one afternoon. In the car on the way over, Aaron's father said that there was more to it than the mine closing, that Petey had stopped working even before that. "He woke up one day and he was afraid of the dark," his father said, chuckling as he usually did when discussing other people's fears, while Aaron's mother stared out the window.

The tour was led by former miners, who spoke to one another in a language that was not English. "Damn Finns," his father whispered. "They run this place." It was dark in the mines and wet, and when his father said "Finns" like that, Aaron felt as if he were underwater with everything closing in. He gasped for air.

Halfway through the tour, the group stopped walking. The Finns began ushering people over the edge of what appeared to be a drop-off, but as Aaron got closer, he saw that they were actually stepping onto a ladder and disappearing into the darkness below. Soon, only he and his parents remained at the top, along with one of the Finns. Aaron's father swung over the edge and onto the ladder. "Let's go," he called to Aaron.

"I can't do it," Aaron whispered to his mother.

"It's like walking down stairs," she said. He knew this was not true.

"You go now," the Finn told him, the light on his helmet shining into Aaron's eyes. "It's not hard," he added in a kind voice, and Aaron knew the Damn Finn had seen that he was crying. Below them, the others were getting restless.

"Aaron, get your ass on this ladder now or I'm coming back up there and we'll see if a good spanking won't help," said his father from the darkness. The others stopped talking, and without their chatter the mine seemed vast. With the Damn Finn's help, Aaron knelt, his right foot reaching down for the top rung. A hand seized his ankle. He kicked, but his father held on, pulling him into the darkness.

His sheets were tangled around his legs. He worked himself free, got out of bed, and tipped the photograph forward, bringing his father face-to-face with the nightstand. He found his mother sitting at the kitchen table with the map of Fargo-Moorhead open before her. She could no longer go anywhere near the parade route, which had turned simple errands into full-day events that began here at the table with his mother marking out a route and ended with them driving in circles through newly developed neighborhoods that did not exist on the map.

"You need shoes," his mother said. "Remember, school starts Monday." The very thought of starting kindergarten filled him with dread. It was not that he did not want to learn. He did, but he did not want to sit in a room full of other children to do so. "Go get dressed," his mother said.

"I like my shoes," he said, but he did not argue because after the funeral Uncle Petey had pulled him aside. "The doctor says your mother needs lots of peace and quiet," Uncle Petey told him, in a tone suggesting that *peace and quiet* was something he believed a boy Aaron's age could not provide. Aaron wondered when the doctor had said this to his mother. She hadn't been sick. It was true that she slept a lot, but that was something she did not do when she was sick because she always said that the best medicine was having him sit by her bed and tell her things.

He went into his bedroom and put on his pants, dividing the pennies between his front pockets. Then he sat on the floor and wiggled his feet into his shoes. They had become tighter, but that did not change the fact that these were the shoes with which he had kicked Paul Bunyan. He could not imagine starting school without them.

The store carried only children's shoes and was decorated to appeal to its audience: a carousel horse stood out front, its coin slot filled with gum, and just inside the door was a gumball machine, flanked by dusty statues of Buster Brown and his dog, whose tail had been broken off and propped against his leg. When they entered, a bell above the door rang.

"And what can we help you with today?" the saleswoman called out to them.

"Aaron is starting school next week," his mother told the woman.

"Starting school?" the woman said, bending toward him. "And what grade are you going to be in, young man?"

Aaron looked up at the woman. Everything about her was

exaggerated—the tone of her voice, the redness of her lipstick, the puff of her hair—each feature rivaling the others like choir members who had decided to out-sing one another. He put his hands in his pockets, letting the pennies trickle through his fingers. "Kindergarten," he said.

"Kindergarten!" the woman repeated, making her eyes large as if to suggest that meeting a boy about to start kindergarten was rare indeed in her line of work.

"Do you carry cowboy boots?" he asked.

"We do," she replied, looking at his mother for guidance.

"Absolutely not," his mother said. "I'm not going to spend all day polishing boots."

"I would polish them," Aaron mumbled.

His mother picked up a pair of dress shoes, checked the price, and held them out to him. "Now aren't these nice?" she said. Aaron looked at them. They were not nice.

"That's a really snazzy pair," the saleswoman said. "They've been very popular with boys your age."

Aaron succumbed to the process, allowing the woman to pry off his old shoes, measure his foot, and lace him into a pair of the cheap dress shoes.

"How do they feel?" his mother asked. He stood and paced for her, realizing that the carpet was so worn because all day long other children did as he was doing, walked back and forth while their mothers looked on. His mother and the saleswoman took turns pressing on the toes. "I guess we'll take them," his mother said, sighing as she got to her feet, and he could tell then that she did not think the cheap dress shoes were nice either.

"I like them," he declared.

They moved to the counter, where the saleswoman wound a length of string around the shoebox while chatting about the weather. His mother stood writing a check, her lips moving as though she were dictating the information to her hand. In the past, she had been able to carry on a conversation while writing checks, but lately most tasks required her full concentration so that even when she did get out of bed to make supper, for example, she no longer invited him to cook with her, did not show him how to measure salt in the palm of his hand or check the temperature of the roast.

"Looks like we'll have a lot of rhubarb this year," the saleswoman said.

"I used to make rhubarb crisp," his mother told the woman as she handed her the check.

"I love crisp," the woman replied. "May I see your driver's license?"

His mother fumbled with her purse. "Of course, that was before the parade," she said, handing the woman her license.

The woman began copying information onto the check. "The parade?"

Aaron looked at his mother. Large, evenly spaced tears rolled down her cheeks, what she called "crocodile tears" when he produced them. Once, she had pretended to catch his crocodile tears with a needle and thread, stringing them into a necklace. She had done it to make him laugh, but his mother no longer seemed to be thinking about his laughter.

"Yes, the parade," his mother said.

He backed away, feigning interest in a pair of Hush Puppies.

"I'm afraid I don't know what parade you're talking about, dear," the saleswoman said. She returned his mother's license and pivoted toward the cash register.

"The parade," his mother screamed. The woman jerked back around. "The parade," she said again, this time with quiet authority. "Don't you know anything?" She shook her head as though she pitied the woman and then rested it on the counter, atop the nest that she'd made of her arms.

Everything that happened next would remain in Aaron's memory as a set of images and sounds, devoid of chronology. He knew that the saleswoman had called to him repeatedly, "Young man, there's something wrong with your mother," and that he had stood with his back to them, focusing on the gumball machine by the door. He recalled the feel of his hands dipping repeatedly into his pockets, the way they seemed separate from him, not his own hands at all, and the things he told himself as he turned the metal crank of the machine, things like

"If it's blue, she'll stop crying and we'll go home." He remembered the whirring as the saleswoman dialed the telephone and what she said first: "I'm calling to request medical assistance." She said other things, but those things he did not remember because nothing had impressed him like that first sentence.

By the time the ambulance arrived, his pockets were empty, his dead-father pennies converted into bubblegum, which had formed a wad in his mouth the size of a Ping-Pong ball. "What's your name, son?" one of the paramedics asked. Aaron stared up at the man, cheeks puffed out, lips pulled back menacingly. His jaw had gone numb, so he did not know that he was drooling, his spittle tinged green and pink and blue. With his pockets empty, he felt as though he might float away, so he stood very still, watching as they strapped his mother to a gurney and wheeled her to the ambulance and as the saleswoman ran after them with the cheap dress shoes. She returned looking satisfied, her transaction complete, but she saw him then and stopped.

"How can you just stand there chewing gum?" she asked in a cool, steady voice.

He stared back at her, feeling the familiar urge to vomit, but he knew nothing could get past the gum. He panicked, the pastel spittle foaming around his mouth as he struggled to breathe.

"What kind of a boy are you?" the saleswoman said just before he passed out.

His jaw ached as it did after a visit to the dentist, but the bubblegum was gone. He kept his eyes closed and breathed in, focusing on the smells: metal, ointments, and Band-Aids fresh from the wrapper, as well as something unfamiliar, a thick odor that he thought might be dead people, for he knew that he was in a hospital. He had never actually smelled a dead person, not even his father, but he knew they smelled. His father had said so at supper one night, describing, almost gleefully, the odor of an old woman, five days dead, whom he had found that morning after the mailman noted an accumulation of mail.

"We had to break in," his father said. The idea of the police breaking into a house had shocked Aaron. "Found her tipped back in her recliner with a bowl of grapes in her lap. She choked." His father paused. "The stink of the human body," he said with awe. He took a long drink of milk, got up, and retrieved the shirt he had worn that day. "Smell here," he said to Aaron's mother as he held it to her nose repeatedly, wanting her to be impressed by the stink of the old woman also, but his mother said, "It just smells like you, Jerry."

Aaron opened his eyes. On a chair was the box with his cheap dress shoes. He remembered the saleswoman running out to the ambulance with it, and he wondered whether this meant his mother was nearby. A man came in. "How are you, Aaron?" asked the man.

"Are you the doctor?"

"I'm a nurse," the man said. He held Aaron's wrist and stared up at the clock on the wall. Aaron had not known that men could be nurses.

"Do you feel groggy?" the man asked. "We had to give you a sedative to loosen your jaw." *Groggy* was a word Aaron knew. The man was looking at a chart, and when he glanced up and smiled, Aaron was startled to see that he was wearing braces.

"Yes," he said, "I feel groggy. Is my mother here?"

"Your uncle's here," the man said, as if that were the same thing.

When the door opened, it was not Uncle Petey but a stranger with a nub for an ear, the skin smooth and pink. "Hello, Aaron," said the stranger. "I'm your uncle."

"My uncle is Petey," Aaron informed the man politely.

"Ah, yes, Petey," the man said. "A name better suited for a parakeet, don't you think?" He gave Aaron a moment to agree, but Aaron did not. "Lives up on the Iron Range. Fine country, the Iron Range. They're really doing God's work up there, though I suspect your uncle Petey's not involved with any of that."

"He works in a mine," Aaron said. He did not tell the man that the mine was closed or that Uncle Petey had quit even before that because he was afraid of the dark.

"My name is Irv Englund," said the man. "You can call me Mr. Englund. We need to get going because it's nearly suppertime, but let's have a prayer first."

He took Aaron's hand and prayed aloud in a fast, rhythmic chant, asking God to make Aaron into a child worthy of becoming a lamb. When he said "Amen," he pressed Aaron's hand hard against his nub. It was as smooth as Play-Doh. Aaron pulled away, and his uncle laughed.

Mr. Englund drove an El Camino, a type of car Aaron knew because his father had always pointed them out. "The car that wants to be a truck," his father liked to say, "or maybe it's a truck that wants to be a car." He had smirked as though they were talking about much more than automobiles.

They got into the El Camino. "Ready?" said his uncle. He slapped Aaron's leg as though they were pals, but the pain was sudden and sharp. Aaron nodded.

Several minutes later, they exited the interstate and stopped at the top of the ramp to wait for the light to change. Aaron thought they were in Fargo, though the two towns were connected and he could rarely tell them apart. Just outside Aaron's window was a man perched on a backpack, a sleeping bag and pan attached to it, a crutch across his lap. His uncle leaned over and locked Aaron's door. "Homeless people like to sit here and wait for the light to turn," he said. "Just when you're rolling away, they reach in your window or yank open the door and grab something."

"What do they grab?" Aaron asked.

"Whatever they can get their hands on—a purse or briefcase, even a sack of groceries." Groceries, his uncle explained, were not as popular because the homeless people wanted money. "For their vices," he added.

Aaron knew what a vise was. There was one attached to his father's worktable in the basement. When his father was away at work, Aaron used to go down and look at his tools, trying to make sense of them but really trying to make sense of his father, who was attracted to them. The vise had perplexed him. When he finally got up the courage to ask his father what it was for, his father said, "Here, I'll show you," and he took Aaron's hand, held it in the air between the two sides of the vise, and began to turn the handle so that the sides moved toward each other, toward Aaron's hand. Aaron felt an unpleasant pressure, which crossed over into pain. He tried to pull away but couldn't. His father was watching him, waiting. Aaron whimpered, and his father loosened the vise. "Now you see how that works," he had said.

"They use the money to buy vises?" Aaron asked. It made no sense to him.

"They're addicted," said his uncle. "Vices cost money, so they take what they can get and run down under the bridge over there."

Aaron looked out at the homeless man, who gazed steadily back at him as he brought his empty hand to his mouth, fingertips pressed together. "I don't think he can run," Aaron said. "He has a crutch."

"The crutch?" his uncle snorted. "That's a prop."

Aaron did not ask what a prop was. The light changed, and they drove in silence, finally pulling into the driveway of a white brick house, a house that looked like every other house around it. Aaron wondered whether he had driven by the house before, on family outings or trips to the dentist. His father had known everything about both towns. He took shortcuts and never got lost and told stories as he drove, like a tour guide pointing out important sites. "You see that house with the red roof?" he had said as they left town on the Englund family vacation. "I answered a call there a few weeks ago, a girl, maybe twelve or thirteen. Cute thing. A garter snake got inside the pipes and came up through the bathroom faucet. It was stuck halfway out of the tap, and the kid was afraid to call her parents because they told her never to call them at work unless it was an emergency. She told me she'd shut the door and tried to forget about the snake, but she couldn't stop thinking about it wiggling around in there."

"What did you do, Jerry?" asked his mother.

"I yanked it out and lopped off its head with my pocket knife." His father laughed, perhaps recalling the weight of the dead snake in his hands.

"I hope you didn't just leave it there," said his mother breathlessly.

"Of course not," his father said. "Why would I do that? The kid was in tears. She hugged me when I left. You think I'd just leave a dead snake in her bathroom?"

Aaron had not been able to stop thinking about it: that the girl,

afraid to call her own parents, had called his father. Even more con-
fusing was that his father had not laughed at her for being afraid or
dangled the dead snake in front of her. He had not yelled at her to stop
crying. Instead, he had helped the girl, and she had hugged him.

His father had pointed out houses belonging to drug dealers and
a park where a homeless man who eschewed shoes, even in winter,
had been found beaten and tied to a swing set by his hair. While they
waited for the paramedics, his father had freed the man by cutting off
his hair. "I did him a favor," his father said. "It was filled with bugs and
leaves and shit, actual shit, but Rapunzel there actually swore at me for
cutting it."

Everywhere they drove, his father had told stories like these, the
town as familiar to him as his own living room, but never once had he
said, "That house over there, the white brick with the perfect yard?
That's where my brother lives." He had never even said that he had a
brother.

"Ready to meet your cousins?" asked his uncle, and they went
inside the white brick house, where a woman and too many children
for Aaron to make sense of at once were waiting at a long table. His
uncle sat down at the head and motioned to the empty chair beside
him. Aaron wanted to wash his hands first, but he was too nervous to
ask. They bowed their heads and recited a lengthy prayer, and because
Aaron was not familiar with praying, he kept his head down longer
than the others. When he looked up, everyone was staring at him.
There was no talking during dinner, just the impressive sound of many
forks and knives being utilized at once. A girl slightly older than him
tipped over her milk, and his uncle turned to her and said, "What's that
good for?," which was what Aaron's father had always said when he
spilled. At the end of the meal, they prayed again, and the girl who had
spilled her milk was told to apologize.

"God, I'm sorry I spilled my milk," she said, her voice delicate as
porcelain.

"That you have so graciously provided," her father said.

"That you have so graciously provided," she repeated.

"Fine," Aaron's uncle announced. "Everyone who has eaten what was put before him is excused. Devotions will be read in one hour."

Two boys remained at the table. They sat with their backs straight, staring ahead rather than down at the onions that they had extracted with great care from the potato salad. "So, Matthew, Mark," their father said, sounding strangely jovial. "No onions for you boys tonight?"

The boys did not answer.

"Well, I guess you know what to do."

They rose and pushed open the sliding glass door that led out to the backyard, and their father called after them, "And not from the elm."

Aaron's aunt came in from the kitchen. "Popcorn with devotions?" she asked.

"Yes," his uncle said, "but none for Matthew and Mark."

She spoke to Aaron for the first time. "Do you like popcorn?" she asked hopefully. He told her that he did, and she said, "I'm glad." He picked up a plate from the table to help the way he did at home. "Aaron," she said, "that's not for boys." He could see the girls moving around in the kitchen, washing dishes and making order.

Matthew and Mark returned, each carrying a stick from which the bark had been peeled. They handed the sticks to their father, turned, and lowered their pants, revealing buttocks as pale as the flesh of the stripped branches. Only then did Aaron understand that the boys were about to be spanked. He wondered what they had thought about as they searched for the perfect sticks and prepared them with the knowledge that the sticks would soon be used against them. His father had delivered spankings with his belt, which he unbuckled and slid slowly from its loops. If he was still wearing his uniform, there was an extra step, the removing of the holster, a step he had conducted with great ceremony, as if the spanking were an official duty.

Aaron did not want to watch his cousins getting spanked, so he studied a clay reproduction of the Last Supper that hung on the dining room wall. The hanging had broken and been mended poorly, the largest crack creating the appearance of a rift between those to Jesus's left and those to the right, with Jesus himself at the epicenter. Behind

Aaron the sticks whizzed through the air, but Matthew and Mark were silent. At last, he heard his uncle leave the room, his cousins zippering their pants and leaving also.

Next to the Last Supper was a painting of a man. "Your uncle painted that," his aunt said from behind him. "He made it for my birthday a few years ago." Aaron tried to imagine his uncle sitting in a room holding a paintbrush, but he could not. "It's the nicest gift I ever received," his aunt declared. "It's not paint-by-number. It's all freehand."

"Who is it?" he asked.

"It's Jesus," said his aunt. She sounded horrified by his question, but Aaron had seen pictures of Jesus and this looked nothing like him.

"Why is he wearing a stocking cap?"

"That's the crown of thorns," his aunt said. With her finger, she traced the rivers of blood that ran from the crown down Jesus's face. The blood was cherry red, which gave the painting a festive quality. She went back into the kitchen, and Aaron crept over to the table by the door on which his uncle had dropped the box with his dress shoes. When he lifted the lid, he missed his mother and their house with a sudden, sick longing.

His uncle came back into the room carrying a rolled-up newspaper. "Don't stand there gawking," he said, swatting Aaron across the head with the paper.

"May I use the bathroom?" Aaron asked.

"You've got ten minutes before devotions."

Aaron could hear the sound of popcorn popping in the kitchen. His aunt peeked out. "Aaron, what do you like to drink with your popcorn?" she asked.

She didn't list possibilities, so he said, "Water, please."

"Water," said his uncle angrily, as though Aaron had requested beer.

"You can't drink water with popcorn," his aunt explained. "The water will taste like fish." Aaron had drunk water with popcorn plenty of times and never noticed a fish taste, nor did he understand why a fish taste would be bad.

"How about root beer?" his aunt suggested, and Aaron nodded, though he did not like root beer. Occasionally on Sunday evenings, his father had said, "How about we drive over to the A&W for supper?" His father liked the A&W, where one could stay in the car instead of having to go inside and eat surrounded by strangers. Aaron always asked for orange pop, which his father nixed. "This is A&W," he said. "You'll have root beer like everyone else." The root beer came in Goldilocks sizes, and because his mother always ordered the Baby Bear even though there was a Mama Bear, Aaron knew that she wanted something other than root beer also.

"You better get to the bathroom," his uncle said. "I warmed the seat up for you."

The smell began in the hallway, like rotting potatoes. When he pushed open the bathroom door and stepped in, the odor was so thick he thought he could feel it on his skin. He picked up a towel and held it to his nose, but he could not urinate like that, so he held his breath, set down the towel, and lifted the toilet seat. When he had finished, he flushed and watched, first with interest and then alarm, as the water rose in the bowl. A plunger sat in a rusted coffee can nearby, and he jammed it into the toilet, but it was too late. As the water streamed over the sides, he opened the bathroom door and called for help. His aunt came running, and they stood together beside the toilet, his aunt pumping the plunger up and down.

"My goodness, Aaron," she said, not unkindly but with some dismay as they stared at the coil of feces floating on the surface. It was as big around as his arm. He reddened, wondering how she could possibly believe he had produced such a thing.

"Hurry up," called his uncle from the living room.

"You better go," his aunt said. She knelt and began mopping up the dirty water, wringing the rag into an ice cream bucket. He went into the living room, where the others sat waiting. They stared at him, this boy who had come home with their father, plugged up the toilet, and delayed devotions. One of the girls handed him a cereal bowl of popcorn, which she said he could not touch until devotions began. When his aunt joined them, she set her bowl on the floor away from her.

His uncle handed Mark a small booklet, from which Mark began to read a story about a young man who had been wounded in Vietnam. Aaron knew that Vietnam was a war because his father had talked about it at the supper table, especially about the Draft Dodgers, of whom his father spoke with great contempt. At first, Aaron did not know who the Draft Dodgers were or why his father hated them, but he did know what a draft was. When his mother came into his room at bedtime, she wiggled his window shut, saying, "You need to keep this closed, Aaron. There's a draft. You don't want to get sick." Then, she laid her hand on his brow for just a moment. There was nothing better than the feel of her warmth against his coolness.

"What are Draft Dodgers?" he asked her one night after his father had spoken of them angrily throughout supper yet again.

"They're young men who run away to Canada to escape the draft," his mother said, adding softly, "They don't want to die." From the way she said this, Aaron knew that she considered it perfectly reasonable not to want to die. Then she reached up and wiggled his window closed, keeping him safe.

In the story that Mark read, there were no Draft Dodgers. The young man who came home wounded from Vietnam wrote to his mother from the hospital, asking whether he might stay with her until he got his strength back. He also requested permission to bring a friend who had lost both legs and had nowhere else to go. The mother wrote back, explaining that she looked forward to her son's homecoming. "But," the letter went on, "I am not strong enough to care for someone without legs. I am sure that your friend has family that can take him in. I know you will understand."

His aunt began to sob, and Mark read the ending quickly: the mother was soon visited by an army officer, who told her that her son had wheeled himself out a hospital window to his death. "It's like that sometimes," the officer said. "A young man loses his legs and can't figure out how to go on." His aunt gasped and sobbed even more, pressing her reddened hands to her mouth while his cousins stared into their empty popcorn bowls.

Aaron did not know what to make of the story. It was not until he recalled it as a teenager that he realized the son had been talking about himself, that he was the legless friend. However, he would never understand—not as a teenager, not even as an adult—whether the son had killed himself because he felt his mother would no longer love him, or because he could not bear knowing that she had failed his test. Never did he consider that it had nothing to do with the mother at all.

"We're putting you in with Zilpah," his uncle said. Zilpah was the cousin who had spilled her milk. "I know you might not like sharing with a girl, but she's the only one with her own room." His aunt brought him a pair of Matthew's pajamas, and after he had changed, she told him to kneel on the floor to pray. He knelt on the orange carpet next to Zilpah, and then they stood and crawled into bed together, his head at her feet, as his aunt instructed.

"We're not allowed to study dinosaurs," Zilpah said once they were alone in the dark room.

"Why?" he asked, though he had little interest in dinosaurs.

"My father says they're sinful." Her voice floated up from his feet. "We also have to leave the room if the teacher talks about Edgar Allan Poe. He wrote a story about a man who cut up a heart and put it under the floor but it was still beating, like this—*boom, boom.*" She sounded like a flute impersonating a drum. "Ruth's teacher read them the story, and then Ruth told us the story at supper, and my father was very angry."

"Why did he cut up the heart?" Aaron asked.

"Put your head under the blanket and I'll tell you." He felt a rush of air on his feet as she lifted her end, and he did the same. "The devil told him to," she whispered. He pulled his head back out because it frightened him to be under the blanket with her saying "devil" just to him.

"What's your name?" he asked, because all he could recall was that it was something strange.

She pulled her head out also. "Zilpah," she said. "Z-I-L-P-A-H." Aaron did not tell her that letters meant nothing to him because he had not yet started school. "It's very uncommon to have a name that starts

with Z. It's from the Old Testament. My father says the great achieve-
ments have been made by men and that makes it hard to find good
Bible names for girls."

"My mother named me after a lake," he said. "Lake Aaron. She
used to go swimming there with her grandfather when she was little."

"Well, Aaron's a Bible name. The lake was probably named after
the Bible," Zilpah said. She giggled. "Do you ever wet the bed?"

"Not much," he said, which was true.

"Me too," she said. "Do you know that I have a condition?"

"What's a condition?" he asked.

"I have a condition with my heart. I was born that way."

"Can the doctor fix it?" According to his mother, doctors could not
fix everything.

"My father doesn't want them to," Zilpah whispered. "He's healing
me with prayer. The doctor told him he was being irresponsible."

"What does *irresponsible* mean?" Aaron asked.

"It means he's not taking care of me," she explained.

"The doctor said that?" It astonished him to think of someone saying such a thing to his uncle. "What did your father say?"

"He was very angry. He called the doctor 'O ye of little faith.' Then
he told my mother to get me ready to go home, and he went to get the
car. The doctor talked to my mother outside my room, and when she
came back in, she was crying. She put my things in the suitcase, and I
got to ride in a wheelchair, and we came home."

"My mother is in the hospital," Aaron said.

"I know. Our mother told us. Does she have a condition?"

"I'm not sure," said Aaron. "She cries a lot. Is that a condition?"

"Well, my mother cries a lot because of my condition. I don't really
cry, except when I can't play with Matthew and Mark."

"Is playing fun?" Aaron asked, for there was something about the
dark room and Zilpah's voice that made him feel he could ask such
things.

"Of course playing is fun," Zilpah said. "Don't you like to play?"

"I don't know," he told her. "I don't think I've played before."

"That's silly. You must play sometimes."

Aaron gave this some thought. "No, I'm pretty sure I've never played. Not with other kids. I play by myself sometimes." He could feel Zilpah's breath on his toes.

"I know what," Zilpah said. "I'll ask Matthew and Mark to play with you. That way, you can see if you like it." Her voice was so kind that he felt he might cry. "I love Matthew and Mark," she said in a slow, sleepy voice.

"Don't you like the others?" he asked. The topic of siblings interested him.

"Not so much," she said. "I love them, but they never do anything that would make my father angry, even if it's something really fun."

"What are their names?" Aaron asked, wanting to keep her awake because he could not imagine being awake without her.

"Leah is the oldest, then Ruth. They always wear braids. Jonah is next. He's the fat one, and my father always says to him that he named him after Jonah and not the whale and to go out and ride his bike." Zilpah giggled. "Then Matthew and Mark are the ones that got switched after supper. They get switched all the time, but they don't care. They hate onions. My father tells my mother to put onions in everything so they'll learn to eat what's put in front of them. My father loves onions."

"My father liked them also. He hated pancakes, so we only had them when he was at work. He died, but we still don't have pancakes because my mother forgets to go to the store. Do people who don't have legs eat less?" he asked, now that he knew people could be legless.

"I don't know," said Zilpah. "I don't know anybody who doesn't have legs."

"You didn't meet any in the hospital?"

"The only person I met in the hospital was the foster. She was my roommate."

"Who's the foster?" he asked.

"She's the one who helped my mother clear the table after supper."

"Is she your sister?"

"She is *not* my sister," Zilpah said.

"Who is she then?"

"She's just . . . foster."

"Why don't you like Foster?"

"Her name's not Foster. It's just what she is. She doesn't belong here."

"Am I foster?" Aaron asked, thinking it sounded awful to be foster.

"No," Zilpah assured him. "You're not foster. For one thing, I wouldn't let you sleep with me if you were foster. They wanted her to sleep with me, but I said no, so she has to sleep with Ruth and Leah. They like her, so it doesn't matter. I get to have my own room because of the condition. I need lots of rest. But I don't mind if you're here. Besides, my mother said you wouldn't be here long, just until your mom's better."

"She said that?"

"Yes, and she said we have to pray because she might have the devil in her like Edgar Allan Poe."

Aaron sat up. "She doesn't have the devil in her."

"How do you know?" Zilpah asked.

It was true. He didn't know. His aunt opened the door. "I'm going to have to move Aaron if I hear anything else out of the two of you," she said.

After she shut the door again, they giggled quietly, and soon Zilpah's breathing became slower. He had awakened that morning in his own bed, his father squinting at him from the night table, but he would fall asleep in this bed, a bed belonging to a stranger who was his cousin, and when he woke up, still in this bed, it would be a new day and there would be nothing connecting him to his real life. He closed his eyes, and when he opened them, it was morning.

6

Three days later, school started, but Aaron was not allowed to go, despite the new dress shoes. He stayed behind with his aunt. Each morning she packed lunches while his cousins readied themselves, chaotically, for school, the mood in the house lighter because his uncle had already left for his job managing the first shift at the beet plant. At eight o'clock, somebody—usually the Foster—announced the arrival of the school bus, which led to one final burst of activity before the house became still, the front door standing open in his cousins' wake because the last one out never knew he was last. Closing it became Aaron's job, and because he craved duties, was comforted by routine, he liked being in charge of the door, though his heart ached at how easily he had stepped through the gate into this new life.

Only then did Aaron and his aunt have breakfast. She said a prayer, and they ate English muffins, which were his aunt's favorite, but he could not get used to their sourness or the way they scratched the roof of his mouth. While they ate, she told him stories that would have scared him at any time of day but seemed particularly terrifying at breakfast. She said that if he passed a pigsty and the pigs were leaping in the air, it meant the devil was floating overhead and the pigs were trying to devour him. Another morning, she took a can of corn from the cupboard and pointed at the bar code on the back. Someday, they would attempt to put a bar code just like it on his body, she said, taking his wrist and tapping it to show where the bar code would go. It was called the mark of the beast and he must never let them do it. He did not know who "they" were, but he liked the way she held his wrist, leaving buttery fingerprints behind, and he assured her that he would not.

Next, they took out the cleaning supplies, and his aunt let him help her clean, though it had to be their secret. He discovered that he liked cleaning, and he thought that his aunt liked having his help. It was always noon when they finished, so they sat at the table and ate again, usually bread with a slice of Velveeta and cottage cheese, his aunt chatting the whole while about everyday things that did not involve the devil or the mark of the beast. Mainly, she talked about a church luncheon that she was in charge of planning. "It's a big responsibility," she said. He nodded, and she turned over an envelope to take notes. "There will be buns with ham. Do you think it's better to serve them open-faced or with the tops on?"

"What will you do with the tops if you don't put them on?" he asked.

"Well, the tops will be another open-faced sandwich," she explained. "With ham on them." Her reddened hands made a somersault, demonstrating how this would work.

"That sounds nice," he said.

"Do you think so? I just don't know." This was where the conversation about the luncheon usually ended.

One day as his aunt sat looking defeated and he sat wondering how to reassure her, the telephone rang. She stood up and answered it. "Yellow," she said, her voice sunny like the color, and in a quieter voice, "Oh, Dolores. How are you?" He moved closer so that he could hear his mother's voice. "Rusks," his aunt said, and then, "I'll put him on."

He took the receiver, which was still warm and carried a cheese smell. His mother sounded far away, like she was asleep and was calling him from inside her dream. "Are you being good for your aunt and uncle?" she asked.

He nodded, unaccustomed to using the telephone, and then, realizing she was waiting, he said, "Yes, I am. Are you in the hospital?"

"Yes," she said.

"Are you sick?"

"I guess I am."

"Where does it hurt?" he asked.

"I'm very tired," she said. "Have you ever felt like that? So tired that you only wanted to sleep?" He waited for her to say more. He could hear something in the background, a television maybe. Finally, his aunt said, "Time to hang up, Aaron," and she held out her hand for the receiver. He turned away and said what his mother always said to him after the book and the kiss and just before the dark. "Sweet dreams." He handed the phone back to his aunt because *sweet dreams* was always the last thing.

At his aunt and uncle's house, the day after Saturday was not called Sunday; it was called the Sabbath, a name that appealed to Aaron because it sounded clean. On the Sabbath, the entire family—his aunt and uncle, his cousins, and the Foster—went to church, his uncle driving them in two batches. Aaron wore his new dress shoes on the Sabbath because his aunt said that sneakers were not appropriate in God's House. God's House was not a house at all; it was a church, of the sort that he had passed with his parents many times though never entered because his parents were not interested in churches. On the second Sabbath, all the adults in the church, including his aunt and uncle, took turns going to the front and kneeling while the pastor stood over them. Aaron was used to seeing his aunt on her knees because they scrubbed the floors together each morning, but he could not reconcile his stern, unbending uncle with the contrite figure kneeling at the front of the church. When they returned to the pew, his aunt had purple commas turning up from the corners of her mouth. The sight of them made him queasy.

"What do you do when you go to the front of the church?" he asked his aunt at breakfast the next morning.

"We eat the body of Christ, and then we drink his blood," his aunt said.

"Does God know you do that?" he asked. She had explained that Christ was God's son.

"You're such a funny boy," his aunt said. She giggled as if he had said something clever. "Of course, God knows. Remember what I told you? He knows everything."

His father had had a name for people who wanted to know everything, like their neighbor Mrs. Severson, who spent her days peering out the window. When his father pulled up each evening, she'd rushed out to ask him how many arrests he had made that day. His father called these people *busybodies*.

"Is God a busybody?" Aaron asked.

"Oh, Aaron," said his aunt, her voice like a slow shattering of glass. She stared at him the way that people at his father's funeral had, then took his hand between her own, which were sticky with jam. He could tell that he had disappointed her, though he wasn't sure how. He took in one, tiny breath, but it exited his body in great, hiccupping sobs.

As he cried, his aunt continued to hold his hand, her mouth forming words he could not understand. After a while, she led him to Zilpah's bed, where he fell into a deep sleep. When he awakened, she was still there, peering down at him, her face flushed. "You beat him," she said. He lay still, his right hand flung up across his sweaty forehead, breathing in and out and missing his mother, who always awakened him from naps with a glass of water in hand because she knew how thirsty it made him to rest. "He was in you, Aaron. I prayed, but you did it."

"Who was in me?" he asked, alarmed.

"Satan," his aunt said. She too was sweaty. "You called God a busybody, but he was making you do it. He was using your voice. Satan is clever, but you defeated him." She stood up. "You rest some more."

"I already rested," he said.

"You weren't asleep even fifteen minutes," she said. "You must be exhausted. I'll take care of things around here this morning."

He stayed in Zilpah's bed, listening to the now-familiar sounds of the toaster being depressed and the tapping of a spoon inside a cup. He could picture his aunt measuring sugar into her coffee as she sat in her robe beneath the broken Last Supper eating a second English muffin. Finally, he heard what he had been listening for: the muted swish of his aunt's slippers against the hallway carpet, the bathroom door being closed partway.

His aunt suffered from constipation. *Constipation* was not a word he'd known when he came to stay, but during one of their first breakfasts together, she explained it to him with a clarity that was rare for her. She spoke matter-of-factly, and he tried to match her tone, though he was deeply embarrassed by talk of bathroom activities. "I've tried everything," she said. "Now, your uncle, he eats one minute and goes the next."

Aaron nodded, knowing this to be true.

"Do you know, I've suffered from constipation since the day I married him."

He thought about this, remembering how the doctor who talked to him and his mother after his father's accident had said that his father had not *suffered*. His aunt had stood then and trudged down the hallway to the bathroom, leaving the door open several inches. While he sat at the table nibbling his English muffin, she labored loudly to expel waste from her body. When she reappeared, her face pale and sweaty, she shook her head, indicating failure, and he felt then, keenly, that his aunt did indeed *suffer*.

The morning he defeated Satan, Aaron listened to his aunt moving around in the bathroom, before covering his head with his pillow against the sounds he knew she would soon make. After what seemed a very long time, he removed it. Nothing. He rose and remade the bed and walked quickly down the hallway, noticing too late that the bathroom door still stood ajar. "Aaron," his aunt called from inside. "Are you up?"

"Yes," he said. "I want to clean."

"You're not tired anymore?" she panted.

"I'm not tired."

"Well, then, I need you to bring me a roll of toilet paper."

"What?" He was sure he had misheard.

"I didn't check the roll before I sat down. I need you to bring one, from the closet at the end of the hallway," she said.

"Do you really need it?" he asked.

"Someone else will need it if I don't." She sounded glum, but then her voice lifted, as it did when she was about to pray. "It's best to be prepared."

Aaron had never seen anyone sitting on a toilet, but he knew how he felt—awkward and ashamed, his legs dangling helplessly, ankles bound by his trousers. His father had been the opposite. He'd thought nothing of pulling to the side of the road and urinating as cars whizzed by. "Taking a leak," he called it. His father had also liked to tell *bathroom stories,* though not all of them took place in the bathroom. His father's favorite, which he retold at the supper table every few months, involved a man with a name that was not really a name at all, more of an adjective—*Stinky something or other.* Each fall, Stinky and Aaron's grandfather, as well as several other men, went on a hunting trip together, and when Aaron's father turned thirteen, he began accompanying them. These men were willing to rise at four in the morning and sit for hours in the cold inside a blind, which Aaron found a strange name for a place from which one did nothing but *watch.* They also trekked through the woods, sometimes for twelve hours before giving up and returning to the cabin. The story that his father liked to tell at the supper table was one that had been told in the hunting cabin one night at supper by Harvey, who was the town barber as well as Stinky's hunting partner, and when his father told the story, he liked to pretend he was Harvey telling it.

"It must have been around seven that we came across this buck," he always began, his voice slowing and deepening to imitate Harvey's, taking on a slight lisp, "but to tell the truth, we weren't really thinking about deer yet. We were just trying to get as much coffee as possible inside ourselves when suddenly the buck's right there, maybe forty feet off." His father's pace quickened. "Well, Stinky throws down his thermos and fires off three shots, and one of them nicks the back leg of the buck. It takes off, limping, and me and Stinky are running after it, when Stinky announces, 'I've gotta shit something terrible.' We run a few more steps, and he says, 'I can't take it,' and he unzips his suit. I'm a half step behind, and I see his left hand snaking along to the back. We keep running, and before you know it, he pulls his hand out and he's holding a steaming mound of shit—like a goddamn magician pulling out a live chick. I swear. Didn't even break stride."

Here, his father had slipped back into his own voice to explain how Harvey repeated this last line over and over—"Didn't even break stride"—and how everyone at the table laughed so hard that they actually threw down their forks and stopped eating. What Aaron had always wanted to know—but never asked—was whether Stinky laughed with them.

The only time his mother commented on the story, it was to say, "It's just not possible," as if the only thing that troubled her was its feasibility.

"Have you tried, Dolores?" his father asked. His mother looked at her plate and said nothing. "Not a damn shred of humor between the two of you," his father said then, which was what he always said at the end of his stories.

Unlike his mother, Aaron had never doubted the story's veracity. He just did not understand why his father found it funny, for no matter how many times his father told it, it was always the same: a man called Stinky chasing a dying deer, wanting that deer so bad that he shit in his own hand to get it. Standing outside the bathroom with a roll of toilet paper, Aaron wondered what his aunt would make of the story, whether she would laugh also or cry in envy. She called to him, and he went in. There she sat with her elbows on her knees, her pink robe tented over her, covering everything but her calves. She looked up at him, as if it were the most natural thing in the world to have another person seeing you like that: hunched and vulnerable and straining.

"Thank you," she said, adding, "You're a good boy."

He went into the kitchen and began extracting cleaners from beneath the sink, lining them up on the counter—Pledge, Lysol, Comet. His favorite was the Lysol. He unscrewed the top and breathed in its powerful, antiseptic odor. Soon, the smell would fill the room and then the house. Several years later, as he was cleaning the bathrooms in the café before school one morning, he would breathe in the Lysol's omnipresent odor and finally understand: his aunt, who had believed God was everywhere, was used to being watched, not just when she was cooking and cleaning and praying, but even when she was on the toilet. And though Aaron did not believe in God, he hoped she had found comfort in having a steady witness to the suffering that would otherwise have been hers to bear alone.

* * *

One morning, Aaron and his aunt drove past the spot where his father had tumbled from the float and died. His aunt said nothing. They were on their way to Target. He had never been to Target. They started in the Men's Department, where his aunt picked out undershirts for his uncle, then went on to Children's. "What do you think about this for Mark?" she asked, holding up a blue plaid shirt that looked just like the shirts Mark always wore.

"I think he'll like it," Aaron said.

"Do you think so? Boys can be so difficult to buy for." She said this as though Aaron were not a boy.

She chose shirts for everyone but the Foster. "What about the Foster?" he said. "What color would she like?"

"Don't call her the Foster. You'll hurt her feelings. Her name is Alice."

Alice. It was a nice-enough name. He did not recall hearing anyone in the family use it. "What color should we get for Alice?" he asked.

"We can't get anything for Alice today," his aunt explained. "She has a stipend. There's not enough money left this month."

Aaron did not know what a stipend was. "Won't she feel bad?" he asked.

"Well, I suppose she might, but she knows the rules."

"Oh," said Aaron. He had not known there were rules.

Nearly twenty years later, as he signed a credit card receipt in a bookstore at the shopping mall in Fargo, the woman behind the counter would look at the name on his card and begin to laugh, pointing at the book that he was purchasing, photographs of nude men. "Now what would your aunt and uncle have to say about your reading material?" she would ask. Only then would he look at the woman, who was pretty in the way of women who work just a bit too hard at it, and realize it was the Foster.

"Oh, my gosh. Foster," he would say, knowing that was not her name, and she would scowl prettily at him, the sort of woman who could not help flirting with a man, even one buying a book filled with pictures of naked men.

"You still haven't figured out that's not my name, Aaron?"

He would apologize, and she would say, "Alice." He would ask about his aunt and uncle and cousins, and she would say, "What a family of freaks."

"Zilpah?" he would ask.

Zilpah was dead, she would tell him matter-of-factly. Right up until the end, her father had refused treatment. She thought there had been a case, something legal, but she didn't know what had come of it. She would suggest they get a drink and catch up, and when he said he needed to get going, she would call after him poutily, "Enjoy your book."

"I have a surprise," his aunt said. "We're going to buy you school supplies." She clapped her hands together. "That way, you'll be ready when you start."

"I don't have any money," Aaron said. He laid his hands on his pockets, recalling the pennies.

"I have money," his aunt said. "It will be my treat. We'll hide everything from your uncle."

"Why will we hide it?" he asked.

"It'll be fun to hide it. It'll be our secret."

They spent forty-five minutes choosing supplies: two fat pencils; a pink eraser; a jar of paste, which his aunt let him smell; and a pair of small, dull scissors. She took down two cardboard boxes with flip lids, one picturing whales and alligators, the other Raggedy Ann and Andy. "Which one do you like?" she asked. "To put everything in."

He liked Raggedy Ann and Andy, who were smiling and holding hands, but he pointed to the whales and alligators.

"They sure are cute," his aunt said, gazing at Raggedy Ann and Andy before returning that box to the shelf. She held up the one he had chosen. "It says here these animals are endangered."

"What does *endangered* mean?"

"It means there aren't so many left," she explained.

"Where did they go?"

"People kill them," she said, "even though God wants us to protect animals." She put the box in the cart.

In the car on the way home, he said, "Thank you for my supplies." They were stopped, waiting for a train to pass. He wondered whether the conductor had noticed them and thought, *There sits a boy with his mother*.

"It's my pleasure," she said. She asked whether he liked trains. When he said no, she began to cry. "You'll be going home soon." She rummaged in her purse for a tissue. "Your mother called."

"She's not sick anymore?" he asked. "When is she coming?"

"I think she's coming soon."

In fact, when they got home, the Oldsmobile was parked at the curb and his mother stood in the yard wearing a fluorescent orange stocking cap with a pompom. It was not cold yet, so the cap puzzled him, especially since his mother did not like bright colors. She raised her hand, not quite waving, and he began to open the car door. "Wait till I stop," said his aunt. Then, they were stopped, and his aunt said, "I didn't think it would be so soon," but he was already out the door and running toward his mother.

"Aaron," said his mother in a surprised voice, as if she were not expecting to find him there.

"Why are you wearing a hat?" he asked.

She laughed self-consciously. "Oh, I'm just feeling chilly these days. One of the nurses found it in the lost-and-found box and gave it to me." In a teasing voice, she asked, "Does it look so awful?"

"No," he said. "It's nice. I like orange."

He did not like orange, which his mother knew. He put his arms around her waist, and she squeezed him back, and they stood like that, not speaking. Finally, she bent down and brushed his face with the fat, orange pompom. "How's that?" she asked.

He made a laughing sound. "It tickles," he said and broke free.

"Hello, Dolores," said his aunt.

"Hello, Jean."

His aunt went into the house and packed a grocery bag with the clothes he had been wearing the day he arrived as well as the hand-me-downs he had been wearing since. On top was the box with his new dress shoes, inside of which she had tucked a small Bible. He wondered whether she'd hidden it because of his mother or because she thought he would enjoy the surprise of finding it. She carried the bag outside, and after his mother set it on the backseat, his aunt said, "Can't you stay a bit? Irv'll be home any minute."

"We really need to get back," his mother said, speaking as though they'd been home all along and had just stepped out, leaving a pie in the oven.

They got in the car, and as they drove away, Aaron looked back at his aunt, who was staring down at the ground as she waved.

They avoided the parade route. That had not changed. When they were almost home, he said, "I forgot my school supplies," but his mother said they did not have his supplies yet, and he did not explain, even though it made him sick to think of his aunt unloading the car alone and finding the supplies that were meant to be their secret.

January

7

His first month in San Francisco, Aaron's thoughts were consumed by earthquakes. He began to wonder whether his subconscious knew something, even though this kind of thinking—thinking that involved talk of the subconscious—made him uncomfortable. He did not discount intuition or careful observation but found that people too often relied on superstition and wishful thinking, which he grew impatient of being expected to accord the same weight as logic. He spoke aloud of his fear only once, to Taffy, who told him that the school had recently employed a woman from Oklahoma. She had moved home after just one month because she could not stop thinking about earthquakes. Moving back to Albuquerque, moving anywhere, was not an option, so he decided to control his anxiety by not speaking of earthquakes again, a Midwestern approach that he had employed successfully in other situations. It seemed to work in this case also, except on elevators, where his standard fear—that the doors would not open—now wedded itself to a new one. As he stood waiting for the elevator car to tremble and plunge, he began to have what he thought were panic attacks, but these, too, he approached like a Midwesterner, which meant that while everything exploded inside him, from the outside he looked like a man stoically riding the elevator.

He had ridden his first elevator on the Englund family vacation. In a rare gesture of enthusiasm, perhaps even love, his father had parked the Oldsmobile in a loading zone in downtown Minneapolis and pointed to a tall building nearby. Aaron thought that they would look out the car window at the building for a minute or two before driving on, but his father had instructed Aaron and his mother to go inside the building, which he said would surely have an elevator. When they got out of the car, he called after them, "Make it fast. We're in a loading zone," as though riding the elevator had been their idea.

Aaron did not know what an elevator even was, but he followed his mother into the building, where they stood in the lobby with a group of men in suits who stared at the two of them, dressed in shorts and grubby T-shirts. Everyone got on together, the other riders rising up around him like corn. When the elevator began to move, he took his mother's hand and held it tightly while she laughed in a way that suggested she was not entirely at ease either.

On the way down, when they were alone, he asked his mother how the elevator worked. "Cables," she said. "You know, ropes pulling it up and down." He imagined people sitting above them, turning these ropes day after day.

"What if the ropes break?" he asked.

His mother showed him the numbers above the door, which flashed as they passed each floor. "Here's what I want you to do," she said. "Right after we pass the second floor, I want you to jump in the air as high as you can. That way, if the ropes break, you'll be in the air when we crash." He had done it, but that night, as he lay in bed in their motel room, he heard his mother telling his father the story, the two of them laughing. His father said something he did not understand and laughed again, and his mother said, "Jerry, come on. He's a child. It was sweet." Lying in bed, Aaron had felt her betrayal.

Aaron continued to think about earthquakes each time he passed beneath scaffolding or visited a museum or movie theater. Once he sat up from a deep sleep, sure that he had felt *something,* but everything around him was still. When an earthquake finally occurred, a small one, though he had not known this at the time, he was calm. It lasted six seconds. Automatically, he reached for the shoes he kept tied to his futon frame, in accordance with the earthquake preparation manual he had studied with his students.

"Why we must tie shoes on bed?" asked Cheng, a student from Taiwan, where they were accustomed to earthquakes. "Is for luck?"

"Luck?" Aaron said. He considered this. "No, it's so you can find your shoes easily, even in the dark. Windows break during earthquakes, so it's dangerous to walk around barefoot." He wrote *barefoot* on the board.

"My friend from motorcycle club said me that the streets can be filling with glass, higher than my head even," Paolo said.

"Your friend *told* you," Aaron corrected him, but he was picturing the futility of shoes when faced with a snowbank of glass.

Aaron had not yet met the owner of the school, who lived up in Bodega Bay but kept an office on the first floor, walled off by glass and never used so that it resembled a museum diorama. A placard on the door read RICH PULKKA, EXECUTIVE DIRECTOR. Mr. Pulkka claimed the school as a not-for-profit, a status that annoyed the teachers because they said he made plenty of profit, some of it fraudulently, though nobody dared to report him lest it mean trouble for the students. Aaron did not know exactly what the fraud entailed, but he thought it had to do with the attendance requirements for student visa holders. His roll sheets, for example, contained the names of several students who had not once appeared in class. He marked them absent, but when the sheets were returned to him each Monday morning, the *A*s had been painstakingly turned into *P*s, no doubt before the roster was photocopied for the official file.

Aaron deduced the sort of person that Pulkka was simply from observing how the building was maintained. It was like getting to know the flaws on a lover's body, for there was something intimate about standing in the men's room after having relieved himself to discover that the sinks worked, in order from left to right: cold only, hot only, not at all—which meant he had the option to either freeze or scald himself, or go with hands unwashed. One morning he came up the backstairs and found puddles of water pooled on the landing, yellow like urine, and when he went into the unused classroom across the hall from his in search of an eraser, he found mushrooms, at least a dozen, sprouting from the mold on the wall beneath the lone window, the sight of them oddly obscene.

When Aaron asked the other teachers what Pulkka was like, they laughed. "I'm the only one who's met him," Eugenia said. "Once, right after I started, he threw a faculty holiday party in the basement, but he drank too much and ended up sleeping with one of the instructors. Barbara. This was a problem because he lives with his girlfriend. Actually, she's on the payroll, though no one's met her either. He pretty quickly realized he better get rid of Barbara, which wasn't hard because Barbara was a mess. There'd been complaints from the students for a while, but after the party, it came out that she'd gotten trashed with her students one night and took off her shirt right there in the bar in front of them."

"Why would she do that?" Aaron asked, his question largely rhetorical. He knew that teachers were like everyone else: varying in their degree of competence and good judgment, not always able to keep their loneliness or dysfunction from pressing in on the workplace. Some of his colleagues, the younger ones, went out drinking with the students, the sort of drinking that made it nearly impossible to stand before the class the next day and make demands about homework and attendance. His own boundaries, he had been told—by other teachers, not students—were rigid. He agreed, though did not consider it a problem. He liked that his students were intimidated, just slightly, by him. He felt that a small dose of fear was conducive to learning. During his nearly twenty years as an ESL teacher, he had taught in a variety of places and knew that privately owned schools such as Pulkka's were especially susceptible to unprofessionalism because they paid poorly and thus attracted a mixed bag of teachers: the inexperienced; the inept; the improperly credentialed; those in transition, like him; and those like Taffy, who preferred to remain on the profession's periphery for personal reasons.

In the classroom next to his, Felix prepared students to take the TOEFL, an ESL exam on which they needed to do well in order to enter college here, but the truth was that Felix's class offered very little preparation, for Felix prioritized having fun. His morning curriculum included showing movies, playing practical jokes on his students, and listening to music at a high volume. In the afternoons the students sat at their desks, taking practice exams if they were actually interested in improving their scores, and sleeping with their heads on their desks if they were not. Aaron had quickly realized that the TOEFL class was a holding pen for students who needed a student visa but had little interest in being students.

Aaron was familiar with men like Felix, a homely underachiever who had gone to Korea in his twenties to teach and found himself suddenly successful with women. He did not care that his success had nothing to do with who he was as a person and everything to do with his being American. That he had neither an interest in teaching nor aptitude did not prevent him from continuing on once he was back in the United States because the school afforded him a supply of sexual partners. When Aaron looked at the female students and then at Felix, he did not understand it, for not only was Felix unattractive but he seemed determined to accentuate his worst features. He wore T-shirts that fit snugly around his fleshy waist and a wig tied in a loose ponytail similar to that of John Adams. He was overly fond of accessories and wore a utility belt, to which he snapped or tied various nonnecessities: a money pouch, though he often borrowed bus fare; a walkie-talkie; a container of aspirin that rattled like a maraca when he walked; and a light of the sort that bicyclists wore after dark, nestled into the small of his back, flashing attention on his buttocks as he walked down the hallway or, more disconcertingly, stood at the urinals, urinating.

Aaron initially heard about Felix's trysts from Taffy, but Felix himself had recently described for everyone in the faculty room how he had gotten caught breaking into the school with Akiko, one of his Japanese students, the night before. "We didn't technically break in," he clarified. "I still had the key from when I taught nights last semester. I just didn't know Polka Dot changes the alarm code, like, all the time. But you know how he is—he doesn't trust anyone." Aaron wondered how Felix could think that his complaint had legitimacy, given that he had engaged in the very behavior that Pulkka was guarding against. "FYI, the alarm's silent," Felix added, as though sharing information meant to make them better teachers.

When Marla and the police arrived, he and Akiko were up in his classroom. He said it that way—"we were already up in my room"—as though the evening had involved nothing more than a scheduled tutorial. "We didn't even hear them coming. Things got, you know, sort of loud."

Aaron stood up then and left the faculty room, though it was too late. He could not erase the image of Felix bent over Akiko, naked but for his utility belt, the bike strobe pulsing as the two of them, teacher and student, worked away atop Felix's desk.

Most weekends Aaron felt as if he were tumbling over a waterfall, floating and struggling for footing, and then Monday morning came, he entered his classroom, and the ground appeared beneath him again. He had wanted his life to change—had believed he might lose his mind if it did not—and just like that, it had. He had changed it. But after the initial euphoria, which reached its apex in Needles as he broke down the door of Jacob's room, he felt discouraged. He thought of Walter often, with what seemed like grief some days and simple nostalgia others. He could not tell whether he missed him, the sum of him, but he knew he missed parts of their life together. He missed feeling like an adult in the world, cooking proper meals and eating them at a real dining room table while he reported on his day. He missed the comforting familiarity of knowing a person for twenty-three years: they had known how to occupy space together, how to be quiet together. He had thrown that away, and if he ever met someone new, they would have to start from scratch. They would have to learn how the other smelled first thing in the morning or when he was sick, how he smelled just after a bath or when he wanted sex. They would have to learn these smells and then how to be comfortable with them.

He did not miss sex with Walter. In fact, he did not miss sex at all. He felt far away from his body, from desire. The last time they had had sex was on Thanksgiving. Aaron had eaten too much, yet when Walter touched him, his mouth still greasy from the turkey, he gave in to Walter's need. It was still light out, and as Walter moved behind him, he could hear the neighbors tossing a football in their backyard. Afterward, as they lay on the king-size bed, Walter said, "Well, someone certainly was thankful," affecting an arch tone, both the tone and the words taking Aaron back to those early days with Walter and his group of middle-aged, closeted friends. Walter burrowed his nose under Aaron's arm while Aaron stared out the window, watching the football arc through the air. He felt something wet, salty, on his lips and realized he was crying. He knew then that he needed to be gone by Christmas.

Aaron did not miss the king-size bed. He liked this bed, a twin-size futon, which reminded him of the bed he had slept in as a boy. When he and his mother first arrived in Mortonville, they had rented a furnished house from Mr. Rehnquist, where Aaron had occupied the lower half of a bunk bed. He used to tuck a blanket under the top mattress and let it hang down around his bed like a curtain, pretending it was a house or a cave or a boat, this last his favorite because he liked imagining storms that flung the boat about. In the midst of the storms, he would throw himself from the bed to the floor, where he pretended that he was swimming, staying afloat and saving his own life because there was nobody else to save him.

8

The day Aaron's mother picked him up from his aunt and uncle's house, after she unlocked their front door and they stepped inside, she said, "Does it feel strange to be home? It's the longest you've been away, you know. Almost a month."

It did feel strange, though stranger still was the disarray in which he found the house: dirty dishes stacked in the sink, mail piled high on the counter, a box of clothes open in front of the hallway closet. He had believed they were returning home together, but he saw then that this was not the case. Nor could he make sense of the mess. His mother had always washed dishes as soon as they finished with them. When she brought in the mail, she did not set it on the counter to be dealt with later. He had seen her toss the whole stack in the trash because she cared more about neatness than bills or correspondence.

Her own parents were pack rats. Perched on his bed one night, she had told him this as if it were a bedtime story. He had met them just once. "I vowed never to take you to that house again," she said. "It's no place for a child." He wanted to point out that *she* had lived there as a child, but instead he asked what a pack rat was, and she said it meant that her parents were burying themselves alive beneath stacks of paper and plastic containers and instruction manuals for appliances that had stopped working years ago. When they did die, several years later, it was not because of garbage. His grandfather's heart gave out on a Monday, his grandmother's succumbing by Thursday. Aaron, who was ten, stayed with the Rehnquists while his mother went to oversee the joint funeral, and when she came back, she said, "Well, that's that," and they did not speak of his grandparents again.

His mother came home from the hospital and walked through their house like a stranger, running her hands along walls as she searched for light switches, bumping hard against the edges of things, the couch, the refrigerator, the sliding doors that led into the backyard. On his third day back, as they sat eating pork and beans for breakfast yet again, she announced, "Aaron, we're moving," and though he feared change, he felt relieved, for he saw that they could not remain in Moorhead, where he had always lived but where his mother could no longer find her way.

They were going to a town called Mortonville. Before he was born, his mother and father had spent a week there at a fishing resort run by a couple who had probably purchased the place with high hopes, the way people do, though by the time his parents stayed, the couple was far past the honeymoon phase of ownership. The resort, which was several miles outside of Mortonville, was called Last Resort. His mother said their cabin was a dark, filthy box, and though she had brought along food to cook their meals, she had become queasy at the thought of eating off the plates she found in the kitchen. She pictured other people using them, people who gutted fish, picked at themselves, and rarely bathed. When she lifted a water glass to her mouth to drink, she was sure she smelled stale milk and fish. They had ended up going into Mortonville twice a day to eat at the Trout Café, an unexpected expense that so enraged his father that he ended their stay early, packing up the car in a huff and refusing to speak to Aaron's mother, even when she begged him to pull over so that she could vomit. They did not know it yet, but she was pregnant. Each time she told Aaron the story, she ended it the same way: "Later I couldn't help but wonder if it wasn't you that made me so sick." She would sigh, and as he got older he understood that she thought him responsible for all of it, not just the queasiness and vomiting but his father's anger and their abrupt departure, precursors of the life they would have as a family.

After his mother announced that they were moving, she said, "Now's as good a time as any," and she unfolded a slip of paper with the telephone number of a man who had a house to rent in Morton-ville. She did not like telephones, an aversion that Aaron would come to share, so she spent a few minutes pacing before she dialed. The man with the house answered. He did most of the talking, and when Aaron's mother hung up, the only part of the conversation that she related to him was the man's cheerful last words: "Let's just meet at the café in town. You'll never find the house on your own because I guarantee I give the worst directions in this entire county." Aaron looked forward to meeting the man. He had never met anyone who actually bragged about being bad at things.

"That's him, I bet," his mother said when they pulled up in front of the café one week later, pointing to a short man who was standing with two tall men. "Our new landlord." The man removed a handkerchief from the back pocket of his overalls and wiped his hands, rubbing each finger carefully, as though he'd just eaten something greasy, and then he came over to the Oldsmobile, where Aaron was struggling to extricate himself from the household items that his mother had packed around him.

"Name's Randolph," the man said. He shook both of their hands. "Randolph Rehnquist. You probably saw my initials by the train tracks when you came into town. Got my own crossing. Course, you're welcome to use it." He was bald and had a habit of removing his cap when he laughed, as though it were improper to laugh with one's hat on. "Looks like you brought the necessities," he said. He nodded at the car, which was filled with clothing and bed linens, kitchenware and a few keepsakes.

His mother had also called these things *the necessities*. "Only take the necessities," she had instructed, but Aaron did not understand what made something a necessity. Each time he brought out one of his belongings and asked, "Is this a necessity?," she looked up tiredly and said, "If you can't live without it, then just pack it. Okay?"

"What about my bed?" he asked, but she explained that their new house had furniture that they could use for now; they would get settled and then come back for everything else. But as he watched her wedge plates under the seats and stack frying pans and a colander where his

feet would go, he realized that there would be no back-and-forth between this old life and the new.

The three of them went into the café and sat in a booth, and a man
came over with a pot of coffee. Mr. Rehnquist said, "Frank," and the
man said, "Randolph," and that was the end of their conversation.

It was from this man, Frank, that Aaron's mother would buy the
café two years later, but that day, Aaron had no reason to think of
the café as part of his future, only his past. His father had sat in these
booths. He had not been dead yet, and Aaron had not been alive. He
could not make sense of this. His mother did not tell Mr. Rehnquist
that she had once eaten a week's worth of meals at this café with her
husband. She did not say anything about a husband. When Aaron
got older, he realized his mother had known that it would not do to
arrive and begin talking about parade floats and dead husbands. Of
course she knew that in a town this size a woman who showed up with
a young son and no husband invited speculation, but Mr. Rehnquist
was not the prying sort. He talked about himself instead, in a friendly,
uncomplicated way. He told them that his former tenants had left
suddenly. The Packers, he called them. "Packed up and left," he said.
"That's what you get with Packers."

He laughed, but Aaron's mother, fresh from the hospital, was
not thinking about things like laughing along companionably. Mr.
Rehnquist didn't seem to mind. He told them that they could have the
house for six months, a year tops, because he was waiting for his son
to get married. "When a man gets married, he needs a house," he said,
addressing Aaron as if this were a matter for his immediate consideration.

They sipped their drinks. "Yut, well, I suppose then," said Mr.
Rehnquist, and somehow Aaron's mother knew that this meant it was
time to leave. They drove out of town, Mr. Rehnquist's truck crawling
along in front of them, turned onto a gravel road and then into a driveway, at the end of which lay a house. His mother shut off the engine
and stared. "What do you think?" she asked. All around them were
fields.

"I think we'll like it here," he said.

"I think so too." She reached over to pat his leg, but her hand curled into a fist and she instead knocked on his knee three times.

Mr. Rehnquist said that he wanted to point out some things before they went inside—*features of the property* he called them—like the birch trees on the other side of the empty garden and a rusty wheelbarrow that he said they should feel free to use. He nodded at the house. "This here's the house where I was raised, and that's my field over there," he said, sweeping his arm toward the field across the road.

"What do you grow?" Aaron's mother asked in her making-conversation voice.

"Oh, corn mainly. That's about all I know how to grow." He laughed. "My wife's the brains in the family. She's a schoolteacher. Fourth grade." He studied Aaron. "How old are you then, Aaron?" he asked.

"I'm five," Aaron said. "I'm going to be in kindergarten this year."

"Going to be?" said Mr. Rehnquist. "School started over a month ago."

"Yes," Aaron said. "I'm getting a late start." This was how he had heard his mother describe it when she called the school in Mortonville to let them know he would be enrolling.

Mr. Rehnquist took off his hat and laughed. "Miss Meeks," he announced. "That's the kiddie-garden teacher. I guarantee she's anything but meek." Aaron did not know the word *meek*. Mr. Rehnquist gave a half chuckle and exposed his head again. "Good luck," he said gravely and winked.

Aaron's new room contained three beds, two of them bunked, the third beneath the window. That night, he climbed into the bottom bunk and fell asleep quickly, exhausted from unpacking and adjusting to a new house. When he awakened, he was not sure how long he had been asleep or what had roused him. He thought it was the silence. His mother had said it would take time to adjust to the stillness of the country after living in town his whole life. He drank the water that she had set by his bed. Then, because the hallway light was on, he got up to look for her.

Everything about the house felt wrong, not just the placement of walls and doors and rooms but even the small things: the resistance of the bathroom faucet handles, the way his chair caught on the linoleum when he slid back from the table, the quiet of the refrigerator at night. He went through Mr. Rehnquist's house, turning on lights, but when he reached for the switch in the kitchen, it was not where he thought it should be. He was years from developing an affinity for metaphor, years from the moment that his eighteen-year-old self would stand in Walter's house on his first night there, his hand fluttering like a moth against the wall as it searched for the switch, and think, *This fumbling in the dark is how life will always be.*

He could not find his mother anywhere. He walked through the house again, calling for her, but there was no answer. His mother was gone.

Finally, he opened the door of her closet and there she was, sitting on a chair beneath a bare lightbulb. "Aaron!" she said, sounding happy to see him. "Can you believe the size of this closet? I don't know what to do with all this space."

"It's really big," he agreed. He did not tell her how scared he'd been, did not ask whether she had heard him calling. He knew she had.

"Come sit with me," she said, and he went in, closed the door, and crouched on the floor. He thought it must be late, but he did not remind her that he was starting school the next day because he liked sitting with her in the closet, which smelled of trees and something chemical-like.

"Aaron, do you remember the time your father let me drive his squad car?"

"No," he said. "I don't remember."

"Of course you don't, Silly Billy. You were just a baby. We set your carrier on the backseat, went out in the country, past Dilworth, and switched places. I drove and ran the sirens. You slept through it all. It was a magnificent feeling, Aaron."

She smiled and touched her hand to her hair. Her nails were pink. "You're wearing nail polish," he said. His mother had always scoffed at nail polish.

"My roommate in the hospital gave it to me. I was trying to stop biting my nails, and she told me the polish would taste so awful I'd just quit." Her nails looked as chewed up as ever. "It didn't help at all," she said sadly. "The problem is the polish doesn't taste that bad, not like my roommate said it would, but tonight I thought I'd give it another shot."

His mother had said nothing about a roommate. He pictured them lying side by side in their hospital beds, watching television, because his mother had explained to him after he came back from his aunt's house that in the hospital everyone watched a lot of television. Until then, he had imagined her days filled with shots and thermometers, doctors and nurses giving her medicine and taking her temperature.

"What else did you do in the hospital?" he had asked.

"Well, I slept a lot. And we went to the cafeteria to eat. I always tried to sit by myself, but the nurses put other people with me, people who were very sick, and sometimes I had to help these people because they didn't know how to do things."

"What things didn't they know how to do?" he had asked.

"Oh, you know," she said. "Cut their food or open their milk or spread butter on their bread. There was one man who always sat holding an unopened ice cream bar against his forehead until it melted and ran down his face, so finally one night I took it from him and ripped it open, but when I handed it back to him, it fell on the floor."

"Then what happened?"

His mother shrugged. "He cried, and after that I ate my meals in my room."

Aaron tried to imagine people who couldn't open a milk carton or spread butter on their food, a man who cried about ice cream. "Is that why they were in the hospital?" he asked. "Because they didn't know how to do those things?"

His mother thought about this. "I guess so," she'd said, and that had been the end of the discussion. Not once had she mentioned a roommate.

He looked up at her sitting on her chair, the Packers' chair, with her pink fingernails. "What was your roommate's name?" he asked.

"Her name was Helen," she said. "Helen Ludtke. She was from Barnesville."

"Where's Barnesville?" he asked.

"I guess I don't know exactly where it is," she said. "Near here. Well, near Moorhead. Her husband used to drive in after chores, so it couldn't have been far."

"Was she very sick?" Aaron asked.

"Yes," said his mother. "I think she was. They finally took her to a different hospital where she could stay longer. She didn't want to go, but her husband begged her. The doctors told him he could either take her home or send her to the other hospital but there was nothing more they could do. They had eight children. Can you imagine?"

"It must be very noisy," he said, thinking about how his cousins sounded when they were getting ready for school. His mother had not said anything about his time there, except when she found the Bible his aunt had slipped in with his dress shoes. "They never miss a chance," she'd said, but added, "I don't know how the hospital tracked them down, but it was good of them to take you in."

"Yes," his mother agreed. "It must be very noisy. Both his mother and Helen's mother were staying at the farm to help out with the kids. I think it was actually relaxing for him to come to the hospital. He'd pack his supper, or probably one of the mothers packed it, and he would sit on Helen's bed and talk to her while he ate."

"What did they talk about?" Aaron asked.

"Once he told her the well was running silt and he needed to get the witcher out. Another time he said, 'I had to put the little dog down. It took a bite out of Henry.' He brought her things from the kids, drawings and cards, some dream bars the girls made. Almost every night, he said, 'Your mother, my mother, the kids. I'm going nuts.' The night he talked to the doctor, he turned around as he was leaving. 'You need to get over this 'cause I can't take much more,' he said. He was crying. The next morning, Helen was gone. She left the nail polish on my nightstand." His mother studied her pink-tipped fingers. "I liked Helen Ludtke. She was a fine roommate."

"What was wrong with her?" Aaron asked.

His mother did not answer right away. Around them everything was quiet—the closet, their new house, the world outside. He thought about what his mother had said when she told him they were moving to Mortonville: "It's not a place for starting over."

"Well," his mother said finally, "she had another baby, and then she got scared."

"Scared of what?"

"She was scared the baby would get hurt."

"Hurt how?"

"Well, she was afraid to clean the house because she thought she might vacuum the baby up. That was the first thing. Then she started worrying she might bake the baby in the oven while she was making supper, so she was afraid to cook."

None of this made sense to Aaron. A baby was too big to get sucked up by a vacuum cleaner and could not climb into the oven by itself. He did not understand why Helen Ludtke did not know these things, or why they put her in the hospital instead of telling her. "Helen Ludtke had to go to the hospital because she was afraid?" he asked.

"Something like that," his mother said. "Listen, you've got school tomorrow, so back to bed with you." When he stood, she reached out and wrapped her hand around his arm just below the elbow, caressing the roughened skin with her thumb.

"Are you going to bed also?" he asked.

"I am," she said. "But first I'm going to sit in the closet a little longer."

9

His mother wanted him to wear his suit for his first day of school. He had left it in Moorhead, wrapped in a bag and still smelling from when he wet himself at his father's grave. "Nobody wears a suit to school," he said because he had not told her about urinating in the suit or leaving it behind.

"Of course they do," she said cheerfully, but she left him to dress himself while she went into the kitchen to make breakfast. "Don't you look sharp," she said when he appeared wearing his brown pants, a button-down shirt, and the dress shoes. She tied a dishtowel around his neck. She'd made cinnamon toast with the crusts removed.

"When will the bus be here?" he asked.

"I thought we'd walk today. What do you think?"

"Isn't it far?" He did not want to disappoint her, but school had started six weeks earlier and he could not afford to be any later.

"It's two and a half miles," his mother said. "I checked the odometer when we followed Mr. Rehnquist out yesterday. We've got plenty of time."

He went into the bathroom, brushed his teeth twice, cleaned the crumbs from his trousers, and presented himself to his mother, who stood waiting on the front steps. He could tell that it was early by the way it smelled outside. She set off briskly, and he ran after her, his satchel banging against his leg. They walked single file along the road, his mother in front while he stared at the ground, taking inventory:

four dead snakes, a rotting skunk, and a turtle, still alive but with a large crack across its shell. They did not speak.

On the outskirts of town, several split-level houses were being built, and across from them were trailers lined up in neat rows. "What does that sign say?" he asked, and she read it to him: "Mortonville, population four hundred twenty-eight."

Thirteen years later when he left, this sign would be the same, though the sign south of town, which he and Walter would pass on their way out, would say 441. "I wonder if they counted me and my mother," he would say, because the second sign had been erected after their arrival. "I suspect it's not a terribly accurate reckoning," Walter would reply. "Nor do I imagine anyone will be out changing the signs tonight once they realize you've gone."

A woman in front of the school began waving at them when they were still half a block away. "That must be Miss Meeks," said his mother, lifting her hand with its chewed-up pink fingernails to wave back. He waved also, but the woman kept waving, and he turned to look behind them. There was nobody there.

"The new boy!" Miss Meeks said when they stood in front of her, declaring dramatically, "The new boy has arrived."

"You must be Miss Meeks," his mother said, placing her hand on his shoulder, which meant that something was expected of him.

"Good morning, Miss Meeks," he said. He swung his satchel hard against his leg, but his hands were slick with sweat and it slipped and landed near Miss Meeks's feet.

"Oh, goodness," said Miss Meeks. "The new boy is nervous."

"I'm Aaron," he said.

As they entered the school, Miss Meeks turned to him with a severe look on her face. "We do not run in hallways," she said, and Aaron, who was walking sedately behind her, nodded. They paused outside the classroom, and Miss Meeks turned to his mother. "I recommend that parents say good-bye at the door—to discourage outbursts."

He had pictured his mother entering with him, the two of them enduring his classmates' stares together. "Fine," said his mother, and she left.

He walked in with Miss Meeks, who took him over to where several children stood in front of easels. "This is Ralph Lehn," said Miss Meeks, gesturing at a boy who had painted a large truck and stick figures holding giant soup cans over their heads. "His father drives the garbage truck in town." Her lips pursed in what Aaron would come to think of as her *vowel lips,* a poutiness that occurred when she exaggerated her vowels or disapproved of something. "Mr. Lehn, say hello to the new boy."

"Hello, new boy," said Ralph Lehn. He dipped the tip of his brush into the black paint and jabbed it at the paper, creating a series of black specks above the truck. "Flies," he explained, looking at Aaron for the first time.

"Ralph, why don't you show the new boy where to hang his jacket, and then I'll help him with his cubbyhole." She left, and he and Ralph Lehn stood looking at each other.

"My name is Aaron," said Aaron. "I'm new."

"So?" said Ralph Lehn. "What's the big deal about being new?"

"Nothing," said Aaron.

"You put your stupid jacket over there. What else do you want to know?"

"What does your father do with the garbage after he picks it up? Does he bring it to your house?"

"Why would we want everyone's stinking garbage at our house?" said Ralph Lehn. "He takes it to the landfill and dumps it in a big hole, and then a cat covers it up with dirt."

Aaron loved cats. His neighbors in Moorhead had had two cats that used to climb over the fence and defecate in his sandbox. He rarely played in the sandbox, so he did not mind, particularly as he had admired how neat and focused they were, crouching with their tails erect and twitching, then turning to sniff at what they had created before covering it with sand. He tried to imagine a cat so large that it could bury a truckload of garbage.

"Are you allowed to pet the cat?" he asked Ralph Lehn. His father had forbidden him to pet the neighbors' cats, but he had done it anyway when his father was at work.

"It's not a real cat. It's a Caterpillar. Don't you know nothing about machinery?"

Aaron thought that caterpillars made even less sense than cats, but he did not ask Ralph Lehn any more questions. He was not interested in machinery. He hung his jacket on an empty hook and took his satchel over to Miss Meeks, who showed him his cubbyhole. When he had finished arranging his school supplies inside it, she pointed to a table and said, "You're at table five." He sat down and waited, and finally Miss Meeks clapped, and everyone else sat also.

"We'll begin Show and Tell today with the new boy," Miss Meeks said, pointing at Aaron. "This is Aaron Englund. He just moved to Mortonville with his mother." She sat down at her desk, hands clasped atop it. "Aaron," she said, "you may take over."

"You better go up," whispered a boy at his table.

"Mr. Englund, please come to the front. Your classmates have questions for you."

Aaron rose and went to the front. "Questions for the new boy?" Miss Meeks said, scanning the room.

"Moo," said a thin boy with great feeling, and Miss Meeks ordered him into the corner.

A bored-looking girl in a cowgirl outfit asked, "What did you do this summer?" Her nose was turned up so that her nostrils appeared gaping.

"I went to the Paul Bunyans, the sitting-down one and the standing-up one. We stayed at a motel. Mainly, my father drove a lot, and I was in the backseat."

"Did your father come here with you?" asked a girl with black glasses and a small, curious face. She was from his table.

"My father died," he said. Everyone was listening now. "Then my mother had to go to the hospital. I stayed with my uncle and aunt and cousins. They also have a Foster."

"How did your father die?" asked the girl with glasses, kindly.

"He was in a parade with some other policemen, and they were on a float. My father fell off and hit his head."

His new classmates stared. Even the boy in the corner turned around and stared, and the girl with glasses took them off as though they had become too heavy for her face. Miss Meeks stood and rapped on her desk. "Aaron Englund, you may return to your table. That's enough Show and Tell for one day."

When he sat down, the girl with glasses leaned toward him. "My puppy died," she said. "The hired hand ran him over with the combine. We buried him by the barn."

"Were you sad?" he whispered.

"Class," said Miss Meeks, "we would expect the new boy to be more interested in making a good impression than in carrying on side conversations during precious class time. But perhaps rudeness is common where he comes from."

"I'm sorry, Miss Meeks," he said, but she did not respond to his apology except to hold up a large cutout of the letter *V* made from green construction paper, the two legs framing her face as though a giant frog were doing the splits in front of her.

"This is our letter for today. Can anyone tell me what letter it is?"

Several children raised their hands. Miss Meeks called on the pug-nosed girl. "V," said the girl. "V as in Valentine."

"That is correct, Kimberly. Valentine starts with V." Miss Meeks faced the class, panting "vuh, vuh, vuh" at them, and they repeated it: "Vuh, vuh, vuh."

"V-v-valentine," said Miss Meeks. "Who can think of another word that starts with V?"

"Vegetable," said the girl with the dead puppy, almost apologetically, which made Aaron like her even more.

"V-v-vegetable," said Miss Meeks. "Good."

"Vickie," shouted the boy who had sat happily in the corner during Show and Tell. Everyone turned to look at a girl at Aaron's table who had bread crumbs dusting her mouth and what appeared to be dried egg yolk on her chin.

"Vickie," said Miss Meeks, "can you come up and write your name on the board for us?" The girl shook her head, scattering crumbs. Miss Meeks said, "Fine," as though it were not really fine. "Other words, class?" she asked.

A very tall girl said, "Veterinarian," which Aaron had never heard of, but when Miss Meeks said, "Does everyone know what a veterinarian is?," the class nodded, so he did not ask.

He raised his hand shyly, and Miss Meeks said, "Remember, it must start with V."

"Vacancy," he announced.

"Vacancy," said Miss Meeks. "Perhaps the new boy would like to explain his word to the class." He did not understand why she was mad, only that she was. She noted his confusion and looked pleased, and he realized that Miss Meeks did not think he knew what *vacancy* meant. His eyes burned. *It means when there's room for you,* he wanted to say.

"Remember, children," Miss Meeks said, "in my class there are no show-offs."

His mother was waiting for him after school. On the way home, she walked far ahead of him, only turning once to ask how his day had gone.

"Okay," he said, and she said, "Just okay?"

"Yes," he said.

"What did you do?"

"I answered questions," he said.

"Questions about what?" He could tell that she was interested.

"Moorhead," he said. "Paul Bunyan." He did not say his dead father.

Aaron did not know where his mother went after she left him at school each morning, but she was always back at noon, waiting for him on foot as the other children boarded the bus and rode home. This routine—walking, school, walking—became the order of their days, one he grew to appreciate because his mother seemed happiest as they walked. Their afternoons also followed a new pattern. When they arrived back at the house, his mother went into her bedroom and closed the door, and he waited—at the kitchen table or in his bedroom—while she rested. She never offered to make lunch first, but he did not mind because he knew that she was tired. Besides, he liked to prepare his own lunch. He always made the same thing, saltine crackers dipped in ketchup.

"I'll have a dozen today," he would say, out loud, to himself. *Dozen* was the word for twelve. He would count out twelve crackers, which he lined up around the rim of the plate like fallen dominoes. In the middle, he squirted the ketchup. After he finished eating, he drank a glass of water, gulping loudly, a sound that had always angered his father.

"How am I supposed to eat with you making that goddamn noise?" his father used to yell. "It's like listening to a clogged drain." One time, his father had jumped up from the supper table and retrieved a red plastic bottle from under the sink. Gripping Aaron's head in the crook of his elbow, he tried to force Aaron's mouth open as he held the red bottle above it. What had frightened Aaron most was the way his father trembled.

"Jerry, stop," his mother had said, her voice low and scared. His father had stopped. Years later, when Aaron asked his mother about that night, she explained that it was Drano his father had threatened to pour down his throat. "He never would have done it," she assured him. "He was just like that, always trying to scare people into changing."

Mr. Rehnquist was part of their new routine also. On the first day of each month, he came by after supper to pick up the rent check. During these visits, he seemed awkward, not jolly and at ease as he had been the day they met him. Aaron's mother said that it probably made him shy to be a guest in the house that he'd lived in as a boy. "Why?" Aaron had asked, and his mother said, "Well, there are things that happen in a house, things you don't always like to think about. Maybe Mr. Rehnquist remembers those things when he comes here."

Mr. Rehnquist's visits always ended at the kitchen table with the adults drinking coffee while Mr. Rehnquist quizzed Aaron about school, about what he was learning and how he was getting on with Miss Meeks, the latter a question to which Aaron gave brief replies because he did not want Mr. Rehnquist to think less of him for failing to win over his teacher.

"How's crazy Betty behaving?" Mr. Rehnquist asked one night in the silence after they'd finished discussing school.

"You'll have to ask Aaron," his mother said. "They're good friends, you know."

Aaron realized only then that Mr. Rehnquist was referring to Betty Otto, who lived in the house behind them, but he did not understand why his mother would say they were friends. It was true they sometimes chatted, but he did not think that chatting constituted a friendship, though he did not really understand what friendship involved. His mother said it was natural to want the company of others, sounding almost suspicious of those who did not, despite her own friendlessness.

"She still busy with that garden?" Mr. Rehnquist asked him.

"Yes," Aaron said.

"She's also busy shooting off her gun," his mother said.

"She shoots squirrels because they ruin her garden," Aaron said.

This garden lay on the other side of a row of tall pine trees that served as a boundary marker. When they first moved in, Aaron had often knelt on the bed in his new room, staring out the window at the garden and the house beyond. He soon discovered that a woman lived there, thin with milky skin and curly hair as red as a clown's. She had a dog that she usually kept tied to a pole beside the doghouse, which sat in front of the real house like its shadow. Aaron always noted the dog's location because he was afraid of dogs. Those first several weeks, he had spied on the house as he waited for his mother to finish resting, until one afternoon he knew that he could not stay inside even one second longer. He rose and went out into the front yard, where he paced with frantic anticipation. When nothing happened, he walked around to the backyard and stood in the knee-high grass beside the pine trees.

"What are you looking at, little boy?" called a voice. He moved closer and saw the woman, stretched out on her side in the garden. She was wearing a large straw hat.

"My name is Aaron," he said, then added, "Nothing."

The woman sat up and removed the hat in order to scratch vigorously at her scalp. "My name is Betty Otto," she said. "You may call me Miss Otto, as I am an unmarried woman, or you may call me by my full name, but you may not call me by my Christian name alone because I do not abide such familiarity from children." She waved him closer. "I don't recognize you. You must not be one of those awful Packer boys."

"No," Aaron said. "The Packers moved away."

"Good riddance," she said. "They were unusually mean children." He could tell that she considered all children inherently mean.

"What did they do that was mean?" he asked.

"Well," she said, struggling to her knees and then her feet. "First, they were cruel to Princess." She pointed at the dog, which sat, untied, at the edge of the garden. "She is pure German shepherd, which you will realize if you know anything about dogs. I've had her since she was a pup, and in that time I've spoken to her only in German. It is her mother tongue and the only language she responds to."

The dog lifted its head. "Princess," Betty Otto called. *"Heil!"* The dog stood and trotted along the perimeter of the garden to its mistress. When it barked at Aaron, Betty Otto said *"Heil!"* again, and the dog fell back on its haunches, whimpering.

"You see?" Betty Otto said. "But those Packer boys insisted on screaming at her in English, which confused her, so she bit one of them. Right here." She tapped her own cheekbone. "Just missed the eye." She sounded pleased. "The parents tried to pretend it was my fault, but I wasn't having any of that."

"Maybe the Packers didn't know German," Aaron said.

"Nonsense. Did you ever meet the Packers?" Aaron shook his head. "Well then. After Princess bit the boy, I told them to stay on their side of the trees, but do you know what those horrid boys did?"

"No," said Aaron.

Betty Otto bent and scratched the dog's ears. "Those hoodlums came out in the middle of the night and moved the trees, a good foot and a half, I'd say. Just look how close they are to my garden now." She pointed to the garden, as though this were proof. "They didn't think I'd see them," she continued, "but I was expecting them. I waited right over there." She pointed at a shed. "I fired off a few shots, just to scare them. You should have seen them run." She gave a pleased chuckle, which Princess echoed with a growl.

"Is that why they moved?" Aaron asked.

"They moved so that Mr. Rehnquist's son could move in," said Betty Otto.

"But we moved in," said Aaron.

"Mr. Rehnquist's just teaching his son a lesson. You'll be gone soon enough." She regarded him slyly. "You know, your mother spends a lot of time outside at night."

He did not know this. "Would you shoot at her?" he asked.

"She just looks at the sky. Would you shoot someone for looking at the sky?"

Miss Meeks never warmed to Aaron. Everything about him seemed to displease her: his politeness and earnestness and timidity, his overwhelming need to learn. She did not hide her feelings, and this set a tone, the model for acceptable behavior toward Aaron Englund, the new boy, which his classmates emulated. All of it, Aaron concealed from his mother. The next year, he and the other students moved across the hallway to Mrs. Lindskoog's room. He still saw Miss Meeks and greeted her courteously each morning. She sniffed in return, crossed her arms, and nodded, but when the children who had been her pets appeared, she hugged them and said how much she missed them. These same children stood around on the playground laughing about the thick veins that covered Mrs. Lindskoog's calves and about the way they could hear her urinating inside the tiny bathroom attached to their classroom, everyone falling silent when she went in.

"Aaron lacks enthusiasm," Mrs. Lindskoog wrote on his first report card.

"Lacks enthusiasm?" his mother muttered scornfully, pointing at the string of *Excellent*s and *Very Good*s that Mrs. Lindskoog had also given him, but Aaron knew that Mrs. Lindskoog had offered this criticism to help him, just as she hoped to improve his printing by gripping his hand tightly in hers and forcing it down on the page.

Upon entering first grade, he grew quickly enamored of phonics, which taught him that words were not just bunches of letters clumped together arbitrarily. Of course, there were exceptions, groupings that didn't add up in a logical way, but he came to accept, almost relish, these minor glitches in an otherwise perfect system. It was why the word itself—*phonics,* with that odd *ph*—seemed so appropriate. As they walked home each day, his mother usually inquired what he had done in school, to which he replied, "We did phonics." Sometimes, he followed this with a question related to what he had learned, a question such as "Do you prefer *hard g* or *soft g?*"

"Soft," his mother had immediately answered, for she had no preference and knew that thinking about it would not reveal one.

"Really?" he said, disappointed. "I prefer hard."

"They're both fine sounds," she said. "You wouldn't have giraffes without soft."

It had not occurred to him that things could not—even did not—exist without names. "What would happen to them?" he asked finally.

"Who?" said his mother. She was often distracted.

"The giraffes," he said. "What would happen to them?"

"Nothing would *happen* to them. They just wouldn't be giraffes."

"What would they be?"

"Well, of course they would *be* giraffes. They just wouldn't be *called* giraffes."

A farmer drove by, lifting his index finger at them, which was how people waved in Mortonville. Aaron waved back.

His mother had told him once that his grandmother, the pack rat, had phoned the hospital right after he was born to suggest a name for him. Lars. Sometimes he tried to think of himself as a boy who came when his mother called "Lars!," who printed *Lars* at the top of each page of homework and was intimate with a capital *L.* No, he had concluded, Lars would be a different boy and there would be no Aaron.

Another time he asked his mother, "Do you know about *sometimes y?*" But that time she was tired from doing nothing all day.

"Why what?" she said.

"The letter *y,*" he said, about to explain, but she turned to him and snapped, "No nonsense today, Aaron." After a few more steps, she said,

"I'm not myself. I have a headache," so they walked the rest of the way in silence.

The headaches were why his mother rested so much. He had seen her lying in bed pushing her palms against the sides of her head in an attempt to make the pounding stop. He had never had a headache, not that he could remember, but he knew that she was in pain. He was good at imagining what others were feeling. It came naturally to him, this desire to be inside someone else's head, to escape his own.

One afternoon he tiptoed down the hallway to his mother's room, carrying a cold washcloth. He'd wrung it out carefully: if he twisted too much, it would be tepid before he reached her, but neither did he want water running down her face and onto the pillow. In the last year, he'd become an expert at fashioning the perfect washcloth. His mother was lying with her eyes closed in the king-size bed that had belonged to the Packer boys' parents. When he laid the washcloth on her eyes, she said, "Did I ever tell you about my name?" Her lips moved, but with her eyes covered the words did not seem to belong to her.

He lay down beside her and stared at the ceiling. "No, you didn't tell me," he said.

"Do you know what missionaries are?" she asked. He did know. His aunt had corresponded with missionaries. She had shown him the envelopes bearing stamps that were colorful and strange. "Well," she said, "when I was just a bit older than you, maybe eight or nine, a missionary came to our town to raise money for her mission work."

"To Park Rapids?" he asked. Until recently, he had thought the town was called Park Rabbits, which he imagined as a grassy place full of benches and trees, people sharing picnics, and, of course, rabbits.

"Yes, of course to Park Rapids," his mother said impatiently. "Our teacher, Mrs. Olsen, invited the missionary to talk to us about the country where she'd lived for years. Guatemala, it was called. All of my classmates laughed when she said it. I didn't laugh, but that didn't really matter because the others did."

"Why did they laugh?"

"Because of the way she said it. *Gua-teh-mal-ah,*" his mother intoned, imitating the missionary. "But they were really laughing because they were scared."

"Why were they scared?"

"Because people feel scared sometimes when they have to think about the world."

"Why?"

"I guess because there's a lot to think about," his mother said.

"Does it scare you to think about the world?" he asked.

Instead of answering, his mother said, "She was an unusual woman. Do you know what she was wearing? Denim jeans. It was maybe 1950, and the female teachers and students all had to wear dresses. That's just now changing—do the girls in your class still wear dresses?"

"Some of them wear scooter skirts."

"What in the world is a scooter skirt?"

Aaron paused, feeling his face become hot. "It's a special skirt so the boys can't see the girls' underwear. It has shorts underneath."

"Do the boys try to see the girls' underwear?"

"Some of them do. At recess usually, but also when they're getting on the bus."

"Aaron, have you ever tried to look at a girl's underwear?" his mother asked.

"No," he said, which was the truth. Sometimes he sat on his bed and studied his underwear, which was white and had a discreet opening for his penis, but he could find nothing interesting about it. If he ever became friends with any of the boys, he thought he would ask why they did it, spent so much time and risked getting in trouble as well for a glimpse of something that surely was as ordinary as their own.

"You know how disappointed I'd be if I heard you were involved with anything like that," his mother said. She pressed on the washcloth with her fingers.

"Should I fix it?" he asked.

"Please," she whispered. He lifted the cloth gently and went down the hallway to the kitchen sink, where he thought the water ran cooler.

"You were telling me about the missionary," he said when he

returned, "and about your name." He settled the washcloth back across his mother's eyes, and she whimpered.

"Well, we came in from recess, and there she was at the front of the room. We all got quiet right away. Even Mrs. Olsen seemed a little scared of her."

"Because she was wearing jeans?"

"I guess the jeans were part of it. We just knew she was different somehow, and then after everyone stopped laughing about *Gua-teh-mal-ah,* she pointed at the map and said, 'Well, children, a nickel to the student who can actually point out Guatemala.' We all just sat there, and she looked at us, one by one, challenging us to look away. I couldn't help it—I looked down before she even got to me.

"Finally, when she'd out-stared us all, she shouted, 'Ha!' and slapped her thigh. We all jumped. We weren't used to adults acting that way. She said, 'I see that your uniformly maintained ignorance does not amuse you nearly as much as the names of countries about which you know nothing, not even where they are located in this great world of ours.' Then she turned to Mrs. Olsen and said, 'I am wasting my time here.'"

"What did Mrs. Olsen say?"

"Nothing. That was the worst part. She just bowed her head. I couldn't bear it because I knew where Guatemala was. In the evenings after I finished my schoolwork, I was allowed to spend ten minutes studying my father's atlas. Mrs. Olsen knew this. She often sat with me at lunch, quizzing me on geography, but I was so shy in those days, and she didn't want to put me on the spot."

"Did you go up and show her?" He wanted the story to end well, wanted his mother to rise as the hero and Mrs. Olsen to be redeemed.

"I didn't even raise my hand. I just ran up and pointed to Guatemala. You should have seen me. I was shaking so hard that my finger pattered against the map, but when the missionary reached into the pocket of her jeans and pulled out a nickel, I took it. Then, as I turned to go back to my seat, she said, 'What might your name be?' I told her, and she said, 'Ah, *Dough-lor-ace,*' so grandly I didn't even recognize my own name. *Dough-lor-ace.*" His mother laughed softly. "Aaron, do you know what my name means in Spanish?"

"No," he said. It shocked him to think of people saying his mother's name but meaning something else altogether.

"*Pains*. Dolores means *pains*. Isn't that amazing? That people in other countries, countries like this Guatemala, are walking around saying my name when they stub their toes, or cut themselves, or visit the doctor. I think about that every day, Aaron—how lucky I was to have that missionary visit our class."

10

On a July morning two years after Aaron and his mother moved to Mortonville, she announced at breakfast, "Today, we're going on an excursion." He did not know what to make of this. During these two years, they had traveled no farther than Florence, which was just eleven miles down the road, the place where people went to buy shoes or visit the dentist. "Come on," his mother said. "I want you ready in one *Adam-12*."

"I know how to tell time," he said.

His mother said nothing, so he gave in and asked where they were going.

"We're going to visit an old friend of mine. Gloria. I met her years ago, before your father even."

"Did my father know her also?" He did not know why this interested him, just that it did.

"Yes, but they didn't like each other, and Jerry didn't want me to be friends with her." Aaron liked when his mother referred to his father as *Jerry,* because it usually meant she was going to talk to him as if he were an adult.

When they were in the car and driving, Aaron asked, "How did you meet Gloria?"

"I was nineteen. I'd gone down to the Cities to work and I got the job with the electric company. Gloria worked there also, so we ended up getting an apartment together, but when I met your father, he didn't want me living with Gloria anymore, didn't even want me around her, so I quit that job and got a live-in situation doing housework and cooking for a family. Mr. and Mrs. Gould. They were Jews." She paused. "They were nice to me. They insisted I take Sunday mornings off for church, and I didn't have the heart to tell them I'd left home to escape Sunday mornings. I just thanked them, and every Sunday morning I left the house and went away for two hours."

"Where did you go?" he asked.

"Oh, I don't know. I took walks. I went bowling and out to breakfast with your father."

"What happened to those people? The Juice?"

"Not juice. Jews," his mother said, drawing out the vowel. "Your father made me quit that job also—because they were Jews. At least that's what he said was the reason, but I'd been there a year already, so I think it was something else."

"Like what?"

His mother turned from the road to smile at him, and he saw that she was wearing lipstick. "I think he just didn't like how happy I was with the Goulds."

A memory came to him, of his father leaning toward him at the Paul Bunyan Park in Bemidji, saying, "Look, son. There go some Jews."

"Were there Jews at the Paul Bunyan Park?" he asked.

His mother looked over at him again. "Sometimes you ask the oddest questions, Aaron. I suppose there were Jews there." She paused, but he did not realize that she was waiting for him to explain his question. Finally, she went on with her story.

"The Goulds had big parties, twenty or thirty people, and I did everything—cooked, baked, served—and you know what? I was good at it. All of their friends told them how lucky they were to have me. And when I told them I was leaving, Mrs. Gould cried. Your grandparents didn't cry when I left home. On my last night, they took me out for supper because they said it wouldn't be right for me to cook. We had wine, and Mr. Gould made a toast and said they wished me all the best. While we were waiting for our desserts, he pushed an envelope across the table to me. He said it was just a little something to express their gratitude, but I didn't realize it was money, so I opened it—right there in front of them—and they both looked away. Inside was a brand-new fifty-dollar bill. Fifty dollars for no reason, and I chose your father."

His mother was quiet then.

They drove for a long time, hours he thought. Eventually, his mother took a piece of paper from her purse and held it above the steering wheel, studying it as she drove. They passed through a small town, and she glanced at the paper and began counting mailboxes. Just past the sixth one, she turned right onto a narrow gravel road, but after a few minutes it forked in front of them. She stopped the car and tossed the paper onto the seat between them. "Well, what do you think?" she asked Aaron. "Left or right?"

"I don't know," he said.

She spotted a tractor that had just crawled into view in the field to the left of them. "Stay put," she said, as if he were a different sort of boy, daring and naughty, and not the boy he was, a boy overwhelmed by open spaces. She climbed down into the grassy ditch beside the road, making her way toward the tractor. When Aaron saw the man driving it lift his hand at her in greeting, he picked up the paper from the seat. Along the bottom was a map, hand-drawn with directions. The short letter on top was written in cursive, which he was just learning.

Dear Dolores [it read],

   Surely you don't expect condolences for him from me. Still, I'm glad to hear from you. I've been living back on the farm with Clarence, who needs some help. Mother died several years ago. A visit would be [here a word had been scribbled out completely and replaced with another] *fine.*
   Try to come alone. We have lots of catching up to do.

Gloria

When his mother got back in the car, she took the right side of the fork and soon pulled up beside a tilting mailbox. "Does it say *Bjorklund?*" she asked, and Aaron climbed partway out his open window to get a better look. The letters were faded, but he could make out a capital *B*.

"I think so," he said.

Before he could pull his head back inside, his mother stepped on the gas. His forehead jolted hard against the window frame, but she seemed not to notice. She turned into the driveway and followed it between a stand of trees, curving past a school bus with missing front tires, weeds growing up around it.

"Why do they have a bus?" he asked.

"I have no idea," said his mother.

"Can I look at it?"

"No." She spoke sharply. "Later maybe."

They stopped in front of the farmhouse, which was gray and sat on a small incline that sloped up from the driveway. As they got out of the car, five dogs emerged from a barn at the end of the driveway and ran toward them, barking and growling. Aaron started to get back inside the car, but a woman came out onto the porch and yelled at the dogs, and they stopped barking and began to wag their tails. The woman stepped off the porch and stood with her hands on her hips, regarding Aaron and his mother. She was not old, but her hair, clipped in a bowl style, was the same weathered gray as the house. She wore striped overalls with a white tank top cut low under the arms and crusty work boots, and her torso was like a tree trunk, solid with no variation in circumference to mark her hips or waist. Aaron had never seen such muscles on a woman: it was as if someone had slit open her arms and stitched oranges inside.

"Gloria," his mother said, holding her purse up in front of her.

The woman ducked her head. "Dee," she replied. She did not step closer.

"This is Aaron," his mother said.

The woman ducked her head again, said, "Aaron" and "You'd better come in then," and they followed her up the porch steps to the door, where his mother gave him a shove so that he entered first, tripping slightly into the room.

There were doilies everywhere, on the furniture and under

knickknacks and even hanging over the couch, that one the size of a car tire and stiff with starch. "I learned to tat a few years ago," the woman said, sounding apologetic.

His mother fingered one of the doilies. "You were always good with your hands," she said.

A flush spread from Gloria's neck to her chin and cheeks. She spun and left the room. Aaron's mother settled on the couch, patting it to indicate that he should join her, but he remained standing. He did not feel at ease in other people's homes. To demonstrate that she did, his mother lifted a bowl of walnuts from the coffee table and rummaged through it, selecting one, which she fit into the nutcracker. It resembled the vise in his father's workshop. As his mother turned the handle, a large screw applied pressure to the nut. Aaron drew closer, waiting for the nut to burst, but when it did, he still jumped, his heart knocking hard in his chest. He looked up, and there was a dwarf. The dwarf sat in a wheelchair, perched atop a cushion. He wore a bright red shirt buttoned to the very top, the deep creases along both sleeves pointing the way to his inordinately large head. His hair was the color of the rust that collected on cars that had faced numerous Minnesota winters, and it clashed—wonderfully!—with his shirt and with the lurid pinks and purples of the afghan wrapped like a skirt around his legs. His feet, clad in black sandals over brown socks, dangled just above the foot-rests. All of these features Aaron noted only later, for he could not stop staring at the man's nostrils, from which protruded tusks, slick like melting icicles. The man scowled at Aaron.

"This is Clarence," Gloria said. "My brother." She placed a hand atop the man's head, and he scowled again.

"I'm pleased to meet you, Clarence," Aaron's mother said. She rose and went to shake his hand.

"Clary has really been looking forward to meeting you," Gloria said. "Haven't you, Clary?"

He grimaced at Aaron a bit longer before turning to Aaron's mother. "Quite," he said and took her outstretched hand. "Dolores, Sister has told me a good deal about you. I understand that you are widowed?" His voice was high and nasal, but he had acquired the dual habits of enunciating and speaking slowly, pausing to breathe through his mouth. Aaron's mother nodded, her hand still gripped by his. "From what Sister has told me of your late husband, it would seem very little grieving is required." He released her hand. "Hit by a pack of Shriners, Sister claims. Can this be true?"

He looked coyly up at Aaron's mother, who nodded uncertainly. Clarence laughed, which triggered a coughing bout.

"Poor Clary," Gloria said. "He has such trouble breathing these days." She patted his head again. "Why don't you take Aaron to your room and show him your collection?"

"They are called archives, Sister," Clarence said. "And I am quite certain that they would be of little interest to a fellow his age." He glared at Aaron. Gloria bent and whispered in her brother's ear. "Fine, but will you push me, Sister?" he said in a whining, peevish voice.

"Aaron can push you," said Aaron's mother. "I think he'd enjoy that." Aaron could think of nothing he would enjoy less, but he knew of no appropriate way to express his reservations, so he positioned himself behind the chair and gripped its handles. It was heavy, but he managed to push it across the room while Clarence gave orders.

"They want to be alone, you know," Clarence informed him, but Aaron, who was focused on maneuvering the chair down a narrow hallway, did not reply.

"Are you afraid of me?" Clarence asked a moment later.

"Yes," Aaron replied, truthfully.

"Because of my tusks, no doubt. I noticed you staring at them. Your mother, on the other hand, feels obligated to avert her eyes. Tell me, young Aaron, at which do you suppose I take more offense—your fascination or your mother's revulsion?"

"Are they like elephant tusks?" Aaron asked. He did not fully understand Clarence's question.

Clarence snorted. "Elephant tusks are made of ivory, which is quite sought after in most places in the world, while mine are nothing more than adenoids run amok. You may touch one if you like, but only if you are extremely careful."

Aaron came from behind the wheelchair and leaned against the left armrest, steadying himself. Clarence's eyes were closed, but as Aaron placed his index finger against the nearest tusk, Clarence sighed, the air from his nostrils rippling across Aaron's finger. "Does that hurt?" Aaron asked.

"On the contrary," Clarence said. "You have an exceedingly light touch."

Aaron stroked the tusk once, then retracted his hand. "Do they grow?" he asked.

"Indeed they do—and far too fast. I had them removed just a few years ago, but I fear that another operation is imminent."

Aaron continued to lean against Clarence's wheelchair, gazing at the tusks. "I love them," he said.

The walls of Clarence's room were covered with books, the spines of which faced inward. "If you turn the books around," Aaron said, "it will be easier." He spent a good deal of time in the school library and knew how it was done.

"What will be easier?" inquired Clarence, who sat where Aaron had parked him, before a large desk.

"It will be easier to find the book you want."

"I want all of these books," Clarence said. "That is, in fact, why I purchased them. When I wish to read, I simply select one." He picked a book up from his desk and beckoned Aaron over. On its cover was a black-and-white photograph of two girls: twins. "This book," he told Aaron, "arrived in the mail several weeks ago. It is a masterpiece by one Diane Arbus. Do you know of her?" Aaron shook his head. "Sister wanted it out of the house immediately. She's not prudish, but her spirit is a bit"—he paused, thinking—"compromised we shall say, for lack of a more precise word."

He opened the book and thumbed through it, Aaron looking over his shoulder. The book, Aaron noted with surprise, consisted entirely of photographs.

"What is your opinion of this fellow?" Clarence asked, holding up a photograph of a bare-chested man wearing a fedora. A towel was draped over the man's lap, and a few wisps of hair curled from his underarm. He was small, like Clarence.

"Who is he?" Aaron asked.

"According to the caption, he is a Mexican dwarf. Beyond that, I know nothing of him. It is the photographer who has captured my interest. In fact, I have composed a letter to her. Would you care to hear it?"

Aaron nodded, and Clarence extracted a sheet of onionskin from the top desk drawer and began to read.

Dear Miss Arbus,

I am a recent admirer of your work, a book of which was sent me by a friend in Wisconsin, a man of normal stature. I reside on a farm in central Minnesota with my elder sister, Gloria Bjorklund, who, in addition to being a devoted steward of the land, is quite skilled in the art of doily-making.

My reason for writing is twofold. First, I would like to express my appreciation for your photographs, particularly those featuring nudists. I have long disapproved of nudism, yet found myself oddly moved by these photos.

I come, now, to my second point—namely, that I am a dwarf. Moreover, I have been endowed with a pair of protuberances—some would call them tusks—that have begun growing in recent years from the vicinity of my nostrils. I should add, for the sake of full disclosure, that I have no formal training in front of the camera. Nonetheless, I would welcome any inquiries on your part.

Sincerely,
Clarence A. Bjorklund

"Did she write back?" Aaron asked.

"She did not, for I did not mail the letter. You see," Clarence explained, his voice cracking, "Miss Arbus is no longer."

"Is she dead?" Aaron asked.

"Quite," Clarence responded. "Barbiturates. Slit wrists. Nothing as grand as a parade float and a pack of Shriners, though equally effective." He refolded the letter and returned it to the desk drawer.

"The Shriners didn't kill my father," Aaron said. "The doctor said he cracked his skull on the street when he fell off the float."

"Ah, but that is really more accuracy than I care to be presented with. Come, let us speak of something else. I understand that these Shriners are involved in the circus business. Certainly a boy of your age must have an interest in circuses."

"I've never been," Aaron said. "I've been to both Paul Bunyans. In Brainerd he's sitting down. He talks, but he's not real. Have you been?"

"Perish the thought! I abhor giants. They're so"—Clarence paused to think what charges might be brought against giants—"large." He laughed delightedly at his own response, and Aaron laughed also. "Well, we mustn't engage in too much frivolity, or they will hear us and become suspicious."

He glanced at Aaron. "I've got an idea. Why don't we spy on them? I'm not as stealthy in this contraption as I would like to be, but you could easily tiptoe down the hallway, listen a bit, and report back. What do you say?"

Aaron nodded, pleased to be given so much responsibility.

"Splendid," said Clarence, bringing his small, plump hands together in a celebratory clap. "I shall await your return with bated breath. Be sure to note all. And be cautious. You know what they do to spies."

"What do they do?" Aaron whispered, but Clarence waved him out the door.

In the living room, his mother and Gloria sat side by side on the couch, a single afghan covering their knees. Aaron heard his mother say, "So, that's what I told him. It was right after we got back from the vacation, and I just couldn't take it anymore."

Gloria said something, breathing the words toward his mother.

"Well," his mother said, "he was angry, but I knew he would be. He said, 'If that's the game you want to play, fine. But I'll take Aaron, and you'll see what I do to him, the mess I'll make. Just try me.'"

Gloria took two walnuts from the bowl and cupped them in her hands, pressing them against each other until one gave way. She extracted the meat and offered it to Aaron's mother, who accepted the bits of flesh and sat holding them in her palm.

"Sometimes," his mother said, "I can't help but think it was my fault. That he wasn't holding on properly because he was distracted by—" She began to cry, but Aaron was relieved that she did not make the low moans he heard coming from her bedroom at night. Gloria tucked the afghan more tightly around his mother's legs.

"Well?" Clarence demanded as Aaron crept in and closed the door.

"They're eating walnuts," Aaron said.

"Where are they sitting?" Clarence asked. "How would you describe their body language?"

"They're sitting on the couch," Aaron said. He had never heard of body language.

"Together?" Clarence cackled, and Aaron nodded miserably.

"Talking?"

Aaron nodded again.

"About what?"

"About my father."

"What about your father?" Clarence asked greedily.

"My father was going to take me," he said. He looked up at Clarence. "My mother said they were arguing because he wanted me with him."

Clarence sniffed. "Would you like to see the wasps now?" he asked, as though seeing the wasps had already been discussed.

Aaron knocked his shoe against one of Clarence's wheels.

"Stop that god-awful kicking," Clarence said, and Aaron turned away. "Fine, if you don't want to see the wasps, then you shall not."

"I *do* want to see the wasps," Aaron said in a low voice.

"Well, you mustn't be petulant, or I can assure you that the wasps will *not* want to see you. Now, slide open that door and see that my ramp is clear. Sister's troublesome dogs are fond of sitting on it whilst gnawing bones."

Aaron went over to the drab white drapes that covered one wall and managed to open them, revealing a sliding glass door. On the other side of it, a ramp sloped gently to the ground. It was covered with leaves and several well-chewed bones. Aaron walked down the ramp, kicking it clean, then back up to where Clarence waited, a pair of oversize sunglasses perched on his nose.

The wasps, it turned out, lodged in the school bus. "I've seen them only once," Clarence explained as Aaron pushed him along a path beside the driveway. "Sister carried me inside."

Aaron listened at the open door of the bus. "They're at the back," Clarence called. "Be sure not to rile them."

Aaron climbed the steps and sat in the driver's seat. The steering wheel was covered with cobwebs and desiccated insect husks. He pretended to drive, using both hands to flip out the sign that said STOP FOR CHILDREN. Mainly, he was thinking about what he had heard his mother telling Gloria.

"What are you doing in there?" Clarence asked fretfully, but instead of replying, Aaron walked to the back of the bus, where the wasp nest hung from the emergency door. He listened for the wasps again, but all he heard was Clarence calling to him from outside. He reached up and shook the nest, hard.

The wasps were on him instantly. As he ran back down the aisle of the bus, he felt small explosions of pain, first on his arms and legs and then across his entire body. He stumbled down the steps of the bus and fell to the ground.

"Sister," Clarence called weakly. "Sister, come at once."

The dogs came first. They circled Aaron, howling. When he opened his eyes next, his mother and Gloria were there. Gloria pulled the afghan from Clarence's legs and began swatting Aaron with it. She stripped away his clothes, shaking out the sluggish wasps lodged in the folds of his shirt and stomping them into the ground with her boots.

"Vile creatures," Clarence announced.

Aaron lay on the ground in his underwear, his body covered with red welts. This time when his mother cried, she did make the low moans.

"This will require poultices, Sister," Clarence declared, the last thing Aaron heard before he passed out.

*   *   *

He opened his right eye. The left was swollen shut. His mother was there beside him, Gloria behind her, Clarence at his feet, head tipped back so that he seemed to be sighting Aaron along his tusks. Aaron sniffed, aware of an odor that was coming from him, a combination of grass and mustard. He did not like mustard because it reminded him of hotdogs.

"Do you like hotdogs?" he asked Clarence. His mother sniffled.

"Certainly not," Clarence said. "I dislike hotdogs in all of their permutations, though I particularly despise the bratwurst." Something about Clarence's response, the way he said "permutations," calmed Aaron, and he closed his good eye again. Soon, he heard his mother and Gloria stand and leave the room.

"Your mother was quite hysterical," Clarence whispered. "She seemed to think you were hallucinating because you kept crying out that you were"—he paused dramatically—"the king of pain."

Aaron did not remember calling out, nor how he had come to be on the sofa, but he knew he had never experienced pain like this, pain that was everywhere, burning and throbbing and itching. He fell back into a sweaty, listless sleep in which he dreamed that he was on a parade float, calling, "I'm the King of Pain" as he rolled down the street, waving to the people below. He could hear Gloria, Clarence, and his mother talking, their voices blending with his dream, their conversation punctuated by a clinking sound that he later realized was the repetition of cup meeting saucer but in his dream became the steady tapping of a pair of cumbersome tusks that collided with everything in their path. When he awoke, he studied Clarence, relieved to find him still in possession of his small, elegant tusks and not the monstrosities of his dream. Only then did he realize that the tusks in the dream had belonged not to Clarence but to him.

"Where are we?" he asked, looking around the small, sunny room.

"We're at the Bjorklunds, Aaron," his mother said. She glanced at Gloria, who prodded one of his poultices.

"I know that," Aaron said. "I mean this room."

"This is the sunroom," Clarence announced grandly. "As you may know from your studies, the sun has tremendous curative powers."

Gloria and his mother rose and gathered the cups. Once they had disappeared into the kitchen, Clarence wheeled closer. "You provoked them, didn't you?" he said.

"Who?" Aaron asked. He sat up.

"The wasps," Clarence said impatiently. "You must have provoked them."

"I don't know what that means," Aaron said. In fact, he did know, but he did not want to talk, not even to Clarence, about the clarity he had felt as he reached toward the wasps intending to do just that—*provoke*.

"Do you like rabbits?" Clarence asked after a moment.

Aaron recalled the rabbit at the petting zoo at the first Paul Bunyan Park, the sleekness of its ears and the way it trembled when he held it. "Yes," he said.

"Splendid," Clarence shrieked. "Sister is preparing one of the little rascals for our supper."

He did not look at Clarence because he knew that Clarence was waiting for him to respond, that Clarence was upset with him for refusing to discuss the wasps. Though his mother had said he was to rest, Aaron stood up. He felt weak, but he took a step and then another, keeping his hand on the couch. He noticed a pile of newspapers, stacked in a beam of sunlight. Atop it was a cat, gray with white-tipped ears.

"May I pet the cat?" Aaron asked.

"Indeed you *may*," Clarence said. "Nothing gives me more pleasure than a child who has learned to use the English language properly, except for an adult who has done so. That, of course, is a good deal rarer."

Aaron let go of the couch and took several slow steps toward the cat. Though it hurt to do so, he crouched beside it, wanting to appear less threatening. He whispered, "Hello, cat," and then, more loudly, "Do you have a name?"

"Of course he has a name," Clarence said. "His name is Aaron."

Aaron turned to look at Clarence. "Is that really his name?"

"Do you take me for a liar?"

"Maybe you're teasing me," Aaron said.

"I can assure you that I *tease,* to use your word, with far greater so-phistication. Really, Aaron, what would be the purpose of such simple-minded game playing?"

"I don't know," Aaron said. He did not understand exactly what he was being asked, but a word came to him and he said, "I guess it's a coincidence."

"A coincidence indeed," Clarence agreed, looking in no way sur-prised at his use of such a word. "Sister named him."

Aaron turned back to the cat and tapped gently on its paw. It stretched and opened its eyes. Except there were no eyes, just two empty sockets where the eyes should have been.

"Oh!" Aaron cried, tipping backward onto his buttocks.

"Did I forget to mention that our feline friend is eyeless?" Clarence crowed.

"What happened to his eyes?" Aaron asked, his voice shaking. The empty sockets seemed to be staring at him.

"Sister found him in the barn several years ago. The ants had made a picnic, as it were, of his eyeballs." Clarence laughed. "His mother had moved the rest of the litter elsewhere. He was a tiny, starving thing when Sister found him, but she nursed him back to health, and that was that. She's quite devoted to him."

"Doesn't he get lost?" Aaron asked.

"Lost?" Clarence said. "There's no opportunity for him to get lost. He's not allowed outdoors except when Sister takes him on a leash, and then he just sniffs the geese droppings and eats a bit of grass. Other-wise, this room is his world, and though it's small, I imagine he feels quite safe here. You know, there's something to be said for the security of the familiar, in all its confining glory."

Aaron did not think he could fall asleep again, not with the eyeless cat nearby, but he returned to the couch and soon he was sleeping. He awakened to the smell of food cooking and the soft whistle of Clar-ence's breathing.

"Clarence," he said, sitting up, "will you ever get bigger?"

"Bigger?" said Clarence. "What sort of dwarf would I be if I were bigger?"

"I don't know," said Aaron.

"Are you familiar with the expression 'I've seen bigger dwarves'?"

"No," said Aaron.

"Well, it's a first-rate expression. You may be young for irony now, but I've no doubt you'll grow into it nicely, so it's an expression worth remembering. I daresay it will provide you with something on which to ruminate when you're older and experiencing the proverbial rainy day. There are sure to be many in that hamlet of yours. What is it called? Mortonville?" He spoke as if Mortonville were a bitter herb he had been forced to sample.

"Have you been to Mortonville?" Aaron asked. He tried to picture Clarence there, peering through the plate-glass windows of Bildt Hardware, rolling past the Trout Café.

"Certainly not," said Clarence. "Were I able to travel and inclined to do so, I can assure you that it is not to Mortonville I would go." He added with an air of finality, "Indeed not."

Neither did Aaron want to think of Clarence in Mortonville, where he imagined people staring, then looking away, putting their hands over their mouths to conceal their laughter each time he spoke because they would not be able to see Clarence as the author of humor, only as its object. In Mortonville, Clarence would not be Clarence at all.

"Of course, I cannot take credit for the expression," Clarence went on. "It was submitted to me by a pen pal from Iowa."

"What are pen pals?" Aaron asked.

"Pen pals are people with whom I correspond via the postal service."

"You write letters?" Aaron said, by way of confirming his understanding.

"That is precisely what we do. I've numerous pen pals, almost all little people. It is thanks to them that I have managed to compile my archives."

"And all of these people—the pen pals—are they your friends?" Aaron asked.

"Friends?" Clarence said. "If pressed to do so, I would place most of them firmly in the category of acquaintances."

"*Pal* means friend," Aaron pointed out.

"They are most certainly not *pals,* for that is a word I despise. In fact, thanks to you, young Aaron, I shall refrain from using the term *pen pals* ever again. Dreadful," Clarence muttered, raking his tongue loudly against his teeth.

"What will you call them?" Aaron asked.

Clarence thought for a moment. "I shall refer to them as my correspondents."

"What do you and your correspondents write about?"

"Everything. I am compiling what I hope will be the definitive collection of artifacts and documents related to dwarves in our society. This is the archive of which Sister spoke earlier. I dare say it shall be my life's work. Already I've been at it—informally, of course—for most of my adulthood, though my fascination truly began in adolescence. As a boy, you see, I was quite convinced I was an anomaly, and though my parents assured me that there were others of my stature—even shorter—I refused to believe it. I measured myself daily and took to hiding in places too small for anyone else in my family to fit. The big pot in which my mother melted lard and the valise that my grandfather carried when he came to live with us were my favorites. Finally, when I was fourteen, my parents resorted to desperate measures to prove me wrong."

"What did they do?" Aaron asked.

"They hired a dwarf. They ran advertisements in several newspapers, and a man replied, an older gentleman, unrelentingly tedious. He arrived on a Friday dressed in what appeared to be a boy's church suit and departed after dinner on Sunday. While I normally despise Sundays, I was never so relieved to see Sunday arrive and that fellow depart."

"What was his name?" Aaron asked.

"Otto. He was a clerk in a grocery store in Winnipeg and had been for thirty-some years. The first night he described for us, in detail, the special stool he'd had fashioned so that he could reach the register. At meal times, as we discussed various trivial matters, he would shout out the prices of the food we were consuming—'potatoes this or that much a pound'—his finger punching the air frantically. He was ringing up the meal, you see. As my sisters cleared the table the second night, I turned to him and asked, 'Well, Otto, what is our grand total this evening?' I was teasing, but his index finger shot out, tapped an imaginary *total* key, and he pulled himself up in his chair to better make out the figure. Of course, we leaned forward to hear it, at which point the silly man became quite flustered and tucked his hands beneath his buttocks. We laughed, both to ease the moment and because it was funny. He tried to be good-natured, but his job was really all he had and he wasn't clever enough to be self-deprecating, so I think the visit upset him greatly."

"Did he cry?" Aaron asked.

"He may have, though not in our presence."

"What happened to Otto?" Aaron asked.

"Nothing *happened* to him. He went back to his stool at the grocery store in Winnipeg. I've received archival scraps from him over the years, nothing significant."

"I wish I had correspondents," Aaron said. "It must be wonderful."

"It can be," Clarence agreed. "Take Olga, my correspondent in Iowa. It was she who contributed the 'bigger dwarves' expression I mentioned earlier, after learning of my archives from Otto. That was nearly a decade ago. She told me nothing of herself in that first letter. Olga requires coaxing. Later she explained that she had been given Otto's address by a well-intentioned cousin of her husband who knew Otto from the store." Clarence coughed and spat delicately into a large handkerchief, inspected the contents, and folded the handkerchief around them. "'He's of your ilk,' the cousin said when she presented Olga with Otto's address. Isn't that a delightful introduction?" He laughed. Aaron laughed also because he liked Clarence's laugh, but he thought the word *ilk* sounded awful.

"The truth," Clarence continued, his voice becoming more nasal, "is that Olga wrote to Otto because she was lonely, but they were not of the same ilk, not at all. I received my first letter from her on June sixth, 1962. It was, as I have already noted, a pithy epistle. I wrote back, thanking her for her fine contribution to the archives, and over the years we have become well acquainted." He cleared his throat again. "In fact, Olga's is a sad tale. Have you any interest in hearing it?"

"I like sad tales," said Aaron. "In school we read only happy ones. My mother says I'm too young to be interested in tales of woe. That's what she calls them."

"Yes, I suppose you are young, though I have found that there is no better way to forget your own tales of woe than by listening to those of others."

Clarence's fingers had crept out from beneath the afghan. They were plump, like breakfast sausages, and Aaron found himself thinking *pigs in a blanket,* which he had ordered once in a restaurant based solely on the name. He remembered how happy he had been when his breakfast arrived and he discovered that pigs in a blanket were sausages, the beauty of their name matching their tastiness.

"You seem distracted," Clarence said querulously. "Perhaps we should speak of something other than Olga's sad story?" A rattling began in his throat, which he tried to clear, but the phlegm seemed to build. "You'll forgive me for making such a racket," he gasped. "It has been a difficult week." He stared straight ahead, his sausage fingers clutching the afghan.

"I believe there has been a settling," he announced finally. "Sister and I have a little joke that we engage in at such times. She tells me I am sounding phlegmish, and I reply, 'I should say closer to Dutch, Sister.' It never fails to amuse her. I must admit I've come to find the joke tiresome, but it would disappoint her if I were to stop."

"I'm afraid I don't understand the joke," Aaron said.

"What is there to understand?" Clarence said. "Surely you've *heard* of Flanders?"

"No," said Aaron.

"What grade are you in?"

"I'm starting second grade."

"Second grade?" Clarence cried. "Second grade and you are unfamiliar with Flanders? I am quite sure that by the time I began second grade I was well versed in European geography, inclusive of its subtleties."

Aaron said nothing. He did not understand how this place called Flanders had even entered the discussion. "What about Olga and the tale of woe?" he asked.

"We shall speak no more of Olga," said Clarence severely, then, less severely, "Come. Supper awaits us. You shall be my valet."

11

Aaron studied the meat on his plate. He had thought that rabbit would be easy to recognize, but without the telltale ears, this was not the case.

"Sister constructed this table," Clarence announced. "She completed it in a single afternoon."

"Gloria, you made this table?" said Aaron's mother.

It was higher than other tables. Aaron had to reach upward for his food.

"For Clary's wheelchair," Gloria said. She pulled her head into her hunched shoulders in an unflattering, turtlelike way. "I've always been pretty inept with my hands."

"Inept," Clarence squealed, and Gloria hunched her shoulders even more.

For several minutes they ate in silence, Gloria occasionally reaching over to Clarence's plate in order to cut his meat into even smaller pieces or to add green beans to his already large pile. When she plopped a pat of butter onto his potato, he threw down his cutlery. "Sister," he hissed, "we have agreed, numerous times, that you will not touch my plate unless I ask for your assistance. I have made no such request, as our guests can surely confirm." He pinched the butter between his fingers and flung it back at her.

Aaron's mother turned quickly to Aaron. "Gloria has invited us to spend the night," she said, "since it might not be wise for you to travel after your wasp ordeal."

Aaron nodded and reached up for his milk. The thought of spending more time with Clarence made him happy, but he did not know how to verbalize his pleasure. They all continued to nibble at the meat that might or might not be rabbit until Clarence sniffed the air as one would a past-due carton of milk and announced, "When I was a bit older than young Aaron, I had a schoolmaster who suffered from an abnormal fear of dwarves. Do you remember, Sister?"

"Mr. Nordstrum," she said. "There'd been some scandal at his previous school."

"Ah, yes, Nordstrum," said Clarence. "He was let go because he'd taken to attaching love notes when he returned homework."

"How do you know such things, Clary?" Gloria asked.

"Little pitchers have big ears," he responded with a giggle. "It's an expression," he added when he saw Aaron studying his ears. "And I know such things, Sister, because I make it my business to know. He was a ridiculous little man, writing love notes to fifteen-year-old girls who no doubt laughed behind his tonsured little head. He had a penchant for robust farm girls and had become inspired by a particular young Heidi, whom he liked to imagine perched atop a milking stool with her plump hands patiently coaxing milk out of one stubborn udder after another."

"Clary, our guests," Gloria said, inclining her head toward Aaron.

"I am merely quoting from his letters, loosely of course." He addressed Aaron directly now, as though that was what Gloria had intended. "I doubt that our beloved schoolmaster was capable of much eloquence. Eventually, his secret came out." He looked back at his sister. "As secrets always do."

"Clary, can we please have a nice evening?" Gloria said. "We so rarely have guests."

"You mean an evening where nobody says anything interesting and certainly not anything they really mean? Tell me, Sister. What fun is a *nice* evening?" He turned to Aaron's mother. "Dolores, were you frightened when you first set eyes on me?"

"Of course not," said Aaron's mother, answering quickly, as she did when she was nervous.

"Ah, splendid." Clarence picked up his fork and dangled it from his fat fingers.

"Clary, stop it," Gloria said. "Why do you insist on this?" She reached over and began sawing at his meat again.

"What is it that I am insisting on? I am merely chatting with our guest, who has confirmed that she was pleased to meet me." As he spoke, he brought his fork down on the back of Gloria's hand, applying pressure. "In fact, I am delighted to hear it since most people, upon making my acquaintance, can think only about what a queer little creature I am—though I prefer *that* to being mistaken for a child." He looked down at Gloria's hand, trapped beneath his fork. "As you can see, Sister, I am quite capable of managing cutlery."

"I'm sorry, Clary," said Gloria.

"I know you are, Sister." Clarence lifted his fork, and Gloria's hand fluttered up. He smacked his lips. "The hare was superb," he said.

At home, Aaron's nightly chore was to dry the supper dishes, so when his mother called to him from Gloria's kitchen, he rose—though he would have preferred to stay with Clarence—and stood, a dishtowel in hand, between his mother and Gloria. His mother washed, and Gloria received the dried dishes from him, inspecting each before she put it away.

"How are you feeling then?" Gloria asked.

"Fine," he said.

"Gloria, show Aaron your trick," his mother said. She stopped washing, halting the whole chain of labor. When she turned, he could see the strain of the visit on her face.

"Ah, the trick," said Gloria. She took two walnuts from her overalls pocket and held them out, one in each palm, for him to see before bringing her hands together, fingers laced as if in prayer. Her muscles bulged and Aaron heard the crack of a nut bursting open. His mother cheered, and Gloria opened her hand—the intact walnut at its center, its shell slick with perspiration—and offered him the meat of the other.

"I don't feel good," he told his mother. He handed her the dishtowel.

Gloria and his mother took him into the sunroom, where he would sleep that night. His mother said she would be back in ten minutes to tuck him in, but he could hear the two of them talking in the dining room and knew they had forgotten about his bedtime. He looked for the cat. The thought of sleeping with its hollow sockets staring at him seemed unbearable. He was bent down, searching beneath the couch, when he heard Clarence roll in behind him. "I imagine you're looking for Aaron," said Clarence. "Sister has taken him to her quarters for the evening." Aaron got up from the floor. "I've come to see whether you need anything, and I've brought you these." He indicated the neatly folded pajamas on his lap. They were covered with Santas and reindeer. "Yet another of Sister's poorly conceived though well-intentioned gifts."

"Thank you," Aaron said. He took the pajamas. "What happened to the teacher who was afraid of you?" he asked.

"Ah, Nordstrum has caught your interest," said Clarence. "I am not surprised to learn that classroom injustice interests you. In fact, I would be happy to finish the story, particularly since justice prevails, but first you must take those wretched pajamas down the hallway to the bathroom and get yourself ready for bed. Agreed?"

"Yes," said Aaron. He ran down the hallway, changed into the pajamas, folded his clothes, urinated, rinsed his mouth because he had no toothbrush, and returned.

"You look ridiculous," Clarence said as Aaron stood before him in the Santa pajamas. "But there's nothing to be done about it. Climb beneath the covers at least, so I don't have to look at you."

Aaron did, and Clarence began his story immediately. "This Nordstrum was bothered by my presence in his classroom to the extent that he wished to have me removed from it altogether. The principal—who was not a bad man, merely limited in his sensibilities—did not grant his request, could not, for ours was a tiny school. Nordstrum was in charge of not just my fourth-grade class but fifth and sixth as well, which meant that he had three years of my unsettling presence to look forward to.

"Instead, the principal summoned me to his office, and perhaps because he too found me freakish, he spoke with candor. Mr. Nordstrum's fear had nothing to do with me personally, he said. It was caused solely by my appearance. He seemed unaware that his assessment contradicted itself. In closing, he noted that Nordstrum would adjust to my oddness, just as everyone else had managed to do. What he asked of me was patience. Though I've outgrown it admirably, patience was one of my virtues as a boy, for hadn't I waited, day after day, year after year, to grow? Of course, a man like Nordstrum never gets over his fear because it's nothing but a stand-in for prejudice. Nonetheless, justice was served." He paused and patted his chest. "By me. From that day onward, I made a point to be always in front of Nordstrum. I sat in the front row so that when he glanced up, I was the first thing he saw. I arrived early for school and stayed late, and when we went outside for recess, I trotted behind him like a shadow so that when he turned, I—"

"You could walk?" Aaron interrupted.

"Of course I could walk," Clarence said. "I walked to school, several miles each way, though in winter my sisters—Gloria, whom you know, and Frances, who is a year older than Gloria—took turns pulling me on a sled."

"Were you afraid of snow?" Aaron asked.

"Quite the opposite. Sometimes my father would hoist me on top of a big bank of snow and I would run across it, liberated by the realization that no one was light enough to follow me."

"But now you have to be in a wheelchair?" Aaron asked.

"I was an active child, and when it became clear that I had weak bones, my parents began to restrict my activities. They lacked money for medical bills and did not like to see me suffer. Moreover, my mother felt secretly responsible for my overall condition because of an incident that occurred in my infancy, involving my grandfather, her father, who had come to stay with us around the time I was born. I don't remember him well—he died when I was still young—but I have been told that he liked to drink. Over the years, he lost everything, all the land he had farmed with decreasing success. He had come from Sweden as a child with his parents and six siblings, but only he and his parents survived the journey. Later, everyone marveled that it was this weak, easily crushed man who had had the stamina, or simply the luck, to remain alive as his siblings fell like flies.

"After he had sold off all his land in bits, he was shuffled around until he came here to be with his youngest daughter. By then he had become like a child again. My mother said that he would chase my sisters around the house making animal noises, quacking like a duck for hours until even my sisters, who were two and three at the time, begged my mother to make him stop. Of course, my mother allowed no alcohol in the house, so at night, while everyone slept, he would sit in his room at the window, seized by tremors and longing, before rising to pace the house. The years of drinking had affected his motor skills, so he clomped along noisily, bumping into things.

"One night, he passed by my sisters' room, where I slept in a clothes basket. Later, he explained that he had heard me crying and, wanting to be useful, had gone in and lifted me from the basket, thinking he would rock me back to sleep. My parents awoke to the sound of my howling outside their window and jumped from their bed to look. They couldn't see me there on the ground because it was dark, but they could hear me. My mother said that my father pried open the window and climbed right out to retrieve me. They found my grandfather asleep upstairs, still leaning on the sill. He remembered nothing more than sitting down to rock me."

"What happened to him?" Aaron asked.

"He killed himself several years later," Clarence said matter-of-factly. "As I began to grow—or rather, as I began *not* to grow—he became despondent. Though he had become childlike in most ways, it seemed that he still possessed an adult capacity for self-recrimination. Often he was up at three or four a.m., before my father rose to attend to chores even, and I would occasionally join him for breakfast. He always made oatmeal, and we rarely spoke, though he would giggle over something silly—a chair scraping across the floor that sounded like gas being passed. When we were finished, the bowls and spoons rinsed, he would remove the yardstick from the old butter churn and gesture for me to stand. I would, and he would press it to my back, hold his hand level across my head, and mark a spot on the stick with his finger. He would study that spot, muttering to himself, and then return the yardstick to the churn and go outside."

"I have a bully," Aaron announced to Clarence after breakfast the next morning. Gloria had served eggs, and their runniness added to the nauseated state in which he'd awakened, the result of having slept poorly. The night before, his mother had not returned to tuck him in, but even after Clarence shut off the sunroom light and the house became still, he'd been unable to sleep, his mind looping back through all the stories that Clarence had told him. It was pleasant, like watching reruns of his favorite television shows, except he realized that he had told Clarence nothing of himself in return, nothing to keep him alive in Clarence's memory the way that the stories about the schoolmaster who hated Clarence and the grandfather who dropped him out the window would keep Clarence alive in his. He resolved to tell Clarence the story of his bully the next morning, and only then had he drifted off to sleep.

"Of course you have a bully," Clarence replied. "Men like us always have bullies. You must think of it as a badge of honor. In fact, I consider it one of my requirements for friendship. I have little interest in the unbullied masses."

Aaron looked down, scuffing the toe of his shoe along the ground in pleasure.

"Does your bully possess a name?" Clarence asked.

"Yes," said Aaron. "Her name is Roberta."

"Ah, a female bully. I have always found female bullies relentless."

"What does *relentless* mean?" Aaron asked, adding, "I know it's an adjective." He had recently learned about the parts of speech and appreciated adjectives most of all because they were not essential like nouns and verbs.

"It means that quite often there is no dissuading them. Boys, you see, tend to bully for the sheer joy of it and are, therefore, indiscriminate. They are motivated by the pleasure of bringing pain and welcome any opportunity to do so, provided it can be achieved with ease."

Clarence paused. Aaron nodded to indicate his interest in Clarence's commentary, even if he did not fully understand it. "The female bully, on the other hand, is loyal. It is you she is after, and she will not be distracted by substitutes."

The bullying had begun in the spring, when the weather turned suddenly and unbearably warm and Aaron and his classmates twitched in their seats and sighed at Mrs. Lindskoog's demands upon them. For weeks they sat, brains dormant, the air rotten with a smell like turning milk, which was the odor of their bodies ripening in the closeness of the room. Then, on the last Thursday of April, a day on which the superintendent announced over the intercom that the temperature had reached ninety-six degrees, a girl named Roberta Klimek sauntered past Aaron's desk on her way to the pencil sharpener and delivered a single blow to his right arm. She had not spoken—in warning or explanation—and nobody else seemed to have noticed the attack, the first of what was to become a daily ritual. Soon, both of his arms were covered with bruises, dark like thunderclouds, and he began wearing long sleeves to conceal them, despite the heat. Still, it intrigued him to think of his body creating and hosting such rich, deep colors, and as he got ready for bed he took to standing with his shirt off before the bathroom mirror, admiring the contrast of blues and purples and yellows against his pale skin. It was in this pose that his mother found him one night. She opened the bathroom door, unaware that he was inside, and as she backed out, the flash of color caught her eye.

"Where did those bruises come from?" she asked quietly. His father's anger had been loud, drowning out everything else. It was only after his death that Aaron realized anger came in quiet forms as well.

"It's nothing," he said.

"It doesn't look like nothing."

"It's a game," he said, and having thus committed himself to mendacity, he added, "They don't even hurt."

"A game?" she said. "Who exactly do you play this game with?"

"Just some kids."

"Brush your teeth," she said at last.

It was working in pairs that had first brought him to the attention of Roberta Klimek, after he had been paired not with her but with Kimberly, the pug-nosed girl who had been a favorite of Miss Meeks. When Kimberly heard her name coupled with Aaron's, she blurted out, "Can't I work with somebody else?"

"You can, but you may not," Mrs. Lindskoog answered sternly, as if grammatical impropriety were the issue. She believed in the benefits of working in pairs, which Aaron dreaded even more than group work, for in groups he could keep quiet and do a disproportionate share of the work while in pairs there was no room for silent diligence.

He and Kimberly pushed their desks together and turned their attention to reading about another pair, Dick and Jane, who were a steady and tedious presence in their readers. After several minutes of boredom, Kimberly announced, "You know that nobody likes you."

"I know," he said.

"Miss Meeks didn't like you," she tried again.

"I know," he agreed.

The two of them sat then, books open, neither making further attempts to read aloud, but Kimberly was not content to while away their reading period in a state of benign idleness. She gazed around the room for inspiration, and her eyes fell on Roberta Klimek. "You love Roberta," she announced with such authority that the other children began to giggle.

Aaron stared down at his book, shocked by Kimberly's casual invocation of the word *love,* then peeked over at Roberta Klimek, whose hands lay on top of her reader, twitching like fish too long out of water. As Kimberly continued her taunting, Aaron watched those hands draw together into fists.

Roberta Klimek was large for her age with long, straight hair and a blotchy complexion, a shy girl who carried out her attacks covertly, for she did not crave the fanfare that often marked bullying as a public event, a factor that he soon realized was not in his favor. He began to study her in the same way that she tormented him—furtively and with persistence. He learned that, unlike his other classmates, who settled into one or two "good" subjects and tolerated the rest, Roberta Klimek had the distinction of being poor at everything. She remained

steadfastly unable to alphabetize, seemed not even to see the relationship between this skill and the alphabet itself, that series of letters that
she had spent kindergarten, and now first grade, struggling to keep in
order.

Finally, on a sweltering day in May, Aaron approached Roberta
Klimek on the playground, where she stood by the monkey bars, alone
like him. "Excuse me," he said, the first words he had ever spoken to
this girl whose fists he knew intimately, wanting to establish himself as
a polite boy, a boy who said "excuse me" even to his tormentors, but as
Roberta Klimek leaped on him and began to pound him with her fists,
he knew that this trait was what flamed her hatred.

His mother was summoned to a meeting attended by the principal,
Mrs. Lindskoog, the school nurse, Aaron, Roberta Klimek, and her
father, who sat beside his daughter with similarly clenched fists and explained that she was in training. She planned to become a boxer, and he
supported her dream. That was the word he used—*dream*—and Aaron
would always remember how everyone looked down at the floor at the
very sound of it.

"What can I do?" Aaron asked Clarence as he finished telling the
story.

"I've never had much success thwarting bullies," Clarence told him,
"though if it's any consolation, bullies, in my experience, eventually tire
of you and move on."

"It's time to go," said Aaron's mother from the doorway of the sunroom. "I don't like driving on gravel roads after dark." It was not yet
noon, so her comment made no sense, but Aaron did not say so. "Five
minutes," she said and left.

"Please, Clarence," he said. "Tell me about Olga's tale of woe before
we go."

"Impossible," said Clarence. "Stories should never be told quickly.
One must always leave time for creative embellishment and digression,
or what are we left with?" He looked at Aaron, who shrugged. "The
dreary facts. That's what," said Clarence. "And I can assure you that
Olga deserves much more than the dreary facts."

Though Aaron would not grasp until he was much older that

Clarence had been in love with Olga, he could see that Clarence would not be convinced to tell the story. Already his mother was yelling, "Right now, Aaron" from the other room, and so he took the handles of Clarence's wheelchair one last time and pushed him down the hallway and onto the porch, where the four of them regarded one another awkwardly, as people often do when it is time to say good-bye.

"Well," said his mother as they pulled out of the driveway, one of Gloria's doilies on the seat between them. "That's finally over."

He had always liked sleeping in cars, waking up in a different place. It was the closest he came to understanding the passage of time. He shut his eyes, listening to the pleasant sound of gravel rattling beneath the car. "What would you think if we moved?" his mother said.

Aaron opened his eyes.

"We already moved," he said.

"I mean into town. I'm thinking about buying the Trout Café. I've already talked to Frank, and he's interested. We would live there."

Aaron tried to imagine it: he and his mother stretching out in the booths to sleep each night, awakening in them each morning, his mother going into the bathroom marked *Ladies* while he used the one for *Men*. "Do people live in cafés?" he asked.

"We'll live over it," his mother said. "You'll help me in the kitchen, washing dishes and chopping things. It'll be a lot of work, you know, so I'll need you." It was only then that he understood what his mother meant. They were going to *run* the café the way that Frank did, frying hamburgers for people and bringing them ketchup and pie.

"We don't know how to live in a café," he said.

"We'll learn," his mother said. "Sometimes you're such a scaredy cat." She laughed, but he heard his father's voice saying "chickenshit." "I can cook," she said. "Remember what I told you yesterday, about when I worked for the Goulds."

Only later, years later, did he understand that she had needed him to say the things she did not yet believe: that she *could* run a café and cook for people and be happy.

"What will Frank do?" he asked instead.

"Frank will retire. He'll go fishing whenever he wants and sit in his garden. Maybe he'll drop by for a cup of coffee sometimes. First, though, he'll teach us everything we need to know."

"Like about the cash register?" Aaron asked.

"Well, yes, the cash register, for one thing. And we'll need to learn how to manage in such a large kitchen. I've got some ideas of my own also."

She sounded happy when she said this, happy to have her own ideas.

"What kind of ideas?" he asked.

"Oh, just some ideas about how to fix things. Frank's getting old, and when people get old, they shouldn't have to think about those things anymore. But we're not old, are we?" she asked brightly. "For starters, I'd like to change the menu a little."

"Won't Frank feel bad if we change the menu?"

"Why would he feel bad, silly?" she said. "It will be our café. Besides, people expect change. They look forward to it."

He thought about Frank sitting at home in his garden, wondering what had been wrong with his menu. He tried to feel excited because his mother was, but he could not. He did not believe that people looked forward to change.

February

12

February started warm (unseasonably so said his colleagues), but over the course of a weekend, the temperature dropped thirty degrees. Aaron woke up late that Monday. There was not enough time to walk to school, and anyway, it depressed him to imagine the bison in Golden Gate Park huddled together on such a bleak day. He added a second sweater under his corduroy jacket and walked down to wait for the bus, which arrived late and fuller than usual, everyone on it subdued, the way people get when the weather has tricked them.

His classroom was like stepping into a freezer vault. When Chisato arrived just after him, he greeted her, and his breath hung like smoke between them. "Excuse me," he said because he was on his way downstairs to inquire about the lack of heat, but she blushed as if he were asking her to ignore some bodily indiscretion.

Chisato had begun arriving earlier each day so that now she was often there when he came in, sitting in the half darkness of the room, her feet swinging above the floor. She was short, well under five feet, and coy about her age, though Marla had let slip that she was in her mid-forties. She often dressed like a teenager, a chaste teenager, in plaid skirts with fringe and knee-high boots, her hair held back by matching barrettes. That morning, she had on thin white gloves of the sort librarians wear for handling rare documents. Chisato did not interact with the other students, though they were friendly toward her. The Brazilian boys flirted, but Aaron knew that the flirting meant nothing. That was just the way the boys communicated, standing close and touching, laughing easily with their mouths wide open so that you could see their teeth. They all had beautiful teeth, white and not overly corrected the way American teeth were.

At first, he had imagined that Chisato must be terribly homesick, here without family or friends, but as he got to know her, he decided that she was probably lonely in Japan also, that Chisato would be lonely wherever she went. When she started coming in early, he feared that she was developing a crush but soon realized that she viewed this time before class as an opportunity for individual instruction. He appreciated her studiousness yet had begun to feel oppressed by it and by the way she planned out precisely what she would say to him, obviously with the aid of a dictionary and a grammar book, so that even when she described simple things—her landlord's dog or the bar where she played darts—she sounded like a child reciting a poem that she did not fully understand, her sentences technically correct but without the rhythm and inflection that imparted meaning.

"I was quite moved," she had told him recently, describing her first bowl of miso soup since leaving Japan, her delivery so lacking in spontaneity or proper inflection that he had understood neither the words nor the emotion they were meant to convey. At his urging, she repeated the story—three times, each telling exactly the same, right down to the intonation of "I was quite moved"—and then, also at his suggestion, she had written those final words out on the board, along the bottom so that he had to crouch to read them.

"Ah," he said, finally understanding what she had been trying to tell him, though by then the words had meant nothing.

Several of the teachers were already in Marla's office, where she was explaining that Mr. Pulkka had come in during the night and placed a padlock on the small storage room that housed the heater controls. At the end of her explanation, she looked at her watch and announced enthusiastically, "It's time for class," not giving them the opportunity to complain. The teachers turned and went back to their freezing rooms. As Aaron climbed the stairs to the third floor, he thought about how Walter would have stayed right there in Marla's office until heat had been restored because that was how Walter was. He argued and complained and made demands—to hotel clerks and customer service reps, managers and stewardesses—while Aaron stood by, looking apologetic and embarrassed but still, as Walter had always reminded him, ultimately benefiting from the results that Walter achieved.

Aaron had never learned to be comfortable with anger—because of his father, he supposed—though Walter's anger was nothing like his father's. Walter did not get angry often, but when he did, he did not hide it from the world. On the contrary, anger was Walter's way of getting everyone else to see what was right. It was a public event. Aaron understood all of this. He did. But understanding it did not change the way he felt, and the way he felt was sick inside every time he witnessed anger—not just Walter's—or felt it rising in himself. He preferred to think of himself as someone who did not get angry, except that he did, his anger seeping out in small bursts of sarcasm or heightened politeness.

Aaron found his students huddled at their desks, bundled up in coats and scarves so that he could not make out who was who at first. They peered at him, sure that he had rectified the problem because they believed he would not let them freeze. "It's time to start class," he said, echoing Marla without realizing it, and his students opened their notebooks and prepared to learn. Soon, Bart, a work-study student from Ukraine, appeared with a space heater in each hand. He plugged in the heaters, ceremoniously, one on each side of the room, and then loitered for a moment, like a luggage porter expecting a tip. The heaters' singular effect was to remind the students that they were paying tuition to freeze. And they were freezing. Each time they answered a question, their words crystallized in the air, shocking the Brazilians and Thais in particular. After an hour of this, Aaron tossed his chalk on the desk and went back downstairs.

"Come in," Marla called when he knocked at her office door. As he opened it, a wave of heat rolled out.

"I'm glad at least one of those space heaters works," he said.

In response, she flapped her arms, a gesture he interpreted as "shut the door and stop letting out the heat." She had not yet taken down the Christmas lights above her desk, and they blinked off and on, making the sweat on her brow and nose glisten. He shut the door but remained standing, despite her suggestion that he sit, while he described the impossibility of teaching under such conditions. "They're trying to take notes with mittens on," he said. "It's like watching some silly party game."

"Do something that doesn't require writing," Marla said. She sounded tired. "It's supposed to warm up again by Wednesday."

"What are you saying? That Mr. Pulkka won't turn the heat back on?"

He knew that she had not asked. Taffy had told him that when Pulkka and Marla looked over the books together, Pulkka questioned each expense and hinted that he could always find a new director, someone less blind to waste. Their work relationship was complicated by the fact that they had dated briefly, years earlier. "She dropped him," Taffy said, "so he enjoys making her feel insecure about her job, especially now that she's divorced with two kids to support." It shocked Aaron that Marla had confided in her employees about such things.

"It's more than just the wasted time," he declared. He was still wearing both sweaters and the corduroy jacket and could feel the sweat pooling under his arms.

Marla looked up, responding to his tone, but he did not know how to explain to her that it made him feel foolish, like a failure really, to stand there before his freezing students blowing warmth into his cupped hands as he scribbled sentences on the board, aware that they were all watching him, watching him accept these conditions. He looked at Marla, her desk piled high with papers, photos of her children on the walls, a sprig of mistletoe—he noticed it only then—hanging over her head.

"Never mind," he said. "The students are waiting."

Lila was leading the class in calisthenics. She had become interested in what she called "American-style fitness" during the year she worked at Disney World. He waited for the class to complete a round of jumping jacks before announcing, "The heater is very broken. It cannot be fixed today." He wanted to tell them the truth—that the owner had locked up the controls—but he maintained an old-fashioned belief in basic workplace loyalty, even when it seemed so obviously misplaced.

They spent the rest of the morning playing the Culture Game, which he had invented when he was teaching at the community college in Albuquerque. The game, which required them to discuss questions that focused on small cultural differences between their countries and the United States, had started as a way to fill leftover minutes at the end of class, but his students had begged to play it at other times because they knew firsthand that the small differences were what bred confusion and distrust. Over the years he had created a lengthy list of questions, which he added to constantly:

What should you do if you see an old man kicking a dog?

When someone on the street asks for directions, should you make up directions if you are not sure how to get there, just to be polite?

If you are invited to a friend's house for dinner, should you help with the dishes?

The rules were simple: he read a question aloud, blew his whistle, and the students rushed to discuss it with someone who was not from their country. Four minutes later, he blew the whistle again and the class reported their responses. Of course, they liked this part of the exercise, enjoyed explaining how things worked in their countries, but soon enough someone always asked, "What is the correct answer here in America, Aaron?" They liked to believe there was a correct answer.

The cold had made the students listless, so Aaron began with this question: *Is it okay to ask someone how much money he pays for rent?* He had found that money questions had an energizing effect. Their answers were nuanced, most of them having to do with the motivation behind the asking. "Is not okay if you are just being nosy," said Pilar, though she pronounced it "noisy."

When it was Aaron's turn, he told them that once when he hosted a class party in Albuquerque, a Vietnamese student had inquired how much his house cost.

"Were you embarrassed by this question?" Katya asked.

He admitted that he had been.

"This I do not understand," said Katya. "Americans are thinking all the time about money but always they are saying it is bad manners to talk about money. Maybe if they are talking about money more, they will not be thinking all the time about it."

The others nodded.

"Maybe," Aaron said. He knew they were expecting a better answer than this, but he put the whistle to his mouth and blew. "Next question: *Is it okay to drop in on a friend uninvited?*" They had just learned the phrasal verb *to drop in on,* and he noted their excitement at encountering it.

Ji-hun, one of the Korean students, began the group discussion by acknowledging that it was best to call ahead, his reasoning practical: one should not waste time driving to visit a friend who was not home. Beyond that, everyone agreed that it was okay—not just okay but a happy surprise. They seemed perplexed that it was even a question.

Finally, Diego asked, "And for Americans?"

"It depends on the person," Aaron said, an answer that always displeased them. They wanted a set of rules that they could draw upon without having to consider individual desires or preferences.

"Is like this in London," said Neto, one of the Brazilians. He had studied there for two years and claimed to miss it, but now he told them a story about an elderly couple who had lived in the apartment above his and invited him for dinner once a week and on holidays. "They were my family there," Neto said. "But one day I received good news at school, and when I arrived at my apartment that night I went up to tell them. It was ten o'clock, and they were wearing their robes and watching television, which I knew because I can hear the television from my ceiling. I only go because I know they are awake and because I am very exciting, but they told me it was too late, that I should not come to their door like this, unannounced."

The others listened, but Aaron could tell from the way they shook their heads that this made no sense to them.

"The next day," Neto continued, "I told my news, and they made a special dinner. I did not tell them, never, that I felt so sad when they scolded me."

The class was quiet. Finally Paolo asked, "What is your idea about drop-in, Aaron?"

He considered blowing his whistle or correcting one of their grammar errors, but he looked at his students there before him, coats zipped, hoods up, all of them shivering yet focused, wanting to know what he thought.

"I do not like when people drop in," he said.

They shifted in their seats and waited for him to explain, but he could not tell them about the hostility he felt each time his doorbell rang unexpectedly, how he pressed himself against the wall out of sight or tiptoed into the bathroom and turned on the shower, hoping that the unwanted visitor would hear it and leave. Once he had even crouched under his desk until he was sure the person had gone.

His students were looking at him, waiting for him to elaborate. Eventually, Katya said, "Americans are so friendly when you meet them, but they will never invite you into their homes." The others nodded, and she added, "Russians are opposite people. We are very moody outside people, but we will invite you into our hearts." Katya believed that *heart* and *home* were the same thing.

His students wanted desperately to make American friends and came to him for advice, considering him equipped to offer instruction in the art of befriending Americans. He gave them pointers—eating out was good, but karaoke made many Americans uncomfortable. He did not tell them that he too was alone in this city, that as he walked down the street each day, he wondered about everyone he passed: what they had eaten for breakfast, whether they cursed more when they were happy or when they were sad, whether they were smiling because of something they had just observed or because they always smiled when they were out in the world alone. Lately he had found himself deeply curious about the details of strangers' lives, yet the thought of engaging in meaningful conversation struck him as unbearable. He was perplexed by his conflicting emotions but accepted that he felt oddly liberated by his loneliness, just as he accepted that he could not tell his students any of this without changing everything between them.

*   *   *

On Thursday, the fourth day without heat, there appeared inside each faculty member's mailbox a small candle in the shape of a heart, which Aaron interpreted as a token apology, an attempt at appeasement. The candle only intensified his frustration, for it was so small, the school so cold. Worse, when he turned it over, he saw that the price tag had not been removed—*49¢*, which meant that the collective apology had set the school back less than five dollars, though he suspected that Marla had paid for the candles out of her own pocket.

By then, it was colder indoors than out, so at the start of class he pulled up one of the yellowing shades along the far side of the room and opened a window. Yoshi went over and leaned out, joking that he wanted to warm up his ears, which was a big deal for shy Yoshi. As he pulled his head back inside, the window slammed, almost guillotining him, and then, in such quick succession that the two events seemed connected, the entire third floor went dark. Aaron supposed it was a blown fuse. He also supposed he should do something about it—report it at least—except weren't the cold and the dark and the broken window all Pulkka's doing?

Soon, he heard the jangling of Felix's belt in the hallway. When he looked out, Felix's bicycle strobe was flashing eerily from the stairwell.

Ten minutes later, the lights came back on. "Okay?" Bart asked, poking his head into the room. Aaron thanked him but could not make his voice sound sincere. He knew that it was not Bart's fault that nothing in the building worked, that he was just a student working to defray tuition costs, yet Aaron could not help but believe that Marla chose students who were sympathetic to the school's ways. Bart pointed at the two heaters he had brought up on Monday, which had yet to produce heat, and shook his head as though the heaters had nothing to do with him. He unplugged them and paused in the doorway, a contraband heater in each hand, to say, "Meeting in Marla's office at noon. Bring your own lunch."

Of course, the meeting had not been called to address anything as urgent as the lack of heat, though Aaron noticed that Marla had let her office cool down. Her mistletoe and Christmas lights had been replaced with hearts that said WILD THANG and U R MINE, and she began by wishing them all an early Happy Valentine's Day. "Did you guys get the candles?" she asked, and they gave mumbled responses, like children who had been asked about a topic that embarrassed them.

"I have some exciting news," she said next. "Are you ready?" She paused dramatically. "Mr. Pulkka has rented out the spare room." She said it as if they were all getting raises.

"His office?" asked Valerie, whom Aaron did not really know because her classroom was on the first floor and she rarely came up to the faculty room.

"No," said Marla. "That little room on the third floor that nobody uses—right across from Felix and Aaron."

"To who?" said Felix.

"Yes," said Aaron, "to whom?" He hoped that Felix had noted the correction.

"A private eye," said Marla excitedly.

"What's a detective want with a room in an ESL school?" asked Eugenia.

"He's going to teach classes," Marla explained.

"Classes in sleuthing?" said Aaron, and everyone except Marla laughed.

It turned out that sleuthing was precisely what the detective planned to teach. That afternoon, the mushrooms were scraped from the wall, a table, chairs, and a whiteboard carried up from the basement. When Aaron arrived to a warm building the following Monday, a function entirely of the weather, he got his first glimpse of the detective. He could see him across the hallway, attaching a hand-lettered sign to his door: THE PRIVATE EYE SCHOOL. He resembled a Hollywood version of a detective—ruddy and big-bellied with a shambling walk and, Aaron would quickly learn, a penchant for tobacco. Unlike priests and professors, who surely benefited from looking priestly and professorial, Aaron imagined that the man's appearance only made his job—much of which he pictured taking place undercover—that much harder. Perhaps he had turned to teaching as a way to finally cash in on his detectivelike looks.

Aaron always gave a quiz on Monday mornings, his way of nudging the students back to English. Most of them retreated to their native languages over the weekend, except Paolo, who spent weekends riding with the San Mateo Harley Club and always had questions on Monday morning. What Paolo wanted to know this Monday—waiting until the others were working away on their quizzes to ask—was why the Chinese were such bad drivers. He picked up his pen, preparing to take notes, and the others, even the Chinese students, looked up from their quizzes expectantly. Aaron studied his chalk while the class studied him. He hated stereotypes, particularly those that struck him as somehow true, but he envied his students their ease in asking such questions.

They asked one another such questions also. The Brazilians asked the Chinese whether they could spot a Chinese American, for example, and they said of course they could because the Chinese Americans walked a different way. "How do they walk?" the Brazilians asked, and the Chinese students said, "Aggressive like Americans. They are not humble anymore." It was the "anymore" that intrigued him, for it implied that they had been born humble and then had it squeezed out of them. They asked about one another's features, the shapes of their eyes, the color of their skin, always turning to him for vocabulary: what was this type of nose called, this shade of skin? Most often, he replied that there was no word, at least none that he could think of, and Lerma, the lone Filipina, said, "How do you speak about noses without words?"

"I rarely talk about noses," he said, then, "Let's see. We have hooked noses, aquiline, hatchet, pug." He tried to recall whether any of these were derogatory.

When his students had these discussions, he listened carefully but did not take part, except once when he overheard Chaa, one of the Thais, say that Thais liked to own businesses in the Castro. "Why?" Aaron asked, and Chaa said because gay men liked to spend money.

"You can raise the price very high," he explained, "and still gay men will pay because gay men care most about pleasure."

Aaron knew that some gay men would take offense at this comment, at the notion that they could be duped into buying anything provided it made them feel good, but he also believed that real conversation ceased the moment a group turned inward, toward communal indignation fueled by a constant parsing of the comment. *What did pleasure mean here? Wasn't this just one more case of hyper-sexualizing gay men?* And if the conversation stopped before it really began, could people ever become comfortable with one another? Could straight people understand what it meant to be gay if they were too afraid of making mistakes to ask questions? He had come to prefer dealing with people who barreled in with questions that might be regarded as insensitive to those who maintained a careful distance, forming measured comments that all demonstrated the same studied sense of what was correct. Listening to his students ask questions had taught him this: that nothing could truly get better in this country until people learned to ask the kinds of questions that they had been taught never to ask.

Still, the truth was that he did not know how to ask these questions either, certainly not about race. Mortonville had existed in a racial vacuum, its citizens not just white but primarily northern European. The only diversity he had known was a handful of Poles who lived along one of the lakes and two boys who were half Vietnamese. Their father was a local man who had gone off to Vietnam to fight and returned married. His name was Richard Schultz. Aaron's mother said Richard Schultz had left as one sort of person and come back another.

"What kind of person was he when he left?" Aaron asked.

He knew what kind he was when he returned. Once when Richard Schultz ordered his eggs scrambled but Aaron's mother accidentally sent out fried, Richard Schultz karate-chopped his hand down on the edge of the plate so that the eggs flew into the air and landed in a mess on the floor. "Now they're scrambled," he had said.

"I only knew him briefly before he left, but I remember him as a sweet boy, shy and so polite," Aaron's mother said, a description that had terrified Aaron because he'd heard these very words used to describe him. He wondered how it was possible to go away to a place—a place like this Vietnam that nobody in Mortonville wanted to talk about—and come back a man who was angered by eggs.

The two boys spoke Vietnamese with their mother when they were young, but their father put an end to this because he said he wanted his sons to be American. The mother came into the café sometimes and sat alone drinking coffee filled with sugar and milk. When Aaron approached her table to see whether she needed anything, she tried to engage him in conversation, but he could not understand what she was saying, which embarrassed him. Eventually she stopped trying to converse with him and with everyone else in town. He wondered whether living in Mortonville was more difficult for the sons, who thought of Mortonville as home yet looked different from everyone around them, or for the mother, who passed her days keenly aware that it was not home, despite the fact that she would spend the rest of her life there. Aaron always smiled at the boys when he saw them in the hallways at school because even though he looked like everyone else, he knew how it felt not to fit in.

What Aaron came to understand as a boy was that people focused on difference. He had learned his first real lesson about this the way that people often learned lessons, by doing something that it still made his face hot to think about. It had happened during Show and Tell, which was not actually called Show and Tell anymore because they were sixth graders, though this did not change the fact that each Friday six of them had to go to the front of the room to perform something—a joke, a poem, a story. This was meant to teach confidence, which Aaron suspected could not be taught. He spent long hours memorizing Longfellow's "The Village Blacksmith" and recited "Trees" by Joyce Kilmer to bored silence while the next boy got up and told a *knock knock* joke that left everyone hooting with laughter. They laughed when Aaron finished also, but only because he had worked so hard.

Over the course of the year, he grew tired of their ridicule, which outweighed even the deep pleasure he felt when he passed Mrs. Korkowski's desk on his way back to his own and she whispered, "Aaron, that was just lovely." Finally, one Friday he decided to prepare nothing and then learn a joke during lunch. He ate his tuna casserole quickly and presented himself at the library, where he asked for joke books. The librarian pointed him toward an entire shelf, from which he chose one at random. The book was called *Fifty Polack Jokes,* and the assistant librarian, who was not really a librarian but one of the mothers, flipped it open and scanned a page, chuckling. "This has got some good ones," she said, and she stamped the book and handed it to him.

That afternoon, Aaron stood before the class and asked, "What did the Polack say to the garbage collector?" His classmates sat up from the slouch they had slipped into, but before anyone could respond, Mrs. Korkowski called out, "Aaron Englund, sit down." They all laughed.

"That's not the end of the joke," Aaron said weakly, desperate to deliver the punch line—"I'll take three bags, please"—which he considered very funny.

"Now," shouted Mrs. Korkowski. "Right now." A few of the students laughed again, but when Mrs. Korkowski stood up, her chair flew backward, and the room grew silent, as though she had actually picked the chair up and flung it.

After school, Aaron went right home and told his mother what had happened, determined to make sense of it. His mother thought for a while in that distracted way of hers that did not always resemble thinking, and then she said, "*Korkowski* is a Polish name." He nodded and waited, and his mother said, "You do know that *Polack* is a bad word for Polish people?" He did not know about the "bad" part, though of course he had heard the word *Polack* many times, mainly from the men in the café.

The next morning he wanted to stay home from school, but his mother said that staying home was not a solution, and so, stomach sour with dread, he went early and found Mrs. Korkowski sitting at her desk, grading their vocabulary assignments. "Yes?" she said when she saw him standing in the doorway.

In a rush, he told her how sorry he was. "I didn't know you were Polish," he said.

She put down her pen and rubbed her eyes as though she were

already exhausted by the day. "My name is Polish," she agreed. "But Korkowski is my husband's name. I hope you understand that I would be disappointed to hear you tell a joke like that no matter what my name was. I've always thought better of you than that." Years later, he would realize that he had been chastised for delivering a joke from a book that came from the school library, a book with *Polack* right in its title, but at the time he had not known to consider any of this. "There's a whole world out there," Mrs. Korkowski continued, more gently now. "I want you to remember that, Aaron, to remember that there are things out there beyond what you know or can imagine right now."

Aaron generally avoided the faculty room during break, but that morning he went in, hoping to avoid answering Paolo's question. He found his colleagues sitting around a box of pineapple buns, purchased from the Chinese bakery next door by Marla, which meant that someone had been in her office asking for something—timely photocopies, perhaps even a raise. He reached for a bun but stopped when he saw the Post-it note taped to the box: *Thanks for the hard work. Love you guys, Marla.*

Aaron felt increasingly old-fashioned and cranky amid this new social topography: business transactions sealed with a hug rather than a handshake; cell phone conversations carried on in public places, offering the sorts of details traditionally reserved for the bedroom or doctor's office; and now this, people who hired you to teach English professing love on a Post-it note. Once, when he and Walter overheard a teenager and his parents bid each other farewell at the shopping mall in Albuquerque, Aaron had asked, "Why must they say 'love you' as though the kid's shipping off to war? He's obviously just heading over to the Gap for a few hours while his parents buy him way too many Christmas gifts."

Walter had replied carelessly, suggesting that maybe Aaron needed to become more *comfortable* with his feelings, as though these rote declarations signaled people at ease with emotion. In fact, Aaron suspected the opposite was true, that people had become so removed from their feelings that they were not bothered by what he viewed as emotion-devaluing gestures: words and actions that undermined the very senti-ments they purported to evoke by turning them into commonplace, all-purpose responses.

Only Winnie had understood, because she was Winnie. He looked again at the Post-it, missing her terribly.

13

On his way back from the faculty room, Aaron paused in the doorway of the detective's classroom, planning to introduce himself, but only the detective's students were inside: a man in his forties, who, he would later learn, was from Kenya; a young woman with neck tattoos, dressed primly in a pale blue sweater and slacks; and a woman in her sixties, who he would come to suspect was a transsexual, though not because she fit any stereotypes of transsexuals. She was, in fact, a diminutive woman who wore tailored pantsuits, no makeup except lipstick, and little jewelry. Aaron's suspicion would be based on one small but curious detail, a habit the woman had of stepping back and letting other women pass through doorways before her, as though unable to dispense with years of gentlemanly decorum. The three students were reading from handouts, and he did not ask them where the detective was. He assumed smoking. Four times that morning, he had seen the man slip out of his room and head toward the smoking balcony at the end of the hallway.

Aaron followed his own students back into the room, where he wrote instructions for the next activity on the board while they were getting seated:

On a half sheet of paper, in 3–5 sentences, write an anecdote or detail about yourself that is surprising, amusing, interesting, or even embarrassing. It should be something about you that no one in this class knows. Do NOT include details, such as place names, that would make your identity known. When you are done, fold the paper in half twice.

"Please," said Yoshi, pointing to the board. "What is *anecdote*?" He pronounced it with a soft *c* so that it sounded like a type of headache medicine.

"An an-ik-dote," said Aaron, "is a little story about something that happened to you."

"Can you give us one example?" said Pilar.

"Okay, here's *an* example of something about me," he said. "I love to eat different types of animal feet—pigs' feet, chicken feet, duck webbing, sheep hooves. This is a detail about me that is surprising. Now I want you to write down an anecdote, and then we'll read them and see whether the class can guess who wrote each one. It will be a way for us to get to know one another better and to learn about the two new students." The two new students had arrived the week before, a Turkish woman named Aksu and a young Korean woman who cried when he asked her to introduce herself to the class. Later, she told him that she had never spoken in class in her life, that back in Korea she had received a doctor's dispensation from public speaking.

The students composed their anecdotes slowly, recopying the final drafts onto fresh pieces of paper, which they folded and dropped into a punch bowl that Aaron had borrowed from the faculty room. He drew a slip and read it to the class. It was about a boy getting his penis caught in his pants zipper and screaming in terror when his father said that he would need to cut it, believing his father meant his penis and not the zipper. Everyone laughed and looked at Luis, who was pleased to be recognized as the obvious author. The next two were in a similar vein, sweet childhood memories that made the class giggle. But the fourth slip described how the narrator had pried open the window of his family's nineteenth-story apartment and thrown his mother's cat out. He was eleven and had been egged on by a teenage cousin, who assured him that cats had nine lives. When he rode the elevator down to retrieve the cat, he found it flattened on the sidewalk below. The class grew quiet as Aaron read. Nobody wanted to guess whose anecdote it was because doing so seemed akin to voting for who among them seemed cruelest. Aaron was sure that Neto had written it—he recognized his handwriting—but when Aaron asked whose anecdote it was, Neto sat quietly, refusing to claim ownership.

"Okay," said Aaron. "I guess that was our mystery writer."

They learned that Aksu, the new Turkish student, was a couch potato and that Ji-hun went to Golden Gate Park on the weekends, because people gathered on the sidewalk near the museum each Sunday to swing dance. Finally, Aaron pulled his own slip. He had thought about the stories he could tell—his father falling from a parade float, his mother disappearing, saving Jacob's life—but in the end he wrote down a story that August, his great-great-uncle, had told him the summer of the Englund family vacation. The story was about how his family on his mother's side had lived above the Arctic Circle for ten years with six other Norwegian families and the Lapps. They had nearly starved because the only thing that grew in the frozen ground was potatoes, and even those grew poorly. At last, they moved to America, where they once again became farmers in a very cold place. Aaron had imagined that the students would relate to the story because it was about coming to this country, but instead they seemed perplexed.

"Why would they farm in the snow?" Chaa asked.

"They needed to eat," he said, but he knew that what Chaa was asking—what everyone was wondering—was why they had moved above the Arctic Circle in the first place and why they had stayed so long once they realized that the situation was hopeless. He was five the summer that August told him the story, and so he had not questioned his ancestors' reasoning. But now, assessing the story via the detached logic of his students, he thought that maybe it ran in his family—this attraction to what was futile, this inability to see it as such—for hadn't his mother chosen to marry his father, even though she was happier working for the Goulds, and when his father died, hadn't she moved both of them to Mortonville because she said it was not a place to start over? And what about him? It was true that he had once loved Walter, but then, for many years, he had not—yet he had stayed. He had stayed above the Arctic Circle because what was familiar was important, even when it felt like growing potatoes in the half-frozen ground.

His students were still staring at him, waiting.

"I guess they wanted a challenge," he said. "And they wanted land, even if it was above the Arctic Circle." He reached into the punch bowl. "Next story."

He unfolded the paper, which read: *I am engaged to Bulgarian woman. We meet last year in my country. Now I am in USA and she is in her country. I am waiting for H-1B visa, and she will come here and marry with me.*

The students called out the name of every man in the class, including Aaron, every man except Melvin. Aaron wondered how it made Melvin feel, to seem less likely than his gay teacher to have a fiancée. Of course, Aaron was not sure that the students understood he was gay. He had referred once or twice to his "former partner," but even native speakers had trouble with the nomenclature of gay relationships, and he knew that for many of the students, Nico, in his chaps, was the model for gayness.

"You're forgetting someone," Aaron said, though it had taken him a moment also to realize that Melvin was the author. Melvin was Korean. His real name was Man-soo, but here in the United States, people had begun shortening it to Man, a nickname that had discomfited him, and so he decided to create his own, Melvin. "Melvin, is this yours?" Aaron asked. "Are you engaged?"

Melvin began to stammer. "Her name is Nikolina," he said.

"How did you and Nikolina meet?"

"She was cleaning in Korea."

"A maid?" said Aaron.

"Yes," said Melvin.

"Your maid?" Aaron asked.

"No." Melvin shrugged, licked his lips, which always looked painfully chapped, and said nothing more.

Of all his students, Aaron had the least sense of Melvin, who tended toward one-word responses and never smiled. The others treated him politely, but they did not tease him as they did one another, perhaps because he was older, thirty-two, though Paolo was in his fifties and everyone in the school joked with him. Aaron knew that their careful, almost deferential, treatment of Melvin had to do with his face, which was crumpled in on the right side, as though a horse had stepped on it. Melvin never mentioned his face, but he carried himself like someone accustomed to people's stares.

"Congratulations, Melvin," Aaron said.

That afternoon, Tommy, who was not so secretly one of Aaron's favorite students, stayed after class with the other Thais to ask whether there was a word in English to indicate that someone was in love with a person who didn't love him back. As they huddled around his desk, Aaron noted that Melvin, who was usually the first to leave, was still seated. "Unrequited love," Aaron said. "*Unrequited* means unreturned."

They repeated it—"unrequited love"—and Bong, the most serious of the three despite his unfortunate nickname, asked questions aimed at pinpointing how the word might be used, questions along the lines of whether *unrequited* could be used to talk about unreturned library books or food that customers wished to send back to the kitchen.

"No," Aaron told him, and "No."

"I have unrequited love," Tommy announced tragically, and Aaron and the other Thais laughed. Tommy tried to look miserable, but he was an optimist with a natural goofiness that he took care to cultivate, all of which undermined his occasional attempts at angst.

"Are you sure that your love is unrequited?" Aaron asked, which made the other two laugh harder. They apparently knew the object of his affection.

"Yes," said Tommy. "I am definitely sure. It's Aksu."

"Ah," said Aaron, then regretted sounding surprised.

Aksu, the new Turkish student, was a quiet, beautiful twenty-four-year-old who had just arrived in the United States, having completed her studies to become a French teacher. When she explained this to the class her first day, Aaron asked, "Why didn't you go to France instead of coming here?" and she replied sadly, "I hate French."

"Then why did you study it?" he asked, and she said, either logically or illogically (he wasn't sure which), "How could I know I hated it until I learned it?"

"Aksu is quite a bit older than you," Aaron said, trying to make her seem less desirable, not easy given her wistful smile and doe eyes. Tommy was just nineteen, fresh from high school.

"I've decided I prefer older women," he said. "They're worldly." Aaron laughed. *Worldly* was a vocabulary word. "And we're perfect for each other. We're both couch potatoes."

"You'll need two couches," said Aaron.

"Tell us the couch potato story again," said Chaa.

"You already know the couch potato story," Aaron said. He deeply regretted telling them the story, which had only reinforced their notions of this country.

"Yes, but we like to hear it again," Chaa said. "Please."

The story, told to him by an ER nurse at a party in Albuquerque, was about a man who had been brought in with chest pain. "He was four hundred and eighty-two pounds," the nurse said. "It took four paramedics to lift him off his couch. So I'm undressing him and trying to get him into a hospital gown—nothing fit, we ended up wrapping a sheet around him—and I felt something hard in his stomach area. I started massaging the region. You know what it was? A TV remote, folded into the rolls of his stomach."

He had told his students the story because they were doing a unit on uniquely American court cases, among them the case of a man suing an airline for charging him for two seats because he had not fit into one. Pilar said that when she flew back from Spain after Christmas, she had been made to sit in one of the crew fold-down seats because the woman next to her had spilled into hers, making the flight uncomfortable for both of them. "Even though I paid for my seat," said Pilar, "I could not occupy it."

"Does a ticket represent a person or a seat?" Aaron had asked the class.

"Why is this a case?" Katya asked. "The man is using two seats. He must pay for two seats."

It was then that he had told them about the patient with the remote control folded into his stomach. The truth was that when the ER nurse told him the story, there at the party, they had both laughed at the notion of a man's vice melding with his body, impressed by the symbolism, but as he told his students the story, it no longer seemed funny or symbolic. It seemed cruel. He felt cruel for telling it, particularly as it aligned too neatly with their stereotypes of America: a place where a man could lie on his couch and eat himself to death because, in America, you were free, free to be lonely, to become so big that you could not get off your own couch.

Melvin was still at his desk. Already he had taken out and put away his notebook twice, feigning busyness.

"No story," Aaron told the Thai boys firmly. "I need to talk to Melvin."

Melvin's head snapped up.

"Good-bye, Aaron," said the Thais. "See you tomorrow."

"Be on time," he called after them, knowing they would not be. "And don't fall in unrequited love." They laughed from the hallway.

Melvin sat waiting with his crumpled-in face. Aaron wondered what he had thought of the couch potato story. Did he think to himself that everywhere in the world, people looked at those who were different and said unkind things, or did he hear the story of a fat man and think that it had nothing to do with him?

"Melvin," he said. "You've been very patient. Do you have a question?"

He was expecting a grammar question, a request for clarification on the passive voice, for example, but Melvin began to stammer. "I have romantic question," he said.

"Oh," said Aaron. "Okay. Well, it's certainly the day for that. What is it?"

"Nikolina and I do not have a language together," he began.

"What do you mean?" said Aaron.

"I do not speak Bulgarian, and she does not speak Korean."

"But you met her in Korea. She must speak Korean."

"She was maid," Melvin reminded him.

"English?" suggested Aaron.

"She does not speak English."

"Okay," Aaron said. "Can you explain to me how the two of you communicate?"

"I write in English, and when she receives email, she uses computer translation program to change to Bulgarian. She writes in Bulgarian, and I translate to English. Soon, I will send money to her for English class, but right now, we are using system."

"And?" Aaron coaxed him.

"Two days ago I sent first romantic letter," Melvin said, looking as though he might cry.

How, Aaron wondered, had their engagement preceded any kind of romantic declaration? "Okay," he said. "And what happened then?"

"Yesterday, she sent response."

"Great," said Aaron.

"It is not romantic response." Melvin's eyes got watery. He handed Aaron a copy of the email and looked away:

Dear Man-soo,

Thank you for your letter. I am very like meat. I am very like big steak with potato and sour cream. I hope we are eating steak in America very soon.

Yours truly,
Nikolina

"It is a strange letter," Aaron agreed. He did not know what to say. "Did you ask her opinion about meat?"

"It was romantic letter," Melvin said.

"Well, may I see what you wrote? Maybe she misunderstood?"

"She used computer translating program," Melvin repeated firmly.

Melvin had arrived in the United States a poor man, but he had spent several years acquiring a very specific computer skill, a skill rare enough that the American government had granted him an H-1B visa, a skill so complex that even though he had described it in detail the first day of class, Aaron had no idea what he did. Computers had gotten Melvin a job, a visa, and, in a roundabout way, a fiancée; he was not about to doubt them, to speculate about their fallibility.

Finally, he opened his backpack and extracted a second sheet of paper, which he handed to Aaron, who read it and began to laugh. Melvin looked down, embarrassed, and quickly Aaron said, "I've found the problem. Your thumb has betrayed you. Space bar, Melvin." He placed his finger under the last sentence, which read: *I would like to keep you near meat all times.*

Melvin stared at it, not speaking, so Aaron picked up Melvin's pen and underlined the word *meat*. "You didn't space," he said. "You meant to write 'near *me* at all times,' but accidentally you wrote 'near meat.'"

Melvin stared at the paper, at his feeble attempt at romance. Two weak *haha*s escaped from his mouth. It was the first time Aaron had heard him laugh.

"I wouldn't worry, Melvin. I'm guessing she found your desire to keep her near meat very romantic."

Melvin pondered this. Then, he wrapped his spindly arms around himself and laughed, the crumpled-up side of his face like a second mouth gasping for air.

14

The day Aaron left Mortonville, he did not think of himself as following in his mother's footsteps, for she had disappeared in the middle of the night, telling no one, while he left on an ordinary Sunday afternoon in July. At precisely two o'clock, Walter pulled up outside the Hagedorns' house, where Aaron had been living since his mother left. He came up from his basement bedroom, leaving behind the bed and dresser that Mr. Rehnquist and Mr. Hagedorn—Rudy—had moved from his room above the café the year before. He carried a suitcase in each hand, into which he had packed his clothes, a photo album, and some books, and set them by the front door before he went into the living room, where the three Hagedorns sat waiting, for they realized that he was going.

They had been kind to him, but Aaron assumed that they would be happy to have their home back because that was how he would feel. He did not consider their kindness diminished by the possibility of their relief. He shook Rudy's hand, and Rudy, who had been drinking already, slapped him on the back and wished him well. Mrs. Hagedorn asked where he was going and why and with whom because even though she would miss him, she still planned to report the details of his departure to her phone friends later. Bernice stood to the side, pretending to be uninterested. When he reached out, awkwardly, to hug her, she pulled back, her hair a black curtain closing over her eyes. He did not know whether she was reacting out of anger or an unwillingness to let him experience her body that intimately, but Walter would later assert that she was in love with Aaron and had pulled away to show him that he was making a choice.

As Aaron lifted his suitcases into Walter's trunk, he could hear cheering and horn honking from the ball field several blocks away, which meant that someone had hit a home run, the ease with which he interpreted the sounds only reinforcing his desire to go. As they drove down Main Street, he thought about the day he and his mother arrived, how they had pulled up in front of the café that meant little to him then. Thirteen years later, he was driving out of town and away from the boy he had become here, the shy, polite boy who had few friends, whose mother had abandoned him. Once people thought they knew you, it was almost impossible to change their minds, which meant that it was almost impossible to change yourself. Maybe this was why his mother had gone also—because she did not know how to be anything else here but his unhappy mother.

When his mother first took over the café, she had done all the baking and cooking herself, as well as much of the waitressing, hiring women from town as needed to take orders and serve food during the busy parts of the day, but eventually the baking became too much for her and she hired Bernice. Sometimes Bernice also handled the grill while his mother ran between kitchen and dining room, though Bernice refused to enter the latter, would not even carry out a plate of eggs that was growing cold. Customers loved her baked goods, especially her hamburger buns, which surprised everyone with their sweetness. "That Bernice has the best buns in town," the men said as they ate their hamburgers. They never got tired of this joke, which had to do with the fact that Bernice was a large woman—359 pounds she informed Aaron matter-of-factly one morning, information he did not know how to respond to, beyond arranging his face so that it did not suggest any of the things that he imagined she was expecting, horror and shock and repulsion. She had particularly large buttocks, which Lew Olsson described as "two pigs in a gunnysack fighting to get out." Aaron did not care for vulgarity or meanness, both of which the joke hinged on. The men, sensing his discomfort, did what men sometimes do. They added to it, making a point to refer to Bernice as his girlfriend. It was true that they were friends and that this struck people as odd because Bernice was a good bit older than he, twenty to his thirteen when she began working at the café, which meant it was an "unlikely friendship," but unlikely friendships, he had since learned, were often the easiest to cultivate.

Each morning at four, Bernice made her way up the alley that ran from her house to the back door of the café, where she let herself in and immediately turned on the small coffeemaker that Aaron readied for her each evening as he and his mother closed up. His bedroom was directly over the kitchen, and in his closet was a vent that brought the smells directly into his room, a sort of olfactory alarm clock: first the odor of coffee wafted in, and then, like a snooze alarm, that of eggs and bacon (Bernice's standard breakfast), all of it waking him in the most pleasant of ways. He dressed and tiptoed to the bathroom to brush his teeth and wash his face, by which point Bernice was ready for him. "I'm fit, just barely, for company," she would say when he appeared, because that was the way Bernice talked. Early on, she told him that she was a misanthrope, which had pleased him, the admission as well as the word itself, which he found beautiful.

"Homebody," she announced another morning as she pounded away at a lump of bread dough. "What do you picture?" This was a game they sometimes played. He saw the word as the claustrophobic juxtaposition of two nouns—*home* and *body*—that had been pushed up against each other. He told her this, and she nodded indignantly, encouraged by his assessment, but said nothing more.

Most mornings, he measured out the ingredients—baking soda and sugar, cup after cup of sifted flour, salt—lining them up in bowls so that all Bernice had to do was follow the trail down the counter, adding and mixing as she went. This system allowed her to concentrate on the conversation, which revolved around words, the possibilities that they presented as well as their inadequacy. They were kindred spirits, Bernice said, two people more comfortable with words than people, though Aaron came to see the irony in this: words existed because of people, because of a deep human need to communicate with others, not as an end in themselves.

Bernice had gone away to college, planning never to return, but something had happened there, something that caused her to pack up halfway through her first quarter and return home. She said that this made people in town look at her a certain way—like she had thought she was better than they were but had learned she was not. This was all Aaron knew of the story for the first two years of their friendship. Then, one morning as they stood making pies, she told him that after she dropped out of college, she had not left her bedroom for six months, except to fetch food in the middle of the night and to use the bathroom. Over time, he would learn that this was the only way that Bernice discussed her life, parceling out details at unexpected times.

"For the first three weeks," she added, "I ate only meat."

"Why?" he asked.

"Meat makes me constipated."

"And you wanted to be constipated?" he asked, trying to sound casual. He had not gotten over his childhood discomfort at discussing bodily functions.

"Yes," she said. "Yes, I did." She sounded angry, as though his question was obviously foolish.

"What did you do in your room all day?"

"I read, mainly my textbooks because I wanted to keep up with my classes. I practiced my Spanish verb conjugations. We'd only gotten as far as the present tense when I left, but I didn't mind. I liked being cut off from the past and the future. Some mornings I heard my mother outside my door, listening. Once, I heard her telling Dad that I'd joined a cult, that I was in there speaking in tongues." Bernice laughed. "It scared her, I think, not to know what I was saying, but I wanted her to be scared."

"Why?" Aaron asked.

"Because every night after I came home, I heard her on the phone telling her friends that it was true, I was back for good. 'Bernice is just a real homebody,' she'd say. So you see, I wanted her to be confused and scared, to realize that she would never know why I'd returned. I wanted her to understand that she didn't know me at all. Does that make any sense?"

Aaron opened a can of cherries and poured it into one of the crusts that she had lined up for him. "Yes," he said. "It makes sense."

"I hate her," Bernice said. She made it sound simple.

Mornings at the café went like this: his mother came downstairs at seven twenty, and just ten minutes later, after a quick check to make sure that everything was in order—tables set, shakers filled, coffee brewing—they unlocked the front door and turned the sign to OPEN, and the dining room became instantly busy. Aaron assisted his mother, filling coffee cups and taking orders, until eight twenty, when he gathered his books and ran out the back door and down the same alley that Bernice crept up at four. Sometimes, as he passed the back of her house, a tiny place squatting between two much larger houses, he saw her mother through the kitchen window, standing at the sink in her robe. It felt strange to see her there, knowing what he knew: that her daughter hated her.

The day he found his mother gone, as he and Bernice sat in the kitchen waiting for her to come down because they did not yet know she was gone, he recited the Canadian provinces for a map test he was taking that day. Bernice had made him spell Saskatchewan for good measure.

"Do you think she overslept?" Aaron asked. It was only seven twenty-five, but his mother had not come down late since the day they opened ten years earlier. It was just the two of them that first day, and he had risen early, too excited to sleep, and sat in a booth waiting for her. He knew when it was time to open because the farmers had gathered on the steps outside, including Mr. Rehnquist, who finally tapped on the window and beckoned to him. When Aaron unlocked the door, Mr. Rehnquist said, "I'm sure it's first-day jitters. Go on up and give her a boost."

And he had. He had gone up to his mother's room, where he found her sitting on the edge of her bed, dressed. "Do you have a headache?" he asked.

"I don't think I can do it," she said.

He sat down beside her and said that she could do it, that he would help her do it. They would go down together and open the door, and once they did that, everything would be fine. He told her this even though he was not sure it was true.

"What would I do without you?" she said. She stood and smoothed the bed covers because she believed in the small comfort of entering a tidy bed each night, and together they went downstairs and opened the café.

"Better go up and check on her," Bernice said, but he could no longer imagine doing what he had done just ten years earlier: entering his mother's room, sitting on her bed, speaking to her encouragingly. Once a week he set a basket of clean clothes, folded, outside her closed door. Other than that, he did not go near her room, nor she his.

By seven thirty, he had no choice. He dragged himself upstairs and down the hallway to his mother's room, where he found the door open, bed made, his mother gone. He looked out her window, to the alley where she parked the aging Oldsmobile. It was not there either. When he reported this to Bernice, she said that come to think of it, the Oldsmobile had not been there when she arrived at four. She asked whether his mother had seemed strange the night before. He said no, that his mother and Pastor Gronseth had sat in a booth talking as they often did, that after he finished memorizing the Canadian provinces, he had stacked his books on the edge of the table and stopped beside their booth to say good night. There had been nothing strange.

Bernice appeared skeptical but did not waste time arguing because the crowd of customers outside was growing. Instead, she made a sign that read, CLOSED INDEFINITELY. FAMILY EMERGENCY, which he wanted to amend to CLOSED FOR PERSONAL REASONS because he thought the word *emergency* implied that someone was dead, but Bernice said that nothing made people gossip more than the word *personal*. In the end, it would not have mattered what they wrote: news spread and people came, making a show of pulling at the locked café door and reading the sign aloud, of peering through the window. "It's closed," someone else would say, someone who had engaged in this same series of actions just minutes earlier. Then, they all milled around together, shaking their heads and comparing information.

The news exploded into full scandal just before noon, when it was learned that Pastor Gronseth was gone also. Aaron and Bernice had sequestered themselves in the kitchen, and even after Bernice's mother phoned with this second wave of news, they continued to bake the bread and rolls and buns that had been rising since morning. As they worked, they talked about keeping the café going, though they both knew that this was impossible: Bernice was a kitchen recluse and Aaron was about to begin his final year of school. In the end the Trout Café would stay closed, the title reverting to the bank, but that day they had appreciated the distraction that pretending provided.

Around five, they decided to sneak out the back door and walk up the alley to the Hagedorns' house. While Bernice stayed in the kitchen wrapping up baked goods, Aaron went up to his room to pack a bag and to confront the new reality of his life: overnight, he had become jobless, homeless, and motherless. He found himself in his mother's room, looking for clues but mainly for something that would catapult him forward, toward anger or clarity or grief. As he opened her dresser drawers, he saw that she had taken every bit of clothing she owned, shorts and sleeveless blouses as well as wool pants and sweaters, the broadness of her needs suggesting that she had not known where she was going, only that she would not return. In the bottom drawer was the family photo album. He picked it up, imagining her shifting it out of the way in order to access all the entirely replaceable items she had chosen to take. He dropped it back in the drawer and kicked the drawer shut, hard.

The following week, when Mr. Rehnquist helped him move, he found the album there in the drawer where Aaron was determined to leave it. "It's a sacrifice," he told Aaron. "She's depriving herself of these memories in order to give them to you." Though it would be years before he allowed himself to accept the possible truth of this or feel anything but rage at the sight of the album, he let Mr. Rehnquist pack it.

That first night, as he lay on the makeshift bed that Mrs. Hagedorn had made for him atop one of their couches, Aaron flipped through his textbooks, stopping on the map of Canada. It seemed so long ago that he had stood with Bernice in the kitchen of the café, spelling Saskatchewan and waiting for his mother to come down. The note was tucked into his chemistry book. His mother had put it there, believing that he would find her gone, pick up his books, and go off to school. She thought she knew him, and he was angry all over again. *You're old enough now,* the note said, only that. He lay awake in the Hagedorns' living room, wondering what he was old enough for and how long she had been waiting for him to get there.

15

The Hagedorns were large people who occupied the smallest house in town, a dollhouse that the three of them had been forced to move into when Bernice was a teenager, after their old place burned to the ground, the three of them awakening just in time to escape. Bernice and her parents ended up in the only house they could afford, where, she told Aaron, they were like three cabbages rolling around inside a produce drawer. By the time Aaron came to stay, they had occupied the house nearly a decade. It had grown even smaller with their belongings, yet they made room for him. Their living room contained three couches, and most nights he and Bernice lay on them, reading or talking. She never mentioned his mother, never asked whether he missed her. He knew that this was partly his fault because in those first weeks after she disappeared, he had pretended not to care; at the time, with his teachers looking sorry for him and his classmates ignoring him for a change (a gesture of kindness he supposed), it had seemed the only way to make it through the day.

Instead, over the course of the year, Bernice told him the story of her life, in installments, each one perfectly composed so that he wondered whether she wrote it out and practiced telling it beforehand. On those nights when her voice slipped into confessional mode, he rolled onto his side so that he could watch her as she spoke, the mountain of her stomach dwarfing the twin hills of her breasts. Her story, which she referred to as "the story of my expanding girth," began like this: "For the most part, it has been a steady climb, one without shortcuts or the occasional dips and plateaus. As a baby, I watched from a high chair in the corner of the kitchen as my mother chopped and pounded, rolled and sprinkled. When I cried, she paused long enough to pop a bit of something—cookie dough, fried potatoes, a fingerful of Cheez Whiz— into my mouth so that by the time I was two, I had become a corpulent child who could not yet walk but demanded treats incessantly. My entreaties, according to my father, were frighteningly eloquent, marked by the syntax and diction of a child twice my age. 'You were a little queen holding court,' he likes to say, which has always bothered me, not the image itself but the clarity with which he recalls it, for in my memory of those early years, my father does not exist. There is only the kitchen—the oven, its door opening like a warm mouth, the potholders hanging beside it—and my mother, who exists as a fat finger smelling of nicotine that delivers these 'shut-up' treats into my mouth.

"By third grade, I had outgrown all the desks that the school had to offer, so one was created for me, a space-consuming contraption made of an old door that the janitors balanced across the tops of two tin barrels, each of which was big enough to have fit any of my classmates inside. I remember the wonderful racket the barrels made as they were rolled down the hallway to our classroom. The desk, which was larger than the teacher's even, accorded me an authority that I had not experienced before. When, after a few days, the atmosphere threatened to return to normal, I began tapping my pencil steadily against the barrels, keeping this up for minutes at a time. I pretended to be deep in thought, unaware of my actions, though I simply wanted to see whether anyone would tell me to stop. Nobody did, not even the teacher.

"From there, I discovered that if I stayed at my desk feigning busyness when the others got up to go outside for recess, my absence went unchallenged. I particularly hated recess since I've always felt most keenly aware of my size outdoors. I despised, as well, the games we played, each of which afforded my classmates another forum to ridicule me. During kickball, they cheered mockingly when I ran the bases, and during Farmer in the Dell, whether I was chosen as the cheese or the cow, there was always the opportunity for a joke. But dodge ball was the worst. My peers all seemed to have unusually good aim, though I helped them along by providing an ample target. It reached the point where even my own teammates could not resist taking aim at me. The first time this happened, I was caught off guard, and the ball hit me squarely between the shoulders and jolted me forward onto my knees. Both sides laughed merrily."

Bernice laughed also as she described this. Aaron watched her stomach quiver gently. He did not laugh.

"I went home sore and bruised on dodge ball days, and at night I would lie in bed and press hard on the bruises to intensify the pain."

"Why?" Aaron asked.

"I thought that if I could increase my tolerance for pain, I would eventually inure myself to it altogether."

"And did you?"

This question she seemed to consider only briefly before declaring that the desk had been her "salvation," saving her from physical activity, which tired her, as well as the humiliation of being a spectacle, which tired her even more. "Most days," she said, "I was content to stay at my desk reading, enjoying my solitude in the empty room, but occasionally I would go over to the desk of a classmate who had been particularly cruel to me that day, open it, and handle the items inside. Later, as I watched him prop his desktop open with his head and rummage around inside, a pencil gripped between his teeth, I liked to imagine myself sauntering over and informing him of what I had done, liked to imagine his repulsion. I never did. It was enough to sit at my desk and watch him sliding his hands back and forth, back and forth, across all of the places that mine had been."

Bernice had told him the story of the desk in October, five weeks after he moved in. The next installment did not come until Christmas Eve. They were alone in the house, despite the late hour, for her father had taken a bottle of spiced rum and retreated to his fish house and her mother was at church, the midnight Mass, which actually started at eleven. It was a particularly cold Christmas—cold even by Minnesota standards, which were far beyond the standards that people elsewhere applied when assessing the cold—but the cold did not keep people home. Indeed, Aaron had noted over the years that morning coffee hour at the café was often busiest the day after a blizzard, as though people needed to make clear that the weather did not dictate their actions. After Mrs. Hagedorn left, Aaron and Bernice lay on their sofas listening to cars crunch by and to families discussing Christmas light displays as they walked past the house on their way to church. They competed to see who could identify the voices first, a contest that Bernice won, despite Aaron's years of having waited on these people at the café.

Bernice sampled a roll of *lefse* from the stack she had buttered and sugared for the two of them. The *lefse* had been dropped off earlier by Agnes Olsson as partial payment on a plumbing bill. "Agnes's potatoes weren't dry enough," Bernice observed, "but I guess it's a fair trade since my father's not the best plumber in town." It was true that Rudy was not the best plumber, though he was cheap and did not mind getting dirty.

Bernice's voice turned confessional then, as it had when she told him the story of the desk. "In the fall of 1976, I enrolled at Moorhead State University," she began, moving from elementary school straight to college, as if the years in between had been too uneventful to mention. Aaron rolled onto his side to listen. "My graduation marked a crossroads: I had come down a path of uninterrupted disappointment, also known as my youth, to find myself in a clearing, a flitting moment in which I allowed myself to feel hopeful, to feel that life just might jag crazily off in a new direction. In short, my life became like a Robert Frost poem."

Bernice disliked Frost. She had told Aaron so repeatedly over the years, but that night she told him again, noting that her aversion had been heightened by the fact that her teachers all seemed to find his poetry compelling and insightful and not at all trite, despite its overt symbolism, decipherable even by a group of uninterested fifth graders, for fifth grade was the year they had been introduced to poetry, a poem a month chosen by their teacher. " 'Stopping by Woods on a Snowy Evening' was our November poem," Bernice continued, though this too she had told him before. "We had one month in which to recite it from memory in front of the class, without errors or excessive prompting. Three more Frost poems were similarly imprinted in my brain over the next seven years. So it was that, at eighteen, I stood in the clearing, contemplating a road not taken, and there was nothing I could do about it. It was the only language I had to describe this unfamiliar feeling known as optimism." She paused to take a bite of *lefse*.

"The 'clearing' appeared courtesy of the newly hired guidance counselor. Matthew Brisk was his name. He was the first person who seemed not to notice my size. He didn't smirk when I turned sideways to fit through the doorway of his office, didn't hold his breath when I lowered myself onto the flimsy folding chair across from his desk. Instead, he talked to me about something called My Future. He spoke with full-on exclamation points. 'Your grades are stupendous! What a transcript! You have so many options with grades like this!' With the same enthusiasm, he asked, 'How about clubs? Are you much of a joiner?'

"Well, the merging and mingling and coming together of people had never interested me, though I could not say so to Matthew Brisk. You see, from that very first meeting, I felt a shameful need to mold myself to his vision of me, so I said I had belonged to FHA, which was true. I had joined my sophomore year at the coaxing of the club advisor, a dull woman with firm orders to breathe life into the organization. I did not tell Matthew Brisk that after I joined, someone crossed out the word 'Homemakers' on the sign above the meeting room, changing it to read 'Future Hogs of America,' or that I quit just three weeks later after my fellow 'homemakers' filled my chocolate cake with grape bubblegum as it baked in the oven during our meeting.

"I filled out the applications that Matthew Brisk gave me and took the SAT exam, which I enjoyed because it was rife with archaic vocabulary words and obscure second meanings, words like *husband,* which I certainly had no interest in as a noun, despite my brief membership in FHA, but found rather attractive as a verb. When I began receiving acceptance letters, I took them to Matthew Brisk, who slapped me on the back and said, 'Nice work!' I chose Moorhead State and informed them I would be attending in the fall. Only later did it occur to me that I had been fooled, that Matthew Brisk, with his exclamation points, had no insight into my future at all."

Bernice paused to eat two more rolls of *lefse*. When she resumed the story, she leaped ahead to the point five weeks into her first quarter, when she hitched a ride back to Mortonville with Karl Nelson, a college sophomore who returned home every weekend. "He had spent his high school years working to attain even a modicum of popularity and was not willing to begin all over again," Bernice explained. "He retained a girlfriend here, a semipopular girl who was a senior, and together they attended sporting events, at which Karl received more attention as a college man than he ever had during high school."

"Did Karl Nelson tell you this?" Aaron asked. Karl Nelson owned an accounting business that catered to farmers, with whom he had often held meetings at the café, so, of course, Aaron knew him, but not in the way that Bernice described him, with the emotional depth and motivations of a character in a book. He knew him simply as a man who talked to farmers about *depreciation* and *yield* and never consumed more than two cups of coffee at a sitting because coffee made him "jumpy."

"Of course not," Bernice said. "He drove with his transistor radio pressed against his ear the whole time. The only time we spoke was when we stopped in Fergus Falls for gas. While it was pumping, he leaned in and said, 'Ten bucks,' which was the amount I had offered when I called him the night before, an amount I knew would ensure a ride. I spread two fives on his car seat, which was unpleasantly warm from his buttocks, though I'm certain neither of us wanted the greater unpleasantness of touching hands as we exchanged money. I had contacted him because I knew of his weekly trips home from my mother, who brought them up each time she called. Until the day I came back for good, I had not made a single visit home. I told no one that I was coming, not even my parents, but when they saw me hoisting my belongings out of his trunk, they deduced that I was home to stay, that I had attempted the road less traveled and failed." She stopped speaking, as though she had reached the end of a recitation.

"And then you stayed in your room studying Spanish?" Aaron asked, referring to the conversation they had had several years earlier.

"Yes," Bernice said. He could tell that she was pleased he remembered. "In high school we were obligated to study German, which never appealed to me, but I took to Spanish immediately, in part because I liked the professor, Dr. Baratto. He was Italian, he told us the first day of class, and in Italian his name meant 'barter,' but in Spanish it meant 'cheap.' 'When I go to Mexico,' he said, 'everyone thinks, *Here comes that stingy guy.*' The whole class laughed. I thought, then, about the way people had always overstressed the first syllable of my name, *HOG-a-dorn*, and about how I'd never met an Italian before and now I was learning Spanish from one. From that very first day, I knew that college was the thing for me."

Bernice yawned, letting him know that the story was over. Perhaps she had simply looked at her watch and seen that her mother would be home soon—indeed, she walked through the door humming "Silent Night" five minutes later—but Aaron was sure that Bernice had chosen that specific spot to stop, as if she had gone away to this magical place called college and never returned.

16

Aaron would later wonder whether Bernice had sensed something about him that he had not yet allowed himself to see, namely that his reasons for not desiring her body had nothing to do with her body itself. He did know that she did not want him to leave Mortonville, but he suspected that this had nothing to do with love or sexual desire.

On the night of his eighteenth birthday, she told him the end of the story, presenting it like a gift. First, though, Mrs. Hagedorn had cooked him a special dinner, lamb chops, his favorite. After supper, she brought out a cake with eighteen candles, and all three of them sang. They gave him gifts: a tie from Mrs. Hagedorn because he would need one for graduation; from Bernice, a book called *Jude the Obscure* that she had read in college and enjoyed and that he read but found not at all enjoyable because in it three children hanged themselves to lessen the burden on their parents; and a fishing pole that Rudy had made by sinking two large nails at either end of a piece of wood and wrapping a line back and forth around them.

The last birthday that Aaron had celebrated was his tenth because his mother had come to believe that celebrations should be reserved for actual accomplishments, and she said there was no achievement in being born. Each time she said this, he tried hard not to think about the party that she had made for him when he turned five, how she had blown up a whole bag of balloons while he was napping and he had found her lying on the floor of the living room, light-headed from the endeavor. He'd lain down beside her, and she told him that he'd been born during a snowstorm. His father had driven her to the hospital in the squad car, the lights flashing. "You were nearly born right there in the backseat. Your father was a nervous wreck," she said. "I'll never forget it, driving through all that whiteness, and then, at the end of it all, there you were." When his mother, the one she became after the parade, said that there was no accomplishment in being born, he went up to his room and cried because he knew she had forgotten about the snowstorm.

Aaron ate three pieces of cake and tried to look pleased instead of uncomfortable with the attention. Afterward, Mrs. Hagedorn went to her bedroom to talk on the telephone and watch television and Rudy went across town to the liquor store. Aaron sat at the kitchen table, where he studied most nights because the light was best there. He had a math test the next day. Soon, Bernice appeared. "I'll tell you the story of why I left school," she said, "but you must not ask any questions, not while I'm talking, not after I've finished. In fact, we must never speak of it. Those are my conditions."

He was on the cusp of a B+ in his math class, had worked hard to get there, but he could not tell Bernice that a test was more important than her story. He thought that maybe she was testing him also. He stood up and followed her into the living room.

"You understand the rules?" she asked.

"I understand."

"And you want to hear the story?" She needed him to say it.

"I really want to hear it," he said. This was true. He lay down on his side, as usual, so that he could watch her as she spoke.

"Don't look at me while I'm talking," she said. "I need you to listen."

He did not argue with her. He just rolled onto his back and stared at the spackled white ceiling. "I'm listening," he said, and she began to talk.

"My roommate's name was Gladys Moore. I was sent her address by the housing department, a standard practice allowing future roommates to exchange information about themselves. While I was still considering whether to make contact, Gladys Moore wrote to me.

The letter was on onionskin paper, though she'd clearly composed it with a piece of lined notebook paper beneath. Her handwriting replicated perfectly the cursive we'd been taught in the second grade, right down to the odd capital *G*s and *F*s and *S*s that nobody ever uses, and I thought then that Gladys Moore and I would get along just fine. The gist of the letter was that she would be bringing a toaster, which I would be welcome to use. It would be a two-slicer. I remember thinking the tone apologetic. She added that if I felt uncomfortable sharing a toaster with a stranger, she would use the left slot, I the right. She would not mind this at all. She signed the letter *God Bless You,* followed by *Sincerely* and *Your Roommate,* and finally her full name. I wrote back two days later, having debated whether to mention my size, which I decided against. I said only that a toaster would be useful and that I would bring an iron, which we would consider the room iron. I signed it *Sincerely, Bernice.*

"The next month, my mother drove me to school. She was slow about everything that day—getting into the car to leave, driving, choosing a parking spot—so by the time we checked into my dorm, it was nine o'clock. As we walked down the hallway, we passed open doors revealing rooms that already looked lived in, beds made, posters on the walls, girls lounging in sets of four and five. I knocked on my door as a courtesy, but when there was no response, I went in. It was clear that Gladys Moore had not yet arrived. My mother was suddenly in a hurry to leave, nervous to be driving home so late, which I felt obligated to point out was entirely her fault. We argued briefly, and she left.

"I chose the bed nearest the door, away from the window, believing the window bed to be more desirable. It was a gesture. I had not brought much—a large suitcase of clothes, my typewriter, two boxes containing sheets and towels, toiletries, a dictionary, the aforementioned iron, and snacks. It was eleven when I finished unpacking. Gladys Moore still had not arrived, and the front desk was closed by then, which meant she would not be coming that night, so I shut off the light and went to bed.

"I awoke to find the room lit by the dim glow from the hallway light, three people standing over me, mother, father, daughter, all of them tall and very thin, like a family of flag poles. I sat up, and they jumped, as one, backward. 'Heavens,' said Gladys Moore's mother, and Gladys Moore, who was holding a toaster, *the* toaster, said, 'I'm Gladys Moore,' and her father said, 'Oh, you're up. We were trying not to disturb you,' and he turned on the overhead light. I glanced at my watch. It was one o'clock.

"I thought it improper to get out of bed wearing just a nightgown, more improper than not helping, so I lay under my covers while they carried Gladys's things in and her mother made up her bed. 'I left you the window,' I pointed out, and Gladys said, 'That's fine,' like she was reassuring me. When they were finished, her father said, 'I guess I wouldn't mind a slice of toast before we get on the road, Mother,' and Gladys's mother, who had obviously done the packing, located the bread and margarine and a butter knife. She made us each a slice, bringing mine to me in bed, and we ate our toast without speaking, me propped up in my tiny new bed, the three of them standing and chewing.

"'Okay, then, you've got everything?' asked her father, and Gladys said she did, and her parents went over and stood in the doorway to say good-bye, no hugging, just three people with their hands raised like they were taking an oath.

"'Sorry we woke you,' said Gladys after they'd gone. She turned away from me to remove her shirt and bra and pull on her nightshirt, and then she turned back and said, 'We actually got here at six, but I felt a little nervous, so my mother got the key, and we went out to supper. We've been sitting in the car praying.'

"I would learn that Gladys Moore was like this, apologetic in a way that made her overly disclosing. I said that I'd arrived late also. I mentioned again that I'd left her the bed by the window, and this time she said, 'Don't worry about it,' like she realized that reassuring me was not enough and forgiveness was in order. She shut off the light and made her way back to the bed by the window. I heard her knees tap the ground as she knelt, the rushed murmur of praying, the whisper of my name. She got into bed and fell asleep, but I lay awake for hours, feeling alone and lonely and frightened."

Bernice paused. Aaron wanted to ask whether she had felt the usual loneliness that comes with new surroundings, or whether it had been something more, something related to the intimacy of sharing a small space with a stranger and hearing that stranger pray for her in the dark. Later, it occurred to him that she had paused precisely at that moment so that he could ask, for when it came down to it, that was what people needed, almost more than sex or love—the reassurance that others wanted to understand them and their fears. He understood this as an adult, but only because of Walter, who had set out to learn everything about him. What a heady feeling that had been, Walter quizzing him on every detail of his life and Aaron answering, flattered and too inexperienced to know how to reciprocate. Eventually—it had taken years—Walter's questions had stopped seeming flattering and started to seem like one more form of control, especially as Walter continued to offer little in return. Their conversations began to resemble a board game, the details of their lives like play money, both of them trying to get around the board without having his dollars end up in the other's stack.

But that night in the Hagedorns' living room, he had still been a boy who believed that what people *said* they wanted from you and what they wanted were the same thing, so he had lain on the sofa listening to Mrs. Hagedorn snore in her bedroom, her television on, while he waited for Bernice to continue. And at last, she had.

"Gladys Moore and I developed a routine. I got up early and left for my first class, and when I came back at ten, she would be running out the door and I would have two hours alone in the room. I'd unhook my bra and flop on the bed to read. Once, I clipped my toenails. Usually, I made toast, two slices with margarine because I did not like the dining hall in the morning. A few weeks passed, during which Gladys Moore and I did not become close, not the way that other roommates appeared to. I preferred this. She spent her time either doing homework or holding Bible study with several other girls. They met in the lounge so that everyone could see them poring over their Bibles because they liked the attention, though Gladys was different. I once asked her what they did at these meetings, my motive purely conversational, and she said,

'Oh, Bernice, you should join us. We're discussing scripture.' She didn't seem to get that people sometimes asked questions simply to grease the wheels of social discourse.

"Occasionally, after we turned off the lights at night, we talked for a few minutes in the dark about our families and the towns we had come from and what we hoped to do with our lives. Gladys Moore came from a town just across the North Dakota border, the kind of place that most of us were from, a small farming community. Her parents raised pigs, and she said that what she liked most about going to college was leaving the smell of the pig farm behind. She had very specific goals. She wanted to marry a pastor and live in a town like the one she had come from, where she planned to teach third grade. I'd never cared for children, nor had I considered that I might one day marry, but that was fine because I did not want us to have too much in common. It made living together in such close quarters easier, I thought. Still, there was something comforting about lying in bed, one of us talking while the other listened until she fell asleep.

"One morning when Gladys Moore came back from class, I was listening to the radio, and she demanded that I shut it off. I did. She said that she had been listening to the radio once, rock music, which was forbidden in their house, and the DJ began speaking directly to her, in words that only she could understand. 'I knew it was Satan,' she told me in a whisper. 'It was just what my parents had warned me about, all of these tricks he would use to get to me.'

"I asked her what everyone else listening to the DJ at that moment had thought they were hearing, but Gladys said of course they had not heard what she did. They heard him still speaking in his normal voice because that was how Satan worked. I said that maybe it was her imagination punishing her for disobeying her parents. 'Our psyches work that way,' I added. I was taking an introductory psychology course.

"At hearing me interpret what had happened not as a battle for her soul but as a matter of simple human psychology, Gladys Moore looked terrified. I saw it in her eyes before she turned away, gathered her books, and left the room. The next day as I passed through the lounge during their Bible study session, Gladys whispered something to the others, and they all turned to look at me and then joined hands and began to pray. After that, the others made a point of pressing up against the wall when we passed in the hallway or moving to another sink if I stepped up beside them to brush my teeth. Only Gladys did not. She remained polite and apologetic, but something had changed. I came back from class one morning a few days later, assuming she'd already gone, but as I stood there fiddling with my bra, I realized that she was still in bed with the covers pulled over her like a tent. It was the same the next morning and the next. She stopped going to classes and then to the dining hall, and just like that, this became our new routine. She survived on the care packages that her parents sent each week, filled with her favorite foods: a fresh loaf of bread and currant jam, nacho chips and salsa, beef jerky, all of which she now consumed inside her tent.

"Her parents began calling more often, but she instructed me to tell them that she was at class, and I did, even though she was right there listening to us talk, listening to me answer questions about whether she seemed to be getting enough sleep and was enjoying her classes, whether she read her Bible and went to church on Sundays, whether anything seemed *funny*. I always gave the answers that I supposed they wanted to hear, which were also the answers that I supposed Gladys wanted given, and sometimes, Gladys would chuckle, as if maybe something did seem funny to her.

"'Your parents want you to call,' I would say when I hung up.

"'Roger,' she would say from under her covers.

"One morning as I made myself toast, Gladys peeked out. 'You're using my side,' she said. I asked what she meant and she said in a panicky voice, 'My side. Your side. We have sides.' I apologized and said I hadn't realized we had sides, and she said, 'Don't you remember the letter I sent?' I said I remembered the letter, of course, but that I had thought she was just being polite, establishing what kind of a roommate she would be. 'So when you make two slices of toast, you do it one slice at a time?' I asked, not arguing but clarifying. By then she was completely out of her bed.

"Yes, she said, yes, of course she did, and I said, 'Even when I'm not here?'

" 'Yes,' said Gladys Moore. 'It's still your side.'

" 'Is it because you think God's watching?' I said.

" 'God *is* watching,' she said, so I said, 'I don't mind if you use my side.'

" 'We have our sides,' she said. 'And he's watching you also.' She picked up the bread knife and held the blade against my forearm. 'Remember that.'

"She got back into her tent, and I went to the library, where I couldn't stop thinking about how she'd pressed the blade into my skin. I stayed there until it closed, so it was late when I got back to the room, almost eleven. Gladys Moore had turned on my desk lamp, which I thought she maybe intended as an apology. I undressed quietly and got into bed, but once the light was off, she whispered, 'Be careful.'

" 'Careful of what?' I whispered back.

" 'Of me,' she said. 'The devil is trying to make me do things.' I could hear that she was crying, but the next day she seemed fine, not just fine, better. She was gone when I came back from my first class, and that night she sat at her desk, typing. I assumed she was writing a paper for a class, so even though the clatter of the keys made it difficult to sleep, I said nothing because I was relieved to have her out of bed and back to being a student.

"I woke up to the smell of smoke. Gladys was crouched over the wastebasket, tending a fire inside. I jumped out of bed and tossed a glass of water on it, but it was still smoldering, so I picked the wastebasket up and hurried down the hall to the bathroom, holding it out in front of me. I set it inside a shower and let the water spray on it. The remnants of the paper she'd been typing were inside, charred and soggy, and I emptied everything into the garbage bin in the bathroom and covered it with wet paper towels.

" 'What were you doing?' I said when I returned. 'Are you crazy?'

"She was back in bed, inside her tent, and when she didn't answer, I went over and pulled back the covers. A smell rose up, the sour stink of unwashed bed linens. She looked up at me. There were dark circles beneath her eyes, as though she hadn't slept in days, and her hair had been singed. 'It wasn't me,' she whispered. I could see that she believed it, believed that she'd had no more to do with the fire than I had. I took the blanket from my bed and went to the study room, where I slept on the floor, poorly. In the morning when I returned to our room, Gladys was curled up asleep with the toaster in her arms like a baby. I tiptoed around, foolishly imagining that all she needed was a good sleep, but when I opened my drawer to take out a pair of underwear, I saw that the crotch—indeed, the crotch of every pair—was smeared with currant jam.

"After class I went to the housing office to fill out paperwork for a room transfer. I had to state my reasons, so I wrote down something about differences in religion and schedules because I didn't want to tell them about the tent or the toaster or the fire or, most of all, the jam in my underwear. When I arrived back at our room, Gladys's four Bible study friends were in the doorway, holding hands and praying. Inside, Gladys stood in front of the mirror, clutching a pair of scissors, which she'd used to chop her hair down to the scalp. I went in and took the scissors away from her, swept up the hair. 'Time for you to leave,' I told the girls, who were watching but doing nothing to help their friend.

"'She asked us to come,' said Beth, who was quieter than the other three and had, for this reason, struck me as more reasonable. 'She needs our help.'

"'How're you going to help her when you're too afraid to even come in the room?' I said.

"'We don't need to come in to pray,' said Beth, and I saw then that I had been wrong about her, that she was quiet because she was in charge. 'We're going to do an exorcism. We were just waiting for you.'

"I knew vaguely what an exorcism was, though not the specifics of what it entailed. 'I don't think I'd be much help,' I said.

"'Gladys said to wait for you,' Beth said. The four of them looked at one another but not at me or at Gladys, who sat on her bed, shorn, flipping through her Bible and acting as though we had nothing to do with her.

"'She said we needed you because there was no other way to know when the devil was out of her,' said one of the other girls finally.

"From her bed near the window, Gladys began reading from her Bible: 'So the devils sought him, saying, If you cast us out, suffer us to go away into the herd of swine.'

"'We're praying for the devil to leave her,' said Beth.

"'And how will you know when such a thing has occurred?' I asked.

"'When pigs jump,' explained Gladys calmly, 'it's because they're trying to snatch the devil out of the air.'

"'So we're praying for pigs to jump,' Beth added.

"'Well, I've got a test tomorrow,' I said, 'so I'll just leave you to it.'

"I picked up my book bag, but as I walked down the hallway, away from Gladys Moore, who believed the devil was inside her, I heard her call out, 'Is she jumping?' and I felt something inside me move. I leaped upward, nipping the air, and from our room, I heard Gladys Moore say, with clear relief, 'He's gone.'"

Until he came to live with the Hagedorns, Aaron knew Rudy only through the stories narrated by the men at the café, where Rudy Hagedorn had been a frequent topic of discussion and amusement. He knew that Rudy spent his winters on the lake, drinking himself into a stupor inside his fish house. When Mrs. Hagedorn had not seen him in a few days, she phoned the café and a party of men was sent out to check on him. Once, he had been found asleep beside a Monopoly board, only one game piece, the shoe, wending its way around the track. Another time, he was passed out over his fishing hole, naked but for a pair of wool socks. After they had determined that he was still breathing, alive and eligible for teasing, the men wanted nothing more than to get back to the café, where they could have a cup of hot coffee and deadpan that they had found Rudy with his head stuck in his own hole—his *fishing* hole, they would clarify, timing it for humorous effect. With this to look forward to, they hurried him back into his clothes and pulled up his line, only to discover a walleye on the hook, spent from hours of trying to free itself. It was bigger than anything any of them had pulled out of the lake that winter, they said in telling the story later, their voices somber as they recalled how they had all stared at the fish, shaking their heads.

When Aaron first moved in, he rarely saw Rudy, who often did not come home after work, the first part of his day bleeding into the second, particularly when his final plumbing call involved a relieved homeowner expressing gratitude with a bottle. Other times, he came home briefly to put something in his stomach before going back out. While he sat in his recliner eating, a bottle of beer poking up from between his legs, he engaged Aaron in conversation, choosing unexpected topics, though Aaron was quick to hide his surprise. One night, for example, as Aaron sat reading *My Ántonia,* Rudy said that he preferred *Song of the Lark,* which Aaron had not read, though he was making his way through all of Cather's work.

"I'll read it next," Aaron said. "Did you read *Death Comes for the Archbishop?*"

Rudy sighed. "I tried, but I didn't care for it much."

"Me neither," said Aaron, the first time he had admitted this to anyone because his teacher had told him that many people considered it Cather's masterpiece.

He had never seen Rudy with a book, but that spring when Rudy started taking him fishing, Aaron discovered that he carried one in his glove compartment and another in his tackle box, that he sat each night in his gently rocking boat reading until the light was nearly gone and just enough remained for him to steer to shore by. Rudy taught him how to drive his truck and manage the boat and determine how much line to let down. Aaron looked forward to these evenings, and though Rudy did not talk a lot, he thought that maybe Rudy liked having him around too.

One night, as they sat in the boat staring down at where their lines disappeared into the water, Rudy said, "It was the goddamn desks, you know. They always came around her too snug." They had not been talking about Bernice before this. They had not been talking at all. Aaron pulled up their lines and turned the boat around, rowing the whole way back instead of using the motor while Rudy sat quietly in the bow. Rudy stored his boat at Last Resort in exchange for handling their plumbing needs, but when they pulled to shore that night he was not sober enough to help Aaron get the boat out of the water. After Aaron had struggled several minutes on his own, a voice came from the dock, asking whether they needed help.

"Walter," Rudy called back. "Give this boy a hand."

Together, Aaron and the man hauled the boat out and got it stored while Rudy gave orders from the dock, where he sat, still drinking. When they were finished, they went over to join Rudy, who introduced them by saying, "Aaron, this here's Walter Shapiro. He's a professor at the university in Moorhead and no doubt the only goddamn Jew in a thirty-mile radius." Walter laughed at the introduction and shook Aaron's hand, and the three of them went into Walter's cabin for what Walter called "a nightcap." It was there in the lighted cabin that Aaron recognized Walter as the man who had come into the café for breakfast three years earlier, the man who read a book in French while he ate.

"You came into my mother's café for breakfast," Aaron said. "The Trout Café?"

"I remember," Walter said. "Your mother was an excellent cook. That's why I had to stop coming, or I would have started to look like Rudy here." Rudy laughed, though Aaron would later learn that men did not always like to have their weight discussed either. He would also learn, after he and Walter had become lovers, that he was the real reason Walter had not come in again. "You were such a lovely boy," Walter would explain. "So wistful and polite and filled with yearning."

Just like that it became the three of them motoring out in Rudy's boat each night, Rudy listening as Aaron and Walter conversed quietly, often about poetry. The poetry that Walter read aloud to them out there on the water was nothing like the poetry that Aaron had been forced to memorize in school, poems about the loveliness of trees. He started with several by Anne Sexton and T. S. Eliot, followed by a poem that he had driven all the way back to his house in Moorhead to retrieve because he had realized at breakfast that they needed to hear it. It was by a man named Richard Hugo, a poem that began so beautifully Aaron had found himself in tears: *You might come here Sunday on a whim. / Say your life broke down.*

Walter also asked questions, lots of them, his tone matter-of-fact: What had happened to Aaron's father, and did he know where his mother had gone, and did he think his life would shape up differently because of these factors? He asked Aaron what he planned to study in college, as if college were a given and the only thing left to be worked out was what Aaron hoped to do with his life. Aaron discovered that Walter was a good listener, and he found himself answering honestly.

"Did Rudy know about you, that, you know, that you're gay?" he asked Walter later, when he was just starting to figure this out about himself.

"I never told him in so many words, but I suspect he knew. Rudy is a very perceptive man," Walter said. "Did you know he came out to the cabin one afternoon to talk to me about you?"

Aaron shook his head.

"Well, he did. He wanted my help getting you into college. He wasn't sure what I could do exactly, but he wondered whether there wasn't something, given my position at the university. He said he didn't want you stuck there like his daughter." It had made Aaron's heart ache to picture Rudy doing this. "He's a good man, Rudy is, a kind man. It's probably why he drinks too much. There are some people that the world's just too much for, you know."

"I didn't know," Aaron had said. He was just eighteen, and there was so much he didn't know.

March

17

On the board, Aaron wrote the day's phrasal verb: *turn into*. He added a definition—"to change from X to Y; to become"—and beneath it, examples:

1. *We turned the garage into a study.*
2. *He started studying more and turned into a straight-A student.*
3. *She turned her jeans into a pair of shorts.*

Behind him, the students copied everything into their notebooks, which was always the case when they studied phrasal verbs. To truly understand English, they agreed, they had to know the difference between *turn into* and *turn in*. They sat in pairs writing sentences while Aaron circulated, checking their work. He read aloud what Chaa had written: *Tommy used to be a man, but then he turned into a gay.* The Thai boys laughed, except Tommy, who looked around for Aksu, worried that she might have overheard their teasing.

"You do know that gay men are still men?" Aaron said.

"Yes?" said Chaa. He sounded surprised.

Finally, it was break time, and the students turned on their cell phones and borrowed change from one another for the coffee machine. As Aaron passed the smoking balcony on his way down to the faculty room, he saw that the sliding door was ajar and that smoke was drifting into the hallway.

"Smoke travels," he called to the two smokers, before slamming the door shut.

He recognized them, two young Japanese women who planned to remain in the class one level below his because they were afraid of him. "He looks too serious," they had told his students, referring to his ties and the horn-rimmed glasses, his tallness and the severe part of his hair. The Thais had reported this to him gleefully.

The women began gesticulating. They pointed to the door, their mouths moving, and he pointed to his ear and yelled, "Louder."

"Broken," screamed the one on the right. She tugged on the door. Nothing. Aaron tugged. It was indeed broken, like everything else in this building.

"Okay," he called. "I'll get help." Instead of going downstairs to find Bart, he turned back toward the detective's classroom, assuming that a man who visited the smoking balcony with such regularity would be familiar with the door's idiosyncrasies. He had not actually met him yet, but they often nodded at each other down the hallway. The detective's door swung open just as Aaron reached it, and the two men collided, hard. Aaron extended his hand. "I'm Aaron," he said.

"Bill," said the detective, his grip unexpectedly loose. "Carpal tunnel," he added, as though reading Aaron's mind. "All those years of writing out reports."

"I was wondering whether you might have some advice regarding the sliding door on the smoking balcony?"

"My advice is 'whatever the hell you do, don't close the damn thing.'"

"Well, I've already done so—slammed it, in fact," Aaron said.

Bill put an unlit cigarette in his mouth, jiggled it up and down. "Let's go take a look," he said. Students had already gathered around the door, but they stepped back, no doubt reassured by Bill's capable appearance. "Yup, it's definitely off the track," Bill confirmed. He turned to Aaron. "I remember seeing a toolbox in the basement when I got the tour—in the corner by the Christmas tree."

Aaron understood that he had created the problem, which made retrieving the toolbox his responsibility. Generally, he avoided the

basement, a dark, low-ceilinged place used for storing extra desks
and blackboards as well as the numerous holiday decorations of
which Marla was fond—bats and leprechauns keeping company
with Chinese lanterns and turkeys. It was also used for hosting
school-wide parties, the only space big enough to accommodate all
the students. They had begun the term down there, the teachers and
students collectively welcoming the new year and the new semester,
and because he was new, they had welcomed him also. He recalled
how uncelebratory the event felt, the dirty windows and flickering
fluorescent lights, the ceiling pressing down on them. Marla had run
off copies of "Auld Lang Syne," which they sang together, ruining
for Aaron, possibly forever, a song that had always invoked in him a
sweet nostalgia.

He made his way down the back stairs and paused to let his eyes adjust. He did not know where the light switch was, but he could discern
the Christmas tree, which lay on its side like a giant tumbleweed. Near
it was a pair of chairs, facing each other as though they'd been set up
to facilitate an interrogation, an interrogation of the sort that required
a dim, isolated, innocuous place. He stepped carefully over to the tree
and saw the toolbox, just as Bill had described, but as he bent to retrieve it, he heard a low, throaty exhalation of air. It frightened him, the
way that human sounds do when you think you're alone, and he jerked
his head toward it.

There, almost close enough to touch, was a young man leaning back
against a column. His eyes were closed, but his mouth was open wide,
like that of a thirsty man trying to catch a drop of rain.

Perhaps Aaron made some small noise, or the boy simply sensed
a presence, but his chin dropped and his eyes opened, and he was
looking right at Aaron, each regarding the other with surprise. Just
as quickly the boy looked down, though not before Aaron had seen
the fear in his eyes. Aaron followed the young man's gaze, down to
where darkness shrouded his body. From this darkness rose a form
that became another human being, a man with black hair that stood
on end as though mussed from a pillow or a lover's restless hands. It
was Melvin.

* * *

Two stories up, in the well-lit faculty room on the second floor, it was easy enough to believe that he had imagined the whole thing, for there in front of him sat Felix eating a potato still steaming from the microwave while Kate passed around a bag of preserved plums, her weekly gift from a Japanese student who was concerned about her digestion. Eugenia was looking through a box of cassette tapes, and when she saw Aaron in the doorway, she said, "Aaron, do you have the *Lake Wobegon* tapes?"

"I have no interest in *Lake Wobegon*," he said. He was tired of people assuming he did. Nobody asked why he was carrying a toolbox.

Even Taffy was there, sorting through magazines, no doubt in preparation for a cut-and-paste activity of the sort that introductory ESL teachers relied on, snipping out pictures of people and labeling them with straightforward adjectives: *HAPPY, SCARED, CONFUSED, EMBARRASSED.*

"Taffy," Aaron said, "may I speak to you in the hallway for a moment?"

He needed to tell someone what he had seen, to try to put into words the mix of emotions he had felt as he walked away from the two men. Taffy followed him out and stood with her hands on her hips. "What is it?" she asked in a voice that made it clear she had more magazines to sort through.

"Actually, it's nothing," he said, put off by her tone, but then the words tumbled out anyway. "It's just that I went down into the basement to get the toolbox, and I came upon two students." He held up the toolbox as though his story hinged on it.

"They were skipping class?" asked Taffy.

"I'm not sure." This was a lie. Melvin had been sitting in his desk right up until break began, but noting this meant implicating him.

"You didn't ask? The basement is off-limits to students. You should've asked."

"They were . . . busy."

"Busy?" said Taffy loudly, as though she took offense at the notion of students being busy, but then, perhaps noting his discomfort, she said, "Busy how? Are you telling me that they were doing something down there?"

He nodded.

"Did you recognize them?" she asked.

He thought about the look of shame in their eyes, shame not just at being caught but at the need that had brought them to this moment.

"No," he said. "It was dark. I didn't recognize them."

The sliding door had been removed and propped against the wall. Bill and four students stood on the balcony smoking, as though being on the balcony were what mattered, the door itself inconsequential. The freed Japanese women regarded Aaron warily. He looked at his watch and saw that somehow only half an hour had passed since the break began. His students were filing back into the room, but Melvin, who never missed class, did not return with them. Nobody commented on his absence, perhaps because Melvin's absence felt much like his presence. Later, when the afternoon session began, he was back, sitting at his desk, not laughing or smiling or talking—in short, acting as he always did, which meant that there was no way to know whether what had happened in the basement had upset him.

It had upset Aaron, his sense of decorum, for there seemed something unsavory about engaging in such activity in a school, the place where one went to improve one's mind. The incident had reminded him of something else, something from his childhood that he did not like to think about because thinking about it reminded him of his own shame, never far away, even after all these years. When he was eleven, a man from Mortonville named Ronnie Hopkins was arrested and sent to jail. He was an older man with large hips who was married to a much younger woman with no hips at all; she had a "boyish" figure, people in Mortonville liked to say knowingly, after Ronnie Hopkins was arrested for having sex with a student—a *male* student—at the vocational school for the developmentally disabled where he worked.

The student was technically an adult, forty, but mentally a boy, and so the police had come to the house where Ronnie Hopkins lived with his hipless wife and three children, and arrested him. While he was in prison, his wife divorced him and his children refused to write, yet when Ronnie Hopkins was released two years later, he came back to Mortonville and settled in one of the trailer houses on the edge of town. That Ronnie Hopkins chose to return had made no sense to Aaron— no sense to anyone in town really—and as Aaron worked to understand, he considered two possibilities: Ronnie Hopkins was punishing himself, or he simply had no sense that the world beyond Mortonville might offer something different. He had always kept to himself, had never sat with the other men in the café, drinking coffee and rolling the tumbler of dice to determine who would pick up the tab for the table. Instead, he came in alone and sat alone, generally to eat a hamburger before work. He was polite, almost apologetic, when he needed something, ketchup or a refill of pop.

After prison, Ronnie Hopkins stayed even more to himself than before. He no longer went into the bank, where his wife, his ex-wife, was a teller, nor did he buy gasoline or groceries in town or come into the café for a hamburger. Yet he still went into Bildt Hardware to pick up some necessity like batteries or nails, even though everyone in town knew that Harold Bildt had become fixated on Ronnie Hopkins. Each night after he finished his paperwork, Harold drove by Ronnie Hopkins's trailer house, making sure that Ronnie was inside and accounted for. Often, Aaron overheard Harold and his friends discussing Ronnie Hopkins, so he knew also that Harold refused to wait on him when he came into the store. Even if Edna, Harold's wife, was not around, Harold stayed in his office with his pals, laughing loudly and ignoring Ronnie Hopkins, who would never dream of demanding assistance. He had not been that kind of man before his arrest, and he was certainly not that kind after.

One afternoon Aaron's mother sent him across the street to let Harold know that the dishwasher was acting up again. Aaron did not like going into Harold's office, where Harold and his friends talked about sex in coarse language that often made no sense to Aaron and about everything else in the world according to a rigid code of right and wrong that seemed never to require examination or recalibration. As Aaron made his way through the quiet store, past Gardening and Hunting, he came upon Ronnie Hopkins standing in Households, scrutinizing the Scotch tape as though he were picking out a wedding ring, but Households was near the office, so Aaron knew that he was actually listening to the men talk. While Aaron stood observing Ronnie Hopkins, he heard Marvin Hultgren say loudly, "What kind of man wants someone's business up his rear end anyway?"

Aaron had always thought of blushing as a public function, but that day in Bildt Hardware, hearing for the first time a graphic description of what men did to each other sexually, he learned otherwise. His face grew hot. He watched Ronnie Hopkins put a roll of tape in his pocket and turn to leave.

"When I joined the army back in '42," Marvin Hultgren continued, "the first thing was they had us strip down to nothing. There we were, buck naked, and we had to line up and bend over with our palms on the floor, asses straight up. This feller comes by with a fire hose and lets each of us have it—straight up the ass. I'm telling you, if that didn't clean you out, nothing would. Hurt like hell. We walked around like sissies for a week."

The men laughed and then one of them passed gas loudly, and so they laughed again, and Aaron knew that all of it—the story and the laughter and the passing of gas—was meant for Ronnie Hopkins. Ronnie Hopkins knew this also, and he stood still for a moment, unaware that he was being watched, and then he took the roll of tape back out of his coat pocket, slid it onto the display prong, and left.

Aaron could not tell his mother that he had failed to relay her message to Harold Bildt, so he walked quietly through Households, waiting for his face to cool, but everything he looked at—the corn skewers that went into the ends of cobs, the ketchup and mustard squirt bottles—reminded him of what he had heard. He took a breath and went into the office and told Harold Bildt about the dishwasher.

Harold looked at the calendar on his desk, trying to figure out a time that he could walk across the street to fix it, and Aaron looked down at the floor because he could not look at the other men, now that he understood: what they hated about Ronnie Hopkins was not that he had done what he had to a retarded man but simply that he had done it to a man.

18

After classes were dismissed that afternoon, Taffy appeared in his doorway, wanting to go out for a drink in order to talk about what he had seen in the basement. Taffy had never come up to his room before, but he knew that the incident had aroused something in her, brought out the part of her that liked being in charge, handling situations, maintaining order. He suggested that they have a drink in the Castro, knowing she would decline. Taffy did not like the Castro because she did not like the way gay men regarded her. The truth was that he did not feel at ease there either, especially when he saw men walking around almost naked or couples holding hands, but he had begun cutting through the Castro on walks and had recently stumbled upon a café that he liked, a busy place, not the type of place he normally chose, but as he sat in the corner with a beer and a slice of pie, he discovered that the café's busyness made him feel invisible.

He liked feeling invisible, and he sat with a poetry book open before him because he had learned that reading was a way to help that feeling along. At Milton's, he had sometimes read through an entire week's worth of newspapers, and the last time he ate there, the Friday right before he left Albuquerque, he had come across an article in *The New York Times* that he read with great interest and now wished he had clipped and saved. It was about the letter writers of India, a disappearing breed of men who set up shop—makeshift desks, paper, ink, stamps—day after day under the same trees in the same village markets in order to take down the letters of those around them who could not read or write but wished to record and share the details of their lives. It was a natural desire, this need to account for one's life, to say it out loud or see it written down before abandoning it to the dusty shelves of memory—to suggest, in some way, that it mattered.

As he sat with his book and his pie that day in the Castro, a man, a very nice man named George, had come up and asked what he was reading. As this man George stood next to his table, his head inclined toward the open poetry book, Aaron considered how much of his life had been spent listening to the stories of others. It was not a complaint. He had felt nothing but fondness for the tellers. But now, nearly forty-two and alone for the first time, he had begun to think that his own life added up to nothing more than the stories of other people. He looked up at this stranger with kind eyes who wanted to know what he was reading and said, " 'Degrees of Gray in Philipsburg.' "

The stranger smiled, which made his eyes appear even kinder, and began to recite: "You might come here Sunday on a whim. / Say your life broke down." He stopped abruptly because the next line was about a kiss, and they both looked down awkwardly. Aaron felt a tightening in his chest, a jolt to his groin, and he thought about how long it had been since he'd felt either. He recalled the farm boy he'd slept with in college, the boy from his poetry class. He had known so little about poetry then, only what Walter had taught him, but put off by the boy's veneration of Wordsworth, he had used poetry as an excuse not to engage in sex with the boy again. He looked up at this man who could quote from Richard Hugo and said, "I'm Aaron. Would you care to join me?"

George sat down, and Aaron tried hard not to think about Walter, who had first read this poem to him all those years ago as they sat in a boat together fishing, just before Walter took him away and helped him become the person he was meant to be, which he now thought of simply as the person he was, the person this stranger, George, had seen reading poetry and wanted to get to know.

They talked for two hours, eating their individual slices of pie and then sharing a third (apple again) to prolong the conversation, forks intertwining for one awful, glorious second as they both reached for the same bit of crust. Most people were not interested in the specifics of teaching, perhaps because they had spent their youths in school and thought they already knew every boring detail of what it meant to be a teacher. They offered overly zealous praise for teachers and all that they had to endure, right before changing the subject. But George wanted to know everything—why Aaron had become a teacher and whether he ever regretted it, where he taught and what his students were like and whether he got along with his colleagues—and Aaron found himself describing it all: Melvin's fiancée, Paolo's motorcycle club, the week without heat, even that Marla wrote "Love you guys" on the box of pineapple buns.

"But she's your boss," George said, voice rising, and Aaron wanted to lean across the table and kiss him. "So what was the thing that surprised you most when you started teaching?" he asked next. "I don't mean about education." He looked flustered. "I mean something more personal, I guess, about how it feels to be in the classroom."

"When I first started teaching, I couldn't sleep most nights because I was so worried I wasn't teaching them enough," Aaron said, but as he spoke, he remembered something else: Walter lying awake with him, listening to him talk through the details of his teaching day. Some nights, he got up and brought Aaron a plate of saltine crackers and ketchup, that childhood snack for which he had never lost the taste. "You need to sleep," Walter would whisper, but he always lay beside Aaron, stroking his brow for as long as it took because he understood that sometimes the only way to fall asleep was with the knowledge that someone was awake beside you.

George smiled encouragingly. He did not know that Aaron was thinking about lying in bed with the man with whom he had lived for more than twenty years. "But you just sort of get used to it," Aaron finally continued. "To the overwhelming sense of responsibility, I mean. Or maybe you just get better at teaching."

George nodded. "What else?"

"Well, one of the little things I really wasn't expecting was how intimate being in a classroom feels, like you're all on this long trip together. Sometimes the students act like they're invisible, like I can't see them doodling and rolling cigarettes, yawning and staring at the clock when they're tired or waiting for the break. The strangest thing—I guess this is where intimate and invisible meet—is that an inordinate number of them poke their fingers into their ears and noses, beneath their arms, even into the little crevice between their shoe and foot. They poke, and then they bring their fingers to their noses and sniff deeply, taking stock of their hygiene. And even though they're sitting right in front of me, it's as if they have no idea that I can see them."

George smiled again, and Aaron noticed that his front tooth was chipped, that one eye crinkled up slightly more than the other when he smiled. He was handsome, Aaron thought, the type of handsome that had to do with being slightly awkward and not caring about a chipped tooth.

"Sometimes, when all the twitching and poking and sniffing becomes too much, I'll stop what we're doing and remind them that I can see them. 'It's not like at the police station,' I'll say. 'There's no one-way mirror. You can see me. I can see you.' They always look a bit sheepish, but then they go right back to twitching and doodling and clock-checking."

"It makes me wonder what I was like," George said. "You know, when I was sitting in my desk feeling invisible." He looked down. "I think your students are lucky to have you." He did not say it like someone who went around handing out compliments, and Aaron felt at once pleased and terrified.

"Actually, I'm lucky to have them," he said. "They're young, and they speak about everything with such passion. They see everything as possible." Aaron stopped, embarrassed by his own earnestness, but George nodded, so he went on. "One of the things I most like about teaching is knowing there's a part of my day that's solely about them. I don't mean that in a 'doing my part to make the world better' way. It's much more selfish. I like knowing that when I go into the classroom, my needs and problems get set aside, that I'll be able to escape my own head, even if it's just for a little while."

"What's going on in your head that needs escaping?" George asked softly.

Instead of answering, Aaron said, "I'm talking too much. What do you do?"

George laughed. He knew Aaron was sidestepping the question. "Do you want to guess?" he asked. "Twenty Questions, maybe?"

"I am extremely bad at Twenty Questions," Aaron said. "I forget what I've already asked and ask questions that are entirely too specific or that have nothing to do with the topic at all. I can assure you that the best approach is for you to just tell me."

George picked up their pie forks and pretended to make a drum roll, which Aaron normally would have found silly or annoying but instead found endearing because he could see how foreign the gesture was to George, that he was not someone who punctuated his conversations with drum rolls. "I'm a Muni cop," George said. "I'm one of those guys that rides around all day asking to see your ticket."

"Do you like it?" Aaron asked.

"I like the hours. I don't like spending my days underground watching people get nervous the minute I get on the train." He paused, and Aaron could tell that he was thinking about something. "Today, for example, I got on the K at West Portal, and I saw this young couple with a baby, all three of them looking like they hadn't eaten in days. I knew right away they didn't have tickets, that they were probably just riding around hoping the motion would lull the baby to sleep."

"How old was the baby?" Aaron asked.

"I don't know, maybe a year. She was at that point where you could tell she was a girl. Anyway, I had to ask them for their tickets along with everyone else. I figured they were going to either hand me expired tickets they'd taken from the garbage or feign some type of ignorance, pretend to be tourists who don't speak English or act like they were looking everywhere for their tickets, and I already knew what I was going to do: make them get off with me at the next stop for appearance's sake, and then just send them on their way. Except the father says, 'I'm sorry, Officer, but the baby grabbed our tickets and ate them.' And I look at the baby, who's hungry and clearly needs her diaper changed and didn't ask for any of this, and I want to punch the guy. I mean, I just felt this rage inside.

"So I say, 'Both of your tickets?' And he nods. 'Without either of you being able to stop her?' And he nods again. 'Well, then, we need to call a medical unit,' I say, and I make a move toward my walkie-talkie, 'because that's a lot of paper for a little thing like her to digest. They might even need to keep her—you know, for observation or something like that.' I was just talking, trying to get the guy to admit he'd lied. Listening to myself tell you the story now, it doesn't make any sense— that I was so angry, that I thought it would change anything for that baby if he admitted he'd lied."

George shook his head, and Aaron wanted to say something to let him know that it did make sense, but George continued with the story. "So then the girl jumps in. 'Please don't call,' she says. 'They'll take her. We lied. Okay? We don't have tickets,' and the guy turns and yells at her to shut up and makes this move toward her with his fist. It was obvious she was used to stuff like this from him because she cowered back in her seat and got quiet."

"What did you do?" Aaron asked.

"You mean did I add even more to the mess I'd already made?"

"It wasn't your fault," Aaron said. "The guy's a jerk."

"I know," George said. "But I also know that I lost sight of what I was supposed to be doing, which was checking tickets. Anyway, you asked what happened next, and that's the best part. The whole time this big butch is sitting next to them, reading. Well, she stands up, sets her book on the seat, and nails the guy. Just *boom*. Then she sits back down and begins reading again. *Jonathan Livingston Seagull,* of all things. The baby starts crying, and the guy shakes his head like something's loose, and he turns to me and says, 'You saw it. I want that dyke arrested,' and I say, 'Saw what?'"

George laughed but his eyes were red. "Anyway, if you ask me a different day, I'd probably say that I like the job well enough. I like the pay and the fact that I can do a forty-hour week in four days and have three left over for other stuff."

"What sort of stuff?" Aaron asked.

George looked embarrassed. "I want to make documentaries," he said. "But that's a discussion for another day because, unfortunately, I have somewhere I'm supposed to be. I'm already late."

"Oh, right. Sorry," said Aaron. He jumped up, and they paid and walked out of the café and onto the street. He wanted to ask something that would indicate whether George had enjoyed their conversation as much as he had or whether this was just the way he passed his afternoons, but he knew that asking would require subtlety, and he did not know how to be subtle in a hurry. They turned in opposite directions, Aaron heading toward the Muni entrance and George hurrying off toward—Aaron imagined—a tryst or a lover at home.

Then, like two men dueling, they spun back around and looked at each other. "You might come here Sunday on a whim," George called, and Aaron laughed and nodded, understanding that he was agreeing to a date.

However, when Sunday came around, Aaron could not bring himself to go because he was overwhelmed by desire, a desire that was not only sexual, though there was definitely that. It was the nonsexual part that frightened him. Specifically, in the days after their meeting, he had found himself wanting to tell George things: that he enjoyed taking public transportation, sitting on Muni surrounded by people from all over the world; that he rode public transportation sometimes just to be near people, not for companionship but because he never felt as keenly alone as when he stood pressed uncomfortably close to strangers; that he needed to feel alone. He wanted to tell George about something that he had recently witnessed in United Nations Plaza. He was on his way to an afternoon concert at the symphony hall, Dvořák's *New World* Symphony, one of his favorites, but he'd arrived early, so he settled on a bench. As he sat there in his suit and tie, a group of young people, grubby and presumably homeless, had engaged in a ritualistic shaving of one another's underarms. They stood in a circle near the fountain and took turns stroking the shaver against the underarms of the person beside them, dipping it into the fountain, then passing it on. Aaron felt repulsed yet could not stop watching. In the end, he had to run to make it to the concert on time. He could imagine telling George the whole story while George nodded and asked questions. He *liked* imagining it, and that was what frightened him, this desire to have George listen and nod as he tried to describe the trust involved in lifting one's arms like that, in letting another person take in your smell and touch a razor to one of the most tender parts of your body.

He had told no one about George, not even Taffy. "The Castro?" she said. "Why don't we have a drink somewhere nearby?" He knew that she assumed he would agree to this request, and he supposed he should, but he also knew that if they were really friends he would have told her about meeting George and standing him up and wanting to go back to the café in the hope of fixing things. He had not told her because they were not really friends. He appreciated her help, he did, but when he thought about his future, he did not picture Taffy in it, except as someone with whom he might occasionally have a drink while discussing nothing more personal than students and pedagogy.

"Rain check?" he said, though he supposed they both knew this was unlikely. They walked down to the first floor together and got on different buses outside the school, and when he arrived in the Castro, he went directly to the café, where he looked through the window. He saw a man—just the back of his head—that might be George, and he did not go inside. Instead, he walked up Market to Civic Center, where he sat for a long while on a bench, waiting for something to happen, for strangers to start shaving the underarms of other strangers, to begin stroking their brows or brushing their hair or feeding them by hand, to begin doing the kinds of things that strangers did not do for other strangers—because he knew now that sometimes they did.

Aaron did not know how the friendship with Bill began, even whether it could be called a friendship, since they had nothing in common. Still, in the weeks following the episode with the broken smoking balcony door, they came to know things about each other, and wasn't that what friendship came down to? He knew, for example, that Bill had been married three times. "First to a black lady, Marabelle," he told Aaron as they stood in the hallway during break, "and then a white lady. That was Peggy. Last was Misclaida from Cuba. So you see, I've tried this marriage thing from different angles, but none of them took. Now I play the dating sites a bit, but that's about it. How about you?"

Aaron wanted to tell Bill that he would never meet a woman if he thought of dating sites as something to be *played,* like slot machines, but Bill had not solicited his advice. Instead, Aaron told him about Walter, and Bill nodded. "I had you pegged that way," he said, clearly pleased with himself.

"What way?" Aaron said. "As someone who could pull off a twenty-year relationship, or as someone who would leave that relationship behind?" He knew that Bill meant neither of these, but he wanted to make him say it.

Bill laughed. "No, I could just tell you were a little light in the loafers."

"You do know that people don't really use that expression anymore? If, in fact, they ever did."

Bill laughed again. He knew all about "the gays," he said. He'd grown up right here in San Francisco—okay, technically in Daly City, which was where you found yourself if you went all the way down Mission and kept going even after it stopped being interesting. Aaron said that he had not explored that part of town yet, and Bill said, "You remember that song 'Little Boxes,' right?" and Aaron said he did, and Bill announced proudly that the song had been written about Daly City.

"My impression of the song is that it's not meant to be flattering," Aaron said.

"I suppose that depends on how you look at things," Bill said. "Sometimes it's just plain nice not to have to think about who's got the better house 'cause 'they're all made out of ticky tacky and they all look just the same.'" He sang this last part. Aaron was surprised at his voice, which was soothing and sweet.

Chaa came up to them with a bag of durian chips, and Bill, who had never heard of durian, took several and then spit them back into his hand. "That is the absolute worst thing I've ever put in my mouth," he said to Chaa, who laughed as if this were precisely the response he had hoped for. After Chaa walked away, Bill turned to Aaron. "I bet it's not the worst thing you've ever put in your mouth," he said.

"You're sure you're not gay?" Aaron replied. "Because you have the sense of humor of an aging queen."

Quickly, they progressed from talking in the hallway during breaks to having a drink together several times a week at a nearby café. Bill referred to it as the hippie café because of the menu, though Aaron pointed out that a true hippie café would not have so many ringing cell phones. It was there that Bill told Aaron the story of his father, who had been one of those people who could figure out a money angle on anything. During the Korean War, he'd gone on a two-week leave to Thailand, where, at a roadside stall that sold gasoline from cans and fixed cars in a small shack behind, he had stumbled across a shedful of old car parts, never used, all still in their boxes and covered with dust. Bill said that his father was the sort of man who was always stumbling across things. He came home from Korea, started a family, and it was only years later that he thought about those parts and went back to Thailand. He made his way through Thailand as well as Malaysia, stopping at any out-of-the-way place that looked like it might service cars. When he came across a stash of parts, especially those for vintage Mercedes-Benzes, he acted like he could not imagine anyone wanting such things—pristine gearshift knobs and hubcaps, mirrors and window cranks—even as he bought everything up, offering fifty cents or a dollar and the illusion that he was the one granting favors.

"We were dirt poor," Bill said, "and then my father came home with that shipping container of parts, and within a year, he'd sold it all, sometimes for a five-hundred- or even thousand-time markup." He paused to drink half of his beer. "He loved to tell stories to anyone who'd listen about how he'd acquired all those parts, but he never let on that it had made him rich. It wasn't until he died years later that we found out he owned buildings all over the city, land up in Napa, but we never moved out of the ticky tacky house in Daly City. He kept locks on the cupboards and the fridge that only he had keys to, and he instructed my mother that we were to eat just one meal a day. It was served at five sharp, and if we missed it, well, we missed eating that day. The rest of the time we drank coffee, gallons of it. He kept a big pot going in the kitchen because he'd heard somewhere, maybe in the army, that coffee was a hunger depressant. We filled our stomachs with it until our insides were bloated and raw and we couldn't sleep, but that was fine with him because exhaustion was also a hunger depressant.

"When I was a teenager, I started going to early Mass before school every day, just to have that communion wafer in my stomach. And to this day I'm the best speller you're likely to meet because every Friday at school we had a spelling contest, and the prize was a candy bar. The teacher didn't know what to make of it: Billy Dawkins, who failed every test he ever took, winning spelling bees. I wanted to tell her that for a hamburger or a box of cereal, I'd learn anything they wanted, ace every test, but I was too proud for that, and besides, my father would have killed me. Not because he worried about what people thought. He didn't. He just didn't want anyone meddling in his business.

"I was sixteen the last time I saw him. I came home from school so hungry I'd almost fainted during PE, and when I walked in, I saw him at the table. Until then, I'd always figured that while he was starving us, he was starving himself also. It was a small consolation to think that way, that we were all in it together—you know, that that's how being poor worked. The thing is, I think most days he did hold himself to the same standard, but not that day. That day he was sitting there with a mound of pickled pigs' feet piled high on a sheet of butcher paper, everything about him slick with vinegar and grease, a pile of bones that he'd sucked clean tossed to the side. The bones were tiny, like children's knucklebones. It was watching him suck those bones that did it. I knocked him off his chair and wrestled him to the floor. I had my hands around his neck, would have killed him too if my mother hadn't come in then and begged me to stop. When I stood up, my father yelled, 'Get out of my house. Get out and don't come back. I'm not spending another dime on you.'

"And I said, 'Right. Because that would mean doubling what

you've spent so far.'" Bill laughed and finished his beer. "I've always been very proud that that was the last thing I said to him, that I had the presence of mind to say something, you know, sort of clever. So I packed a few things and left—never saw the bastard again. It wasn't until he died that it came out about him being filthy rich, a millionaire actually. Of course, he'd written me out of his will the very day I left. My sisters tried to give me my third anyway, but I refused. I didn't want a thing from him."

"How did you survive?" Aaron asked. "You were just a boy."

"Our priest helped. He was a good man—found me a job working construction and a place to live. I had to leave school, but that was bound to happen anyway. I did that for maybe eight or ten years, and then I got hooked up with this whole detective business, apprenticed myself to an old guy and found out I was pretty good at it. He couldn't get around so much anymore, so I became his legs, and he taught me everything I know about the business, which is considerable." He looked down at his empty beer glass as though he wished it were not empty. "It's a funny thing, isn't it," he said. "I drop out of school when I'm sixteen, and here I am, almost forty years later, a teacher. Not a very good one, but it's still a heck of a thing."

"Yet another example of life's abundant irony," Aaron said. Then, afraid that Bill might think he was mocking him, he continued, "When I was a boy, my mother owned a café, which we lived above. My bedroom window looked out over the street facing Bildt Hardware and Swenson's Variety Store, which sold primarily groceries but also school supplies and bed linens. At night I lay in bed, watching the Swenson's neon sign flash off and on: *Variety. Variety. Variety. Variety.* I'd been watching that sign for years before it suddenly hit me that there was actually something very funny about a sign that promised *variety* flashing off and on in the same monotonous way night after night."

It was the first time he had told Bill anything about his childhood, and he stopped there, not explaining about the pleasure he had felt that night at realizing that this was irony. That would mean talking about

Clarence, who had predicted that he would grow nicely into irony. He was not ready to talk about Clarence.

Bill laughed. "Yup," he said, "it's a fine thing, irony."

Bill still attended Mass at Mission Dolores once a week. "Oftener," he told Aaron, "when I'm involved in a really sordid case."

Aaron did not think that he had ever had a friend who attended church regularly. "Give me an example of sordid," he said.

"Cheating spouses. That's my bread and butter, you know." Aaron did know, since Bill had told him several times that his caseload was made up, disproportionately, of adultery and workers' comp scams. "They get messy."

"Tell me about a recent case that required extra attendance at Mass," Aaron said.

"I just went this morning," Bill said. "Fourth time this week 'cause I'm tailing a guy who's a real piece of work. Guess where he heads every night?"

He had also never had a friend who used words like *tailing*. "Where?" he said.

"The Castro. He's got one of those transvestites on the side. You know—looks like a woman, but then the plumbing's all male. Anyway, so I have to tell the wife that her husband's a fag, and—"

"Bill," Aaron interrupted. They were having this conversation in the hallway with just five minutes left of break, and he did not know where to begin.

"What?" Bill said, and then, "Oh, I get it. I shouldn't say *fag* around you, right?"

"You shouldn't say it, period," Aaron said, and Bill looked at him as though Aaron had asked him to give up smoking or stop eating a hamburger for lunch every day.

Aaron knew what Walter would say about his friendship with Bill—Walter, who believed that gay men and straight men could never really be friends, that the former could never fully trust the latter. Though their social lives over the years had involved a preponderance of heterosexuals—colleagues, neighbors—Walter insisted that gay people could only be themselves, their truest, uncensored selves, in the company of other gay people. Aaron found this argument perplexing and reductive. "Do you think that's how it was with you and the guys in Moorhead—that you were being your truest, uncensored selves?" he had asked, referring to the group of closeted men with whom Walter had been friends when Aaron came to live with him. "Because the truth is I didn't feel any more true and uncensored with them than I did sitting around with the men at the café when I was a kid."

Walter had acted incredulous—perhaps he truly was incredulous. "But didn't it at least mean something to you, after all those years in the closet, to be able to say things out loud, to not wonder what people were thinking?"

"Maybe," Aaron had said. He thought about it. "Okay, yes, though I don't think I ever felt in the closet as a boy—that implies a level of awareness that I simply didn't have. And I certainly never felt like myself around your guys either. I always felt the way I do when someone who's really religious suddenly wants to be my friend and I can't help but think that it's not me, Aaron, they want to be friends with—because they don't really know me. That's how I felt with those guys—like I was just some gay boy that you were lucky enough to catch, and their job was to make clever remarks."

"Well," Walter said, "at least they never gave me the kind of look that everyone else did, those here-comes-Walter-with-his-boy looks."

"Of course they did. The only difference was that they approved. But what were they approving of? What did they really know about our relationship? Did they know that we read poetry together at night? That we didn't have sex those first four years? They didn't, because they weren't interested in poetry, and they believed we were having sex because that's what you let them believe." He wondered at what point in the conversation he had become angry.

"You're mad that I didn't clarify that we weren't having sex?" Walter asked.

"No," Aaron said, "I'm not mad about it." This was true. "I guess I just don't know why you can't see that if they were really your friends, you'd have told them the truth."

Walter was silent. "Sometimes," he said finally, "people just need to be around others that are like them."

"That's just it," Aaron said. "I had nothing in common with them, nothing except being gay. Maybe that's something, but it's not nearly enough."

"Surely you don't hold it against them that they don't like poetry?" Walter said.

"No, I don't hold it against them. I'm just saying that if I had to choose between spending time with a straight person who reads and a gay person who doesn't, I'd choose the straight person."

"What if both of them read?" said Walter.

"Well, then it depends on what they're reading."

The argument had ended there, not because things had been resolved but because they saw that they could not be. It had become absurd, yet they were not able to laugh together at the absurdity. Aaron supposed it was ironic that he was the one who had moved to San Francisco, he who had never required the trappings of gay life, the bars and restaurants and entire neighborhoods populated by gays and lesbians; he who did not go out of his way to patronize gay mechanics and plumbers, did not assume that a heterosexual mechanic or plumber—or detective—would say something homophobic until he said it, and then, you dealt with it. You explained why the comment or word or joke was offensive. It was tiring at times, but he thought it was the price you paid for truly living in the world.

"Do you ever feel bad about what you do?" Aaron asked Bill. "About making money by exposing other people's secrets?"

"Everyone's got secrets," Bill said. "Maybe this guy's got the right to his, but his wife's paying me to find out what they are, and I think she's got the right to know. It just proves what I've always said: that you can't really know another person, and if you can't know them, you can't trust them."

"I've always found that people who say you can't trust anyone are actually saying something about their own trustworthiness," Aaron said.

"I guess it's a matter of how you think about trust. For me, if you've got secrets, then I can't trust you."

"Everyone has secrets, Bill," Aaron said. "That's the state of being human. I know you Catholics like your confession, but I just don't believe we need to confess everything about ourselves to the world. That's too much to expect of people."

19

Aaron was awakened one morning by the moan of a foghorn, an anomaly, he supposed, since everyone had said that March would be a respite before heading into the fog of summer. The sound put him in mind of cows, of their low, mournful mooing, which was all that he really knew of the creatures, though numerous people over the years, upon learning that he had grown up in a small town in Minnesota, had called on him to explain not just cows but any number of things: how grain elevators worked and which crops were easiest to grow, how fast a tractor could go and whether it was true that farm boys had sex with sheep. He knew the answers to none of these questions, his only knowledge of farming gleaned from the discussions he had overhead as he served farmers in the café and from the summer he spent pulling tassels from corn when he was twelve, monotonous work that he had enjoyed. His mother had made him quit after just three weeks because she said that she needed his help at the café, but he thought that she resented the way he came home tired but whistling each afternoon.

In fact, she wanted him around the café—around her—even less that summer, and in the fall, she began lending him out. *Lent* was how he thought of himself, like a library book that entered the homes of strangers briefly. His mother said that people in Mortonville could not forgive them for being outsiders, using the word *forgive* as if she would like nothing better than to make an apology and be done with it. Aaron supposed it was this need, the need for acceptance, that led her to begin lending him out to people in town, primarily old people, his job to help with tasks that they could no longer manage—carrying boxes up and down steps, shopping for food, applying rubber pads to the bottoms of things—tasks that made him privy to their vulnerabilities. The old people were always grateful for his help, grateful to his mother for sending him, and as he was leaving, they often tried to press something into his hand—a few coins, a Pop-Tart, an envelope bearing colorful stamps—compensation for his services, all of which his mother required him to refuse. The old people fussed then, telling him to zip his coat all the way up, to be careful walking home, not because there was anything to fear in Mortonville but because they wanted to give him something. He felt that his mother was wrong to deny them this small pleasure.

As he made his way across Mortonville late one afternoon in December, the normally pleasant sound of snow crunching beneath his sneakers nearly brought him to tears. In truth, it was not just the crunching or the day's steady retreat but so many things, all piling up inside him like the mounds of snow that flanked the recently plowed streets, mounds that other children, not he, liked to climb upon. Of course, winter dusk is particularly conducive to melancholy, and though he was young to know such things, to feel them so deeply, his age did not change the fact that he did. He thought about his mother sitting by herself in the café, wanting to be alone, wanting nothing between her and dusk. Back in their house in Moorhead, she used to come into his room some afternoons and wake him from his naps. "It's getting dark," she'd say, "and I thought how nice it would be to have your company." He missed that mother, the one who thought his presence made nightfall more bearable.

He was being lent that day to the Bergstroms. There were no streetlights in their part of town, but all around him houses were aglow, predictably, with Christmas lights and kitchen lights and the steady yellow beam of porch lights, each anticipating a specific event—a holiday, a warm meal, a father's return. He could tell who was having chicken that night, the odors wafting from these well-lit kitchens into the street where he walked. Meanwhile, his mother was back at the café, creating her own good smells as she cooked, but this thought only added to his mood, surrounded as he was by mothers making meals for their families, whom they solely considered as they cooked. He could not remember the last time his mother had prepared something just for him, something that was not a leftover from the daily special or a kitchen mistake, an overcooked hamburger that became his supper.

Aaron did not really know the Bergstroms because they rarely came into the café, and he trudged along, dreading the visit. Mrs. Bergstrom had been a teacher in a town nearby. They lived in Mortonville because Mr. Bergstrom owned the tire store, long closed because they were retired and their son—their only child—had no affinity for tires. Anyway, their son was dead, had gone through the ice the winter before. This son was the reason that Aaron dreaded the visit, for people in town said that the Bergstroms had not recovered, that having a dead son had made them odd.

They had turned on their porch light, and he stood on their front steps, watching them through the picture window, the two of them side by side on the sofa, an afghan tucked round their collective legs and rising partway up their chests. They were staring ahead, both of them focused on something that he could not see—the news, he thought, for they had about them the look of people distracted by problems that were not their own. From outside, they did not look like two people with a dead son. He knocked, and they beckoned him in. He opened the door and stepped in, anticipating warmth, as one did in Minnesota in December, but when he said hello, his breath hung in the air. The room was silent, the television off, and he glanced over to see what they had been staring at, but there was nothing there.

"My mother sent me? She said you needed help?" His voice rose at the end of both sentences, turning them into questions, and he wished that he could start over, could reenter the house making declarations.

"Come here and let us take a look at you," said Mr. Bergstrom, gesturing vaguely toward the middle of the room.

Aaron bent to remove his sneakers, which were covered with snow, and Mrs. Bergstrom said, "What a polite young man."

He came and stood in front of them, and they regarded him without speaking. Then they turned and looked at each other, thoughtfully, as though Aaron were an appliance that they were considering buying, an appliance that offered some but not all the features that they wanted in their appliance. The look that they gave each other seemed to say, "Well, shall we take him anyway? Can we make do?"

"How old are you, Aaron?" asked Mrs. Bergstrom.

"Twelve," he said quietly. "Almost thirteen."

They waited, perhaps expecting him to comment on his impending puberty—to describe his first whisker or the new muskiness beneath his arms—and when he did not, Mrs. Bergstrom said, "Well, it's time for the news, so why don't we let Father watch while we work on our letter." She told Aaron to turn on the television, and he did, the newscaster's voice exploding into the room. She extricated herself from the afghan, and Aaron saw that she had on snow pants, as though she had just come in from an afternoon of sledding. She wiggled herself to the front of the sofa and concentrated, staring straight ahead before she hoisted herself to her feet with a small grunt that embarrassed him.

"Let's settle ourselves in the den," Mrs. Bergstrom said. He followed her down the hallway, her snow pants making a *phit, phit* sound as she walked, and into the den, where she locked the door behind them. The room smelled of cedar, which he liked, and wet cardboard, which he did not. On the wall above the sofa were photos of their son, Tim, their dead son, one from each year of school, lined up chronologically. He was smiling in all of them, and the gap between his front teeth seemed bigger than it had in person. There were no photos of him as an adult, but Aaron remembered him as a sad-looking man who came into the café alone and took a cloth from his pocket to clean the cutlery before using it. He had never ordered anything but water to drink, which Aaron's mother said had to do with his inability to keep a job for long, which meant he could not afford to drink pop, and he always had a bacon cheeseburger, from which he would not take a bite until he had uncrossed the two strips of bacon arranged in an X by Aaron's mother because he preferred his bacon parallel.

The morning after Tim fell through the ice, the café was exceptionally busy. Aaron came down late, so he did not know what was going on, only that something was, for the tables and booths were filled, the room buzzing.

"Something happened," his mother told him later. She explained haltingly that this *something* involved the Bergstroms, who had called the police the night before because Tim had stopped by to visit them and was acting strange.

"Strange how?" Aaron asked.

"He kept telling them he loved them," his mother said.

Aaron considered this: the fact that the Bergstroms had called the police because their son would not stop saying that he loved them. "They called the police because he wouldn't stop?" he said at last.

"Well," his mother said. "There was more to it than that."

The police had come, pulling up in front of the Bergstroms' house as Tim was driving away. They flashed their lights, but he did not stop, and like a parade of two, Tim and the police drove slowly through Mortonville and out of town. When Tim turned onto the dirt road that led to one of the lakes, the lake where people in Mortonville went to swim, the police sensed that something was wrong. They began running the siren and speaking to him over the loudspeaker, but he drove straight onto the frozen surface. The lakes had been tricky that year, with soft spots everywhere, which meant that even people who knew them well were staying off, so the police watched from the shore as Tim continued out toward the middle alone. Eventually, his headlights lurched upward, and within minutes he was gone. "You understand what I'm telling you, Aaron?" his mother said.

"Yes," he said.

"They can't get to the car. It's too dangerous." She tore open a packet of sugar and let it dissolve in her coffee. "Imagine how cold it must have been."

* * *

He and Mrs. Bergstrom sat down at a card table, atop of which was a half-completed puzzle, the picture side facing down. He studied the gray backside of the puzzle for a moment, wanting to say, "This puzzle puzzles me," but he was not the sort of boy who engaged in silliness with others. He used to say such things to his mother, who had been sincere in her reactions, laughing only when she truly found something funny, but it struck him one day that his mother was no longer listening.

"Why are you putting the puzzle together upside down?" he asked Mrs. Bergstrom. "Wouldn't it be easier if you could see the picture?"

"Why must everything be easy, young man?" She pushed the puzzle aside and drew a wooden box toward her, opening it to reveal stationery and pens. "How's your penmanship?" she asked, and he said that his penmanship was fine. "Good," she said. "I'm not interested in faulty penmanship. And your spelling?"

"I have the best spelling in my class," he reported.

"Well," said Mrs. Bergstrom, "that only means something if the class is not made up of imbeciles." She removed the top sheet of paper from the box and put it in front of him. "I assume your mother told you that I require assistance with my correspondence."

"Yes," he said. He glanced at her hands, which looked capable of holding a pen.

"Dear," she began dictating, and then stopped as though she could not recall to whom she had planned to write. "Just leave it blank for now," she instructed before resuming her dictation: "Winter has arrived in Mortonville."

She picked up the paper and examined it. "You must work on your uppercase letters," she told him severely, pointing to the W specifically. "The bottoms should be sharp, like two elbows resting on the line. You see how rounded yours are? You've made knees of them, as though they are kneeling. I do not approve of kneeling," she said. "We are not Catholics in this house." She laughed as though this were funny.

"Should I fix it?" he asked.

"That would just make it unsightly," she said, "and the first line, in particular, should not be unsightly. No, we'll leave it, but it's something to bear in mind."

He held the pen above the paper, waiting for her to continue.

"You seem like a perspicacious young man," she said, her tongue darting into the corners of her mouth as she studied him, slyly, wanting to know whether he would ask what *perspicacious* meant, wanting to know, that is, whether his curiosity would trump his timidity, for he understood that she saw him that way, as a timid boy who would put up with being bullied by an old lady in her den.

Of course, he knew what *perspicacious* meant, but he did not know how to convey this to her or whether she would make too much of his doing so. "I know what *perspicacious* means," he blurted out finally.

She chuckled. "Good," she said. "Because I want to show you something."

They stood, and she unlocked and opened the door. The television in the living room was still loud, but she held a finger to her lips as they tiptoed down the hallway to the next door. She opened it, and he felt her hand on his arm, pushing him inside, into the darkness. The door shut. He heard it locking, her hand fluttering against the wall until she found the light switch.

They were in the bathroom, and he could not look at Mrs. Bergstrom, not with the toilet right there, close enough to touch. She took a flashlight from a cupboard and knelt beside the toilet, putting her hand on the seat to steady herself, and then she looked up at him. "Come," she said sternly. And so he knelt beside her. "What do you see?" she asked, shining the flashlight on the floor around the base of the toilet. She sounded hopeful, and he bent closer, noticing dirt and small bits of toilet paper as well as a few tightly coiled gray hairs. *Pubic hairs!* The sight of them made his throat constrict and he gasped for air.

"You see it?" Mrs. Bergstrom asked in an excited whisper, for she had heard it as the gasp of discovery.

"See what?" He felt miserable.

"The urine," Mrs. Bergstrom said, her voice low and urgent. She leaned forward, her face hovering above the toilet bowl as if she were about to drink from it or bob for apples. "Every time Father comes in here, it's all over the floor, and I have to come right in after him and clean."

"Maybe he can't help it," Aaron said.

"I don't mind cleaning it up." She sounded angry. "It's the way he acts, telling me I'm crazy, that I'm imagining things." She tapped her finger on the seat. "Well, this afternoon I didn't clean up after him. I knew you were coming, so I left it."

Aaron looked away, studying the pattern that the linoleum made, trying to make sense of where the lines ended and began. "Yes," he said. "I see it."

Mrs. Bergstrom gave a low, growling laugh. "I knew it," she said and then, "Help me up." She extended her arm as though inviting him to admire a new watch, and Aaron stood and took her arm, supporting her as she struggled to her feet.

He wanted desperately to wash his hands, but he thought that doing so would be regarded somehow as impolite. "My mother needs me," he said instead, and Mrs. Bergstrom unlocked the bathroom door, and they went back down the hallway and into the living room, where Mr. Bergstrom still sat beneath the afghan watching the news.

"Were you any help?" he asked Aaron, shouting over the television.

"Not much," said Mrs. Bergstrom, answering for him, and the Bergstroms laughed together while he bent to put on his shoes.

"Good night then," Aaron said.

"Yes," said the Bergstroms.

Aaron switched off their porch light, which had been on this whole time, and stepped out into the darkness. Once again, he paused to peer through the picture window at the Bergstroms, who sat huddled beneath the afghan, collapsing in on each other like melting snowmen. He tried to assign a word to what he saw, to what he felt, but he did not know the word to describe the way that the Bergstroms sat on their sofa, an afghan and a dead son between them, or the soft ache of his own heart.

*　*　*

When Aaron returned to the café from the Bergstroms' that evening, Jim Evarold was already there, sitting in his booth. Every Thursday night, while his wife was off at her weekly Weight Watchers meeting, Jim came, sat in the corner booth, and spent a long time staring at the menu. He assessed his options carefully, even though he always chose the special, meatballs, waiting until Aaron's mother turned toward the kitchen to add, "And a large milk. And some of those Tater Tots." He always seemed sheepish about his order, perhaps ashamed to be wanting Tater Tots while his wife was off discussing calories and the hollowness of desire, and Aaron's mother always turned back to him and asked, "That all, Jim?" in a voice that Aaron found aggressive, almost bullying.

Jim Evarold pretended to consider the menu a bit longer then, before clearing his throat to make his usual plea: "Can't you change the Thursday special to meatloaf?"

"Meatloaf is Friday night," his mother replied, her voice sour from tending to people's needs all day. "They're the same, Jim. Just different shapes."

Jim Evarold would look at his hands or touch the napkin dispenser and mumble, "But meatloaf doesn't jump all over the plate when I cut it."

Aaron supposed some form of this conversation had taken place before he arrived, for Jim Evarold sat with his food already before him. Later, when he picked up Jim's plate, wiped clean, as usual, of the unwieldy meatballs and the ignominious Tater Tots, he found a scrap of tinfoil resting on the rim. Jim did not mention the tinfoil, which was about the size of a thumbnail, but Aaron knew that it had come from his food. He blew it to the floor, not wanting his mother to see it and be ashamed.

Over the next several weeks, more detritus washed up on the shores of Jim Evarold's otherwise empty plates: a snippet of butcher string, a scrap of wax paper, rubber bands, twist ties. Still, Jim said nothing, though it was clear that he left them on the plate for Aaron to find. Aaron dispensed with each surreptitiously. Finally, after two months of this, Aaron picked up Jim Evarold's empty plate one evening and discovered a bristle as delicate as a fish bone teetering on its edge. It was too small to have come from any of the brushes that his mother used in the kitchen to clean the grill or scrub potatoes. He held it on the tip of his finger, wanting to breathe it away with a wish. Instead, he brought it to his mother, who stared at it as though it were an object that had been missing for many years, something she had learned to live without so well that its reappearance now seemed a burden.

"Must be from the vegetable scrubber," she said at last, turning to flip a hamburger.

Aaron went upstairs and into the bathroom, where their toothbrushes hung from a rack. He reached for his mother's brush and held the bristle beside it. It matched. He had known it would. What it meant was this: his mother had extracted the bristle from her toothbrush and taken it downstairs, then had cooked Jim Evarold's meatballs with the bristle inside. She had done this intentionally, and as he pictured the whole sequence of events, he was afraid, for he accepted—somehow only then—how deeply unhappy his mother was. Her despair was like a snowball rolling downhill, growing bigger, moving faster, while he stood at the top of the hill watching it go. He was powerless to stop it.

Yet she had put the bristle in Jim Evarold's food, marking the world in this small way with her unhappiness, and he wanted to believe that there was something hopeful in her need to do so. He did not know why she had focused on Jim Evarold, whom everyone in town liked, including, as far as he knew, his mother. Jim was a quiet man. He was polite but never appeared to want company, and others accepted this. They greeted him as they passed his booth and moved on.

Just before he and his mother moved to town, Jim's brother, Matthew Evarold, had killed himself. The skeleton of the story was this: one day after his wife had gone to Florence with the two youngest children, Matthew Evarold went into the barn, looped a rope over a rafter, stood on a feed bucket, and then kicked the bucket out from beneath him. Perhaps he had hoped for someone else to discover his body, but it was his children, returning from school, who found him. Aaron occasionally rode the bus, so he knew where the Evarold family lived, just one stop before his own. Their driveway was long and straight, a dirt path with grass growing down the middle, the house and barn at the end. Aaron imagined the four oldest children trudging up the path that afternoon, laughing and kicking at the grass running down the middle, even as their father was already dead, hanging in the barn directly ahead of them. What had continued to shock Aaron was the way that these two realities could exist side by side, could share the same moment: a man swinging from a rafter in a barn, and his children, laughing and teasing each other just outside.

As a teenager and then as an adult, Aaron had often felt deeply alone and discouraged, had even encouraged himself to feel worse by convincing himself that no one would miss him if he ceased to exist, but those feelings never moved toward the realm of action, for the thought of not existing terrified him. Still, he felt no anger toward people who did consider suicide—who considered it, attempted it, even committed it—which was not the way that people in Mortonville had responded to Matthew Evarold's suicide. They said he had killed himself because he was selfish, but when Aaron thought about what *selfish* meant, what his dictionary said, "Seeking or concentrating on one's own advantage, pleasure, or well-being without regard for others," he could not reconcile these words—*advantage* and *pleasure,* which brought to mind a man grabbing some coveted prize, elbowing others out of the way and claiming the pleasure of it for himself— with the image of a man going into a barn, stepping up on a bucket, and hanging himself.

"Jim took his brother's death very hard," his mother told him one night after Jim Evarold had eaten his meatballs and Tater Tots and gone home to the wife who wished more than anything to be thin. "He felt he should have done something to help him."

"Like what?" Aaron asked. He wondered how his mother knew this.

"Oh, I don't know. Tried to make him happy I guess."

"How?" he asked.

"Listen, Aaron," she said. "You can't make other people happy. It's silly to try."

"Why is it silly?" he asked.

"Because it is," she said. "And because it will just make you feel like a failure."

20

When his mother and Pastor Gronseth disappeared, people in Mortonville felt betrayed, not just by their pastor, to whom they had confessed their problems, but by his mother as well. She knew things about them, secrets that she learned not because she pried but because while she poured coffee and took orders she overheard their stories of an uncle who had done something shameful or a child who had gone away and never come back. It made people feel vulnerable to think that two people who knew so much about them had left *together,* and this vulnerability translated into distrust, aimed at Aaron because he was the one left behind.

Throughout the following year, whenever he walked into Swenson's Variety Store to pick up something for Mrs. Hagedorn, the cashier would stop speaking midsentence. "Why, hello, Aaron Englund," she would call out in an artificially loud voice, and the aisles would fall silent. It was the same when he and Rudy went to pick up plumbing supplies at Bildt Hardware, except in this case it was Rudy shouting back to the men in the office, letting them know Aaron was with him because he feared they might be saying cruel things that a son should not hear about his mother. But the worst was going into the post office, where the postmistress, who stood hunched behind the counter in her blue sweater, announced shrilly, "Nothing for you, Aaron." Though he pretended that he was there only to retrieve the Hagedorns' mail, he felt sick with disappointment, which he hid with a smile because he knew that the postmistress reported on his mail, his *lack* of mail, to the rest of Mortonville. Everyone knew that his mother had not written to him.

At school, it was suggested by first one teacher and then another that he make weekly visits to Mr. Brisk, who came in Tuesday and Thursday afternoons because two afternoons a week was the most guidance the school could afford, perhaps the most it felt was needed. Aaron met with him twice, not because he wanted to but because the visits were already arranged. He had always been obedient about such things. They sat in Mr. Brisk's office, which had originally been conceived as a ticket booth. It had one window, through which the exchange of money—admission to sporting events and school plays—had taken place. It was this office that Bernice would describe just months later on Christmas Eve, and he never let on that he could picture it all: the office's smallness, the rickety chair on which one sat, knees jammed up against Mr. Brisk's desk.

At the first meeting, Mr. Brisk asked Aaron in a general way about his mother, and Aaron said that running the café had made her tired, though she had never said such a thing, at least not the way he made it sound to Mr. Brisk, like she had fled out of sheer exhaustion. The second time they met, Mr. Brisk asked him how he felt about his mother running away with the pastor, but he did not know whether Mr. Brisk was putting emphasis on the *running away* part or the *pastor* part.

Aaron did not believe that his mother and Pastor Gronseth had run away because they were in love. He had sat with them all those nights in the café, listening to them talk while he did homework, and he knew that they had come together out of loneliness, both of them incapable of forging friendships with the people around them because these people were their customers. Pastor Gronseth's customers, his congregants, came to him because they needed his reassurance about their children and marriages and jobs, believing that his reassurance meant something. They brought him maple syrup and freshly slaughtered chickens, but they came with their own needs in mind. What they did not want, could not bear, was to know any details of their pastor's personal life in return.

Many nights, the two of them talked about forgiveness, which Pastor Gronseth said people were keen on, though his opinion was that forgiveness should be difficult to earn. Otherwise, people were too easy on themselves: they acted without considering the consequences, knowing that they could simply request forgiveness later. He likened it to declaring bankruptcy, which allowed you all the fun of spending while other people dealt with the fallout. He had once been that sort of man, he told Aaron's mother, a man who left his first wife and their three children because he was tired of the way things were, *bored,* if you wanted to get right down to it. He had explained all about his past to the church board before he took the job in Mortonville. The three first children visited on holidays and sat in the front pew beside his second wife and their half brother, a loud boy whom none of them liked. Pastor Gronseth had been forgiven by everyone, but he was not sure that he had learned his lesson.

Aaron looked at the two filing cabinets against the wall of Mr. Brisk's office, cabinets that contained notes on everyone in the school, and then he looked back at Mr. Brisk. "I think Pastor Gronseth needed a ride, and my mother had a car. Pastor Gronseth didn't want to steal the car from his wife and son."

After Pastor Gronseth left, there was nothing for the wife and son in Mortonville. They lived in the parsonage, which meant that with him gone, their right to occupy the house was also gone, and though the matter had been handled with delicacy, the church trustees had nonetheless been dispatched to the parsonage to clarify the matter. The wife and son continued to attend church, sitting in the front row each Sunday as pastors from nearby parishes stepped in to give the weekly sermon. All of this Aaron knew from Mrs. Hagedorn, who was Catholic but knew what the Lutherans were up to.

Aaron made a point to avoid the son at school as well as the part of town where the parsonage was located, but one day when he was out taking a walk, the wife and son pulled up beside him and the two of them stared at him through the closed car window. Finally, the wife said something to the son, who rolled down his window.

"Where did they go?" she called across her son to Aaron.

Aaron crouched beside the son's window in order to see both of them. "I don't know," he said.

"Well, they'll end up in hell eventually," Pastor Gronseth's wife said, and his son nodded. They raised the window and drove off. The next day they too were gone.

On the morning of Tuesday, March 13, his forty-second birthday and his first alone, Aaron awakened early to the rare and disorienting sound of his telephone ringing. His first thought was to wonder not who was calling but why he had even installed a telephone. "The human voice carries entirely too far as it is," Mark Twain had said upon the invention of the telephone, words Aaron had repeated to Walter frequently in trying to explain the hostility that a ringing telephone invoked in him.

The origin of his phone antipathy lay in two incidents that had occurred twenty years earlier, when they were still living in Minnesota, the first while he was in college. As he spoke on the telephone to a classmate from his humanities class about a project on which they had been paired, he heard the distinct sound of a toilet flushing on the other end, a sound that, in retrospect, gave meaning to a series of grunts he had discerned earlier in the conversation. It had shocked him to know that while he and this stranger, Franklin (after the president), discussed a mediocre book about an environmental utopia, Franklin had been defecating. It was as if he had been in the bathroom with Franklin.

His distaste for the instrument deepened two years later, as he sat one afternoon in the Democratic headquarters in Moorhead, cold calling on behalf of a candidate whose virtues he could no longer recall. He spent a dull few hours reading from a script that encouraged others to join him in supporting Shirley Lund for state senate, and to amuse himself he invented stories about the people on the list: Marsha Norquist collected antique quilts; Jerold Harvey liked portly cats and bingo; Howard Hofbrau, plagued by a flamboyant name, had become increasingly retiring over the years.

As he dialed the final name on his list, Sadie Thompson, he could not move into the more liberating realm of fiction, for he had known a Sadie in Mortonville, Sadie Sandstrom, a woman in her eighties who painted customized landscapes, though what he remembered most was the way she dressed, in a tweed jacket and men's dress shirt with a loosely knotted tie. The Sadie who answered his unsolicited call that day was also elderly, her voice like chalk, dry and constantly breaking. She was crying, he realized, sobbing to be specific, and he wanted to hang up, but instead he asked whether she was okay.

"Yes, I'm okay," she said, "but my husband is dead."

"I'm very sorry to hear that, Mrs. Thompson," he said. "How did he die?"

"I can't tell," she said. "He was watching the set when I went out to the garden to pull up some weeds."

It registered then that her husband had just died, was lying before her dead even as they spoke. "You need to call an ambulance," he said, looking frantically at his script.

"I called them," she said. At that very moment an ambulance passed by the campaign headquarters on Tenth Street where he sat making calls, and he felt overwhelmed by the small ways that his life was attaching itself to this stranger's.

"What were you calling about, young man?" Sadie Thompson asked, and so he explained his mission, referring to the script as he spoke.

"Bob's a Republican," she said when he had finished, dropping her voice in deference to years of discussing her husband in muted tones. "I'm a Democrat, but we try not to fight about it. We just take turns voting. One year I go in, and the next year he goes, because otherwise what good is it? We'd just be canceling each other out."

Aaron wanted to explain that that was the whole point of voting, that an election was nothing more than a grand process of canceling one another out, but he did not have the heart to point out that the system she and her husband had utilized all these years lacked logic. He stayed with her on the line until he heard the sirens outside her house, and then he said, "I'm very sorry about your husband, Mrs. Thompson" and hung up.

That night at dinner, he told Walter the story. "I'm a stranger," he said at the end. "What right did I have to intrude like that when her husband was lying there dead?"

He was being intentionally dramatic, but Walter responded calmly. "Think of how she was feeling at that moment, sitting there with him. She was probably happy that you called. After all, she picked up the phone."

"She didn't pick it up thinking it was me," said Aaron. "She probably answered because she always answers the phone. Or maybe she thought it was the hospital calling or the police or their children."

"Or maybe she just needed to hear a voice," Walter said, in the soothing voice that made students and friends turn to him for advice and comfort, the voice that had had that effect on Aaron also, until one day it no longer did.

Aaron picked up on the fifth ring. "Hello," he said.

"Aaron?"

"Winnie?" He noted the time, 5:09, which meant 7:09 in Minnesota, far too early for Winnie to be up. "Is everything okay?" he asked. "You? The kids? Thomas?" and then, "Walter?"

She said his name again, sounding at once happy and sad. He had always loved her ability to evoke contrasting emotions and make them seem valid and compatible. "Everyone's fine," she said. "We're fine. Walter's fine." She paused as though expecting him to respond, but when he did not, she said, "He misses you. We all do."

"I miss you," he said. "But I like it here," and then, "I'm in San Francisco."

"I know. Walter told me." Winnie giggled. "My god, Aaron. All those gay people—it must be driving you crazy." They both laughed. "Happy birthday," she said and began to sing a raucous, operatic version of the song, attempting to conceal her terrible voice.

He pressed the telephone to his ear and covered the receiver with his hand because he did not want her to hear his sniffling. "Thank you," he said when she was done. "And thank you for calling. It's the best birthday present ever." He was embarrassed by how trite this sounded, how inadequate, and so he said her name again, whinnying it like a horse, "W-w-winnie," their old joke.

"He's miserable," Winnie said quietly.

"I'm sorry," Aaron said.

"Don't be sorry. He's difficult, my brother. Nobody knows that except us because he's only difficult with the people he loves, and we're it, Aaron. We are the only two people in the world he truly loves. You know that, right?"

He did know, though did not know how to respond to having it stated.

"Are you teaching?" Winnie asked.

"Of course," he said. "You know I love teaching. Besides, I have no other skills."

"That is not true," Winnie said sternly. "You're logical and well read, and, most important, you're the kindest person I know."

Aaron hid his pleasure with a laugh. "You've just hit on the most sought-after qualities in any job market. In fact, I was just reading a job description when you called." He cleared his throat. "Wanted: logical, well-read, kind person for six-figure position." She laughed, and he said, "Anyway, enough about me. How's business?"

"I just got back from my spring trip to Korea. That's why I'm up at this ridiculous hour—jet lag." Most mornings, Winnie rose at 8:52, which allowed her just enough time to drink one cup of coffee, shower, and drive across town in order to open at ten o'clock. "I've been awake since four," she said. "You know what I was thinking about? That time the three of us stopped in Hong Kong on our way back from Bali, and we stayed in that little hotel with the poster taped up in the foyer: *Seeking hairy Caucasian men*. Remember?"

"How could I possibly forget?" he said. "I spent half our stay trying to talk Walter into responding."

"Because you couldn't bear not knowing what they needed hairy white men for. Also, that was a rhetorical 'remember,'" she said. "Oh, and remember—rhetorical again—that short couple from San

Francisco we kept ending up on the elevator with? Every time we got on, there they were, dressed in matching outfits and grinning."

"Panama hats. White linen shirts with khaki pants."

"You forgot the matching fanny packs," Winnie said. "The first thing they said to us was 'you might want to exchange those purses and wallets for fanny packs. We're not in Kansas anymore.' They laughed hysterically, and when we didn't laugh back, they said, 'That's from *The Wizard of Oz,*' as though we weren't laughing because we'd missed the allusion, to which you replied, lying earnestly, 'I've never seen the film. My mother forbade all sorcery-themed cinema.'"

"Walter was so mad at me."

"At both of us," Winnie said. "He always thought I encouraged you."

"Which you did. Remember how he walked way ahead of us all the way to breakfast, and then he refused to eat anything? I don't know why he always thought that he was somehow punishing us by refusing to eat."

"That place had the best congee," Winnie said. "Oh, and when we got back to the hotel that afternoon, they were on the elevator again. 'I'm afraid we didn't introduce ourselves this morning,' the woman said. 'This is Robert.' And he said, 'This is Roberta,' and in unison they said, 'We're from San Francisco, the city by the bay.' Then Walter introduced the three of us, and when they pieced together that I was his sister, not his wife, and that you and Walter lived in Albuquerque, *together,* the husband said, 'We just love gay people, being from Frisco and all.' And you said—"

Aaron groaned. "I said, 'Yes, they're adorable, aren't they?' You know I only say things like that when you're around. I felt awful about it later because they were nice people, Robert and Roberta. They meant well, and I'd much rather deal with people who're maybe a little awkward about their good intentions than with those who lack good intentions altogether."

Winnie was still laughing—except, he realized, she was not. She was sobbing, the two sounds so similar that, on the telephone, there was almost no way to tell them apart, but he could because he knew

Winnie, knew that when she laughed, she gave herself up to it completely, but when she cried, she was always fighting to stop.

"I'm sorry, Winnie," he said, which could mean sorry he had left Walter or sorry he had not told her he was going or sorry he had made her cry; he meant all three. They had always ended telephone conversations the same way, with one of them saying, "Chow mein," a small joke at the expense of Walter, who ended all conversations with *ciao*. Aaron waited for Winnie to say it, but the line was dead.

By six fifteen, Aaron stood in the driveway, finger on the garage door opener, watching the door make its slow, stubborn descent. It took nineteen seconds—he had timed it—which meant that he spent an hour each month waiting for the door to open and close. Once, when he was already running late, it had rolled off its tracks. He'd considered leaving it like that, halfway down, and going off to work. He would have, but he knew that the Ngs would terminate his lease, so he knocked on their door, and Mrs. Ng, whom he rarely saw but whose angry voice he knew well, came out with a hammer and screwdriver and expertly maneuvered it back on track.

It had rained throughout the night. He heard the *thwomp* of sneakers on wet pavement behind him and turned with his finger still on the control, expecting the elderly Chinese woman who walked her portly Pekingese in her robe, but it was a white woman with a Saran Wrap–like scarf binding her hair.

"I found you," the woman called out cheerfully as she stepped toward him and raised a gun. She looked just like his mother, or rather, what he imagined his mother must look like now. Behind him, the garage door jerked up and down like a beast in its death throes, but he could not let go of the button, could not stop thinking, *My mother hates guns,* as if a person could disappear for twenty-four years yet stay the same.

"I've been waiting all night, you rascal," she said, her finger moving against the trigger.

A stream of water hit his tie, the tie Walter had given him, and splashed his neck. It was cold, and he was alive, and the woman was not his mother. He gasped.

"I got you," she cried out as the garage door bounced once more before the opener slipped from his hand and broke open on the pavement. Aaron fell to his knees. "Are you okay?" she asked.

He looked up at the woman towering over him who had stepped out of the mist and shot him with a water pistol—a deadly looking water pistol—on his birthday. He saw now that she resembled his mother in only the most superficial of ways, a fleeting impression suggested by height and age and big bones. Her name, he learned later, was Agnes Nyquist. She was sixty-six, his mother's age, and had moved to San Francisco from Council Bluffs, Iowa, when she was thirty-four. But before he knew any of this, she was a woman offering him her hand, saying, "Dustin, let me help you up."

"My name is Aaron," he said. "Aaron Englund."

"No," she said, insisting. "You're Dustin. It took me two days to find you. You're my next target." She reached into her purse and brought out a photo of a man who was tall and thin. His hair was blond, and he was holding a small dog.

"That's not me," said Aaron. "I don't even like dogs."

"Oh dear," said the woman. She compared Aaron to the man in the photograph and seemed to accept that it was not him. "I'm sorry," she said. "I'm trying to win the prize."

"What prize?" he asked gently.

"I'm competing in StreetWars," she said. "I'm one of the last assassins alive, but this really puts me behind."

"Perhaps you can explain StreetWars to me," he said. "I've never heard of it."

"It's simple," she said. "Everyone's an assassin. We're given the name and photo of another assassin, and we need to hunt him down and shoot him with one of these." She held up her water pistol. "The problem is that someone else is trying to get us at the same time." She looked over her shoulder and back at him. "Actually, we're not part of the official StreetWars. We're a renegade group. A lot of us are retired or don't work regular jobs, so we've got all day to track each other. We don't give out addresses, so there's more research involved. And we make our own pot."

"Pot?" He pictured a band of unemployed and elderly stoners running amok in the city with squirt guns, but he found the image hard to reconcile with this woman standing in front of him, her Saran Wrap–like scarf still snugly in place.

"Winner takes all," she said.

"Ah. That kind of pot. How much are you playing for?"

She lowered her voice. "There were a hundred of us when we started, and we each put in $500, so that's—"

"That's $50,000," Aaron said.

"Yup," Agnes said. "And there are just eight of us left." She turned and looked behind her again, checking to see that she was not being followed. "I don't suppose I could use your facilities?" she said.

"What? My bathroom?" he said. "I guess that's fine. I don't usually have guests."

"I'm not really a guest," she said.

He bent and gathered the parts of the opener, snapped it back together, and was relieved to find that it worked. They did not speak during the nineteen seconds it took for the door to open. When they entered his studio, he showed her the bathroom and then banged around in the kitchen because he did not like to hear people urinating. She came out humming and thanked him. She had removed the scarf.

"I don't suppose you have any tea handy," she said.

"Handy?" he said. "No. I was actually on my way to work when you shot me."

"Coffee?" she asked hopefully. "It's a little hard on my stomach, but I'm usually fine if I mix it with lots of milk."

He looked at his watch. Assuming he took the bus and there were no delays, he had forty-five minutes before he had to leave. He began grinding coffee. While it brewed he prepared a plate of toast because it was the only thing he had that felt breakfastlike, but when he turned back around, Agnes Nyquist was asleep on his bed. He sat down on his only chair and thought about how exhausted she must be to fall asleep in a stranger's home. Then he thought about how he was forty-two years old, an age he had never seen his mother reach because she had left at forty-one. He did not even know whether she had reached forty-two, but he did not want to think about that on his birthday.

Instead, he called Marla to say that he would be late. He did not tell her why because he did not want her gossiping about it and because already the events in the driveway seemed absurd, almost slapstick, an effect that Agnes Nyquist's snoring presence underscored. As they were hanging up, Marla called out, "Wait. Will you be here by lunch?" and he said he thought so. He knew what her question was about. Marla had all their birthdays on file and was planning a lunch "surprise" party, at which he would be given a melting ice cream cake with blue and yellow frosting. He disliked both ice cream and frosting and always passed on the cakes, though he doubted that Marla noticed. She was fulfilling her notion of being a good boss and her love of ice cream. She was having her cake and eating it too.

21

"We were worried," said Katya when he finally arrived, which Aaron knew was their way of asking why he was late, but he said only, "No need to worry about me." What had happened in his driveway was not the sort of thing one told students. The fact of him alive in front of them, the victim of nothing more than a shot of cold water, would not alter the more compelling revelation of there having been a gun. Already, they believed that Americans carried guns as casually as everyone else carried cell phones. A week earlier, Bolor had quit her cleaning job after she found a pistol lying on the foyer table next to a stack of outgoing mail. The students had been shocked by her story, but Aaron said nothing, not knowing how to explain that it struck him as at once startling and mundane.

In Mortonville, nearly everyone had owned a gun. The guns were mainly for hunting, which meant that the men at the café talked about gun legislation as though the government wished to control their very right to eat. Occasionally, one of the young couples from the Twin Cities who kept a summer lake cabin nearby would get involved in the discussion, inserting statistics about gun violence or gangs, these arguments laying bare the divide between urban and rural. Most of the farmers would stir their coffee and keep quiet because they did not like to argue, but Harold Bildt would turn to the city folks and say something about his right to protect himself from the dangers that they had created in the city. Harold sold rifles at the hardware store, and sometimes, when Aaron's mother set his food in front of him, he would say, "I got new stock in. You should come over and pick one out."

"I appreciate the concern, Harold," his mother would reply, "but I wouldn't know what to do with a gun."

His mother always walked away when the conversation turned to guns because she said it made no sense to argue with Harold about them. "He's not going to change his mind, and I'm not going to change mine. In the meantime, we've got to keep being neighbors." Aaron knew his mother was right. There was a fine balance involved in living peacefully with people with whom you did not agree, and nothing changed the fact that Harold Bildt had been a good neighbor. If an appliance was acting up, he came over and fixed it right away. He let them run a tab, and early on when they could not make payments every month, he did not constantly bring it up as a way of keeping them grateful.

"You don't need to do anything with it," Harold called after her. "You just have it around in case someone gets funny ideas about how much money a place like this keeps in the till overnight."

"If someone wants the little I've got in the till that bad that they'd break in here for it, then they can have it. I'm not coming down to stop them."

That afternoon at the hippie café, Aaron told Bill what had happened in his driveway because he knew that Bill would not get so focused on the gun that he would be unable to listen to the rest of the story. When he got to the part about how he had turned around to find Agnes Nyquist asleep on his bed, Bill laughed. "What did you do?" he asked.

"I waited for her to wake up. What else could I do?"

Bill snorted. "Well, to state the obvious, you could have woken her up, maybe given her a squirt of ice water with her own gun."

"I don't know how to explain it, but she looked vulnerable lying there, like it was the first time she'd rested in days. Then, I went into the bathroom, and she'd made everything so neat, the towel folded perfectly, the bar of soap dried off."

"At least you didn't leave her there sleeping and go off to work," said Bill.

"Actually, I thought about it."

"Because she reminded you of your mother?" Bill said. Two days earlier, he had told Bill about his mother's disappearance and Bill had simply nodded, accustomed to stories like this. Aaron thought that maybe he had told him precisely because he would regard it as ordinary. "I can find her," Bill said. "Aren't you at all curious about where she got to, what she's doing, whether she's even alive?"

"I am not," Aaron said. He wondered whether this sounded like the truth. He wondered whether it was the truth. He knew that it was possible to push a thought so far away for so long that you did not even know whether you were lying to yourself. They drank in silence for a bit, and then Aaron said, "I have a picture." He realized that this made it sound like he was agreeing, which was not his intention. He was just talking.

"A picture's good," Bill said. "I need her name, her full name, date and place of birth, even better a Social Security number, and anything else you've got." Bill picked up his beer again, and just before he put it to his mouth, he said, "No charge, of course. Since we're, you know, friends." He drank loudly, as if embarrassed to have made this declaration, but they were friends, unlikely friends, but perhaps that was what friendship always was: two people met and, despite themselves, despite their own fears and oddness and bad traits, somehow liked each other.

"It's my birthday," Aaron announced. He meant to acknowledge the friendship also through this admission, but he realized that it sounded as though he were accepting the offer as his birthday due.

"Happy birthday," said Bill. They knocked glasses and drank. Normally, Aaron drank two beers while Bill consumed twice as many, but that afternoon Aaron drank four also. It was his birthday.

The next morning, as Bill stood smoking on the doorless balcony, Aaron handed him a piece of paper with the information he had requested, everything but his mother's Social Security number, which he did not know. During the night he had awakened with his stomach in knots and gone into the bathroom, where he stood over the toilet trying to vomit. When he lay back down, he finally acknowledged the truth: what he feared was learning that his mother had been living all these years in a town just like Mortonville, working at a place just like the Trout Café, which would prove what he had believed all along, that the reason she left was to be away from him.

"At the bottom I wrote two questions," he told Bill. "It's all I want to know—nothing else. I don't want addresses or telephone numbers or photos."

Bill unfolded the paper, his lips moving as he read through the information. Aaron could tell when he got to the two questions:

1. Is she alive?
2. Is she happy?

Bill looked up. "Happy?" he said. "How the hell am I going to know if she's happy?"

When Aaron was ten—almost ten—he fell into a coma that lasted two days, a coma that the doctors were never able to explain. It started on a Wednesday, after school. He went upstairs to do his homework in their apartment above the café, and when he did not come back down at four to eat a quick meal before helping his mother prepare for the supper crowd, she came upstairs and found him on his bed. When he awoke Friday evening, he did not remember arriving home from school Wednesday afternoon and drinking a glass of milk before climbing the stairs to his room, did not remember sitting at his desk and working out ten math problems (correctly) before going over to his bed to lie down. When his mother could not awaken him, she had run downstairs and across the street to Bildt Hardware, returning with Harold, who carried Aaron, wrapped in a blanket, down the back stairs to the Oldsmobile. Harold had offered to drive so that his mother could sit in the backseat with Aaron, but she had said no, so firmly that Harold turned without saying another word and went back to his store.

Aaron knew these details, the blow-by-blow account of what had happened, because his mother, hoping to force his memory, had described it all for him later, starting with the moment she entered his bedroom and called his name, shaking him harder and harder. As she spoke, he had closed his eyes and tried to visualize it, but he knew that the images in his head were not memories. "Finally I lifted your shirt," she said, "and put my finger inside your belly button."

He opened his eyes. "Why?" His mother knew that he could not bear to have his navel touched.

"I just wanted to be sure," she said.

"Sure of what?"

"That you weren't playing a game," she said, which made no sense because his mother knew he was not a boy who played games. "Now concentrate." He closed his eyes again and willed himself to recall the swaying of the car and the blanket like a cocoon around him, but he could not remember any of it. His mother always ended the story at the moment that she sent Harold Bildt back to his hardware store, which meant that he would never know what she had done as she drove the eleven miles to the hospital in Florence, whether she had spoken to him soothingly or even sternly—"I want you to stop the foolishness this minute, Aaron"—or whether she had not spoken at all.

The café had stayed closed while his mother sat beside his bed, waiting for the doctors to know something, waiting for him to open his eyes. When he finally did open them and took in his surroundings, she was there, sitting at the window, her head turned away from him so that she did not even know at first that he was awake. For several minutes, he had watched her stare out into the darkness as he tried to recall what had happened. He remembered walking down the alley to the café, stopping to feed the stray cat he called Clary that waited for him after school because Aaron always brought the cat leftovers from his lunch. The smell of tuna casserole and Clary rubbing himself against his legs—these were the last things Aaron remembered. Over his bed the nurses had stretched a length of string, on which cards were slung like tiny saddles. They were from his classmates, but when he read through them later, he could not reconcile the sentiments expressed—"Get well soon. We miss you!"—with the names printed after them, for these were the same children who rarely spoke to him and chose him last for their teams, even their spelling teams, though he was clearly the best speller in the class. On the table sat a pitcher of water, a vase with flowers, and a stack of books, *his* books. He turned back toward his mother, who was still staring out into the darkness, and whispered, "Mom," and then, "Mother." Neither sounded right, but she turned from the window, slowly, as though she had forgotten where she was, forgotten that he lay in a coma behind her.

Three doctors came in and stood around his bed, unsure what to say about the coma or his sudden recovery from it. "Welcome back, young man," said one of them finally, as though he had been on a trip. "What's the last thing you remember?"

"Clary," he said. "I was feeding Clary."

"That doesn't make sense," his mother said, not to him but to the doctors. "Clary is a family friend, but Aaron hasn't seen him in nearly three years. He's a dwarf," she added, as though it might be relevant.

"It's nothing to worry about," said the doctor who had asked Aaron what he remembered. "There's bound to be some confusion." He leaned in close and looked into Aaron's eyes with a small flashlight, then wrote something on a chart while one of the other doctors, a tonsured man named Dr. McFarley, fiddled with the water pitcher beside the bed before suggesting that the coma might have been anxiety induced.

All three doctors seized on this. "Is he under stress at school?" they asked. "At home? Anywhere?" Aaron lay in the hospital bed listening.

"His birthday's coming up," his mother said finally. "I told him he could invite only four friends. He looked upset. Maybe he feels bad about not inviting the others."

It was true that he had been upset, upset because he understood that *four* was not a restriction but a quota, even though his mother knew that he did not have four friends to invite. She glanced at Aaron, giving him the look that they had used to signal collusion against his father, a look that meant that his job was to play along. Later, when he was back home, she told him that the coma was a mystery and would always be a mystery and that sitting in the hospital talking about it would not have solved the mystery, that she had just wanted to get him out of there.

In the end, the three doctors agreed that the coma was probably anxiety induced. They told his mother that she needed to find a way to accommodate all of his classmates, so the afternoon of his birthday, she closed the café and the party was held there, amid the booths and tables. All of his classmates came, though Aaron did not know whether they came because their parents had made them or because the coma had temporarily elevated his status or simply because they were attracted by the novelty of having the café to themselves. He received twenty-eight presents, most of them reflecting the tastes and interests of the givers—rubber snakes and magic tricks, various wheeled objects, and lots of bubblegum—but only one book, from Vickie, the messy girl who loved reading almost as much as he did. He knew that she had read the book before giving it to him because there was a thumbprint on each page, although the smudges stopped twenty pages before the end. He wondered whether she had grown bored with the book or run out of time. It did not occur to him that she might have washed her hands.

In the year following the coma, his mother took him in twice for checkups. Both times the doctor said he seemed fine, that there was nothing to worry about. Still, he thought his mother did worry, and he took to making noise as he studied after school—dropping a book, stepping heavily from desk to bed—but later he decided that he had imagined her concern. There was no proof other than the comments from customers about how frightening the whole thing must have been for her, but their comments were not evidence of what his mother actually felt, and beyond taking him in for checkups, she said nothing. Over the years, when he thought about the coma, he thought about waking up in the hospital and looking around for his mother, how that had been his first response, and about seeing her there at the window, how he had wondered—but would never know—whether she was watching something outside in the darkness or just studying her own reflection.

*   *   *

The Ngs' arguments were intensifying, in frequency and in volume. Aaron did not have the courage to address the situation directly, to go upstairs, knock on their door, and stand there explaining that he could hear them, that he had been listening to them scream for three months now. He could not get by on so little sleep, which meant he would need to move soon. This was what he was contemplating as he and Bill sat in the café ten days after his birthday, having a beer though it was not yet two o'clock because classes had been dismissed early, after a jackhammer started up in the street outside the school.

"I found her," Bill said. He was actually well into his second pint.

Aaron did not reply. All around them people were writing essays, eating sandwiches, and talking loudly into their cell phones even though the café had a policy. Bill took an envelope from his coat pocket and set it beside Aaron's beer. It was small, like the envelopes his mother had put Mr. Rehnquist's rent checks in. Aaron recalled how she had placed the envelopes under Mr. Rehnquist's coffee cup instead of handing them to him directly.

"There was nothing in public records," Bill went on. "No tax documents or DMV trail. She doesn't vote or own property. I found a tax bill from 1983, unpaid. That was it. It was like she left that night and ceased to exist."

The envelope remained on the table. Bill finished his second beer, his face, which was always florid, becoming even more so. Three days later, on Monday morning, Aaron would arrive at school, where Marla would be waiting with poorly concealed excitement to announce that Bill was dead, that as he sat in his car Saturday night, conducting surveillance on a man who was cheating on his wife, he had suffered a massive stroke, his body eventually discovered by the very man whom he had been following, who would in this way learn that he was the focus of an investigation. "Can you believe it?" Marla would say, referring not to the fact that Bill was dead but to this strange final twist. Aaron would be one of five people at the funeral, and after the service, he would go home and open the envelope Bill had given him one week earlier, the envelope that currently sat, untouched, beside his beer.

Aaron pointed at Bill's empty glass. "Another?"

Bill nodded and pushed his glass toward Aaron, and Aaron got up and stood in line, ordered Bill's third beer, and brought it back to the table.

"I found the Gronseth guy easy enough through public records," Bill said, "so I called him. Said he hadn't heard from her in years, but he was pretty sure he knew where she was. He's a chatty guy."

They were both drinking fast. When you were drinking, you didn't need to talk. "Did you speak with her?" Aaron asked at last.

"No," Bill said. "That's not my business. I called and pretended to be working for the census bureau, just confirmed that she lived there." He reached over and tapped the envelope. "It's all here," he said. "Telephone numbers and addresses. I know you think you don't want it, but it's here. You can decide what to do with it."

"Okay," Aaron said. "Can I buy you another? Or maybe something to eat?"

Bill's glass was still half full, and Aaron could not imagine him eating beetloaf or quinoa fried rice. Bill looked at his watch and stood up. "I've got a guy I'm keeping an eye on. His wife's suspicious. He gets off work in a few, so I better get going."

"Bill?" Aaron called after him. Bill turned. "Thank you."

Bill nodded. "See you Monday."

"See you Monday," Aaron agreed, because there was no reason to think that he would not, and he picked up the envelope and put it in his pocket.

April

22

The grass around the bus was high, obscuring the wheels and even the black lettering on the side that announced the name of a school whose students the bus had once shuttled. Aaron supposed the school no longer existed, that it had been consolidated like those in so many small towns. He wondered whether there were still wasps living inside the bus but thought that Gloria had probably disposed of them after the attack, the way people put down dogs that were biters. He parked the car, an airport rental, got out, and slammed the door loudly, but no one came from the house to greet him. He shooed away three dogs that barked at him halfheartedly, climbed the porch steps, and knocked. After several minutes—during which he heard nothing from inside—the door opened.

It was his mother. She looked old, not simply *older,* for of course she was older, but old. It was not just one thing—wrinkles or jowls or bad teeth—but all of them combined, years of ignoring dentists and hairdressers and doctors, of ignoring the expectations of the world. During the three-hour drive from the Twin Cities, he had worried about numerous things, including how they would greet each other, so he was relieved when she said, "Hello, Aaron," stepped back, and motioned him inside.

The doilies were gone, but otherwise the room was as he remembered it. His mother sat down on the couch, leaning back into it. She did not fill the silence with small talk, did not ask about his drive up from the Cities, whether he had eaten lunch along the way or gotten lost or seen anything of interest. He was thankful for this. Of all the scenarios he had imagined, the one he dreaded most was the one in which his mother spoke to him with casual familiarity.

"What about Clarence?" he asked finally.

His mother laughed. "Clary? He's dead. He's been gone for a good while now."

He was not surprised to hear Clarence was dead. He had assumed he would be. "When did he die?" he asked. "How?" He did not ask his mother why she had laughed.

"You were like this as a boy," his mother said. "So serious. Always asking questions. You never had any friends because everyone was afraid of you."

"Afraid of *me*?" he said. It was he who had always been afraid: of his father and then of his father's death, the memory of his father somersaulting through the air and the watermelonish thwack of his head; of his mother's illness and the constant sound of her crying; of Miss Meeks and the other children; of being left alone. He had spent his adult life dismantling these fears, but he did not say any of this to his mother. She did not deserve to know who he was, who he had become. She had given up that right.

Gloria came in and rushed toward him, chattering nervously, asking the questions about his trip that his mother had not. It was not how he remembered her. In fact, everything about her seemed different. Usually one confronted the past and it shrank down to size, but when Gloria held out her hand to shake his, it was the size of a man's, her grip almost painful. Of course, she had been strong back then also. He recalled the way she had cracked walnuts open with her hands and then handed the flesh to his mother, shyly, while his mother talked about his father and cried. "Someday, you'll enjoy irony," Clarence had predicted. It was true. He had grown into a man who saw the world in terms of irony and symbol, who looked at these two women before him and thought of walnuts being squeezed together.

"I'm sorry to hear about Clarence," he said.

Gloria nodded. "He lived longer than the doctors ever thought he would," she said. "He fell out a window, you know."

"That's how he died?" Aaron said. He pictured Clarence tumbling through the air as his father had.

"Oh, no. I mean when he was a baby. Our grandfather lived with us. He used to pick Clary up and talk to him when he cried late at night, and sometimes he'd hold him out the window so the rest of us wouldn't be bothered by his fussing. But one night he dropped Clary. He was sure the fall was what made Clary little."

"Clarence told me that story," Aaron said. "After the wasps attacked me. Remember?"

Gloria nodded. "I made mustard compresses."

He felt foolish, for of course she remembered. She remembered everything connected to his mother. He saw that now. He had not seen it as a boy, but Clarence had, and so had his mother. It was why she had come here. *Sad Café Love,* he thought. It was better to be the *loved* than the *lover,* if better meant easier, safer.

"You know, Clary hated nearly everyone, but especially children," Gloria said. "I always thought it had to do with their size, but after you left that day, he told me he thought you might grow up to be 'more bearable' than most folks."

She laughed and Aaron found himself joining her. His mother did not laugh. Gloria was the one who had cracked open.

His original plan had been to show up unannounced. He imagined something useful coming out of the surprise, but he had changed his mind when he arrived in the Twin Cities the night before, once he was back in Minnesota and could feel how easily he might lose his nerve, how he might drive back and forth past Gloria's farm for an entire afternoon without ever pulling in. He needed something that would bind him to action, something beyond his own weakening resolve, so he took out the telephone number Bill had given him and dialed it from his hotel near the airport.

Gloria had answered. "Yut," she said, and he said, "This is—" and she said, "Aaron," as though she had been sitting there by the telephone waiting for him to call.

"Yes," he said. "This is Aaron," and then, not knowing what to say next, he added, "Her son," using the pronoun even though they had not yet mentioned his mother because his mother was all they had between them.

"I'll put her on," Gloria said. Her breathing was off, wheezy.

"No," he said. "Just let her know I'm coming."

"When?"

"Tomorrow," he said. "I'll be there tomorrow."

"All right, then," Gloria said. She did not say that his mother would be happy to see him or that they looked forward to his arrival. He appreciated the lack of pleasantries.

The hotel was not in an area conducive to walking. This he had learned during check-in, when he asked the woman at the front desk—her nametag said IRENE—what restaurants were in walking distance. She looked at him as though he were asking about strip clubs or how to obtain a sexual partner. The last time he'd stayed in a hotel was in Needles. He remembered the way Britta had regarded him as he signed in; he'd been too tired to operate a pen, unable to recall his address, the one in Albuquerque that he was leaving behind. Perhaps it was just the nature of people who worked front desks to act skeptical and uninterested, to make clear that hospitality had its limits.

"Walking distance?" Irene said. She slid a list of restaurants across the counter. The nearest was three miles away. She put an X beside two she thought might still be open at this hour. It wasn't even late, nine o'clock, still seven on his watch, which he had not moved ahead when the pilot suggested they do so just before landing. He was sure that he would not be in Minnesota long enough to make it worth the effort of losing and then regaining time.

He was not hungry enough to do everything required to obtain food: get back into the rental car, follow a map, enter a restaurant filled with people, some of whom he would need to interact with in order to procure a meal. Instead, he took his suitcase to his room and set it on the bed, sat down next to it, stood up and paced, and sat again. It was then that he had called Gloria's number, but when he finished talking to her, he still felt restless. He knew this had to do with the flight, on which he had occupied a window seat for four hours, his knees pressing hard against the seat in front of him. Despite his long legs, he always requested the window. He had come to flying as an adult and hated it, hated especially the moment when the plane veered onto the runway and he could see the long expanse of tarmac before him. The engines revved, the plane lurched forward, faster and faster, while he considered the sheer impossibility of it all. Walter, by contrast, got on a plane, took out a book, and began to read, as calmly as if he were in his study at home. Aaron supposed Walter's calmness should have made him calmer, but it never had. The only thing that made him calmer was staring out the window with a steady focus that kept the plane moving down the runway and into the air.

He left his room and began walking briskly up and down the hallways of the hotel. Until San Francisco, he had never lived so close to strangers. It both shocked and impressed him to know that people did not alter their behavior around the fact of this proximity. The Ngs continued to scream their discontentment day after day, night after night, despite the fact that he, a stranger, lay below them, while behind each door of this hotel, there were televisions on too loud, children crying, even a dog barking. He did not understand people who traveled with dogs. As he paced, he heard other sounds, private sounds: gas being passed, a man saying, "I'm ashamed to even know you," people moaning. In room 208, a woman panted the word *bigger* over and over in a rhythmic, unsettling way. It seemed an impossible demand.

On the landing between the second and third floors he discovered a vending machine. There was nothing in it that he wanted, but he bought two bags of pretzels, a bag of M&M'S, and Cheetos. Back in his room, he emptied everything into the ice tub and began to eat, going from the salty pretzels to the chocolate to the chemical flavor of the Cheetos. Finally, he washed the orange Cheetos powder from his hands and picked up the telephone again, dialing from memory. It was almost eleven, but he knew Winnie would be awake, stretched out on her *gerebog,* a coffinlike, wheeled rice chest from Java. It had taken four large Samoan men to get it into her living room. When they set it down, they were coated with sweat and collapsed onto it, filled with admiration for its solidness. At night after everyone went to bed, even the dog, Winnie lay atop the *gerebog* reading, for though she loved Thomas and her boys deeply, she said that part of maintaining that love was knowing to end her day alone.

Aaron listened to the phone ringing, imagined her resting her book across her stomach as she reached for it. Then, "Hello," she said, right into his ear. She sounded tired, and he wanted to hang up, understanding his own selfishness. She said hello again, and when he still did not reply, she said, "Aaron, is that you?"

"Winnie," he said. "I'm here. I'm in Minnesota." And he began to sob.

It was Gloria who asked him to stay for supper. His mother had gone out to feed the animals, the three dogs as well as the geese and chickens they still kept. They had gotten rid of everything else, Gloria said. It was too much work for a couple of old spinsters. He had not offered to help his mother. He needed a few minutes away from her. He asked Gloria what he could do to assist her with the meal, but she said she had her own way of doing things in the kitchen and did not really know how to factor another person into it, so he stood awkwardly off to the side watching her.

"My mother doesn't help with the cooking?" he finally asked.

Gloria had taken a pint box of fish fillets out of the freezer and was running hot water over it. "I guess you like sunfish?" she said.

"I haven't had them in a while." He did not want her to think he hadn't had them because he didn't like them, so he added, "They're not easy to come by in San Francisco."

The truth was that he thought of sunfish as specific to his childhood, along with lutefisk, which his mother had served in place of meatballs as the Thursday special the last two weeks before Christmas. She prepared it with boiled potatoes and a white sauce of butter, flour, and water, and on the side was a sheet of potato *lefse,* everything on the plate as white as snow. Then she added string beans and lingonberry sauce, the green and red giving the plate a holiday feel. On those two Thursday nights, people lined up outside the café to get in.

"Why don't you serve lutefisk every night?" he had asked.

"That's not the way it works," she said. "Folks are only this interested because I don't serve it every night. That's human nature. Besides, I couldn't stand the smell of it every day."

His mother hated fish. Didn't Gloria know this?

"Your mother caught these sunfish last summer," Gloria said.

"My mother caught them?" he said. She had also hated fishing, though she had gone only once that he knew of, with his father when they stayed at Last Resort on their honeymoon. She had told him the story of that trip numerous times, and always she stressed that she had never been so aware of her life ticking away as when she sat in that boat waiting for a fish to bite.

"Sure," Gloria said. "All summer long she's out on the lake. Winter too. She's got a fish house that one of the neighbor boys hauls out with his truck after the lake's solid. He gets it all set up for her—puts in the stove, stacks some wood, drills a few holes, brings in her card table and chair. Every morning she packs sandwiches and a thermos of coffee, and I don't see her until bedtime most days."

Gloria worked a butter knife between the fillets. "Try not to judge her too harshly," she said now that her back was to him. She plugged in a frying pan and dropped a chunk of Crisco into it. As it melted, she dredged the fillets in flour and then lined them up in the pan. "Anyway," she said, "she's a different person."

At supper his mother dished up several fillets of the sunfish and ate them without comment. "How's work?" she asked him.

"Do you even know what I do for a living?" he said. He took a bite of his fish and thought about how much better it would be fried in butter.

"Yes," said his mother. "Actually, I do. I know some things about you, you know, about your life."

"How?" he said. "How do you know these *things* about me?" He knew that she was lying.

"Well," she said. "I shouldn't say how I know because that involves other people, and it's always best not to involve others, but I know you're a teacher."

She put another piece of fish into her mouth and swallowed quickly without chewing, which was what he did when someone served him onions and there seemed no polite way to avoid them. Gloria was wrong. His mother had not changed. She still hated fish. Except now she was a person who would pretend she did not hate fish, which meant Gloria was right. He felt his chin quiver, which meant he was about to cry. He did not want to cry, not here in front of his mother. He was no longer the same person either, and he did not want her to think he was, to think he was still the boy who cried about everything. At a dinner party once a doctor had told him a trick she used to keep herself from crying when giving families bad news. She pushed out her jaw. He tried it, and it worked. He turned to Gloria and said, "Supper was very good. Thank you for cooking and for inviting me to join you."

"You were always so polite," said his mother. "That was another reason the kids were afraid of you."

"No, that's why they didn't like me," he said. "When you're polite to people who don't deserve it, they think you're mocking them."

"I think Aaron has lovely manners, Dee," Gloria said. "We're just not used to such things." She stood and began stacking the dishes, and Aaron rose to help her. His mother sat staring down at her plate, but Aaron took it from her and carried it into the kitchen. A few small bones from her fish were lined up and teetering on the rim.

"Aaron," said Gloria, "you'll stay the night."

It was after eight. He could not imagine leaving now, trying to locate a town big enough to have a motel. "Thank you," he said. "You're sure it's no trouble?"

"It's no trouble," said Gloria. "We'll put you in Clary's room." They heard his mother's chair scrape back from the table. She did not say good night.

*　*　*

It was just as he remembered, the shelves of books with their spines turned in, keeping their titles to themselves. He sat on the bed, Clarence's bed, and laughed at the memory of his young self advising Clarence to turn the titles outward. In the corner beside the desk, turned inward like a naughty child, was Clarence's wheelchair, the afghan that had covered his legs folded neatly across the back. Aaron rose from the bed and gripped the chair's handles, recalling how he had maneuvered it so carefully down the hallway while Clarence berated him for his clumsiness.

He could hear Gloria moving around the house, closing up for the night. His mother used to engage in a similar routine when he was a boy, a routine that had angered his father, who liked bedtime to be a fast transition into sleep. After checking the doors and windows, she would pause longest at the oven, staring at the dials, and then, still unconvinced, she would open the door and put her head inside. From his bed, Aaron had listened for these familiar sounds, even though the routine often ended with his father screaming, "It's off." Once, as his mother crouched before the oven, head inside, his father had come up behind her and pushed her in. Aaron had seen it happen. He was standing in the kitchen doorway, needing another glass of water, but he had crept back to bed with his empty glass.

His day had started in a nondescript airport hotel in Minneapolis and was ending in Clarence's bedroom. He imagined he would lie awake all night, trying to sort through everything that had happened in between. In fact, he fell asleep immediately. When he awakened— minutes or hours later—he moved from deep sleep to consciousness quickly, aware of something, a *presence* there in the dark. It was the sort of dark that seemed both vast and one-dimensional, and he stretched his hand into it, colliding with something hard—metal and rubber. It was Clarence's wheelchair, pulled up beside the bed.

In the iron ore mine when he was five, the Finns had pointed out stalactites, which he did not touch, though he had imagined how they would feel: cold and smooth and slick. He had thought of the stalactites when he laid his finger on Clarence's tusk. But had the tusk been slick? He could not remember, the tactile part of the memory simply gone.

How was it possible to lose part of a memory, for one of the senses to stop contributing? If he reached out into the darkness again, would his fingers remember how Clarence's tusk had felt in the seconds before Aaron said, "I love them," or in the seconds after?

Clarence had been crying. He understood this only now.

"Aaron," said a voice from the dark, "why are you here?" It was his mother.

23

She had awakened him like this once before, when he was five. Nearly five. It was New Year's Eve. His father had had to work the night shift, and he and his mother stayed up late watching television and eating popcorn with an ease that felt festive, neither of them saying aloud what they both knew: it was his father's absence that made it feel like a holiday. He did not remember falling asleep, but he woke up in his bed, the room dark, his mother beside him. "Welcome to the seventies, Aaron," she said. She smelled of alcohol, though she was not a drinker, and crackers. He recognized both as she leaned close to kiss his forehead, the latter an everyday smell that he associated with soup and upset stomachs, the former a rarer odor that occasionally wafted from his father's glass at the supper table. She remained there with him a long while, her breathing unsteady, her hand warm on his brow, before she stood and whispered, "Don't be afraid of the world." Years later he thought that she had been talking to them both.

"I'm not sure why I'm here," Aaron said. "All these years, I've never tried to find you." He could not see her face or gauge her reaction. Maybe that had been her plan all along—to wait for darkness, believing it would make them both braver. "When I thought of you, I sometimes thought of you alive and other times, dead." Or maybe she had awakened him from the fog of sleep in order to have the upper hand. "But mainly I didn't think about you." Only then did he consider that she had no plan, that she had gone to bed, expecting to sleep, but the need to talk had overwhelmed her.

She did not respond, which unnerved him, though he recalled from his childhood this manner of listening that involved silence. It was not particular to his mother. He was the one who had changed, who had come to believe that a person had to say he was listening in order to be listening.

"Walter always felt I should look for you," he went on, filling the silence. "But that was Walter."

It was the first time he had referred to Walter. He decided that he would provide no clauses or parentheticals to establish the details of his life, to explain who Walter was, who *he* was. He would not make it easy for her.

"How did you and Walter meet?" asked his mother, surprising him.

"In the café." He took pleasure in revealing that Walter was someone for whom she had once cooked. He did not explain the rest of the story, how he had met Walter again after she left, how they had come to live together and be lovers. Let her wonder.

"So you're a homosexual," she said at last.

He had always hated the word *homosexual,* which tended to be used by those uncomfortable with the compactness of *gay,* those requiring just a few more syllables. "Well, yes," he said. "I believe that's been established."

"It was Walter," she said.

"What was?"

"Walter was the one who told me things about you—that you were a teacher, that you were good at it, that you had moved to San Francisco."

"You talked to him?"

"No," said his mother. "He wrote to me."

"When?"

"After you left." She sighed. "But also once before that. Maybe ten years ago. You had just moved to New Mexico, and he wanted me to know that you were fine, that you were a good teacher and a good person. I still remember what he wrote: *Aaron's students love and respect him. He's great at what he does. He is a compassionate human being.*"

"Did you write back to him?" he asked.

"No. What would've been the point? He didn't write because he wanted to make me feel better. He wrote because he was angry at me."

"Why?"

"Oh, Aaron," she said, sounding sad and wise and like a mother. "He wanted me to know that you didn't need me, that you were just fine, that you had managed nicely without me. He didn't say that the two of you were—you know—but I could tell because he was just so angry." Aaron did not know what to make of this, how to reconcile what his mother was telling him with the way that Walter had always talked to him about his mother, patiently, as though Aaron were a student in need of his advice.

"Did you come here to Gloria right away?" Aaron asked, even though he knew the answer. What he wanted to know—what he was trying to bring the conversation around to—was why she had left.

"It's not like that," his mother said. "Why does everything have to be about that?"

"About what?" he said, not understanding her response or the irritation in her voice.

"About"—she paused and even her pause sounded mad—"about love."

The afternoon that he opened the envelope Bill had given him and looked at his mother's address, he had not recognized it as Gloria's. He had gone to Bill's funeral that morning and then to the hippie café to drink several beers in his friend's honor, and though he was not drunk, he thought that the funeral and the beer explained what he did next: he dialed the telephone number for Charles Gronseth, which Bill had also included. Charles Gronseth picked up after just two rings, and when Aaron identified himself, there was silence and then Charles Gronseth said, "Just a minute, please," and Aaron heard him say to someone, his wife he supposed, "It's a client."

Bill had told him that Pastor Gronseth was no longer a pastor. He was just Charles Gronseth, married for the third time and living in Detroit Lakes, Minnesota, where he sold insurance, successfully Aaron imagined, for Charles Gronseth had always been good at talking, at making people afraid of the unknown.

On the other end, Aaron heard footsteps, a door closing. "What a nice surprise," said Charles Gronseth. "I thought you might call." His voice was hearty, but the two statements contradicted each other: one could not be both surprised by a call and expecting it. Charles Gronseth was nervous, which made Aaron feel oddly better.

"I hear you're selling insurance?" Aaron said.

"Aaron, let's cut past the small talk," Charles Gronseth said. "You're calling because you want to know about your mother. I told everything to that detective, but I guess it still doesn't make sense to you, so let me explain it one more time." He paused. "And then I'm going to ask you never to call here again."

Aaron felt a shot of rage, but when he spoke, he said only, "Fine."

"Being a pastor is a very lonely thing," began Charles Gronseth. "Everyone comes to you with their problems. They tell you about themselves, about their marriages and children, their disappointments and failures and weaknesses. And your job is to listen, to offer advice and encouragement, to tell them to pray. But who does the pastor talk to? Nobody wants to hear about his problems. They don't want to hear that he and his wife sleep in separate rooms, that they keep their cutlery in separate drawers because they can't bear the thought of their mouths touching the same thing. And your mother was lonely also."

"I know that," Aaron said.

"She didn't think of me as a pastor. We just talked like two regular people. I understood her. We understood each other. At least, that's what I thought. I thought we were running away together, to be together. I thought we were in love."

"Love?" Aaron said. He was not expecting the conversation to involve love.

"Yes," Charles Gronseth said. "I guess that sounds silly to you. It certainly sounds silly to me now. I've had a lot of years to think about it."

"Whose idea was it to, you know, run away?"

"It was your mother's, but only because it occurred to her first.

Believe me—I was more than willing. Then, it turned out that she was just using me."

"Using you how?" asked Aaron.

"To get up her nerve, I guess. You know how it is. You realize that you need to do something, but you don't always have it in you to do it on your own."

"So you used each other," Aaron said, not defending his mother but stating what seemed obvious.

Charles Gronseth laughed, a bitter laugh. "I suppose we did," he said. "My wife and I were barely speaking. I woke up one day and realized that my son had become just like her—petty and complaining. When you live every day feeling disappointed, it gets harder and harder to go about your daily duties, to pretend that you know about God and forgiveness and love of any sort, human or divine."

"And my mother?" said Aaron.

"Your mother understood these things." He paused. "She was a very unhappy person."

"I know that," Aaron said. He did know it. He did not need Charles Gronseth to tell him. "I guess what I really want to know is about that night. Because the last time I saw my mother, she was sitting in the booth with you the way she did every night, looking like she was going to stand up any minute and go to bed and then wake up and do it all over again the next day." His voice broke, and he stopped.

"I can tell you about it, about that night," said Pastor Gronseth, "but it will only be my perspective. Okay? Because what I've come to accept is that we can never know another person's mind."

"Of course," said Aaron by way of agreeing.

"We left at midnight. I'd snuck my suitcase over to my office earlier that day, and your mother picked me up in the alley behind the church. We got to Gloria's around three. I drove, but I didn't know where we were going. I just followed your mother's directions. She got out of the car and told me to wait. It was so dark, and the only radio was one of those fire-and-brimstone programs, preaching to the sorts of folks who are up at that hour, people who're feeling miserable and sorry for themselves and lost. I remember wondering whether this radio preacher would ever imagine that a fellow man of the cloth was out there listening to him at that very moment while he waited for the woman he'd just run away with.

"After maybe twenty minutes, Gloria came out. I rolled down the window, and she put out her hand, so I shook it. She told me that your mother was staying, that she had nothing more to say to me but that the car was mine if I wanted it. 'I've come for her suitcases,' she said. I sat out there maybe another hour. Eventually all the lights in the house went out again, and I finally realized how it was."

"And that was it?" Aaron asked.

"That was the last time I saw your mother. You know she cried the whole way there. I kept asking if she was okay. She said it was the first time she'd cried in years."

"Why was she crying?" Aaron asked.

He knew that he wanted Charles Gronseth to say that his mother was crying because of him, but Charles Gronseth said, "I don't know." Aaron heard a door open on the other end of the line and Charles Gronseth say, "Sure, honey. Be right there," and then he heard the door close.

"You didn't ask why she was crying?"

"I didn't ask, no. Maybe I was afraid she'd say she was crying because she could see it was all a mistake. There was one thing she did say that I thought about a lot. Still do. She told me that when you lose the ability, the desire, to make your life interesting, then maybe it's not worth staying alive anymore."

"You think my mother was going to Gloria's to kill herself," Aaron said.

"I don't know." Charles Gronseth sighed. "I better go now. My wife needs me."

"Do you still believe in God?" Aaron asked. He did not know why he asked, except that it seemed a way to know who Charles Gronseth was now that he was no longer Pastor Gronseth.

There was a long silence on the other end, and finally Charles Gronseth said, "I don't go to church much anymore, but I guess I still believe. I just find it easier to believe when it's not my job to make sure other people believe also."

* * *

"You do know that Gloria loves you?" Aaron said, but his mother was silent. "Of course you know. It's why you came here. It's also why my father hated her, isn't it?"

"Your father," she said, "hated everyone. Did you know that? Do you remember that about him?"

"I remember that he didn't like me." Even after all these years, he could not bring himself to say *hate*. "I remember that everything I said or did made him angry."

"Yes," said his mother. "I thought that's why you'd come."

"What do you mean?" said Aaron.

She sighed. "What do you remember about that night?"

"What night?" he said, though he supposed she meant the night she disappeared.

"The night before the parade," said his mother. "We never talked about it, and I could never tell whether you remembered, but I always assumed you must."

"No," he said. "I don't know what you mean."

"You don't remember being in the closet?" Not waiting for him to answer, she added, "Because it's all I think about some days." He heard her tap the armrests of Clarence's wheelchair. "I'm glad you don't remember," she said at last, stood and rolled the chair back across the room. "Good night, Aaron," said his mother.

He wanted to call out to her, "Tell me about the closet. Tell me everything," but the door creaked open and then closed, and he had said nothing. He listened to her padding down the hallway, not hesitating or bumping against things because she knew this house. She'd lived here longer than she'd lived anywhere else.

He tried to lull himself to sleep, as he often did, by repeating the last line of his favorite Wallace Stevens poem, *It can never be satisfied, the mind, never,* and when this did not work, he rose, put on his pants, because it seemed wrong to walk around a stranger's house in his briefs, and made his way down the hallway to the kitchen. There, sitting in the glow of the stove light, was Gloria, wrapped in a puffy robe. She did not look surprised to see him. He was relieved to be wearing pants.

"Can I make you something?" she said. "Tea or hot milk?"

He shook his head. She gestured toward the other chair with one of her large hands, and he found himself staring, as he had while he watched her cook, the fish fillets tiny in her hands, and again during supper, as she wielded her cutlery and reached for the carrots. "My feet too," she said, because she had noticed his staring. She held up her right foot, but he could not see it properly in the dim light.

"What happened?" he asked.

She shrugged. "A couple of years ago they just started growing. They ached, so I thought it was arthritis maybe, until my shoes didn't fit anymore. Your mother wanted me to go to the doctor, but I waited until there wasn't a shoe left in the whole house that I could still get on."

"What did the doctor say?" He was trying not to sound horrified.

She shrugged again. "It's rare."

"I would imagine so," he said, and Gloria laughed.

"Your mother told me you had a sense of humor."

His throat tightened. He wanted to pull his chair up close and demand that Gloria tell him everything his mother had ever said about him. Instead, he nodded in a way that invited her to continue the story. She waved her big hand in the air dismissively. "Something was pressing on my pituitary gland," she said, "which caused the growth, like I was right back in puberty. It's under control now. The doctor monitors it. I get measured once a year. I haven't had any new growth in over ten years."

"So it's"—he raised his hands, let them drop—"it's not serious?"

"I'm still here. Dee always gives me a list of questions to ask the doctor, but I like knowing just what I need to know and nothing more." She hesitated. "It started right after Clary died, so I thought it was my imagination at first, some psychological thing. That probably sounds silly."

"It doesn't," Aaron said.

"I'm just glad Clary wasn't around for it," Gloria said. "He hated giants." She and Aaron laughed together, and then she sipped twice from her cup and studied the clock on the wall. "That thing just keeps losing time," she said.

"Gloria, does my mother ever talk about my father? About, you know, what happened the night before he died and the closet?" He was making it sound as though he remembered that night also, but he did not think he was being dishonest, not exactly. He had told his mother that he did not remember, which was true, but as he had lain there, listening to her nervous breathing so close by, a memory had overwhelmed him—a memory of her breathing, panting really, in a small, dark space beside him, the smell of urine and wet wool rising around them.

"When you and your mother visited that summer," Gloria said, "you came down the hallway and stood in the doorway of the front room. You were eavesdropping on us. Do you remember that?"

He nodded. "You were cracking walnuts with your hands, and she was talking about my father," he said. "But I was sure that neither of you saw me."

"Your mother, no, but I knew the sorts of tricks my brother was fond of. I knew he'd send you out to spy. He was very upset about the visit. He didn't speak to me for two days before you and Dolores arrived."

"Because he didn't like visitors?"

"There was that." She fiddled with the belt of her robe. "But he was especially upset that it was your mother coming."

"He was jealous," Aaron said, aiming for matter-of-factness, and Gloria coughed and cinched her belt tighter.

"I guess something like that," she said. "Anyway, what you heard that day, about what your father said? I was very sorry you heard that. Clary was sorry also."

"It's such a strange thing, memory," Aaron said. "I mean, I'm sitting here with you thirty-five years later, and I remember everything about that visit, everything Clarence said to me, even though I didn't understand half of it. How does that happen? Why does our memory cling to certain things and just discard others?"

"I don't know," Gloria said. "I can tell you exactly what your mother was wearing the first time I saw her, but I have no idea what the weather was like the day I got married."

"You were married?" Aaron said.

"It only lasted a day. He was a nice enough man. His name was Donald, and he sold tires. That's how we met. He worked at a place outside Fargo. I was bringing a couple of my father's spring lambs into the lab at the university there. They'd died suddenly, and my father wanted some tests done, just to make sure there was nothing to worry about. I picked up a nail outside of town, and the back tire went. I had to unload both lambs onto the road to get to the spare. I must have been quite a sight, changing a tire with a couple of dead lambs looking on."

They both laughed, and Aaron recalled with a twinge that he had been put off by Gloria as a boy, had not liked the way she doted on Clarence, cutting his meat and patting his head. She was a good person, kind, and he felt ashamed that he had not recognized this then.

"And so you loaded up the sheep and limped over to his tire shop on your spare, and while he fixed your flat, you fell in love?" he said.

"Well, he did fix my tire, but the marriage was really just a matter of convenience, maybe not for him so much—men get away with a lot more—but I was twenty-six, and people were starting to talk. He was impressed that I'd changed the flat by myself, and there was something nice about that, about looking at another person and seeing myself reflected as smart and capable. So when Donald started driving out here on Sundays, I didn't object. It was the first time anyone had pursued me, and there was something nice about that also." She sounded embarrassed.

"I was tired of my life here, tired of the farm, of taking care of everything and having all the attention go to Clary. The truth is, I was tired of Clary and of my parents' guilt and sadness. And Donald really was a very decent man." She tapped one of her giant fingers on the table to emphasize this, to let him know that there had been nothing wrong with Donald. "I thought maybe it could work somehow, so a couple of months later we eloped. We drove down to Minneapolis, got married, and went to a ball game. That was our honeymoon. We were staying with his cousin out in Stillwater, but that night when we got back from the game . . . well, afterward, I realized it wasn't for me."

It took Aaron a moment to understand what Gloria meant: she had had sex with Donald and knew she could not do it for a lifetime, could not do it even one more time.

"The next morning I woke Donald up and told him I just wasn't cut out for it. I didn't go into the specifics because I'd heard men feel bad about such things. He wasn't happy about it, but he didn't try to stop me. I walked to a bus stop, got on the next bus, and rode until I liked the look of things. I got off, found the job with the electric company the next day, and that's where I met Dolores. She started a week after me."

"Did you ever hear from Donald?" Aaron asked.

"No. As far as I know, we're still married, but he's surely passed by now. He was an older gentleman, almost fifty when we got married."

"I could look him up on the Internet," Aaron said. "Put in his name and see what comes up."

"Thank you," Gloria said, "but I'd rather not know."

Aaron nodded. He thought he should say good night, get some sleep so that he could wake up in the morning, which was only a few hours off, and leave. Gloria took her cup over to the sink, where she spent several minutes washing it, several more rinsing it. Next, she opened a cupboard and took down two plates and retrieved a bag from the bread box. He did not know that people still had bread boxes. Inside the bag were homemade caramel rolls with walnuts. She put a roll on each plate and set one in front of him, the other in front of herself.

"When your mother arrived that night," she said, "I didn't know she was coming. You might not believe that, but she just pulled into the yard and knocked on the door. I went out and got her suitcases from the trunk, sent him on his way. I didn't know he was a pastor, not then. I figured it all out later, that he believed they were running away together, to *be* together. I guess Dee let him think that, let him burn his bridges. When I leaned in the window to tell him I had everything and to thank him for bringing her, he started crying, just sat there smoking a cigarette and crying. I guess he was accepting the truth, that she'd just needed—" She stopped abruptly.

"A way out," Aaron said, and Gloria nodded.

"I didn't ask any questions, Aaron. I should have. I should have asked, first thing, where you were, but I didn't. I've never pushed Dee on things, and I guess that's why she's stayed. Sometimes, she feels like talking, and she does, talks and talks, but that's rare. If I ask her a question point-blank, she gives me the silent treatment for days. So I don't ask. I've made it easy for her, too easy, and I'm sorry about that."

He thought about what Charles Gronseth had said on the telephone just the week before, that his mother ran away because she had lost the ability to make her life interesting. "She came here to die, didn't she?" he said.

Gloria's hands were stacked like baseball mitts on the table in front of her. "Maybe something like that was on her mind, but I don't know whether she was thinking about, you know."

"Killing herself?" Then, because he felt he had to know, he asked, "Did she try?"

"There are other ways to stop living," Gloria said carefully.

"Meaning?"

"She never tried anything specific, Aaron. Still, I can't help but think she came here because she was ready to . . . to give up, I guess. She was tired of doing all the things that people do to keep living— working, paying bills, making decisions."

"Taking care of her son," he added.

She nodded. "Yes, but also she didn't want you to go through that."

"Through what?" he said. "Through wondering where she was, whether she was still alive? Or through wondering, every day for years, whether I was the reason she'd left? What, exactly, didn't she want me to go through?"

"I'm sorry," Gloria said. "Clary kept telling me I needed to be harder on her, but I wouldn't listen. I just thought he didn't want me to be happy. Anyway, the truth is that having Dee here hasn't made me happy, or her less unhappy."

"Has it at least made you less lonely?" he asked. "Because being around people you love, even those who don't love you back the same way, sometimes that can at least make you less lonely." He paused. "Though usually it makes you more lonely."

"You were wise as a boy also," Gloria said. "Just seven years old, but you understood Clary so well. You had an instinct for people even then." Gloria did not want to talk about her feelings for his mother, and that was fine. He was not even sure that talking about the past helped. Maybe it did allow you to clarify things so that you could move on. Or maybe it just kept pulling you backward. "I told her plenty of times that she needed to find you," Gloria said, "but I should have insisted."

"Did you know that Walter wrote to her?" he asked.

"Not the first time, but she showed me the letter that came last month."

Gloria picked at the nuts on her caramel roll, and he thought again of her cracking walnuts on the couch beside his mother all those years ago. How strange it must be for her to have him here, a boy who had returned a man.

"I left him," Aaron said. "I left Walter."

Gloria nodded. "I figured as much. You know, from how the letter sounded."

"Right after she disappeared, I moved in with a family in town, the Hagedorns. I don't know how I would have survived that year if they hadn't taken me in, but all I could think about was how to get away. I wanted to go to college, but she'd left just five hundred and two dollars behind in the bank for me. And then Walter came along. He gave me a home. He paid for me to go to college. He taught me everything. This life I have, who I am today? I owe it to Walter."

"Walter sounds like a fine man, but you had something in you, Aaron, something special. You made Clary laugh, and nobody ever made Clary laugh. You were a good, sweet boy, a smart boy. That much I know."

"Thank you, Gloria. I appreciate that, I do, but it doesn't change the fact that Walter made it possible for me to have a different life. And how did I repay him? I got in a truck in the middle of the night and disappeared. I haven't called or written. Nothing."

"Walter did the things he did because he wanted to," Gloria said. "People pretend otherwise, but they almost always do what they want to do. I let your mother stay because that's what I wanted. Anyway, I've learned the hard way what happens when you stay with someone out of guilt or feeling beholden. People do it all the time, sure, but they end up angry or bitter or worse, hating the other person."

"By the end, I felt like I hated Walter," he said quietly. "I kept a journal of all the things he did that drove me crazy. It was a way to make sense of it, I suppose, but also a way to see the evidence lined up, as my friend Bill would say, and to give myself permission to leave.

"Years ago, when we were still living here in Minnesota, I knew this woman who had three cats she loved more than anything, but she also had a husband who did not love the cats. They were always underfoot, he said, doing things—shredding his papers, peeing on his clothes, swiping at him every time he walked by. They didn't do stuff like that to her. One day he'd had enough, so while she was at work, he loaded the cats into his car, drove out in the country, and just left them there by the road. That night, when my friend got home from work and couldn't find them, she asked her husband if he'd seen them. He said no at first, but finally she got it out of him, what he'd done. She left him that very night. When she told me the story later, she said that every time one of the cats peed in his shoes or hissed, she wondered what it was about him that they sensed, so when he got rid of them like that, she was actually relieved because she finally knew what the cats had known all along.

"I used to wish Walter would do something like that, something so terrible or unjust or cruel that it made leaving the necessary thing to do. But that's the thing about Walter. He's a good person. All those years he did everything I needed, but the more he did for me, the more I started to hate him for it."

He was crying now, and he tried to stop himself by taking a bite of the caramel roll, but that only made it worse, his throat tight with his tears and the dryness of the bread.

Gloria nodded. "You wanted Walter to be wrong so you didn't have to be, but there isn't always one person who's right and another who's wrong. Sometimes—usually—it's not that easy."

Neither of them spoke for a long time, until finally Gloria said, "Here's what I know, Aaron. When your mother left, she wasn't thinking about you—for better or worse, she wasn't. She was thinking about herself. Maybe she was planning to end her life, or maybe she was trying to salvage it. I don't know which, but I do know that sometimes the most you can do is save yourself."

24

"Gloria," he said, "I'm sorry to ask, but I need to know about the closet, about what happened the night before my father died."

Gloria pushed her plate with the half-eaten caramel roll aside. "Are you sure?" she asked. "I'll tell you the whole story, but only if you're sure."

"I'm sure," he said. "Was that what she was telling you when Clary sent me out to spy?"

"She told me just part of the story that day, but when she came to stay, that's when she told me the rest, over and over until I was worn out from reliving it with her. Then, one day she just stopped talking about it. She hasn't mentioned it since."

"But you still remember what happened?"

"I remember every detail," Gloria said.

As Gloria told him the story of what had happened in the closet the night before the parade, he felt like he was watching a movie, a movie that he thought he hadn't seen before, except as he watched, he realized he had because he already knew what was going to happen just before it did. She began with their return from the Englund family vacation. In the week after he kicked the sitting-down Paul Bunyan, the three of them had maintained a truce that primarily took the form of silence. He remembered the silence, the way that conversation was tossed like a hot potato around the supper table, and the relief that he and his mother both felt when his father went back to work. He remembered his mother telling him that on Saturday they would be attending the

SummerFest Parade, in which his father would be participating on be-half of the police department. It would be Aaron's first parade, but his mother said that she liked parades and thought he would like them also.

"You'll see," she'd said. "There's something nice about standing on the sidewalk and watching everything move past you, floats and marching bands, clowns and regular people."

"Why?" he asked. He meant why were all these people going to line up in the street and march past them? Why was his father going to join them? What his mother described made no sense.

But she thought he was asking how she knew he would like it, and she replied with something unworthy of her, something about all chil-dren liking parades. "Right after the parade," she added, whispering but excited, "everything will change."

The next afternoon his mother produced his suitcase, just as she had that first night in the cabin after the standing-up Paul Bunyan. It was neatly packed and almost full. "You can choose three more things to put in," she said, "but you need to do it quickly, before your father gets home."

"My father doesn't know about my suitcase?" he asked.

"Not yet," said his mother. "It's a surprise for tomorrow, after the parade."

She made the finger-to-lips gesture that meant this was their secret and then stood by as he hastily chose a blue sweater vest, a book about a boy called Silly Billy, and his stuffed giraffe, whose neck he liked to sleep on. The giraffe was a gift from some people his mother had once worked for. She closed his suitcase, which was not easy with the giraffe neck, and once this was done, she set it in the closet and told him not to touch it.

"When your father gets home," she said, "I want you to stay in your room." He said that he would, and she pulled his door shut behind her.

When he heard the squad car pull into the driveway, he went to the closet and checked on the suitcase that was a secret from his father. He could hear his parents in the kitchen, the low rumble of their voices, and then his father yelling and the sound of glass breaking. His father did not like to be talked to when he first got home.

His mother had said only that he was to stay in his room. She had said nothing about not opening the door. He opened it quietly. "Where?" he heard his father say. "You have nowhere." His mother responded, her voice too low to hear, and just like that Aaron found himself out in the hallway, pulled steadily toward the kitchen, where things were being said that he was not meant to hear.

His mother stood at the stove heating something in a pot, and his father stood nearby, still wearing his uniform, hat on his head, holster on his hip, handcuffs at the ready. Aaron stood to the side of the doorway, for the trick was not to be seen, or else his father would widen the scope of his anger to include him, and that he could not bear, not with the memory of his father's hand on his head, ruffling his hair in front of the sitting-down Paul Bunyan, the other parents applauding what they called his pluck in standing up to the giant because people admired pluck.

Even though his mother's back was to him, Aaron could hear her clearly now. "I can't take it anymore," she said. "I just can't."

"I said, 'Where?'" demanded his father, but she kept stirring, and his father moved up close behind her. "I have a right to know. You're not going to your parents, so where? To that chickenshit brother of yours? To the dyke? Or maybe you think the Jews will be waiting with open arms?" His father laughed. "You could start a baseball team with the band of misfits you've got, Dolores."

His mother continued stirring, and his father grabbed the pot from the stove and dumped the contents onto the floor. It was stew.

"There," said his father.

His mother stood with the dripping wooden spoon in her hand. She still did not speak. "You're not going anywhere 'til that's cleaned up," his father said, his voice smug.

His mother crouched with a handful of paper towels and swabbed up the stew, but her calmness seemed to anger his father even more and he snapped open the refrigerator and began flinging food onto the floor until they were surrounded by a moat of broken eggs and mayonnaise, leftover hotdish and milk. He squirted mustard and ketchup on top, the colors creating a festive icing.

"Jerry," said his mother. "You're just making a mess for yourself."

"You want to see a mess?" said his father. He was panting. "Fine, you go ahead and leave, but Aaron stays with me. Then you'll see what a mess I can make."

His mother rose with the stew-filled paper towels and turned toward the garbage can. "Try to stop us," she said. "I'll call your friends at the station and have them escort us out of the house."

His father lunged, grabbing his mother and twisting her right arm behind her until she was bent over, her upside-down face peering at Aaron. He could see that it hurt, but his father yanked her arm higher.

"Jerry, please," his mother said, and his father stepped back, releasing her. "Let's go," she said, talking to Aaron now, and his father turned and saw him there. His mother walked fast down the hallway to his room, and Aaron trotted to keep up. She boosted him onto the bed and picked up his shoes, the shoes with which he had kicked the sitting-down Paul Bunyan. "They're getting tight," she said. She gripped his ankles hard and forced them onto his feet.

"My suitcase," he said.

"I know," said his mother, and she went over to the closet and bent in.

Aaron saw his father come in and move toward the closet. He could have called to her then. "Watch out," he could have said. "Watch out for my father."

Instead, he watched his father place his hands on his mother's buttocks and push her into the closet the way he had pushed her into the oven, as though he were Hansel *and* Gretel, and she the witch. Her head hit the wall, and his father scooped him up and dropped him inside with her. The door shut. He heard his father fumbling for the key that they kept above the door, fitting it inside the lock.

"Jerry," called his mother. She jiggled the knob and banged on the door.

Aaron heard his bed creak loudly as his father settled on top of it. And then they waited.

Eventually—Aaron was not sure how long it had been—they heard his father rise from the bed and leave the room. His mother spoke to him then, whispering, "He'll let us out. He will. He's just trying to teach us a lesson." She reached for his hand, but there in the dark he imagined that her hand was a snake or a mouse, not his mother at all. He pulled away, startled, and she did not try to touch him again. When his father returned, the smell of bacon and eggs came with him, wafting under the closet door. They could hear him setting things—a plate, cutlery, a glass—on the nightstand and the bed creaking again.

"Jerry, Aaron is hungry," said his mother. He had not said that he was hungry.

His father did not reply, but they heard his fork scraping, the sound of him chewing and swallowing, the glass knocking against his teeth each time he drank. His father belched, as he did at the end of every meal.

"What did you have?" asked his mother encouragingly. "It smells like bacon."

"Did I ever tell you my favorite bacon story?" his father said.

"Why don't you open the door and tell me while I clean up that greasy pan?"

"The pan is fine," said his father. He sounded relaxed, like he was enjoying himself. "Once the grease sets, I might spread some on a slice of bread. I'm going to need a midnight snack."

"I can make dessert," said his mother. "I'll make a crisp. We still have some of those apples left from the motel."

His father snorted. "And have him puke all over my arm again? Anyway, I have my own dessert," he said, and they heard him take another drink.

"Jerry," his mother said, "you know you don't like drinking."

"Actually," said his father, "I do like drinking, and this is a special occasion."

"What's special about it?" said his mother.

His father laughed. "How can you ask such a silly question?" he said. "First of all, do you spend most nights in the closet?" His father paused to take another drink. They heard the steady expulsion of his flatulence. "No," said his father. "You don't spend most nights in the closet, because you have a bed, and Aaron has a bed, but you don't care about that, about how lucky you both are to have beds."

"Jerry, are you drunk?" his mother said.

"I'm celebrating," said his father. "Tomorrow I'm going to be in a parade, and tonight I'm having bacon and eggs for supper, and I was just about to tell you my favorite bacon story. Don't you want to hear my story? Do you have something else to do?"

"No," said his mother. "I do want to hear it."

"It's short, but it's very funny. When I tell the story, I want you to laugh for once in your goddamn life. Okay?"

"Okay," said his mother. "Tell me the story, and I'll laugh."

"Okay," said his father. "It's about the Jews. Do you remember the first time I met the Jews?"

"Yes," said his mother. "You came by to pick me up. We were going out—bowling, I think." She paused. "What does this have to do with bacon, Jerry?"

"Well," said his father, "that's the funny part. You see, I brought a slice of raw bacon with me when I went to pick you up from the Jews. They probably thought I didn't know anything about Jews—they were snobby like that—but I had the bacon wrapped up in tinfoil in the glove compartment, and just before I went up and knocked on their door, I took the bacon out and rubbed it all over my hands, and when the Jews opened the door, I shook hands with them, both of them." From the other side of the closet door, Aaron heard his father laughing while beside him, his mother remained silent. "I don't hear you laughing," said his father. "Don't you get it? I had bacon grease all over my hands, and they didn't even know it. They just acted so polite and pleased to meet me."

His father grunted. "You see—not a damn shred of humor between the two of you." His glass kept clinking, but he did not speak again. Soon, they heard his deep snores on the other side of the closet door.

His mother wet herself first. When Aaron smelled it—a wild, frightening odor amid the smells of dust and wool and moth balls—he thought that it was his own bladder betraying him, even though he had been focusing on holding it in. He relaxed, a defeated letting go, and felt the sudden warmth of urine seeping across his thighs, pooling beneath his buttocks.

"Jerry," called his mother, "we need the bathroom."

His father rolled over heavily on Aaron's bed. "How am I supposed to sleep with all this racket?" he said, his voice thick.

"We need the bathroom, Jerry. Please."

After a very long silence, his father said in the same thick voice, "What if I can't live without the two of you?"

"You don't need to, Jerry," said Aaron's mother. "Open the door so we can all go to bed. In the morning, I'll clean everything up, and then we'll go to the parade."

"I don't think you understand," said his father.

"Understand what, Jerry?" said his mother. "Tell me."

Aaron heard his father moving around on the bed, heard him mumbling. "I don't think the two of you understand what a good life I gave you," he said at last.

The gunshot came immediately, an exclamation point on his father's words.

"My god," screamed his mother. She began to kick at the closet door, calling his father's name.

It was August, a humid month. The heat from their bodies was trapped in the closet with them and gave substance to the smell of urine and sour clothing and fear. Aaron could not breathe. It was like being in the iron ore mines, like being underwater.

"Aaron," his mother said, "ask your father to let us out."

"Can we come out?" Aaron whispered.

"Remind him about how you kicked Paul Bunyan," said his mother.

"I kicked Paul Bunyan," he said.

"He did that for you, Jerry," his mother said, but there was no reply, no sound at all from the other side of the door. His mother's sobs settled into a steady whimper, and the whimpers gave way to silence. Inside the closet and out, there was only silence.

* * *

Aaron awakened to the sound of birds. There were nests in the eaves above his window, which his father sometimes sprayed with the garden hose, blasting them loose, eggs falling to the ground along with bits of feather and twigs and dried grass. But new nests always appeared. Aaron never told his father about the new ones because he liked waking up to the cooing of birds. The closet was still dark, but the light beneath the door had changed. It was morning. His stuffed giraffe nudged his chin, though he did not remember taking it out of his suitcase during the night. His mother breathed steadily beside him, asleep on his leg.

He heard a key in the lock, and the closet door swung open. His father stood over them, haloed in light, still wearing his police uniform. His shirt was coming untucked, the belt hanging undone. His gun was snapped into its holster. Aaron's mother sat up, the smell of urine rising with her, a stench like gas station bathrooms.

"I thought you were dead," she said, her words breaking into sobs.

"I was just having some fun," said his father. "But as usual, you two don't get the joke." He laughed and stretched in a leisurely way, then brought his hand up over his nose. "Jesus, did you two shit yourselves? Get up and get changed," he said. "In five minutes we're leaving for the parade."

May–June

25

Aaron awakened at eight his first morning back. He had fallen asleep at eight the night before, a symmetry that might have comforted him, except twelve hours was a long time to sleep. Ahead lay a day of getting up and going to school, teaching and coming home. Each of these tasks alone seemed beyond anything he felt equipped to do, but he got out of bed and ate, cold, the rest of the spaghetti with butter he had made the night before, after he realized that he had no interest in going out to buy groceries, had no interest in anything.

When he walked into the school an hour later, his colleagues greeted him as if it were a normal day, as if he had not been gone for nearly two weeks, as if Bill were not still suddenly dead, THE PRIVATE EYE SCHOOL sign gone, Bill's students gone also. Aaron had been the only person from the school to attend Bill's funeral, which was held at Mission Dolores. It was easy to pick out Bill's sisters, one large and disheveled like Bill, the other tiny, both of them looking dazed. "Bill was such a joker," they said to Aaron when he went over to offer his condolences. Earlier, he had watched them approach the casket, holding hands and peering inside as though they expected Bill to leap up and scare them. "He had a delightful sense of humor," Aaron agreed, and they looked up at him like he was mocking them.

He walked into his classroom at precisely nine, which meant he was on time, strictly speaking, but the students had all arrived early, imagining he would be excited to see them. "Welcome back," they said.

"We've been looking forward to seeing you." He had taught them that expression right before he left.

He set down his satchel and tried to smile.

"How was your vacation?" they asked. Vacation was what he had told them—anything else, namely a mother he had not seen in almost twenty-five years, seemed too complicated.

"Fine," he said. "It was fine. Thank you. Now, let's get started."

He moved toward the board to write out phrasal verbs for review, but his legs felt weak and he detoured to his desk, where, he told himself, he would sit for just a minute, but his mouth was like a drain: as he talked about the difference between *put off* and *put aside,* his last little bit of energy flowed right out of him. When classes ended at one thirty, he was still sitting. He could see the confusion on their faces, which evolved into sadness over the following weeks as he continued to show up at nine, right at nine, with no time for pleasantries or questions, no time to help with college application essays or explain the best way to ask an employer for time off. When they straggled back from break late like everyone else, he said nothing, just sat at his desk at the front of the room, flipping through magazines that the former teacher had left behind.

After he left Gloria's farm, he had driven back to Minneapolis and straight to Winnie's house, where no one was home because no one was expecting him. It was Wednesday. They were at either work or school. There had been no plan. When he called Winnie from the airport hotel on Monday night, they had spoken for fifteen minutes, just long enough for him to stop crying and tell her about his mother, about how she was living with Gloria and had been all these years, about how Bill had found her and then died, about how he had booked a flight and gotten on a plane and now he was scared.

Winnie listened.

Right before they hung up, he said, "I'm so sorry, Winnie," as he had on his birthday, an apology meant to include everything, from the way he had left without telling her to the fact that he was calling, out of the blue and sobbing. He had taught his students that adding *so* in front of *sorry* made the apology stronger, more sincere, but as he listened to himself say these words to Winnie, now that he had treated apologizing as a matter of semantics, they sounded empty, disingenuous.

"I know," Winnie said.

"I better get some sleep. Big day tomorrow." He laughed.

"Wait," Winnie said. After a long pause, she blurted out, "I love you, Aaron." They did not usually say this to each other, and he tried to make the whinnying sound, but his voice broke, so he set the phone back on the hook without replying, then lay on the hotel bed and cried some more, sick with the realization of how long it had been since he'd said "I love you" to anyone.

For thirty minutes, he sat in his rental car outside Winnie's house. It was a cool, clear day, not unusual for Minnesota in April. Just hours earlier, he had awakened to the smell of bacon and eggs and Gloria's exaggerated cheerfulness, which meant that his mother was being difficult, for that was how couples worked, he knew, one always trying to offset the other's behavior.

"Is she still in bed?" he asked as he and Gloria sat down to eat.

"Yes," Gloria said. "But it's not you, Aaron."

He cocked his head to indicate that he knew better, and she said, "Well, of course it's your visit that's thrown her, but the way she is? That's not about you."

"Thank you, Gloria. I know that." He supposed he did know it. "But it's nice of you to say so." He ate some bacon, drank his coffee. "You know, after we finally went to bed, I still couldn't sleep. I started to think about the day we moved to Mortonville, how I woke up that first night in the Rehnquists' house, and she was gone. I looked for her everywhere. You know where she was? In the closet. I'm sure she heard me calling, but she didn't answer, yet when I finally opened the closet door, she seemed happy to see me. She invited me in. I sat on the floor, and we talked. She was in there almost every night that first year. I thought it was because she didn't want me to hear her crying."

"Maybe that was part of it," said Gloria. "But knowing your mother,

I'm pretty sure she sat in there because she wanted to keep reliving it, wanted to keep the pain fresh. She just couldn't forgive herself, you know."

"Forgive herself for what?" he said. "He was the one who locked us up, who kept us there all night and pretended he'd shot himself."

"I know it doesn't really make much sense, at least not to us, but she believes your father fell off the float because he was distracted and tired from being up all night. She blamed herself."

Aaron had tried to explain the word *blame* to his students once, so he knew what a slippery word it was, that it reflected how a person perceived an event, not necessarily what was true. When his mother followed the causal chain backward, his father fell from the float and died because she had packed Aaron's suitcase, intending to leave. Without the suitcase, there would have been no closet, and the parade would have been just a parade instead of the moment that their lives split in two: before the parade and after.

"I don't understand it," Aaron said. "I don't understand how she could feel that way. You know, all those nights she and Pastor Gronseth sat in the booth talking, mainly they talked about forgiveness. They both felt it should be much harder to earn, that people get off too easily. I always thought it was a theoretical discussion, but I see now that they were talking about themselves." He pierced the yolk of his other egg and thought about how this fork might be the same fork that Clarence had driven into Gloria's hand all those years ago. He wondered whether Clarence had ever apologized, or whether he too had counted on easy forgiveness.

"Her closet was nothing like my closet in Moorhead," he said. "It was big, the size of an office really. There was an overhead light, and she kept a chair in there. But still, I should have remembered something about that night. Right? It makes me feel like I'm crazy— because how could I not remember?"

"You were only five, and memory's a strange thing. Sometimes it protects us from ourselves. Look at your mother. Look at what remembering did to her."

He ate his last strip of bacon. "That was the best breakfast I've had in months," he said. "I'm fortified for the road, so I guess I better get going." He had put his bag in the car before he sat down, preparing for an efficient departure.

"Will you at least go in and say good-bye to her?" He did not want to. Gloria knew this. "Do it for me, Aaron? Because when you leave, I can tell you it will be that much worse if she has to face the fact that she didn't even have it in her to say a proper good-bye. And I'm the one who's going to have to deal with it."

"I'm sorry," he said. "Yes, of course, I'll say good-bye."

"Thank you." Gloria stood up and began removing their plates, and he stood to help her. "I'd like to give you something of Clary's," she said. "It would make me happy to think of something of his with you. Would that be all right?"

"I'd like that," he said. "Very much."

He knew what he wanted: the book Clarence had shown him that first afternoon. He did not recall the name of the photographer, but they went into Clarence's room and looked for it together. Diane Arbus.

"I remember this book," Gloria said. She laughed and put one of her big hands to her mouth. "I was horrified when Clary first showed it to me, but he loved the pictures."

Aaron thought about the letter to Diane Arbus that Clarence had read to him. Clarence had written to a person he thought was alive, a person he believed would understand him and photograph him in a way that made him feel understood.

"Thank you for the book," he said to Gloria. "And for taking care of her."

"I guess you won't be coming back?" Gloria said.

"No," he said. "I guess I won't."

He knew that Winnie was at her store, but showing up unannounced seemed melodramatic, as though he expected her to stop earning a living in order to tend to him. Then he remembered the way she had said, "I love you," the way she hesitated first because she was nervous, and he started his car. When he arrived, she was discussing a Madurese bed panel with a woman who was taking notes and snapping photos with her cell phone, so he pretended to examine a dowry chest. Winnie came up behind him and threw her arms around him. "Go wait in the backroom," she whispered. "I'm almost done with her."

"I'm sorry to just show up," he said when she joined him. He sat contritely atop a teak daybed.

"Don't be sorry. I'm happy you're here. I was worried about you."

"Still, I don't want you losing sales over me."

The front door buzzed. "We'll talk tonight," Winnie said. "You're staying, right?"

"If you'll have me."

"You'll need to earn your keep," she said. She handed him a bottle of oil and a rag, and as she tended to customers, he oiled furniture, his preferred task when visiting Winnie at the store, finding comfort in the way the wood came back to life, in the ease of working beside her without speaking.

At six they closed up. He drove behind her in his rental car, back to her house, where they opened a bottle of wine and began making dinner. Soon Thomas and the boys arrived, all three of them excited to find him there. Thomas hugged him tightly, but even after all these years, Aaron found himself gauging the hug, wanting to be the one who pulled away first. He knew what Walter would say: this was just proof of the distrust that existed between gay and straight men. But maybe it was just proof of the distrust among human beings.

The boys hugged him also and then went to their rooms to change. "We'll be right back, Uncle Aaron," they said. They had always called him that, Uncle Aaron, but after dinner, as he and Winnie talked quietly in the living room, he asked, "Do they know about me and Walter? You know, that we're not together?"

"Of course they know." Then, because Winnie had always sensed what he was thinking, she said, "You're still their uncle. You've been their uncle their whole lives. That's not going to change."

"Okay," he said.

"You know, he called every day that first month. Once he called at two in the morning."

"Walter did?" This shocked him. Walter had always adhered to proper telephone etiquette. He said it was unfair to send people to bed or welcome them to the day with the feeling of unease that a call at an inappropriate hour triggered.

"Just once. He'd been drinking," Winnie said. "He told me he was calling because he finally got what you'd been saying all these years about king-size beds."

"We won't be getting back together," Aaron said. "You know that, right?"

She held up the bottle of wine they had started before dinner, and he nodded.

"I do," she said, "but you have to give me time to get used to it, to keep getting used to it. The two of you were together more than twenty years. And now it's been what? Four months?" She stopped talking and took a sip of wine. "When you left, he waited until Christmas to call, three whole days, and then he acted like it was our usual holiday telephone call, him calling to wish 'the gentile' a merry Christmas. He and Thomas talked for a couple of minutes, and then he talked to the boys and wished them 'half a merry Christmas.' Finally, I asked him to put you on the line, and he said you weren't there. I said, 'What do you mean *not there*? Where is he?' And he said, 'Well, I imagine that by now he's settled in his new home in San Francisco.'" Winnie looked at him. "And that's how I found out you were gone."

"I'm sorry," he said again, because she sounded angry.

"So that's it?" Winnie said. She held up her wineglass as if making a toast. "To the end of a twenty-year friendship." She was definitely angry.

"Okay, you're right," he said. "I should have told you I was leaving. You're the closest thing I've got to family. Still, you're Walter's sister, not mine, and we have to think about his feelings."

"Well, that's the thing," Winnie said. "He won't tell me what those feelings are. Even back in January when he was calling every day, he'd spend the whole conversation complaining about some mix-up with the room scheduling for his Advanced Spanish class. Once, he did note that he'd switched to buying quarts of milk instead of gallons, which was the closest he came to talking about it, about you. So I was actually thankful when he called like that in the middle of the night, drunk."

"I guess you know I haven't called him?" he said, and Winnie nodded. "Every day I think about it, but then I just, I don't know. I can't bring myself to do it."

"Do you miss him?" Winnie asked.

"Of course I miss him. I miss him all the time."

"Then why haven't you called?"

"At first I was afraid I'd hear his voice and want to go back. Now I'm afraid I'll hear his voice and feel nothing. Lately, it's like I've reverted to childhood, when everything made me cry, yet I feel oddly removed from emotion also. When I say it out loud to you like this, I can hear it doesn't make sense." He paused. "Maybe I just don't think I deserve his understanding right now."

Winnie looked away from him. "What do you think Walter deserves?" she asked.

They set out on Saturday, at dawn. Winnie did not like dawn, was no good at mornings. She sat beside him, not speaking, and he considered turning around, worried that she had changed her mind, though it had been her idea to go. The whole thing started when he told her about Jacob. "I don't know why," he'd said after he finished the story, "but lately I can't stop thinking about him, wondering what happened. It's strange. The more my own life seems to be closing in on me, the more obsessed I've become with knowing what happened to some kid I've never even really met."

"Once, years ago, when Thomas and I were in southern Spain, we crossed over into Gibraltar for the afternoon. We were walking along in the park, enjoying ourselves, when this young Moroccan man came up to us. He looked awful, feverish. He was sick, he told us, and didn't know what to do. Go to the hospital, we said, but he said the hospital wouldn't help him. He had no money and was there illegally. We gave him aspirin and ten dollars. There was nothing else we could do. We were tourists. That's what we told ourselves. For years I wondered about that young man, whether he was okay. It weighed on me. He'd singled us out to ask for help, us out of all those people strolling by. We'd looked like the ones who would help, and we got rid of him with some aspirin and ten dollars."

"So what you're saying is that this is not about Jacob. It's about me."

She laughed. "I thought I was being more subtle."

"You might not be skilled at subtlety, but that doesn't mean you're wrong."

"So why not call the motel and talk to that receptionist? She probably kept up with things."

"I've thought about calling her, but it feels strange, especially now that so many months have passed."

"Well, what if we go there?" Winnie said at last.

"Go there?" he said. "To the motel?"

"Yes, to the motel." She sounded excited. "A road trip with just the two of us."

They both knew that there were other ways to find out what had happened to Jacob, more practical and efficient ways that did not involve driving for days, except the driving was the point. Aaron had always been most comfortable talking in cars, staring ahead with the knowledge that he did not have to rush through the conversation because there were miles to go.

They spent the first night in North Platte, Nebraska, at a motel that evoked the artificial peacefulness of a funeral parlor. When Aaron told the man behind the counter that they would like two rooms, the man said, "Well, at least she's not making you sleep in the doghouse," engaging in one of those jokes that husbands make to other husbands. The man winked at Winnie to let her know that he was just having fun, which meant there were two things to be annoyed by: the comment and the winking. Winnie rolled her eyes but did not respond to the man. She knew how Aaron hated confrontations.

After they were settled in their rooms, they decided they might as well take a walk, see a bit of North Platte, Nebraska, since neither of them imagined coming back here. Winnie wanted to see the grain elevator up close, which meant crossing a small bridge. As they paused halfway across it, she asked, "Is this what Mortonville was like?"

"Sort of," he said, "though Mortonville was much smaller."

"Smaller?" she said, as if it were not possible to imagine a place smaller than North Platte, Nebraska.

"Didn't you see the sign when we came in? The population's twenty-four thousand. That means North Platte"—he paused to do the math—"is sixty times the size of Mortonville. But if you're asking whether it feels familiar, the answer's yes, though bear in mind that familiar doesn't necessarily mean comfortable."

"What makes you uncomfortable?" she asked, but before he could formulate a response, she said, "Did what the motel guy said bother you?"

"You mean that he assumed we were married?"

It was not just the motel clerk. The waitress at the diner in Iowa where they stopped for lunch had come by the table when Winnie was in the bathroom and asked Aaron what his wife wanted to drink. He had not known how to respond but thought he might feel foolish if he made a point of insisting that Winnie was not his wife, so he said, "Can you check back after she returns from the restroom?" It turned out that this made him feel foolish also. As they drove, they had become just one more husband and wife eating, buying gas, driving across the middle of the country, together. It was as though he had stepped into another life, the life he might have lived had he not left Mortonville, had he not understood who he was, whom he desired.

"To be fair," he told Winnie, "they're looking at two people who clearly enjoy each other's company, so it's not a stretch to think we're a couple. But if you're asking whether it bothers me that I could be here with a man, looking just as pleased with his company, and these same people would be asking whether we're brothers, and which one of us is older, and nonsense like that, yes, that bothers me."

But he was guilty of making assumptions also, for hadn't he decided that most of these people had never felt on the outside of anything, were incapable of seeing the world from the perspective of someone who was? Without even knowing them, he had concluded that they lacked the necessary imagination.

"When Walter and I traveled, we'd get to a town like this and find ourselves right back in the closet, actually thanking the motel clerk after he'd explained proudly that he'd managed to secure us a room with two beds. The truth is that a part of me enjoys how easy this feels, yet I simultaneously feel like, I don't know, like I'm being erased, like I don't exist here." By then they were in front of the grain elevator, and they stood looking up at it together.

Later that night, after they had eaten dinner and gone back to their rooms, Aaron composed a letter to Walter on stationery from the North Platte Motel. He carried the letter with him, stamp-less, during the rest of the trip.

Dear Walter [he had written],

Do you remember how you tried to teach me Spanish and French, back in the beginning? "With your vocabulary and the ubiquity of cognates?" you used to say. "It'll be a piece of pie." "Piece of cake," I'd always correct you, and then we'd argue about whether it was still a cliché if you changed one of the key words like that. "You've turned it into a cliché and a malapropism, which makes it doubly offensive," I would say, and you'd reply with something like "Well, there's more than one way to skin a mouse." We'd laugh, and sometimes we'd have sex because we had that in common: verbal sparring aroused us. I know it will probably embarrass you that I'm writing about sex—you never liked to talk about it, at least not with me. I wish you would have told me why, but you didn't, and I didn't know how to make you.

But back to language. I always argued that it was my fierce love of English—of its nuances and endless synonyms—that hindered my attempts to learn, that and the fact that you were a language professor. But what I never told you was that I abhorred cognates, that I preferred words that bore no resemblance to English, to the sounds that I formed on a daily basis. I gravitated toward the useless and obscure. In fact,

*I kept secret lists, words that I learned in the countries we visited: in
Japanese, I liked* inushishi, *which is a wild boar; in German, I could
request a sewing kit, a dustpan, or a table runner; and in Spanish, I could
point to a child's curly hair and say "ringlets."*

*Of course, I could also exchange pleasantries and keep myself fed. But
it was only in tossing around those useless words—blurting them out to
children on trains and to the spouses of your colleagues as we sat together
at interminable dinners—that I truly felt I was communicating, letting
everyone know how far I was (and would always be) from ever being
able to say anything that I really needed to say.*

That is, I'm sorry.
Aaron

He finally mailed the letter from the airport in Minneapolis, as he
waited for his flight back to San Francisco. Winnie had insisted on
going with him to the airport, even though he still had the rental car
to return. She was waiting for him just before the security checkpoint,
holding a bag of cookies that she had stayed up making for him the
night before. "Snickerdoodles," she said happily. He'd told her once,
years ago, that they were his favorite.

Then, they stood awkwardly for a few minutes, as people do when
there is still more to say. "Beware of leaving guests," he joked. It was
something that Walter used to say, a Russian proverb he thought.

"You're the one who's insisting on leaving," she said.

He thought about all the things he wanted to say to her. "Thanks
for my cookies," he said. "I love snickerdoodles."

"I know," Winnie said.

As he walked toward his gate, he took out the letter to Walter
that he'd composed in North Platte, Nebraska, bought a stamp, and
dropped it in a mailbox. Immediately, he wanted it back, but wasn't it
always that way with letters? There was that moment right after you'd
put it in the box when you wished you'd said so much less—or so much
more.

*   *   *

Whatever was wrong with him—and there *was* something wrong—had started before he walked into the school and saw Bill's empty room and the smoking balcony door still leaning against the wall, before he awakened, exhausted, from his half day of sleep. He did not understand it. On the plane home he had been buoyant, filled with resolve: there were issues to be addressed, and he was going to address them. He would begin by telling the Ngs that he could hear everything, all their screaming and cursing and furniture shoving. Then he would find a new apartment, something quiet where he could maybe have a cat. Next, he would go to the café where he had met George and would keep going until he found him. He would invite George to take a walk with him, *just a walk*. Maybe they would become friends, maybe something more, but even if nothing ever happened, this nothing would at least be the result of something other than fear. The most important thing was that he was going to call Walter and make sure that the letter had arrived. He was going to apologize for not calling earlier.

These were the things he had planned to do, had thought about on the flight back from Minneapolis and was still thinking about as he rode BART into the city from the airport, but then he entered his studio beneath the Ngs' house, dropped his bag on the bed, and discovered he did not have the energy to unpack it. Instead, he lay down and pulled the covers over his head, making a tent, where he stayed for hours, trying to empty his mind, as people who meditate claim to do, but he did not have a mind for meditation.

He tried an exercise he'd read about in a magazine one time. He was supposed to picture something, let it come into focus. What he saw was a package, neatly wrapped, like a gift beneath a Christmas tree. The tag on it said *For: Walter* and *From: Aaron,* and inside was *An Apology.* Except envisioning it beneath a tree reminded him that he had left just before Christmas and, worse, that he had never given Walter a gift, not once in all their years together. Walter had always claimed not to mind. He probably didn't mind, but Aaron was still ashamed. He had let his mother's injunction against gifts become a rule, and now Walter had nothing to remember their years together by.

When he tried to push these thoughts away by focusing on the gift itself—picturing himself handing the package to Walter and Walter opening it—he found that there was not only *An Apology* inside but so many other things, all the things he had realized during his trip: that he loved Walter but when he was right there beside him, day after day, the love part disappeared. It was only from a distance, without the daily grievances and resentments to obscure it, that he was able to recall this love at all, and even then, he was not sure whether what he felt was love or the memory of love. But if he included *that* in the package, he would need to include the part about how he had also come to hate Walter, in order for any of it to make sense. And what kind of gift was that?

"Did you find a new place yet?" Winnie asked each time she called, and each time he said, "No, I haven't seen anything interesting."

"You are looking?" she asked finally.

He did not answer, and Winnie did not fill the silence because she knew he would answer eventually. "No," he said. "The truth is that I'm not doing anything. I go to school and I teach, if you can call it teaching, and then I come home and I wait to go to bed. I try to make it to nine because that seems like a respectable hour, but I rarely make it past eight. It's like I'm swimming through the day, and the shore's so far off, and the only way I can get to it is by taking one stroke at a time and ignoring everything else around me, and when I do get there, I'm exhausted. All I want to do is sleep."

"What about your landlords?" she asked. He had told her about the Ngs. He had told her everything.

"The same. Everything's the same, Winnie. I don't know what's wrong with me." He did not tell her that he was scared, though he supposed she knew.

"The trip was a lot," Winnie said. "There's also Bill's death. Maybe you didn't know him long, but he was your friend. Sometimes you just need to let yourself be sad, and if you don't take time, your body takes it anyway. You've got a lot on your plate right now."

"I taught my students that expression not long ago," he said, "and now they use it constantly. Last week Melvin told me he wanted to do his upcoming presentation on the Amish because they have a lot on their plate."

"What did he mean?" Winnie asked.

"I'm not sure. I think he meant that they have a lot of rules to follow. I guess I'll find out soon enough—they start presenting tomorrow."

"How is Melvin?" she asked. He had told her about what he had seen in the basement, and she said that he needed to talk to Melvin about it, that saying nothing only reinforced Melvin's feeling that having sex with a man was shameful, which was what had led him to the basement in the first place. At the time he had agreed, but now, talking to Melvin was just one more thing he didn't have the energy for.

"It's always hard with Melvin to tell how he is," Aaron said, "but I suspect Melvin has a lot on his plate also."

The next morning, Aaron asked for a volunteer to begin the presentations. Everyone looked down, as students do when they fear being chosen. As he stared out at their bent heads, the room became once again a great expanse of water. He knew that if he stopped swimming, he would go under, so he sat at his desk and they stared at theirs, until finally Paolo raised his hand and said he would go first.

He went to the front of the room, smiled at everyone, and said, "Today I will tell you about a very important subject, Harley motorcycles in this country, the United States." The students laughed, and Paolo looked pleased. "In August I will go for first time to bike rally in Sturgis, South Dakota. This rally starts in 1938." Aaron did not tell him to watch his verb tenses. Paolo wrote vocabulary words on the board—*rally* and *hog* and *biker chick*—and then he walked over to the map of the United States and traced the route that his motorcycle club would take when they drove to South Dakota. He told them how many miles they would ride each day and gave them data about how many bikers attended each year and how much money Sturgis earned from the rally, because at heart Paolo was still a man who felt most comfortable assessing the world in numbers.

When Paolo was finished, Neto raised his hand and went next. He had attended Burning Man for the first time and spoke with the zeal of a convert. His presentation consisted primarily of pictures of people who appeared to have survived an apocalypse. Normally Aaron would have tried to understand what Neto saw when he looked at the photos, would have asked Neto questions with that objective in mind, but this time he sat at his desk and watched Neto's slideshow in silence. After that, one of the Borols talked about Levi's jeans, which had been invented during the Gold Rush, and then Lila explained the role of the Chinese in building the railroads. She used note cards and a Power-Point, and Aaron was sure no one would volunteer to follow her, but Melvin, surprising everyone, offered to go next.

His first talk, about computers, had been incomprehensible, but this time he stood in front of them and said, "I will tell you about some people I met when I was on East Coast. They are called Amish people. They do not drive cars or use telephones." He showed a picture of an Amish horse and buggy and wrote the word *buggy* on the board. "My friend, who is Amish person, cannot sit at family table. He must sit quietly in corner to eat his food." He turned and wrote *shun* beside *buggy*. "When I visit with my friend's family, I sit at table but my friend, he is on the floor, and we must not talk to him."

"Why?" asked Pilar. "Why must he sit on the floor?"

"Because he buys car and keeps it in secret garage. This is how I meet him. He is selling car very cheap, and I think I will buy car and drive across America to my new home, which is San Francisco. He told me that he had to eliminate the car from his life because now his family knows he has car. They are very angry and also embarrassment because all of the Amish people know about the car, and they criticize his family. The car is called 'stigma.'" Melvin wrote *stigma* on the board next to *shun*.

"Stigma is what Jesus had," Lerma said. "From the nails in his hands."

"Excuse me," said Katya. "I am not understanding this word *stigma*."

She looked at Aaron, and from his desk he said wearily, "A stigma means that other people look at you in a negative way because they think something about you is shameful." He paused. "If you have a mental illness, for example, people might think of you in a negative way, so we say, 'There's a stigma attached to mental illness.'"

"What else?" said Katya. She was taking notes. "What else is attaching with stigma?"

"Well, I guess being in prison, having AIDS, being homeless. But remember, sometimes the stigma disappears."

"How can it disappear?" asked Katya.

"Well, because the stigma isn't real. It's about how people think, so maybe society changes. People become educated about a topic, and then they think the situation isn't shameful anymore."

He could see from their faces that he was not explaining *stigma* well. He should get up and write his examples on the board, but he knew that if he left his desk, he would drown.

"What about Jesus?" said Lerma.

"That's not relevant," he said. He could hear the impatience in his voice. The others looked down. Lerma looked down also.

Each day after class, Lerma took two buses to her job, her *first* job, which involved picking up a brother and sister from school and shuttling them home, where she oversaw their homework and made dinner and got them ready for bed. Their mother was there also, but she did not like to be disturbed. She required "peace and quiet," lots of it, she had told Lerma at the interview. She reminded Lerma about this whenever the children became loud. Lerma put the brother and sister to bed, and then she went to her second job, sleeping in a chair beside the bed of a sick girl. Every two hours an alarm rang, waking her so that she could check on the girl. She did this until the nurse arrived at seven, and then she went home and changed in order to be at school by nine. This was her schedule every day except Sunday because Sunday was church day. She worked hard to improve her English. She did not complain or fall asleep in class. And in return he had yelled at her for wanting to understand *stigma* better. He said her question was "not relevant" because everything felt irrelevant to him now, and he had not stopped to consider that for Lerma it was more relevant than anything else.

"I'm sorry, Lerma," he said. "I'm very sorry. Everyone." His voice trembled. "Let's take a break." He went across the hallway to the room where Bill used to teach sleuthing. It was dark inside, but he did not turn on the light. He went in and sat at the table and cried. He wondered whether his mother had felt this way when she sat in the closet after his father died, as though she had no idea what she was crying about at all.

26

The next morning when Aaron pressed the button on his remote control, the garage door did not open. He tried the wall control, thinking his batteries were dead, but the door remained firmly closed, not even making the whirring sound that meant it was trying. He thought he could hear Mrs. Ng upstairs, so he seized a rake and banged it against the ceiling, but upstairs Mrs. Ng went blithely along with her morning routine, unaware that he was trapped below her. He began to think about earthquakes, for that was the way the mind worked, wasn't it? And the more he thought about them, the surer he became that one would occur any minute. The house would buckle down on top of him, Mrs. Ng's screaming the last thing he heard.

In second grade, when he first learned the unbearable truth that the earth was spinning beneath him, he'd felt a similar panic. He remembered standing outside after school, thinking about it: this earth beneath him that felt so solid was turning at a frantic pace. He had flung himself on the ground and hung on. It seemed the only thing to do, and it had helped. He went back into his studio and lay down, wrapping his arms around the mattress.

The last time he saw his mother, she was in bed also. After Gloria gave him Clarence's book, she took him upstairs to where his mother lay, in a bed that was clearly too small to accommodate a second person, certainly not Gloria with her giant body. The covers were pulled up over her, so he could not even tell which way she was facing. He and Gloria stood in the doorway, and finally Gloria said, "Dolores, Aaron's leaving. He'd like to say good-bye."

His mother did not reply or take the covers off her head to look at him.

"I'm hoping to be back in the Twin Cities by noon," he said, "so I guess this is it." He thought he should say more, but he could not act as though this were a routine visit, one that concluded with him thanking her for her hospitality. "Remember the coma?" he said. "I used to worry about it all the time, wondering whether it could happen again. I still do." He paused. "When I woke up that night, you were sitting by the window in my hospital room. It was dark outside, and for a while, I just watched you. You seemed to have forgotten all about me lying there behind you. Afterward, I could never call up the image of you looking out into the night without thinking that that was the moment I should have known you would leave."

He turned as if to go, but he knew he would regret it if his last words to her sounded bitter, angry. "Anyway," he added, "I want you to know that I've had a good life." It was not that he forgave her. He did not, not yet, but he was giving her permission to forgive herself. He did not think she would. His mother was not ready to be done with guilt or unhappiness.

It was eight thirty. He was going to be late for work, but he did not get off the bed or think about the garage door that would not open. Instead, he thought about how Walter used to get into bed with him when he sensed that something was wrong, about the way Walter would take his hand and hold it tightly and they would lie together, not talking, just staring at the ceiling because Walter had understood that sometimes it was enough for two people to be looking at the same thing. And just like that he could breathe.

He called Marla and told her what had happened. He asked whether Taffy was at work already, and Marla handed the telephone to Taffy, who was sitting right there in her office and who did have the Ngs' number, had written it down when she arranged for him to rent the studio. He listened to the phone ringing above him. He listened to

Mrs. Ng walking across the room toward it. He thought that she hesitated right before picking it up, but then she did pick it up, answering in Chinese, and soon he was free.

Winnie had told him once that when she felt stuck, she tried to find the wherewithal to make just one change. She said that if she could do that, sometimes everything else followed. That afternoon he stayed after school, looking through apartment listings in the computer lab, and three days later he found a new studio. It was near the school, but what he liked most about it was that it was on the fifth floor. When he stood at the window while the landlord pretended to be busy behind him, he could see the ocean just nine blocks away. He had not known until then that just seeing the ocean would make him feel better.

The studio cost more than the Ngs' studio, but he would be leaving the school soon. It was not a place one stayed for long, unless you were a lazy teacher like Felix or ill-equipped for the world like Taffy. Until he found something else, a job that paid better, he would be fine. Walter had sent him a check, a buyout for his part of their house in Albuquerque. It had arrived one week after he sent the letter from the airport, wrapped in a half sheet of blank typing paper. He had not cashed the check yet, but Winnie said he needed to, her reasoning based not on the fact that he needed the money (though he did) but on her observation that he needed to stop giving substance to his guilt.

He told the landlord on the spot that he would take the apartment. Then he walked up Fulton and cut down into the Castro. He went into the café where he had met George, ordered a slice of apple pie, and sat at a table to eat and read poetry and wait. He did this every afternoon for the rest of the week while in the evenings he repacked his few belongings into boxes. He told the Ngs that he would be moving out. They did not ask why, and he did not tell them because there was no reason to tell them. They knew they argued. They did not need him pointing out that they were unhappy.

One afternoon, Eugenia came into the faculty room and stared at him in that way that meant she was waiting for him to look up so that she could start talking. In the past, he had listened to her with a bland expression on his face that Eugenia always interpreted as interested, but today he pretended to focus on other tasks—his timesheet, corrections to Pilar's résumé. Finally, Eugenia could not help herself. "You're going to the Pride Parade this weekend, right?" she said, asking in the same way that she had asked about the missing *Lake Wobegon* tapes, as though assured of his interest.

"No," he said. "I don't like parades." This was true. He had never taken to parades. People who knew about his father treated his dislike as a given, for how could he ever get past the memory of the float and his father tumbling backward through the air? But he believed that his aversion was a response to the overall aesthetics of parades—the gaudy floats, the music that inspired marching, the sun bright overhead—though it was possible everyone else was right.

"But everybody in San Francisco goes to Pride," Eugenia said.

"Well, that's one more reason to stay home," he said. He laughed to show that he was sort of kidding, and then he said, "Anyway, I'm moving this weekend."

In class the next day, Paolo asked whether he would be going to the parade.

"Actually, I'm moving this weekend, to a new apartment, so I don't have time for parades." He pretended to sound disappointed.

"Are you needing help?" said one of the Borols.

"No," he said quickly. He did not like people handling his belongings. He never had, but he especially did not want his students doing so. He did not want to think of Chisato carrying a box that contained his underwear and socks or the Thais lifting his mattress, because how did you carry someone's mattress without picturing the person on top of it, sleeping or having sex, intimate activities that he did not want his students imagining when they looked at him. He had boundaries, and boundaries were a good thing. But letting others help you was a good thing also. Winnie had told him that on the trip.

He took a breath. "Actually, I am needing help," he heard himself say.

"I will bring shuttle van," said Leonardo, who had graduated from delivering pizzas to driving an airport shuttle. "We can fit many things."

"I have car," said Katya.

"I have car also," said Yoshi.

"I will bring pizzas from delivery mistakes," said Diego. "They will be from past night but still very good."

"Old food?" said Aaron. The students laughed hard, so he knew they forgave him.

On Sunday morning they arrived at his place at nine o'clock, as if they were meeting for class, except they were all on time. The Brazilians brought cheese bread and coffee, and the Thais brought bags of dried mango and durian chips. Aaron had everything packed, and he stood with the garage door rolled up, waiting for them.

"Where's Melvin?" asked Ji-hun. Melvin was the only student missing, except for one of the Bolors, who'd had to work. He had not said he was coming, nor had he said he was not coming. He had, as usual, said nothing, letting the conversation swirl around him as though he were not really part of it. Aaron wondered whether the others had actually expected him to show up.

"He left a message on my cell," Tommy said. "This morning before I was awake. He has some problem with his fiancée's visa paperwork, so he will meet us at the new apartment."

Sure enough, when they pulled up at Aaron's new address two hours later, there was Melvin, leaning against the building. The other students greeted him, and he put on gloves and helped them unload the shuttle van.

"Melvin," Aaron said as they carried in boxes together, "can I talk to you after everyone leaves?"

"I must go home very quickly," Melvin said.

"It won't take long," Aaron assured him.

The Thais were the last to go, and when Tommy called to Melvin, asking whether he needed a ride, Melvin turned and said, "Thank you, but I must talk to teacher Aaron." He was at the window that looked out over the ocean, and Aaron wondered whether Melvin was the sort of person who felt hopeful when he looked at the ocean's vastness or overwhelmed by his own insignificance.

"Do you mind sitting on the floor?" Aaron said, because it would be awkward to sit on the bed, awkward even to suggest it. They sat and leaned back against the wall. "Thanks for your help today," Aaron said.

"It is my pleasure," said Melvin, bowing his head at Aaron. Aaron looked at the crumpled side of Melvin's face, remembering how it had risen slowly in the basement, the eyes filled with shame.

"Melvin," he said, "we never talked about what happened in the basement." He saw fear in Melvin's eyes, and he added quickly, "And we don't have to. I understand that maybe you don't want to talk, and that's fine. I just want to say that if you do want to talk, or you have questions, or just need help with something, you can ask me. Okay?"

Melvin kept his eyes down.

"I'm sorry if I've embarrassed you," said Aaron. "Can I get you any-thing? Water? A beer? Leftover pizza?"

"I must go," said Melvin.

"Thank you for your help," Aaron said again.

At the door, Melvin looked up. "It is the stigma of my life," he said sadly.

"What is?" said Aaron, but Melvin had already turned to leave.

When he and Winnie had pulled off the interstate in Needles late in the afternoon, Aaron could not remember which direction to turn to get to the motel. He went right, but after several blocks, he decided he should have gone left, so he turned the car around, and there it was, nondescript and unappealing, the sort of place that people looked for when they wanted to sleep without frills. He pulled into the parking lot, and they got out. He showed Winnie the spot where Britta's boy-friend had punched and kicked him until he announced that he was gay. He laughed and said, "Beaten up *until* I said I was gay," and then,

"What if Britta doesn't work here anymore?," which was what he had been saying since they left Minnesota, and Winnie replied the way she had been replying. "We'll find her," she said. "We'll figure out what happened to Jacob."

She put her arm through his, and they walked toward the front entrance of the motel, but when they got to the door, he stopped. "I can't do this," he said.

"Of course you can. We'll do it together. Okay? You're just nervous."

He leaned against the wall beside the door. "No," he said. "I really think I should not do this. If Jacob's dead, there's nothing more I can do about it. Not really. Right?"

She nodded.

"So what would it change for me to know?"

"Well, you'd know for sure. Sometimes clarity is important."

He remembered the force with which Lex had kicked him that night, desperate to know the truth about what Britta had been doing in his room. But had knowing changed anything? Had it made Lex understand the woman he loved any better? Had it made Britta love him more? Had learning where his mother had been all these years made Aaron forgive her any faster?

"Clarity is important," he agreed. "But maybe clarity is sometimes about knowing what you don't need to know. For months I've been thinking about Jacob, imagining his life before that day and his life after, and maybe I'll go through the rest of my life wondering about him, but it's okay. I saved him. I was running away, saving myself, and I saved him as well. Maybe that's enough."

Winnie put her hand on his shoulder, the shoulder he had used to break down Jacob's door. He remembered the feeling as it gave way, the certainty he had experienced as he saved Jacob's life. Was certainty what Walter felt as he drove out of Mortonville that Sunday afternoon with Aaron beside him? He'd never asked him, but he thought he might, someday soon, because there was so much about Walter he didn't know.

The motel wall was warm against his back. He turned back toward the parking lot. As they drove past the front office, he slowed the car and glanced inside. A young woman stood behind the front desk. He thought it was Britta, but he couldn't be sure. It could be any young woman.

Before he dialed, he planned out what he would say. "This is Aaron," he would begin, "and I'm calling to see how you are and to apologize for not calling sooner." He wrote the words out and practiced reading them aloud, but it was like the script he had used when he was twenty-two and working for the political campaign, like something you read to a stranger. In the end, he decided just to see what happened, even though spontaneity and the unknown were everything he hated about the telephone, but when he heard Walter's voice, Walter sounded like a stranger, like someone who required a script.

"It's Aaron," he said.

On the other end, Walter was running water, washing dishes maybe, and the sound of the water stopped abruptly. "Aaron," Walter said. "I got your letter. I see that you haven't lost your flair for metaphor." Just like that, he sounded like Walter.

"I miss you," Aaron said, but that was unfair because it gave the wrong idea about why he was calling, so he said, "That's not why I'm calling." Except that made it worse.

"Why *are* you calling?" Walter asked. He was not going to make it easy, and why should he? He'd made things easy all those years, and look where that had gotten him.

Aaron did not answer right away. He wanted Walter to know that he appreciated everything he had ever done for him, but all the ways that he thought about conveying his gratitude sounded like clichés. He could not imagine anyone being convinced by clichés, though he knew people were. People listened to pop music, didn't they? They wept at musicals and exchanged Hallmark cards. But not Walter.

"I'm calling to say that you saved my life," Aaron said. "And to say thank you."

Gloria was right—people did what they wanted to do. Walter had wanted to help him because helping him had also helped Walter. That morning, Aaron had opened an unpacked box and found his journal of grievances inside. He had thrown it away because that was what *he* wanted to do, because forgiving Walter was forgiving himself. He stood up and looked out the window of his new studio. He thought about Walter on the other end of the line, looking at the familiar walls of their house with no idea that Aaron was looking at the ocean. Even when they were together, he saw now, they had always been looking at different things.

"Call you next week?" Aaron said, and Walter said, "I'll be here."

Maybe George had stopped going to the café after Aaron stood him up, or maybe he had not been a regular there to begin with. Maybe his presence that day had been a fluke. After two weeks of eating pie and waiting for George to reappear, Aaron got on Muni one afternoon, thinking he would ride the N all the way to the ocean and walk home from there. He got on, and there was George, wearing his Muni uniform and asking to see his ticket. Aaron showed him his ticket and said, "I'm sorry. I got scared. What time do you get off? Do you want to take a walk?"

And George said, "At six. And yes."

When six came, Aaron was waiting. George came up close to him as if he were going to hug him, but he did not. After Aaron had recovered from his fear that George might hug him, he realized that he was disappointed George had not, so he reached out and hugged George. George hugged him back, and Aaron blurted out, "I'm not really much of a hugger" because they were two strangers after all, which meant that everything they did would lay the groundwork for how each came to understand the other. He did not want George to think he went around hugging people, that he crossed over into intimacy with such ease. Except now George would think he was so attracted to him that he could not help himself, that he had felt compelled to hug him.

But George just smiled and said, "Do I contradict myself? Very well, then I contradict myself," and Aaron smiled back and said, "I am large. I contain multitudes."

"Actually, I'm not much of a Whitman fan," said George.

"Me neither," said Aaron. Even agreeing made him feel shy. "Anyway," he said, "while I was waiting for you, it occurred to me that you've been on your feet all day, so it's okay if you're not up for a walk."

"Are you standing me up again?" said George.

Aaron looked down. "It was the poem," he said at last. "The Richard Hugo poem. It reminded me of someone, a man I met years ago, when I was just a boy. He introduced me to that poem, to poetry, to so many things." How strange it felt to be discussing his life in such general terms, to be referring to Walter as "someone." He took a breath. "I loved him very much."

"Okay," George said. "Good. It's important to have been in love."

If he and George began walking now, where would it end? Would a day come when they would say, "Do you realize how many miles we've walked together?" They would try to calculate it. At least ten thousand they would decide. By then, they would know everything about the other. He would know that George always needed to be on his right when they walked because as a boy he had gone to the post office each day with his father, who could not hear from his left ear, so George had always walked on his right. Now George could not walk any other way. They would have had lots of sex. They would have talked and read poetry because poetry was not only who he was with Walter, it was who he was.

Or maybe none of that would happen. Maybe years from now, while eating a piece of pie, he would think to himself, *What was the name of that man I met over pie? He worked for Muni, I recall. We took a walk together once.*

He did not know what would happen because that was the way life worked. You went to a parade, and your father fell from a float and died. You got into bed, thinking about the map of Canada, and woke up the next day to find your mother gone. You went out fishing one night, and met the man who would change your life. You fell asleep at the wheel of the U-Haul in which you were leaving the man you'd met fishing, checked into a seedy motel, and saved a life.

"So, should we walk?" said George.

"Yes," said Aaron, and they started walking.

Acknowledgments

I would like to thank the following:

The organizations and individuals who offered crucial support in the early stages of this book, especially Nancy Zafris, who got my publishing ball rolling and has continued to offer friendship and guidance; The Rona Jaffe Foundation, which provided me with the financial means to reduce my teaching load in 2009–10; the Creative Writing Department at the University of North Carolina at Chapel Hill, where I was the Kenan Visiting Writer from 2010 to 2012 and was fortunate to have wonderful students and colleagues; Bread Loaf Writers' Conference; and all the hardworking editors at various literary journals who have supported my work, especially *New England Review*, as well as those who published early parts of this novel: *The Iowa Review, Bluestem, Beloit Fiction Journal, Nashville Review*, and the *Northwest Review*.

My agent, Terra Chalberg, who is pragmatic and supportive and knows when to set deadlines;

Liese Mayer, my editor, who has been an enthusiastic friend to this book, saving me from myself countless times with her thoughtful, gentle, and judicious edits; as well as Nan Graham, Kate Lloyd, Alexsis Johnson, Rita Madrigal, Mia Crowley-Hald, and the rest of the team at Scribner, all of whom have made me feel continuously grateful to have found a home for my book with them.

My students, who make me feel both useful and hopeful. I'm not sure how much I would write if I didn't feel both of these at least some of the time;

My dear friends, who understand that when I complete a day of writing, I rarely want to talk about it, and who have shown their support in countless ways;

Anne Raeff, my first reader, with whom I have spent nearly two-and-a-half decades of my life.